Bc

STAR FORCE SERIES
Swarm
Extinction
Rebellion
Conquest
Battle Station
Empire
Annihilation
Storm Assault

IMPERIUM SERIES
Mech Zero: The Dominant
Mech 1: The Parent
Mech 2: The Savant
Mech 3: The Empress
Five By Five (Mech Novella)

OTHER SF BOOKS
Technomancer
The Bone Triangle
Z-World
Velocity

Visit BVLarson.com for more information.

Storm Assault

(Star Force Series #8)
by
B. V. Larson

STAR FORCE SERIES
Swarm
Extinction
Rebellion
Conquest
Battle Station
Empire
Annihilation
Storm Assault

ISBN-13: 978-1492149477
ISBN-10: 1492149470
BISAC: Fiction / Science Fiction / Military

The carrier ship *Gatre* hung in space over Eden-8. Dark, imposing and diamond-shaped, the ship had only a few gun turrets. Every cannon it did have was a light laser with an automated brainbox driving it. The real armament was inside her: fighters. Over a hundred of them slept in her launch bays, waiting like wasps to charge out and defend their nest.

Gatre was Captain Jasmine Sarin's ship, but as the overall commander of Star Force I spent a lot of time aboard. The carrier was equipped with some of our best command-support hardware.

There were no other vessels in the immediate vicinity. Stretched out below the ship was the loveliest of the seven inhabited worlds in the Eden system. Eden-8 was a warm planet with amazingly tall forests and lush growth everywhere. It was as green as Earth was blue, being covered with more land than water. Someday, I thought to myself when I gazed down at that glowing jewel of a planet, humanity would fill that vast wilderness. But for now, it was very sparsely inhabited like the other three worlds here that were dedicated to my species.

I sat in a dark chamber which was lit only by the green glow of the world outside my window. The room was my office, and it was late. The ship was deathly silent and still. No one was stirring other than the night-watch people up in the bridge section.

I had a bottle in my hand, and a lot of things on my mind. I'd spent a lot of time doing this lately: sitting, staring and drinking.

After Sandra's death, my mood hadn't *always* been bad…but I knew I'd changed. I was less forgiving, less likely to see the humor in a given situation. I was also quicker to anger. More than once an underling who had screwed up in my presence or bothered me with something trivial found himself kicked through a hatchway—literally. Fortunately, flying headfirst or ass-first out of my office and smashing into a bulkhead was only an embarrassment for my nanotized troops. They weren't physically injured, only their pride suffered.

At first, they seemed understanding and tolerant about my new attitude. They made up excuses for my behavior to one another when they thought I wasn't listening. This only served to further piss me off.

I knew, at some level, that I was being unreasonable—but it was hard to care. I was grieving and drinking and grabbing what fun I could out of life day to day. I was in a slump.

I'd been hanging around with Major Gaines in the evenings, a black guy with the unusual first name of Bjorn. Gaines had become my sidekick during the turbulent days after the fiasco in the Thor System which had cost literally trillions of biotic lives. He seemed to have his own demons he would prefer to forget about, so we never mentioned them. Instead we drank, caroused and put dents in the walls and tables of whatever room we were in at the time.

These dents slowly reformed themselves after our abuse, of course. The smart metal ship never complained, cleaning up after us like a long-suffering parent.

Thinking of Gaines got me to my feet. I put down my bottle on my desk and used my com-link to connect to him on a private channel.

"Gaines?"

"Colonel?"

"What are you doing, sleeping?"

"I was getting around to that, yes sir," he said.

"You want to play some pool?"

He was quiet for a second. Then he laughed. "Sure, why not."

One of our favorite stops was the pool room. I'd had one built on the carrier after the battle for the Thor system had been

2

lost. The ship was big enough—hell, a third of it was still empty. Even the parts of the vessel that had a purpose were pretty bare-bones. I'd decided *Gatre* needed a place for her crew to unwind.

I'd soon found Gaines to be an excellent competitor. He had true predatory instincts. I'd thought he might have been lucky to be one of a handful of survivors from his unit, which had seen heavy action on Yale a few month ago, but now I realized luck had little to do with it. He was a natural. His moves, his focus—if it hadn't been for my microbial baths, I wouldn't have stood a chance against him in the pool room. He was that good.

But fortunately, I had enhancements to my body that were unique, as far as I knew. I was older and a bit slower, but I was definitely much stronger. When I cracked a bat into a ball, it flew with fantastic speed. Gaines needed all his agility and guile to survive when the ball came screaming his way.

Like many games of Star Force pool, the one we began that night became a matter of endurance. Headshots were illegal now and generally considered bad form. But taking careful aim and nailing your opponent anywhere else was perfectly acceptable, as long as you banked it at least once.

Our version of pool was radically different from the earthly version. We played in zero gravity with a baseball bat, a load of colored balls and a few players. The walls were plain flat sheets of smart metal, and the players were the pockets. Nailing one of them was the key to victory, but you had to bounce it off at least one wall for it to be a legal score.

Half an hour later it was Gaines' turn at bat, and he had blood in his eye—literally. I'd nailed him with a scorching four-ball in the clavicle that had ricocheted upward and into his face. On passing, it had plowed away part of his eyebrow. It was unintentional, so we hadn't called it a foul. Still, I could tell he wasn't too happy about that one. His nanites had sewed him up within thirty seconds, but the blood still dripped and glistened on his cheek.

We were both sweating and mildly drunk. We were playing nine-ball, our usual game of choice—you had to be a glutton for punishment to play the full fifteen.

I missed with the five, and it was Gaines' shot. He grinned at me as he took the bat, hefted it and located the bright orange ball. It was well-placed, hanging mid-room with barely any spin on it.

"You know sir," he said, taking his time with his shot, "after all that's happened, I'm surprised you trust me to be in this room with you alone."

I glanced up at him sharply. This was an unexpected comment. He was making a reference to the number of assassins I'd met up with lately. The most recent of them had managed to kill Sandra, my girlfriend and bodyguard. It was a sensitive subject, and he'd brought it up cavalierly in the middle of a game.

Naturally, this was the opening Gaines had been waiting for. The moment my eyes left the five-ball he took his shot. When playing pool with a Star Force marine, you should never take your eye off the ball.

Crack! The ball was in motion, and it took an unexpected course: downward. There wasn't time for me to dodge, I'd blown that fraction of a second by looking at Gaines' face. I had only a brief moment to think. What was he up to?

I knew in an instant. I instinctively reached down with my hands and covered my groin.

The ball came firing up from the floor at a wicked angle. My fingers took the blow and went numb. A normal man's knuckles would have been shattered like a collection of sticks, but mine were too hard for that. I cursed, and he chuckled. The bright orange ball floated away and bounced until it hung near the ceiling, spinning like a lost planet.

"That was low even you for, Gaines."

"Thank you, sir."

When I was ready, he took his next shot. Just as in normal billiards, when you sunk a ball into a "pocket" you got to shoot again. There was nothing quite as painful and humiliating as having some shark run the table on you, bouncing balls off your sorry body until they'd all struck home.

I managed to dodge his next shot, and it was my turn to shoot. I hefted the bat with a grim smile. My hands had recovered enough to grip the bat properly, and I was ready for vengeance.

I pushed off the floor and floated up near the ceiling. The six-ball had come to a halt in a tough spot, too close to the wall for a really good hit. I grumbled at my luck.

"As to your implied question, Gaines," I said, "I *do* trust you. I've fought alongside many men, and I've learned to know if they're assassins or not."

Gaines snorted. My comment seemed to amuse him. I twisted around up there in the corner of the room so I could see his face. He was smiling at me, as if I'd said something funny.

I frowned at him in return. "If you have something to say that isn't just meant to distract me, now is the time to speak, Major."

His smile faded. I stared at him until he dropped his eyes. He glanced down and opened his mouth, then closed it again thoughtfully.

At that precise moment I took my shot. It was a wild one, a swing done with all my power, but only one-handed. I had held the bat loosely so as not to look as if I was ready to make the attempt. Trickery was everything in a half-drunken game of pool.

Although I couldn't hit the ball with my full power, that didn't mean I gave it a love-tap. Of all the marines in Star Force, I'm pretty sure I'm the strongest. I'd been rebuilt to withstand the pressures of a gas giant, and not even First Sergeant Kwon could beat me at arm-wrestling.

Gaines was startled by the sound of whistling doom. He gave a little lurch and his eyes widened. The ball was a blur and had already made two ringing banks, leaving deep dents in the walls behind it. He looked for it, but was already behind him.

Not quite sure where the hit was coming from, he hunched his shoulders, squeezed his eyes shut and wrapped his hands around his jewels. I began to smile, because he'd guessed wrong.

Thump! The ball hit him in the ass. I'd fired a triple-banker, and managed to bring it up hard from behind him. Really, the shot was a lucky one. I almost never made triple-bankers, and when I did, they often didn't hit the spot I'd been aiming for.

But this one did. He made a hissing, gargling sound I found most gratifying. I had plenty of lumps of my own, and it did me good to think Gaines wasn't going to be sitting down comfortably for the next hour. He'd be sore, in fact, until the nanites managed to build him a new ass.

He moved slowly and painfully after that hit, but I could tell he was angry now, and dangerous. There was no more banter between us. I've found after many games of pool that this was a common tendency. It was all fun and giggles for the first three or four hits, but after people got banged up a bit, or after they took a really low blow, they tended to become grimly serious.

We sweated and swung the bat with ferocity. I managed to dodge the seven, then slam it back at him, nailing him in the left shinbone. But then he got into the zone. First the eight-ball and then the nine struck home—I took them both. When he landed the eight my ribs cracked on the left side, I was pretty sure of that. This slowed me enough so that he got me in the thigh with the nine, taking his shot quickly before I could recover.

As we'd been playing nine-ball, the game was over. I congratulated him between clenched teeth and we limped out of the pool room. There was another trio of late-night players outside waiting to use the room and they cheered us as we passed. I took it as good-naturedly as I could. After all, they'd been watching on the consoles and they knew Gaines had beaten me.

We went straight from the pool room to the officer's wardroom. On board ship, the late night had transformed into early morning. The morning watch had begun, so the bar was just opening up. We demanded alcohol, and we were served promptly. I dabbed whisky on the bloody spots, even though there was no chance of infection. I found that the liquid slightly numbed the worst injuries and made the itching of the nanites more tolerable. The rest of my drink I swigged down with a gulp, then ordered more by waving the glass at the barkeep.

"Colonel," Gaines said after he'd drunk his shot and breathed a sigh of relief. "I was a hired killer before I joined Star Force. A pro."

I looked at him in honest surprise. Then I winced, half-expecting a hidden pool ball to smash into my gut. But there was nothing on his face but a look of regret.

I suddenly understood. We'd known he had a shady past—as far as we'd looked. We knew he'd been in the U. S. Special Forces, but not what his missions had been. He'd come to us during the battle for Andros Island, the Saturday Assault, and he'd fought well ever since. That was good enough in our outfit.

As a group, Star Force Marines were pretty accepting of new recruits. Joining us was akin to joining the French Foreign Legion a century ago. We asked very few questions, but in return we demanded total loyalty.

So in response to his statement, I merely nodded to him. "We knew you had specialized training. You came to us ready to fight on a day when we needed every man we could find. I've never regretted signing you up, and I don't regret it now, either."

"I know that, sir," he said. "And I thank you for the opportunity you've given me to serve in Star Force. It's the best thing I've ever done with my life."

"A man's past is his own in this outfit."

Gaines nodded. "Do you want to know what my last assignment was, sir?"

I looked at him with mild curiosity. "Sure."

"I worked freelance for years. I was recruited during the Saturday Assault to assassinate *you*, Colonel."

Now, finally, he had my attention. I studied his face, and I believed him. It made a lot of sense. At that time—and ever since—Crow had been throwing assassins at me. But I frowned as I considered the timing.

"You couldn't have been working for Crow, not then. He was still cooperating with me in those days."

"That's right, sir. I was recruited by General Kerr. I'm happy to point out that I refused the assignment and was effectively kicked off Earth soil. I traveled to Andros Island and joined your forces there."

"I assume you didn't mention this before for obvious reasons. This does go beyond the usual range of acceptable omissions, however."

"Well..." he shrugged. "I didn't think the confession would improve my odds for advancement."

"Wait a minute," I said, staring at him. "You're telling me Kerr recruited you? Way back then?"

Gaines nodded. "Yes sir. He did it personally."

My mind was whirling. I wished Gaines had reported this earlier, but I could understand why he hadn't. We'd told him from the start that his past was in the past, and he didn't have to divulge any details. In accordance with those rules, he'd kept quiet. But, if I'd known Kerr had been behind at least some of the assassination plots earlier, I might have done things differently. I might even have saved Sandra.

"I'm sorry, Colonel," Gaines said, frowning at me. "I didn't even know Kerr was in the Eden system until after he'd left and the assassin was planted. Still, I wish I'd confessed at the time. It might have given you more warning."

With difficulty, I turned to him and straightened. I managed to give him a flickering smile.

"I know how you must feel," I said, "but it's all right. You didn't break any rules. In fact, you're breaking them now by telling me about your past. Have you got any other news for me?"

"Well sir, it's my impression that Earth will never make peace with Star Force. Those in charge have seen this invasion by the Macros as an opportunity to take control of the entire world, to force all humans to bow to a planetary government. Really, the only thing that stands between them and total domination is you."

"*Us*, Major," I said. "*We* stand in defiance of Kerr and Crow. Not just me. And I hope we'll all stand together when the time comes."

Gaines smiled slightly, and I knew I had him. He reached out and we shook hands. It only seemed natural to drink to this statement of solidarity, so drink we did. After that, things

8

became loud and blurry. I awakened some hours later on my bunk.

In my mind, I played Sandra's death over and over. I'd been torturing myself that way for some time now. I saw the pink froth on her lips and her glazed eyes. I'd been dreaming of her dying face every night, and today I saw it in the mirror staring back at me until I washed my troubles down the drain.

It was that morning I made my decision. Kerr had been sending assassins after me for years pretending to be my "reasonable guy" contact inside the Empire. It was intolerable, and I had to respond.

We'd been building up our fleets for months and had six new, sleek carriers. But build-up is one thing and launching an attack is another.

The time had finally come. Star Force was going back to Earth.

My first act was to round up every bottle of alcohol in my personal chambers and my office and dump them on the decking. The smart metal glistened and sheened over for a moment, perhaps surprised by the volume of liquid they were being doused with. But soon the nanites performed their prime function and made the booze vanish. I imagined a stream of it outside the ship, flowing and turning into a shower of icicles. It was a shame, as some of the bottles had been imported all the way from Earth, but it had to be done.

Afterward, I felt better. I told myself sternly that until Earth was liberated there would be no more than a single six pack of beer—and *only* beer—in my daily ration. This might not seem like a small quantity of alcohol to normal people, but a Star Force marine requires more than others to become intoxicated. The problem was the nanites in our blood, they tended to process the stuff out almost before it hit the brain. Beer was especially problematic, because it took longer to consume and thus made it even more difficult to get drunk.

But that was the point. With no more than a six pack a day, I knew I would be relatively sharp throughout the coming campaign without starting any rumors that I'd sworn off adult beverages completely. As a highly visible leader, it was critical that I keep my people confident in my ability to lead. I had to appear stable and unchanging—I was the rock upon which the rest of my followers relied. I didn't want people to say I "had a problem"—even if I did. I was determined not to fail them in this regard.

I frowned to myself as I marched down the corridors toward Medical. It was possible my reputation had already suffered somewhat due to my recent indulgences. I decided I would ask Dr. Swanson her opinion on the matter, and have her give me a physical.

There were two good reasons for this action. First, I wanted her to be able to profess that I was in excellent health despite my recent binges. Second, I'd been having private meetings with her lately and I figured it was time to move things along between us.

She and I weren't romantically involved—not exactly. But she'd made her intentions clear in that regard. I found her attractive and interesting, even fun to be around. Today, however, as I stepped into her office, she was all business.

"I'm glad to see you made it here on time," she said. "Please put your arm into this sling and I'll begin the procedure."

I found her tone rather cold. "What? Am I late for my appointment?"

She glanced at me without smiling. "I'm a person who feels we should all respect and value one another's time."

I frowned while she messed around with some weird-looking instruments. A modern doctor's office didn't bear much resemblance to the last-century look I'd been accustomed to all my life. The differences were due to the nanites, of course. They'd changed everything. They did most of the healing, and the doctors were only kept around to decide if they were functioning properly and if they needed a little help or prodding. Occasionally, the tiny robots ran into something that they couldn't handle. Some viruses were very small and hid in the body effectively, for example. Specialized nanites swarms had to be applied in such cases to affected areas.

She wasn't talking, so I didn't say anything either. The bright, cheery, determined mood I'd had upon entering her office had vanished for both of us. I racked my brain, trying to think why she might be miffed, or what sort of meeting I'd…

Then I had it. Like the proverbial light bulb going off in my head, I recalled the incident that must have been bothering her. We'd had a date about a week back, I remembered. Something had come up, and I hadn't made it to her door to pick her up.

I heaved a sigh. I'd stood her up. Worse, I hadn't even *remembered* I'd stood her up. I began thinking hard. How could I get out of this one…?

I brightened as I came up with a plan. Right about then, she plunged a needle into my arm and sucked out an alarming amount of blood. She was clearly angry and taking it out on my arm, but I barely winced. All Star Force people are tough when it comes to pain, and I had more improvements than most.

As a delayed reaction, I forced myself to pretend it hurt. "Hey, what are you doing, drilling for oil?"

"Sorry," she said crisply, her tone indicating she was anything but.

"So what's that for? Just because I didn't show up for our date? Is that it?"

Her eyes flicked up to meet mine, then lowered back to her work.

"Certainly not," she said. "That would be highly unprofessional."

"I had a good reason, you know."

"I'm listening."

Bingo, I thought. I'd guessed it. Now that the ground was laid for my excuse, I pressed ahead. It's best, I've found after long years of experience, to place a strong grain of truth in one's cover-stories. If there is something real at the core of it, the story becomes an embellishment of reality with an emphasis on a particular detail and everyone feels better about swallowing it. Even the liar.

"I somehow became drunk that night. I didn't want to embarrass myself, so I skipped the date."

"You could have called."

She was right, naturally. Even more right than she knew, because I'd gotten drunk with Bjorn Gaines hours after I was supposed to show up to her place. Also, I hadn't been embarrassed, I'd totally forgotten about her. None of those details were going to help me, so I left them out of the story.

12

"Yeah, I should have. But you know how it is. I knew I was too far gone to go on the date—hell, I too far gone to call you. So I did the no-show thing."

"And what about calling and explaining the next day?"

"I had a headache the next day."

That part was one hundred percent true, but it didn't seem to make her any happier. After she jabbed the other arm and took some readings, she left me sitting on the table for a few minutes. When she finally returned her expression was one of concern.

"Your blood chemistry is off. The nanites have been working overtime to compensate for toxins. You've killed a number of them off. You'll need a new dose—you really have been drinking heavily, haven't you?"

I nodded. "I guess I have. Really, it's been too much."

She looked at her tablet and tapped at it repeatedly, clucking her tongue and shaking her head. "This would have killed a normal man. You realize that, don't you?"

I didn't say anything. I hadn't known that. I tried to look sheepish, and managed to pull it off.

"I poured it all out," I told her. "This morning. Everything. I'm done grieving."

She laughed suddenly. "Drinking yourself blind every night isn't grieving, that's *avoiding* grief."

I shrugged. I didn't want to argue with her. For me, a month or so of drinking every night had done wonders. I hadn't forgotten about Sandra—far from it. I was still angry, in fact, but my state of mind had shifted. I now felt a cold, functional anger rather than the sullen anger I'd been wallowing in, which had bordered on a state of depression. I was now determined to take action rather than crying about the state of the universe.

"I feel better already," I said. "Let's go on that date tonight, okay?"

Her eyes were downcast, not meeting mine. She crossed her arms, holding her tablet to her chest. I could tell she wanted to say yes, but didn't want to get hurt again.

"Maybe you aren't ready for that yet," she said at last.

"Yeah, all right," I said, "some other time, then."

13

I started to climb off the table, but she put a hand on my chest. I stopped, even though I could barely feel the pressure she was exerting against me. She pointed to the chair in the corner.

I looked at it with squinting eyes. Every Medical facility in Star Force had one of those metal chairs. They were equipped with leather straps and bolted to the floor. This one had a layer of smart metal poured over the entire unit, making it look smoother and less medieval, but I knew all too well what it was for.

When applying fresh nanites, there was always discomfort involved for the recipient. A refresher dose was never as bad as the first time when most people lost consciousness and raved for hours in agony, but it wasn't going to be a happy experience, either.

I felt a trickle of sweat run down my back as I eyed the torture chair.

"You're going to enjoy this, aren't you?" I asked her.

"I'm selling tickets for the live show and making a vid for later. I'll clean up."

I forced a laugh then sat down in the metal chair. It was cold and the clamps were even colder.

"Now," she said, "I really need you to behave yourself, Colonel. Can you do that? I'm not sure this chair can hold you—if you really wanted to break free."

I knew that it couldn't. I also knew that I should be able to control myself well enough to bear the pain without tearing the place apart.

"I'm good to go," I said.

"Do you want anything? For the pain, I mean?"

I shook my head, but even that simple gesture was a lie. I wanted a stiff drink. Hell, I wanted the whole bottle. But that was in the past now. There weren't going to be any more easy nights, no more forgetting my problems and blacking out.

The clamps went on and she screwed them down, grunting to get them to lock into place over my arms. Then she prepared the shot, which looked like a glass vial full of mercury. There was a needle at the end of the vial that was as big as a four inch nail.

14

When she plunged it into my bicep and shot the contents home, I made a hissing sound.

"I should have shown up for that date, right?" I asked.

"That has nothing to do with this necessary medical procedure. Please, just try to relax."

"Uh-huh."

* * *

Later that same afternoon I'd scheduled a meeting with my command staff. I staggered out of Medical and down the hallway, heading for my conference room.

Kate was in the hallway behind me, saying something. I didn't get the words. My head was still ringing and probably full of teeming little buggers that interfered with my nervous system. They did that sometimes. But I figured if I could reach my office chair and sit there for a few minutes, I'd make the meeting.

It wasn't until I passed an ensign with a shocked look on her face that I looked down at myself and took stock of the situation.

I'd torn up my clothing. Fortunately, it was smart cloth, and it was trying to reassemble itself even now. But there were holes in the suit that had yet to seal and my skin showed through in places.

I smiled at the ensign and gave her a painful nod. "The smart cloth is knitting up. Just had a workout," I said.

She nodded quickly and scuttled off. I pressed my tunic together here and there, forcing it to make contact with itself. That always sped up the reknitting process.

When I arrived at the conference room, I was glad to see no one was there. I took my seat at the head of the table and slumped down, touching my ear on the desk. A moment later I was dreaming.

I came awake with a start. Kwon loomed over me, and my shoulder hurt a little. I surmised he'd given me a hard whack.

"You missed your calling as a nurse, Kwon," I said. "You have a natural gentleness to your soul that would comfort anyone in your care."

Kwon frowned. "You're drunk again, right?"

"No, not this time."

I explained about the nanite injection. Kwon commiserated immediately.

"I hate that," he said. "Especially when you piss out the extra metal later on."

"Thanks for reminding me. I require the facilities."

"You going to puke?"

"No, I told you I haven't been drinking."

"Right."

A moment later I found the officer's head. As I growled at the toilet and urinated glitter, I wondered if all my command staff was in a similarly poor state of morale. Kwon was certain I was drunk at a meeting. Had they been making jokes at my expense for weeks? I hadn't really noticed...but then I hadn't been on top of my game lately.

When the rest showed up, my smart cloth suit was in good shape. I had a full pot of black coffee in front of me, and the new nanites in my blood had settled down to a level of activity I could withstand.

Still, despite my forced smile, they all looked at me in concern. None of them spoke as I started the meeting.

"Commodore Miklos," I said, "would you give me your report on the status of our fleet build up? What do we have that could fly into battle today, should the need arise?"

He began his report, and I paid close attention, asking questions every page or so. He listed every vessel, its position, mission and state of readiness.

"What about the carriers?" I asked. "I want to know how many we can fly right now."

He gave me a funny look, then cleared his throat. "As you know sir, we've diverted all our discretionary industrial output to fleet production for the last seventeen weeks."

Seventeen weeks? I frowned. Had it been that long? I'd figured it had been a month or so since the Thor campaign, no more. I gave my head a shake and tuned back in.

"Exactly," I said, as if the timespan wasn't a shock to me. "What have you got to show for it?"

"Seven carriers, sir."

I frowned. "Only seven?"

Miklos looked uncomfortable. "We've gone over this several times over the last—"

"I don't care about recent meetings. Just tell me now. We have only seven carriers when it takes no more than a week to produce one. Why?"

"The fighters, sir. And the support vessels. We need more cruisers and destroyers to accompany the bigger ships."

"Hmm, that doesn't seem to be what I ordered, but under the circumstances, I'm going to let it go. Seven carriers...all loaded with the latest fighters."

"The latest? I suppose so. They are the same design that we used in the Thor system."

I frowned. I'd wanted to make upgrades after flying those little buckets around and shooting up the Macro cruisers.

"We're going to have to talk about that," I said. "I think I might have to do a redesign."

"A redesign? Now? Sir, are you sure that you are in the appropriate state of mind to—"

"Yes," I said, trying not to become angry. I knew they had good reason to doubt me. I could tell now that during my AWOL period, they'd all taken on responsibilities and made decisions without me. I could forgive them for that. It was my fault. But now, it was time to reassume command with a firm hand.

"Commodore," I said, "This fleet composition discussion should be for us alone. Everyone else is dismissed, with this last parting order: be ready to fly within a week. It might not happen, but if it does, I don't want any of you caught with your pants down. I want marine invasion ships, carriers—the works. Everyone is on alert, as of this meeting, which just ended. Dismissed."

They looked at me in surprise. They all wanted to ask the same question: "Fly *where* sir?" but I didn't give them that opportunity.

Only Kwon looked happy. He slammed his hands together making a booming clap.

"Riggs is back!" he said.

I nodded to him and then turned to Miklos who had stayed behind while the rest filed out.

"Nicolai," I said, using his first name on purpose. His eyes widened further, as I almost never spoke to him informally. "I know I checked out for a few weeks. But that's over now. I'm done with all that. Let's get back to business."

"I'm glad that you're feeling better, sir," he said cautiously.

"I'm not. But I'm feeling a lot meaner."

I told him then what Gaines had told me. I told him that the assassination plots had begun and ended with Kerr, and that I'd been in the dark about it for years.

He listened with his usual attentiveness.

"I understand how this could be viewed as a personal affront, Colonel," he began when I was finished. "But I'm not sure it qualifies as a good reason to take military action."

"No," I said, "it doesn't. But fortunately, good reasons for military action are not in short supply. Earth is in the grip of Crow, who has become a dictator of the worst stripe. He's got a worldwide cult of personality going—do you know about that?"

"I've read the same reports you have."

"At first, I held out hope that after he had a firm grip on the reins of power he'd be satisfied, that he would see Star Force as an ally rather than a threat. I mean, doesn't it make sense to you? Why attack us? Why not leave us out here as a buffer between Earth and the Macros?"

"There is a certain logic in what you suggest, Colonel. But not if you're Emperor Crow. As long as you're out here, you are a threat."

"You mean we—as in Star Force."

"Yes, and no. I think he fears you personally. On every occasion in the past when he tried to defeat you, you came out on top. The only reason he's running Earth now is because you brought the core of your force out here to the Eden System, leaving the home planet undefended."

I nodded and massaged my punctured arms. The circular spots were already healing, but they itched and burned.

"Yeah," I said, "I can see how it looks from his point of view. In a way I'm worse than the Macros. People tend to side with me over him, a problem he's never had to face with the machines. In his eyes I guess I'm the playground bully, and he's the determined kid who wants to take me down. But I still say this whole thing is insane. He should let me fight the Macros and use me, if nothing else. If I were him, I'd be feeding me supplies and platitudes. I'd even send out shipments of troublemakers from my own armed services as 'volunteers' for the front. The situation should be a win all the way around—all he has to do is respect our independence."

Miklos shook his head. "He can't do that for any reason. He wants to remain the Emperor of the world and to expand his power. His real goal is to be the absolute ruler of all humanity. You're not cooperating in that regard."

"And I never will."

"Therefore, you must be removed."

I nodded thinking it over. Miklos' impression of Crow matched the facts, unfortunately.

"First," I said, "he sent out orders, trying to tell me what I had to do to appease him. When I ignored his wishes, he sent fleets. All along the way he sprinkled in assassins to get rid of me directly, hoping that Star Force would crumble and return to Earth's control without me at the head."

"I would respectfully suggest that he almost succeeded in that regard a few months ago."

"Yeah. If I'd taken the assassin's dose of poison instead of Sandra—well, he would have scored."

"No sir, I don't quite mean that."

I looked at him seriously. "Explain."

"I think I can do so now—now that you are in a recovered state of mind. You have been out of commission for a long time. The assassin missed you, but she crushed your spirit by killing Sandra. I can only surmise that she had instructions to do exactly that if she could not get to you directly."

I stared at him while thinking about it. I slowly nodded, and resolved with greater intensity to get my act together again. I

19

couldn't let Crow beat me by making me depressed. That simply wasn't happening. I refused to go down that way, with a whimper and an empty bottle in my hand.

"I'm going to have to kill him," I said quietly.

"Yes sir. You probably are."

As we spoke these words, I had to wonder if a similar council of war had been held some months ago back on Earth. I suspected that it had, and that Crow, Kerr and whoever else was advising him had come to exactly the same conclusion. I could almost hear their words echoing in my mind: *"We're going to have to kill Riggs, sir. There's no other way."*

And now I'd come to the same conclusion. Crow had to be removed, and the only way he was going out was feet-first.

But exactly how was I going to pull that off?

-3-

The next few days were a blur of furious activity. I got the feeling my officers had been sitting on their hands lately, leaning back and taking it easy while the big dog got drunk every night and slept it off during the days. But those times were over. I was back in the game, kicking butts and high-fiving people in turn, depending on how they were doing.

The results were immediate and almost startling. Looking out the window of *Gatre* I could see the changes. The fighters were on patrol, swooping around in sharp formation. The factories churned relentlessly, and assembly teams floated outside in vac suits around the clock putting the final touches on all the equipment we could produce.

My next major meeting was with Jasmine Sarin, the Captain of *Gatre*. She met me with a worried expression on her face.

Jasmine was as pretty as always. Her eyes were almond-shaped and refined like the rest of her face. I'd been attracted to her since the first time I'd met her. She was small and quiet, but tougher than she looked. Best of all, she always knew what she was doing.

I flopped into an uncomfortable chair. Just about everything on *Gatre* was uncomfortable. The ship had been built with a minimal number of creature comforts. Except for the wardroom, which served a reasonable selection of alcoholic beverages, and the pool room, there wasn't anything fun to do on this ship. Even the bunks lacked cushions. Fortunately, my people were as hard as stainless steel and didn't complain about it much.

"I hear you're a changed man, Colonel," she said warily.

"It's true," I said, "I'm off the sauce and into working again. We're going to take this ship back into battle. Are you ready for that, Captain Sarin?"

She stared at me for a second. Miklos and I hadn't let our plans become public yet, but there were always rumors in any military. In this case, the rumors were dead-on.

"We're really going back to Earth?" she asked. She almost whispered the question as if it was some kind of heresy.

"Yes, we are."

"But sir, how will that go over with the troops? They didn't sign on to attack Earth's forces. They're here to fight the machines."

I put a finger up and waggled it at her. "We're not going to *attack* Earth. That's entirely the wrong way to say it. I never want to hear you speak those words again in front of anyone. Our goal is to *liberate* our homeworld from a dictator."

She looked unconvinced. "I don't think semantic tricks are going to get you out of this one."

I slammed my fist on the table, making a two-inch deep dent and making her jump.

"I don't want to hear that kind of talk, either. Listen, you've been privately suggesting we take out Crow for years. Now that it comes down to doing it, you're balking? Explain yourself, Captain, before I relieve you of your command."

Jasmine looked shocked. That's just what I'd wanted. I had to get her and my other key officers into line on this one. We had to provide a united front to get the rank and file to follow us. I knew part of her hesitancy was due to my recent lapses. I'd lost some degree of credibility with her. This was my ham-handed way of getting it back.

"That won't be necessary, Colonel," she said in a slightly hurt tone. "I didn't say I was going to actively resist your decision. But I think you need to get all the top commanders into a meeting and talk it over. You have to convince them, Colonel. You can't just announce something like this and expect everyone to follow your orders without question."

I sighed, thinking she was right, and that I didn't want to have that meeting. But after staring into space for about ten seconds, I turned back to her.

"Yeah, all right," I said. "We'll have a meet-and-greet with the whole staff. Get every one of the carrier captains, plus the ground force commanders, into the wardroom for a meeting."

"What about the cruiser captains? And the battle station command people? And the Centaur leadership? Now that I think of it, there's the intel team back on Shadowguard, too."

"All right, all right. Invite them all."

"When?"

"We'll meet in three days. That will give people in outlying areas of the system time to attend. A week after that, we fly. That's the plan."

Sarin looked at me for a moment. "Is there any particular reason—"

"Yeah, there is," I said, interrupting her. "In one week, the eighth carrier will be commissioned. When it's stocked and ready to fly, we all go."

She nodded thoughtfully. "Will eight carriers be enough fleet power, sir?"

"I have no idea. But that's what we have, so we're flying to Earth with everything."

She paused again. "This plan doesn't seem to be meticulously worked out, sir."

"No, it isn't. That's because we have little idea what we'll be facing. But in the interval since the Macros blew down Earth's defenses, I don't think the Imperials have had enough time to rebuild anything like the fleet they had before. They don't have the production capacity we do in alien factories."

"Hmm," she said.

I could tell she didn't like my unverified assumptions.

"I would like to point out," she began, "that we have no real intel on what they have in the way of static defenses. We've seen their fleet, but not their battle stations, etc."

"I have to concede that point. Listen, Jasmine, I'm not a fool. We'll quickly fly out there to Earth's doorstep, then we'll take it slow. We'll probe and scout. When we know what we're up against, we might decide to withdraw. I'm not planning a suicidal plunge, here."

She sighed in relief. I felt slightly insulted. Sure, there had been times in the past when I'd flown by the seat of my pants and all our lives had hung in the balance. But each of those situations had arisen out of a series of unique circumstances.

"Jasmine," I said leaning toward her. "This time will be different. This time, *we* will be the ones in the driver's seat. We'll head out there in an organized fashion and make our play. If things look bad, we'll run.

"Run? Really? Do you promise?"

I chuckled. "Yeah, I promise."

She smiled at me. "In that case, I'm in."

"Excellent!" I said, standing up.

She waved me back down, and I returned to my seat reluctantly. "There are some things you might want to know about, Kyle," she said.

I instantly paid closer attention. She rarely called me Kyle, and when she did, she meant business. I gestured for her to speak.

"There have been alterations made to the production schedules. I want you to know about them now."

"Show me," I said, frowning fiercely.

She produced a series of documents by tapping on the desk between us. She expertly flipped them around for me to read. Some had attached images, video and audio recordings. I thumbed through them.

The short version of the story was that the carriers had been redesigned. They now had twice the number of generators as originally planned. They also had additional engines, a single heavy cannon, and a number of other minor touch-ups.

I turned my face up to meet hers and forced a smile. "Thanks for showing me this. I'm looking at Miklos' work, if I'm not mistaken."

She nodded. Her eyes were worried, as if she expected me to start shouting at her about insubordination and alteration of orders without authorization. I have to admit, those thoughts crossed my mind. But I couldn't see taking that kind of a hard line with her or Miklos. For one thing, it wasn't just Miklos' work. There was no way in Star Force that anyone could circumvent my direct orders without the involvement of many people.

I forced my thin smile to broaden. It almost hurt. "This is exactly what we agreed to back before the Thor campaign," I said. "I'm glad he implemented the more robust designs when we had the time and focus to put into the project. What you have here, is a carrier done right."

I flipped the document back around to her with a flick of my fingers and she looked surprised. Almost shocked. I wondered for an instant if she'd planned to sink Miklos with this revelation. I didn't think Jasmine operated that way, but I supposed she might have changed. She was always hungry for a promotion, and she'd been my exec before Miklos had taken the job. I felt that underneath she still wanted that position back.

"So, he had authorization to do this?" she asked.

"Yes. I was out of it, and he handled the details. The original plan was approved by both of us months ago. Recall that when the Crustaceans came to us for help, we had to hurry up with the carrier design. Now that we've done it right, I can already see advantages."

"Such as?"

"Well, I mentioned scouting and running if there is a problem at the last ring connecting to the Sol system. If the carriers fly more slowly than the rest of the fleet, running is problematic."

She nodded thoughtfully. "May I ask permission then to update *Gatre*?"

"That hasn't been done yet?"

"No," she said quietly.

"Then by all means, press ahead and get the extra engines you need. Even if it takes a few more days. I insist."

Captain Sarin ought to be looking pleased at this point, after all what captain doesn't want a major systems improvement on their vessel? But she didn't look happy, which confirmed my earlier suspicions. She had told me about the design changes privately to steer some rage in Miklos' direction. I didn't like the idea, mostly because I didn't like being thought of as easy to manipulate.

When I got up to leave the meeting I was fuming. I didn't like the fact Miklos had gone off and indulged himself with the carrier designs. I also didn't like that Jasmine was jealous of him and trying to undermine him in my eyes.

But I kept telling myself it was my own damned fault. I'd left my people leaderless, and they'd very naturally begun to assume my job. How could I blame them for that? They had to cover for me the best they could. I told myself I should be happy they hadn't thrown me out of office entirely. They would have had the right to do so. Any officer who'd performed as I had under my command probably would have been tossed into a titanium brig to dry out at the very least, and quite possibly demoted as well.

Jasmine followed me to the door. She stopped me with a touch at my elbow as I reached out to touch the smart metal. My fingers were an inch from the wall when I halted them.

"Kyle?" she asked, looking up at me.

I turned to her, feeling mixed emotions. If she kissed me, I knew I would respond. I wasn't sure what would happen after that.

"I'm glad to have you back in charge," she said, giving me a quick hug.

I patted her gently and smiled. "I'm glad to be back, too."

It was good to feel her body pressed up against mine, even briefly. We separated a moment later and I left her office. The frown that had been riding my face had miraculously transformed into a smile.

* * *

Two days passed swiftly. I worked steadily, pulling double shifts. Every time I stepped onto the bridge by surprise at random hours, everyone lurched into high gear. That was part of my purpose in doing so. I wanted them to see me in full uniform and one hundred percent sober at midnight, dawn and dusk. No one was going to be lounging around any longer. Recess was over.

At the moment it was dawn on *Gatre* and the shifts were changing. I was there to watch both groups, the one leaving for their bunks and the one coming in and no doubt groaning inside their heads when they saw me at the command table.

Of course, it wasn't *really* dawn. In space there was no such thing. Outside the ship the sun was simply a bigger, brighter star than the rest and it burned pretty much around the clock with even intensity. But since humans are used to a day-night cycle, we'd decided to run time onboard ship in a twenty-four hour loop. Pretty much all of us preferred it that way.

As I watched the night shift people file out looking ready for their bunks, I saw a new face among the crowd taking their places. Really, it wasn't exactly a face. It was a brainbox with a lot of tentacles attached. We liked to call this creature "Marvin".

"Colonel Riggs?" he asked upon seeing me.

"Marvin," I responded, smiling.

"I'm surprised to see you here."

"I'm surprised to see you, too."

He stared at me for a moment, his cameras rotated to get different angles. Marvin had a large number of electronic eyes and they often focused exclusively on things that interested him. You could always tell if you were boring him: you would rate only a single camera.

Today, I found myself overwhelmed by scrutiny. There were at least ten cameras aimed in my direction from one angle or another, and I wasn't sure if I should be gratified or insulted.

"Why are you surprised to see me, Colonel?" Marvin asked.

"Because the last I'd heard you were assigned to the battle station. Now, you're on the *Gatre*. How did this change of assignment occur?"

"You approved the change, sir."

"I most certainly did not."

""Shall I play the audio?"

I hesitated. One thing that was especially annoying about Marvin was his tendency to record everything around him.

Even now, this very conversation was being stored in some form in his brainbox. I flattened my mouth in annoyance. There were staffers all around looking at us with mild interest. If Marvin played a recording of me in an obviously drunken state, it would do a lot of harm to my efforts to recapture my authority in their eyes.

"No Marvin, that won't be necessary."

"I see. Do you now recall the order you gave me?"

"Let me ask you, robot: what kind of state was I in when the order was given?"

"As I recall, you were very happy about something."

"Happy?"

"Yes. Happy, as in laughing without apparent cause. I'd assumed you found something humorous about my data reports, but I could not determine what it was."

"Fine, yes. Delete that recording, Marvin, please."

His cameras, which had been slowly drifting away from me now coalesced again in number. They came at me from every angle.

"Are you ordering me to destroy documentation, sir?"

"Marvin, I will stand by the orders I gave. Unless I countermand them, you are free to follow them. But I want that one deleted."

"I see. Done."

I nodded, wondering what other kinds of nonsense Marvin might have drifting in his box. Perhaps I'd given him permission to make an army of robots, or to fill one of Eden's sea worlds with transplanted species of plankton. I would have to keep an eye on him from now on. When he got an idea, he could be very evasive and difficult to redirect onto a harmless path.

"Now that your presence has been confirmed and reauthorized, can I ask you what your mission is here on *Gatre*?"

"Why, to monitor the Blues, sir."

I frowned, and seemed to recall having given him that order. Yes, I had done so, back before Sandra had died, and the world had gone gray for a while.

"Right, what do you have for me?"

"You're original assumptions seem to have been correct, sir."

"Could you be more specific? What are they up to?"

The Blues had been working on a large scale project on their homeworld for months now. Ever since we drove the Macros out of the system, they've been releasing huge energy bolts down deep inside their atmosphere. Initially, I'd believed these releases must be from natural causes. After all, the planet is huge and mostly atmosphere. It is never fully stable, and there are frequent violent storms.

"They appear to be building something," I echoed, frowning and working the command table. The Jupiter-like image of Eden-11 appeared. "Something large... How large?"

"Difficult to say. Standard sensory systems can't penetrate the thick atmosphere."

"Estimate."

"I'd say a mass has been displaced—something on the order of fourteen miles of rock."

It was my turn to stare at him. "Fourteen...? What do you mean by 'miles' of rock?"

"As in diameter. If the mass were a planetary body, it would about the size of Phobos, the larger of the two moons that orbit Mars in the Solar System."

"Hold on, let me make sure I'm getting this. You're saying they've displaced a mass equivalent to that of a moon?"

"Exactly."

My mind was racing. There could not be a pleasant reason why the Blues were building something so big. I'd had no idea up until this moment that they were capable of such a technological feat.

"Marvin," I asked. "Why did you pick Phobos as your comparison?"

"Firstly, because the sizes are similar. Secondly, because of the meaning of the term 'Phobos'"

"Enlighten me, what is the meaning?"

"Phobos is related in meaning to the term 'phobia'. Essentially, Phobos was the Greco-Roman god of fear, sir."

"The god of fear," I echoed, nodding. It all made perfect sense to me now. "Bring up the data you've compiled onto my command table."

Marvin moved with alarming rapidity. His tentacles rasped and scraped on the control panels and manipulated the screens with software transmissions and physical movements simultaneously.

A set of images began to collect on the table. They told a terrifying tale, worthy of a Greek god's namesake.

A grainy image appeared, looking like a boulder embedded on a much larger flat surface. This thing—whatever it was— was big. It was spherical and looked like the inverse of a crater—like a bubble of rock. There were indentations at either end of this otherwise smooth round object.

"Some kind of dome, or something," I said. "All the way down there, at the base of their thick atmosphere? The pressures there must be tremendous. I didn't even know they could operate that deep down at the core of the planet. Do you think it's a building?"

"That has yet to be determined."

While he worked, other staffers gathered around. They seemed as surprised as I was at what he revealed. They tapped at his reports and began doing analysis and confirmation immediately. A murmur rose as one told another. Soon they were thronging the table, and I backed away. I'd seen enough.

"Marvin? Why didn't you report the existence of *Phobos* earlier?"

"I attempted to do so on three separate occasions. You weren't receptive, Colonel."

I wanted to hang my head in shame—but I didn't do it. No one appreciated a weak display in their commander. Next, I thought about asking Marvin to delete any recordings of our interviews, but stopped myself. I deserved a little embarrassment. What I'd done, I'd done to myself. The unfortunate part was that everyone else in Star Force was going to have to live with the consequences.

-4-

I never made it to the big council meeting between all the major players in Star Force. I regretted this later because it would have been good to show them all that I was back and in charge of myself again. But it just wasn't in cards.

Immediately after Marvin told me about the strange structure forming on Eden-11, I ordered heavy probing of the planet's thick atmosphere. Like most gas giants, it was a mix of hydrogen, methane and other compounds. We'd never directly seen a solid or liquid core, but we suspected there was one. Marvin's readings indicated there was something down there, on the "surface", which was growing unnaturally large. The conclusion that it was artificial seemed inescapable.

We didn't have to wait long before new data came in. Perhaps our probing triggered the events that transpired next, I really don't know. But what I do know is that in the depths of their soupy world the massive contact began to stir.

The moment I heard the contact had shifted position slightly, I called an all-hands and ordered the *Gatre* and two of her sister ships to fly toward Eden-11, the Blues' homeworld. By the time everyone started obeying those orders, the thing on Eden-11 was moving faster, rising up slowly out of ten thousand miles of atmosphere.

"Colonel?" Captain Sarin called as she pressed her way through the smart metal hatch and stepped on to the bridge. She crossed the deck to the command table. "Why are we making a maneuver in the middle of the night shift? I like to be informed when drills are being executed."

"This is no drill," I told her without taking my eyes from the table.

I zoomed in the perspective and isolated the object itself with spreading motions of my fingers.

"Tell me Captain, what do you make of that?" I asked her.

She examined it briefly. "It's some kind of satellite. An asteroid or small moon. What's it doing? Which planet is it orbiting?"

"None of them. It is, in fact, lifting off from the surface of Eden-11."

I backed up the perspective so the entire sphere of the Blues' homeworld was visible. The ship—if that's what it was—took up a relatively tiny portion of the massive disk representing the gas giant. But the fact it was big enough to be distinguishable at all when the entirety of its huge mother planet was onscreen was alarming.

"That can't be happening," she said.

I looked at her, and her big brown eyes were as wide as I've ever seen them. Her smart cloth uniform was not quite all the way on yet, and I could see her left shoulder under her flowing hair. Usually, she kept her hair tied up and her arms covered professionally while on the command deck, but I didn't think now was the time to bring up regs. She'd rushed right out of bed to the command deck when she'd heard I was giving her crew flight orders without advising her.

I reached out and tapped the smart cloth over her shoulder, and her uniform sealed itself, covering her skin. I turned back to the images on the command table.

"It's a ship," I said. "There's no other explanation. I suspect that it's lifting off in reaction to our probing and increased scrutiny."

"It's too big to be a ship."

"We look big to ants. Size is all a matter of perspective. When under low atmospheric pressures, an individual Blue can be a mile or more across. In order to accommodate such a crew, they appear to have decided to go big."

32

"May I interject, Colonel?" asked Marvin. He came closer, his tentacles all aflutter. I hadn't seen him this excited since he'd asked me permission to resurrect Sandra.

"Go ahead, Marvin."

"This vessel might not have a living crew. The Nano ships indicated in the past the Blues didn't want to leave their natural habitat."

I put up a finger. "But that was because they were under an agreement with the Macros to stay on their homeworld. They stayed there because they didn't want to start a war. At this point, there are no Macros watching them."

"An important tidbit," Marvin said, "but we don't really know why they've never gone into space personally. After all, they built not one but two species of robot to explore the cosmos in their stead. That seems to be a powerful aversion to spaceflight."

"All right, I grant you all that. We don't *know* they're personally flying this moon-sized ship. What's your point?"

"What if they've developed a third species of inorganic being to man this vessel?"

I stared at him, and Captain Sarin joined me, sharing my shocked reaction. I couldn't argue with him—it *was* a possibility. Jasmine and I took a second to absorb this grim thought. Marvin seemed excited about it, but we were horrified. The Nanos and the Macros had both been invented by the Blues, and they'd caused no end of trouble for Earth and many other worlds.

"Given their track record on the topic of creating artificially intelligent crews," I said, "I seriously hope they didn't take that course again. But I thank you for voicing this disturbing thought."

"No thanks are necessary. If, however, I should be proven right...I would like to be given the chance to interact with the new form of machine life. I've met numerous biotic species, but my own kind seem to be relatively rare."

Jasmine cast me a dark look that indicated she didn't think it would be a good idea, but I didn't respond to her expression. Instead, I nodded to Marvin. "You'll be front and center when it comes to talking to that ship, regardless of who's flying it."

33

Marvin churned away happily to check more of his specialized instrumentation. New reports were being processed and transmitted to us by our sensory systems in orbit over Eden-11 every minute. Although we'd always had difficulty examining what was going on down in the depths of the gas giant, we'd set up a large number of orbital probes to scan anything that came near the surface.

"What if he's right, Colonel Riggs?" Jasmine asked me.

I shrugged. "Then we'll either talk our way out of a fight, or destroy this new monstrosity. We've defeated two machine races. A third won't change the situation."

I said this loudly, and with absolute confidence. Internally, I was far less certain. I really hoped that ship was full of talkative cloud-people rather than some kind of new, nightmarish machine.

Really, the more I thought about it, the more I should have expected the Blues to come up with something like this. After all, they'd built the Macros and the Nanos and had to have spaceships to get them into orbit. Those accomplishments demonstrated an amazing technological capability. No matter who was manning that ship, I had to assume the vessel could wield vast firepower.

"How long until we reach Eden-11?" I asked the lieutenant manning the helm.

"We'll have three carriers there with a full complement within four hours, sir."

"Okay then, Marvin, could you stop fooling with that and help me translate?"

Reluctantly, the robot left his instruments and came nearer.

"The reports are fascinating Colonel Riggs," he said. "There's armament aboard the ship, that much is clear, but I don't recognize the variety. Something big, with a nozzle—or maybe it's a projector—at each of the moon's poles."

"The moon's poles? I thought you said it was a ship."

"The composition of the vehicle is largely silicon-based. Since it is made of rock and its big enough to have a significant gravitational pull of its own, I believe it qualifies as both a celestial body and a spacecraft."

I grunted. If we did have to tangle with this thing, the matter couldn't end well. It outweighed my four carriers significantly.

"How much displacement are we talking, here?" I asked.

"Difficult to say. But I would hazard to guess the vessel outweighs our fleet by a thousand to one."

"All four of our carriers? A thousand to one?"

"No sir, I mean all the ships in Star Force put together."

I stared at the moon-ship, which we'd decided to call *Phobos*. I typed the tag in on the flashing contact as it exited the atmosphere and rose up into space.

"What kind of propulsion does it have?"

"I can't measure any appreciable energy expenditure," Marvin said, his tentacles rasping on the command consoles. "There is a considerable amount of disruption in the upper cloud layers of Eden-11, however."

I could see that for myself. There was something of a divot in the top layer of the planet—like a depression that was slowly filling back in. I wasn't up on my fluid mechanics, but I had to assume that the ship's passage through the thick air had disturbed it.

"Velocity?"

"Approximately thirty-six thousand miles per hour now and accelerating steadily."

I frowned. Any normal type of propulsion system would require some kind of released energy. But this ship didn't appear to have any engines, and there was no exhaust—nothing.

"I don't like this at all," I said. "It's bigger than our entire fleet and we don't even know how it flies. We have to assume it can blow us from the sky if it wants to."

"In that case, maybe we should try diplomacy, Colonel?" Captain Sarin suggested.

"That's why the best translation robot in the known universe is right here. Ready a transmission to the Blues, Marvin."

"Ready."

"Do not transmit until I give you that specific order, do you have that Marvin?"

"Understood. Standing by."

"Record this," I said, then cleared my throat. "Blues, this is Colonel Kyle Riggs, the commander of Star Force. We've had peaceful contact with your species on several occasions, but we've also had encounters that were less pleasant. I would like to hear your explanation for the large ship rising up out of your atmosphere. We had an agreement that you would stay on your planet and not attempt to contact the machines."

I turned to Marvin. "Stop recording. Do you have that?"

"Yes."

"When you transmit, can you make it appear it isn't coming from this ship? I don't want them to pinpoint our command vessel."

"Done."

"All right, send it."

Marvin did so, and we all waited. It was a long wait as we were about ten light minutes from Eden-11. The message had to travel there, the Blues had to generate a response, and then that message had to crawl back. I figured we'd hear something within a half-hour.

In the meantime, *Phobos* rose up completely out of the atmosphere but didn't park itself into orbit. Instead the big ship kept coming.

I frowned, studying the data. "What's the escape velocity of that gas giant?"

"About five times as great as Earth, sir," Marvin answered promptly.

"But that ship isn't moving that fast. It's accelerating straight up and up, but not going fast enough."

"With enough power, you can blast away from any world at any rate of speed."

My concerns deepened. What was the vessel capable of? Was attacking it suicidal? I had no idea. I didn't even know if it was going to attack us if we did nothing or if we could even hope to damage it if we struck first. I began to feel hot in my flight suit.

"Sound battle stations," I said, "and get everyone into a vac suit. If you have full battle gear—put it on. Oh, and get ready to scramble the fighters."

36

Sarin stared at me for a moment. "We can't be in range yet, sir."

"Probably not. We're just taking precautions."

"But if we send out the fighters, won't that look like an aggressive move to them?"

"I don't know, and I don't give a damn. I want them out buzzing around for any contingency. Personally, I doubt they know much about carriers and fighters, anyway. They're unlikely to see the move as aggressive."

She relayed the orders. Klaxons rang, and people scrambled over the decking getting their kits in order. The lights changed, dimming and gaining a reddish tint.

"It's been nearly half an hour," I said a few minutes later. "Any response from the Blues yet? Even a blip?"

"Nothing, Colonel."

"Do we even know if they received the message?"

"The transmission was sent using their own language and utilized channels known to work in the past."

I stared at the command table, fuming. Damn these gasbags. They always made me sweat. They often didn't answer any signals until forced to. In the past, I'd bombed them to get an answer. I didn't have that sort of option today. I didn't want to appear as if I was threatening their homeworld.

"They've changed everything with this move," Jasmine said next to me. She'd been standing there quietly for quite a while.

"What do you mean?"

"They built a fleet. Or at least one monster ship. Now we have to give them respect. We can't just order them around because today they have the power to strike at us."

I guessed she was right, but I didn't like it. I glared at the screen. The situation could very easily get out of hand. I'd ordered my tactical teams to come up with a strike plan against *Phobos*, but they weren't having much luck.

When dealing with alien ships in the past, we'd targeted either their engines or their weaponry. With this vessel, we were having trouble even identifying a target. There were protrusions at the poles as well as other, smaller structures here

37

and there on the surface, but I had no idea if these represented vital systems we could knock out.

I finally voiced my thoughts and frustrations. "Hell, for all we know this is a colony ship. Or a freighter full of merchandise to trade."

"Do you really think that's a possibility, Colonel?" Marvin asked.

"No," I admitted. "But we just don't know. Marvin, we're going to send a second message. This one will be more diplomatic."

"Ready."

"Same deal as before, don't transmit until I give you the command, and make it look like it came from someplace else."

"Still ready."

I glanced at him sidelong. Sometimes I wondered if he was a smart-ass or a straight-man. I supposed it was a little of both.

"Blues, friends, comrades," I began. Several people perked up and looked at me in surprise. I did my best to avoid eye contact with them. I didn't want them to distract me from my speech. "In the name of friendship, I ask you to respond. We're willing to discuss new terms. We wish to change the nature of our relationship with your people and come to a new understanding between our two peoples."

I glanced at Marvin. "Did you get that?"

"Ready to transmit."

"Do it."

"Message sent."

The next half hour was worse than the first one. They'd ignored my first message entirely, and we were getting closer by the second. How much range did they have? Was this a battle or a misunderstanding?

"We could fire missiles, Colonel," Sarin said.

"I know that. But that is a very clear attack. Words of peace followed by a flock of missiles? I know where that will end. With one side or the other destroyed."

"Yes sir, but they aren't talking, and we're reaching what I've calculated to be their maximum possible range."

I frowned and went over her figures. I scoffed at the numbers. "That can't be. Millions of miles? What kind of laser is effective and focused at that range? To the best of my knowledge, these people are blind and might not even understand optics."

"I doubt there is any region of basic science they have not mastered," she argued. "A laser would not have to be focused precisely if it was powerful enough. The beam could be as big as this entire vessel and still vaporize us if it was fired with sufficient power."

I shook my head. She was right mathematically, but I didn't think the Blues would use lasers. After all, their natural environment didn't permit vision of any kind. Beams of intense light wouldn't be natural weapons for them.

"I've been down there on their world," I told her, "It's as dark and dense as a sandstorm at the bottom of an ocean. How would you even test a long range optical weapon in such an environment? They would have to have come up into orbit to fire it, and we would have seen it months ago."

"I'm just being cautious and looking after my ship."

I couldn't fault her for that. Ten more minutes passed, and I became antsy again. There was only time enough left for one more transmission and response before our two paths crossed.

"Marvin, prepare—"

"Excuse me, sir," he said. "I'm detecting an energy surge—"

"Kyle, look!"

We saw it on the command screens first. One of our four carriers winked out—or rather, it rapidly reduced in size to a blip no bigger than a gunship. The new configuration was misshapen and irregular. It looked like a wad of gum someone had chewed and spat out on the sidewalk.

"Emergency evasion!" Captain Sarin screamed. "Ready all missile tubes, scramble all reserve fighters, transmit e-code delta-delta to Shadowguard!"

I stood beside her, but didn't interfere, she was listing off every emergency command she had on the books. That was the right thing to do, and I wasn't going to second guess any of them.

"They just destroyed *Defiant*," she said, still in shock.

"Is that confirmed?" I asked.

"Yes," Marvin said brightly. None of our stress or dismay was evident in his voice. "The carrier *Defiant* is now reduced in composition and size, but not in total mass."

"What're you saying?" I demanded. "Didn't they blow it up?"

"No sir. They appear to have crushed it somehow. It is now flat and crumpled. The alloys are fused, and although there are secondary explosions, the central mass seems stable now. I expect no survivors will be found."

"No kidding," I said. "Marvin, when I told you to hide the source of my transmissions, what did you do?"

"I relayed them through *Defiant*, sir," he said brightly.

I nodded. "That's what I thought."

-5-

The next few minutes were like a mass panic. We scrambled every fighter we had and threw every emergency plan into action.

Black metallic tentacles sprouted from the smart metal decking and entwined themselves around our legs. More came down from the ceiling and ensnared our upper bodies. They were programmed to let us move as freely as possible, but the end result was like moving around with car restraints all over you—restraints that had peculiar ideas about what they should let you do.

I let Sarin do her thing. In this action, I couldn't use her as my exec for the overall battle. As I watched she moved to another station where she could manage her ships and her fighters. As the captain of *Gatre*, her first responsibility was to her own vessel. At the same time, she was operating as the ship's CAG, which seemed like more than enough.

In her place stood Marvin and a few staffers at the central command table. The holotank hanging above it was full of contacts. All the missiles and ships were green because they were all ours—except for one big spherical mass the size of a baseball. It was red now, having been reclassified as an enemy target.

"Where's Miklos?" I asked. "Was he on *Defiant* when it was hit?"

"Negative sir," Marvin answered. "The Commodore is attempting to communicate with me right now."

"Patch him through to me."

There was a squawk and a few beeps, then a crackling sound. "Miklos? Do you read me? This is Colonel—"

"Yes sir, loud and clear."

"Good. Did you escape the *Defiant*? If so, what hit you?"

"I've got no clue, sir. I was flying a pinnace between *Defiant* and your ship when the enemy struck us."

I wanted to ask him why he was doing that, but I simply didn't have time. I was very glad he had survived. He was the commander of the *Defiant*, but that didn't mean he had to die with her. I valued him as my second in command more than the ship itself...well, almost.

"Well then, get aboard and come to the command deck. We've got a very hard battle ahead of us."

"Sir, I think that would be a mistake."

"What would be a mistake? Talk quickly and plainly, Commodore, we're under fire here."

"Yes sir. I don't think we *can* fight them. We aren't even in range to strike yet. If we launch every missile and fighter we have left, they wouldn't even notice for twenty minutes."

He was right. My carriers didn't have heavy, long-range guns. They had a few cannons for aerial bombardment but nothing that was going to effective against a target as big as a moon.

"But what choice do we have, Commodore? If we get in close enough and attack, maybe we'll win. If they kill us before that, well, then it's over anyway."

"We can run, sir."

I frowned, looking at the boards. I shook my head. "I don't think so. Have you looked at the tactical situation?"

"Yes, and I still say it's our only option. Every second we spend closing with them is a second we could better use trying to escape."

I gritted my teeth and tried to think. Around me, a dozen voices were shouting at once. The klaxons kept blaring until I ordered them shut off. I figured everyone had gotten the point by now, and they weren't doing anything other than giving me a headache.

"We can't reverse course, our speed is too great."

Miklos tapped my arm. I startled, then smiled. I clapped him on the shoulder, making him stagger back a step. He'd been on his com-link, but had managed to reach me during the conversation.

"Glad to see you make it out of that mess alive, Commodore. Step into my office and use the screens to show me what you're thinking."

Miklos still had his vac suit sealed. He had to struggle out of it and I saw frost inside the helmet. Maybe his escape had been closer than he'd indicated. We didn't have time for chatting about it so I let him do his job.

"We can't turn around due to inertia, but we can veer off at an angle," he said, running a finger in an arc across the screen. The brainboxes immediately interpreted his gesture and plotted a theoretical course with many slight corrections of their own. I watched as he directed our ships toward the homeworld of the Blues, right past the enemy fleet.

"Why do you want to head that way? To convince them we're on an attack run? Or maybe you want us to threaten to bomb their world?"

"Possibly sir, but really I wanted to achieve maximum velocity. If we head for their planet, we'll get the added benefit of the extreme gravitational forces exerted by Eden-11 to increase our speed. We can then slingshot around it, changing course rapidly by using the gravity again, and make good our escape. We can choose practically any destination we want, and they won't know where we're going until we break orbit."

I nodded. "We'll do both. I want our fighters to head at them in a loose cloud formation. They'll do a passing run then rejoin us in orbit over Eden-11."

"Is that wise, sir? That will end any chance of achieving a ceasefire with them."

"Take a look around, Miklos. They aren't even answering my transmissions. They have no interest in peace, and that won't change as long as they think they have the upper hand. Besides, I'm hoping they might shoot at the fighters instead of taking out the rest of the motherships. Execute the plan."

Miklos didn't hesitate further. He turned and began shouting to every navigator present, and they tapped their

43

screens to set the course. Soon, the ship was shaking and we all began sliding toward the aft bulkhead. I had three or four lateral Gs on me within thirty seconds, and it kept building. For the first time since the crisis had started, I was glad my feet were wrapped up by metal vines.

Once our course was established, we had a bit more time to breathe. I didn't feel relaxed by any stretch of the imagination, however. At any moment that ship could reach out and snuff another of my best vessels.

"What was that weapon? Any theories?"

Marvin's tentacles did a dance in response. "I have several, sir."

"Give me the most likely one."

"They have developed a weapon beyond our science and employed it in such a way as to leave no traces as to its origins."

I rolled my eyes. "That's obvious, Marvin. What I want is speculation as to the nature of said weapon. Are there any trace radiation readings? Any chemical signatures? Anything at all?"

"I believe my initial statement clearly indicated we don't have that data."

I turned away from Marvin in frustration. Sometimes his precision was irritating. This was one of those times. "Has anyone thought to ping that wreck? What have we got?"

The staffers gave me startled looks in return.

"People, pull it together. Someone should be out there in a vac suit by now, looking for survivors and taking samples. We have to know what we're up against."

I reached out and grabbed an ensign by a handful of his smart-cloth suit. I pointed toward the airlock. "Get to the Commodore's pinnace, fly out to the wreck and report what you find. Take an instrument kit and a sensor box."

"Both of those items are already aboard my pinnace, sir," Miklos said helpfully.

The startled ensign looked at both of us with wide eyes. He found no comfort in either of our faces. He seemed too stunned to reply.

I decided to help him get moving. I lifted him with one hand until his boots were clear of the floor. The tentacles that

44

were responsible for his feet were upset about that, and tugged to pull him back down.

"Sir?" he asked, as if dazed, "how will I get back? We're accelerating away from the wreck on an angular course."

I ripped him loose from the tentacles and propelled him toward the exit. He had the presence of mind to put his hands out in front of him before he hit the hatch, which turned to liquid at his touch.

"Someone will pick you up later," I called after him. "Be happy, Ensign. You might be *Gatre's* sole survivor today."

As he drifted out of the chamber and into the airlock, he didn't look happy. But sometimes I'm not good at reading people's expressions.

"Sir?" Marvin said at my side. I felt his tentacles tapping and rasping at my suit.

I turned on him, glowering. "What have you got?"

"I believe we were just hit again."

That got my full attention. I scanned the carriers and did a quick count. There were still five. I zoomed in on several in turn, examining their mass and their readings.

"I think you're wrong about that, Marvin," I said in relief. "Every vessel is accounted for and showing green."

"I'm not talking about the carriers, Colonel."

I suddenly understood. A second later Jasmine reported in.

"We just lost three fighters from 2nd Squadron. They were mine, Colonel."

I nodded in sudden understanding. Really, this was good news. If they wasted shots against our fighters when they could take out an entire carrier with one hit, we were winning—well, at least we would last longer.

"Sir, I'm ordering my fighters to spread out farther."

"Belay that, Jasmine."

There was a moment of quiet, then a private channel request began blinking. I hesitated, then took the call.

It was Captain Jasmine Sarin, naturally. She was calling me privately, even though we were only a few feet apart. It was a technique we employed when we didn't want our underlings to see us arguing in public.

"What are you doing, Kyle?" she demanded. "If I spread them out, they might only get one fighter with their next shot. Why risk more?"

"Because I want them to keep shooting at fighters, not our big ships. It's grim, Jasmine, but that is the calculus of war. We only have three carriers left in this task force and I need them all."

"So my fighter pilots are just out there to bait the enemy?"

"If all goes well and they don't get any smarter, yes. Riggs out."

I disconnected and turned back to Miklos. He nodded to me.

"You had no choice, Colonel," he said. "If we make the fighters harder targets we could be cutting our own throats."

"Do you have a timing interval between the first strike and the second?"

"I do, Colonel," chimed in Marvin. "My best estimate is nine minutes and seven seconds. This interval may change as we close with the enemy. I can't estimate the variation until I know more about the nature of the weapon system."

"Nine minutes," I said thoughtfully. "That's a long time. That's excellent news, in fact. I surmise from this data they have a very powerful, long-range weapon, but it has a serious weakness: a slow rate of fire."

"I would agree with that assessment, sir."

I turned back to the boards, thinking hard. We would be past them in roughly twenty nine minutes. Time enough for three more shots.

"When will the fighters hit them?" I asked.

"In approximately two minutes," Marvin answered.

"Any sign of enemy point-defense fire? Any smaller weapons at all?"

"Not yet, sir."

It was hard not to order the fighters to spread out on their final attack run. I couldn't be sure if I was sacrificing them needlessly. But such decisions were the bane of all commanders in a tough fight. In the end, I knew I had to play it safe. The enemy had already struck us a grievous blow, and I intended to get out of this without suffering a second crippling

46

strike if at all possible. In the end, fighters were much easier to replace than an entire carrier.

The minutes crawled by while we all watched the screens, staring until our eyes stung before daring to blink.

We were running, and I didn't like that, but I didn't see any better options. The enemy looked invincible. When faced with an overwhelming force, the only sane choice was to withdraw and study the target, hoping to find a weakness. We'd been surprised, and we had no plan and no real data on which to base a plan. Running was the only thing that made sense.

But my fighter pilots didn't know that. As far as they were concerned, they'd been tasked with taking out a moon that was for all intents and purposes a flying wall of solid rock. I didn't envy their situation. But I didn't know how to help them.

"Two fighters more were just taken out—the ships were from the 6th Squadron," Miklos reported.

"The interval has reduced, but it is still lengthy," Marvin said. "I think the weapon may be limited to the speed of light, Colonel. That may explain why it hit us sooner this time."

"Well, at least we've got that going for us," I said.

My carriers were now passing the big rock and hurtling toward Eden-11. Soon, we would be out of their range. I began, for the very first time, to feel a tiny relaxation in my belly. It was a small thing really, just enough to realize that I'd been clenching up my guts for nearly half an hour now. My muscles ached from the tension. I wanted to rub my neck, but my helmet was in the way.

"Sir? The fighters have almost reached the target. The pilots are reporting a variation in the enemy ship's attitude."

"What's it doing?"

"Uh, rotating sir. It's coming around—to face us."

"Emergency evasive procedures!" I roared. "All carriers, assume incoming fire is imminent."

"It hasn't been anything like nine minutes," Miklos argued.

The ship was rolling and shaking at this point. Both of us clung to our table, and our bodies were whipped about. We must have looked like trees in a hurricane.

"We're a lot closer than we were last time," I told him. "That may have shortened the timespan required to cycle their weapons."

"You think they've decided to ignore the fighters?"

"Wouldn't you? It only makes sense to worry first about the big ships heading toward your homeworld."

"I see. Orders sir?"

"Fire our missiles. All of them. Target the structures at the poles. Maybe that will do something."

Up until this moment, we'd held onto our limited supply of nuclear missiles. We had sixteen of them on each carrier. At first, I hadn't given the order to fire them because we didn't have a clear target. Later, I'd held back because I wanted the enemy to go for the fighters instead of our motherships. Now, it seemed to me I was in a use-it-or-lose-it situation.

I felt the vessel shudder as the missiles left their tubes. They fired in rapid succession. I hoped they'd do some good when they struck home.

There was a short interval then during which nothing happened. *Gatre* was still twisting and jerking from side to side. But there was no evidence of a strike against us, not yet.

Then, with no warning whatsoever, another carrier was hit.

"Hit confirmed. It was *Excelsior* this time, Colonel."

I nodded to Miklos and he brought the data up on the screen. Looking at the ship, I didn't see the damage at first. Unlike *Defiant*, it wasn't a total loss. The ship hadn't been crushed like a beer can. Could the enemy weapon—whatever it was—be weakening?

But then Miklos rotated the view and the secondary explosions became apparent aboard *Excelsior*. A hole gaped in the aft region of the hull.

"It looks like a shark has taken a huge bite out of *Excelsior's* ass," I said.

"Exactly what I was thinking, sir. I think our evasion had some effect. It was not a perfect hit."

"Either our evasion, or the reduced timeframe. Maybe it takes them nine minutes to stoke up to a full charge with their system. Maybe if they fire it faster, it is less effective—or less accurate.

48

"It might be that. In any case, less than a third of the ship has been crushed."

"That's enough to cripple any vessel. Unless I'm mistaken, the engines are in that aft third."

"Confirmed. The engines are gone and the ship is disabled, but what's left is holding together and many of the crew may have survived."

I wasn't so sure about that, but I didn't argue. I decided to let people believe they might survive this terror weapon if we took a hit. It might make them feel less helpless. But I was beginning to think this weapon did something to distort the fabric of matter in a localized area, and if that was the nature of it, human tissue was a lot softer than a ship's steel hull. The ship might be left partly intact while the entire crew died.

"Sir, course corrections on *Phobos*," Miklos said. "The ship is coming about and reducing speed. It is now heading in the precisely opposite direction it was traveling before."

I nodded. "Reversing course and flying back home, eh? That makes sense. At least we know they can think rationally. Maybe we can use that to our advantage."

Miklos gave me an odd look that I ignored. I knew he didn't like the idea of threatening another biotic species' homeworld. In the past, we'd bombed Eden-11 briefly to get them to cooperate. Possibly, this time things would go even more badly for the Blues back home.

Before *Phobos* could take another shot at us, the fighters made their run. The tiny ships had been forced to reduce speed in order to make an effective attack. If they'd just flashed by at a million miles an hour, there would have been little point to the attack. They'd been decelerating, and therefore reached the big ship after we'd already passed by.

We watched as the four squadrons of fighters, nearly a hundred craft in all, flashed over the rocky exterior. It looked for all the world as if they were attacking a moon or an asteroid. The surface was dusty, barren stone. We watched with unblinking intensity as they fired beams and what ballistic weapon they had against the behemoth, focusing on the strange superstructures which were mounted at either pole.

49

They kicked up a lot of dust and looked impressive, but I got the impression they weren't doing much effective damage. The superstructure was still there after they'd passed by.

Our own ships were leaving them behind. We'd passed the enemy laterally and were now heading toward Eden-11 while *Phobos* was still flying away from it.

"Are they taking any flak?" I asked.

"Negative, sir," Miklos said. "The enemy seems to be ignoring them."

"I'm not surprised. They look like gnats annoying an elephant. Have them spiral around and hit again. This time, they can use their bombs."

We'd held in reserve a small cache of fission weaponry for bombing runs. Normally, that sort of weapon would be unwieldy and overkill when attacking a ship. But this ship was the size of a planet, and so it needed to be treated like one.

"They are low on fuel, sir," Miklos cautioned me.

"Yeah, and I'm low on ships. One more run, bombs hot."

He nodded and the orders were given. The tactical display shifted as we watched. The fighters looped out and away, and then swept back toward *Phobos*. This time, explosions blossomed from the surface so thickly it was nearly hidden from view.

I smiled, at last impressed. "That should get their attention."

"I'm getting an energy reading, sir…" Marvin said suddenly. "Something coming from the enemy ship."

"Have you seen this before?"

"Only an echo of it, before the big weapon fired. And also, of course, back on Eden-11."

"You've never said anything about an energy surge."

"You never asked about it."

I glared at him for a second. I was going to have to have a full debriefing from Marvin on exactly what he'd known and when. One of the troubles humans had when dealing with him was his tendency to withhold information. To this day, I was never sure if he did it to keep secrets or because he honestly didn't know what we would be interested in.

I looked back to the tactical display, frowning.

50

"Pull them out of there," I said, "get my fighters away from that moon."

Miklos didn't hesitate or argue with that order. Soon, a river of silver fish zoomed away from *Phobos* in a rush.

They didn't make it far. From our point of view, it looked like *Phobos* shimmered. One second it was shrouded in plumes of dust and escaping fighters, and the next moment there was an odd waver, as if the camera were shooting the scene through a heat shimmer on a hot summer highway.

The contacts, which were green triangles on the screen, winked out by the dozen. I could see it, a wave emanating from *Phobos*, in the form of dying fighters.

"Sir, I..." began Miklos, but he trailed off. His voice sounded ragged.

All over the command deck there were sighs and gasps. I stared at the screen, feeling sick inside.

"Let me guess," I said, "They were crushed. Are there any craft still transponding? Are there any survivors?"

"Yes sir—nineteen of them made it out, sir."

I nodded. "So it has a second weapon. Something with a much wider area of effect. But this weapon has a shorter range. It looks like it extends a hundred miles or more from the surface of *Phobos*. They can reach out and destroy everything that's close all at once. That's just grand."

"Colonel?" Marvin called for my attention.

I looked at him wearily. I'd just lost half my fighters and half my motherships. We'd been crushed in this battle, if one could even call it a "battle".

"What is it?"

"There is a piece of good news. I estimate our motherships are now out of range of the enemy. Due to the combined velocities and widely varied course of our two fleets, they will not have time to recharge their long-range weapon. We've escaped."

"That's great. How long until our missiles hit them?"

"About three minutes."

We all watched tensely until the flock of missiles reached the enemy moon. At the last possible second, the field rose up again and batted down the nearest half.

51

"Signal all the remaining missiles to detonate. Maybe the shockwave will shake them up a bit."

Far from effective range, the missiles self-destructed, blossoming like a hundred tiny pinpoints of brilliant light. I saw *Phobos* blow through the radioactive cloud they left behind as if it was nothing.

I sighed and withdrew from the command table. I took my place in a crash seat, brooding. The command center was quiet and somber. The battle had been depressing. We'd lost a lot of good people and about half the task force hardware. In fact, counting everything Star Force had, we were down by ten percent after a single engagement.

Captain Sarin approached me as I sat and stared.

"Kyle, we've faced new enemies before."

I looked at her, becoming aware of her presence for the first time. I forced a smile onto my features.

"That's right," I said. "We've learned a lot about this new player in the game, and we'll be better able to deal with them next time.'"

She looked relieved to hear my brave, confident words. It never ceased to amaze me when my staff bought statements like that. I guess it was what they needed to hear, so they believed it. In my mind, we were in a grim situation. All the careful preparations I'd made to build fences and keep our enemies outside them had been for nothing. Here was a newly announced enemy, and they were standing right in the midst of our home system.

Worse, they possessed weapons that seemed to brush aside our best attacks and so far, they weren't talking.

Yes, the more I thought about it, the more I was certain. We were screwed.

"Whatever you do, Kyle," Jasmine said to me quietly, "please don't do what I know you want to."

I blinked and forced myself to look at her. I was thinking hard, and coming up with nothing in the way of a solution.

"What's that?" I asked her.

"Don't bomb their homeworld."

I shook my head. I was about to say 'with what?' but stopped myself. We still had some missiles and half our complement of fighters. They carried bombs with them and could release them into the atmosphere of Eden-11.

"Wait a minute," I said, "did you just say you think I want to bomb them?"

"Yes."

"Why would you think that?"

She looked momentarily confused. "Because we just took a hard loss and you've bombed them before. This time, I would find it hard to argue with the move."

"I don't *want* to bomb them, Jasmine. I didn't want to the first time, either. I'll admit that I get tied up in these things. It's hard not to when people you know are out there, dying while under your command."

"I understand that perfectly."

"I'm sure you do. But in any case, they're fighting fairly, and I don't see any logic in attacking their civilian populations."

"They might withdraw if you do. They might go back home and stay there defending the planet."

I looked at her thoughtfully. There was a tightness to her expression. She was maintaining a poker face, I realized. At some level, I figured *she* wanted to bomb them. I thought I knew why, after thinking about it. Her ships had been attacked with impunity. Her pilots had been expunged like fleas in a poisonous bath. They'd never had a chance. She was angry and reacting emotionally. I hadn't thought I'd see that trait in her before, but perhaps being in command of a big ship had changed her somewhat. She felt personally responsible for the carrier crews and the dead pilots.

"Jasmine," I said softly, "If we hit their cities—if they have cities—they may well fly to Eden-8 and erase our farming communities. Did you think of that? What if we lose this fight? You don't want to endanger our own civilians, do you?"

It was her turned to look startled. "Of course not, Colonel."

"Good. Now, have you got anything else to report?"

"Nothing that will help us win this fight."

I nodded, unsurprised. "Carry on, Captain."

On the main displays I saw Eden-11 looming close. Our ships, as big as they were, looked like microbes beside the gas giant.

I did some hard thinking. What the hell was I going to do next? After a few minutes, I thought I had it. There were plenty of dangers involved and some tricky details I hadn't worked out yet—but at least it was a plan.

I walked up to the navigational tables. I watched as the staff plotted optional courses. The commander in charge of navigation waved me closer.

"I'm glad you're here, sir," she said. "I wanted to know which path you want us to take. We're quite near the planet, and we need to make that decision now."

"Give me some options."

"Well, we've preplotted several. You could use the planet as a brake, swing around and face the enemy as they follow us. We could make another high-speed attack pass."

I looked at the navigator and I could tell that she didn't want me to take that option. But she was putting up a good front.

"What else is on the menu?" I asked her.

"You could slingshot around and head toward Welter Station."

I nodded. "Right. If they follow us, they'll have to contend with the heavy weaponry on the battle station. Not a bad choice. Is that it?"

"Well, no sir. We thought you wanted a thorough selection of options. We've worked out a course to take us back to Eden-8, where the rest of the primary battle fleet is stationed."

"Absolutely no way on that one," I said, "I'm not towing this monster back to our primary world. They may well decide to take the time to scrape every human off the surface—after demolishing the rest of our fleet, naturally."

The navigator drew a blank expression. "Well...where do you want to go then, Colonel?"

"I've been giving it a lot of thought, actually. I think we're going through the ring—the Helios ring."

"Ah," she said, brightening. "Let the Worms deal with it. Is that it?"

"Certainly not. Our allies don't deserve that kind of treatment."

"Are we just going to let it chase us forever, sir?"

I smiled grimly. "I know just where I'm taking this big bastard," I said. "All the way to Earth. It will make a nice Christmas present for a certain Emperor Crow."

The navigator looked at me as if I was crazy. I had to admit, she could be right.

-6-

Now that I had a plan, I realized it was going to be difficult to pull off. My staff felt the same way.

"Sir," Miklos said in our first meeting on the subject, "that idea is simply unfeasible."

"Why?" I asked. "So far, the ship is following us doggedly. The first shot they took they attempted to kill me personally. I don't think they'll rest until they've destroyed our entire task force—or until we've destroyed them."

"There are so many flaws it's difficult for me to explain them all at once."

I frowned. "Give it a shot."

Inwardly, I groaned as Miklos raised a hand and began ticking off his complaints on his fingers. He really did have a large number of them. Underneath it all, I think he was mostly upset he'd lost so many carriers and that his beloved fighters had been ineffective against this enemy. He took fleet losses very hard.

"First, we don't know that the enemy will continue to follow us."

"That's a good one," I said, "and I have a plan to keep them on target. But continue your list. It's your turn at bat, Commodore. Swing away."

The second finger came up. This was his middle finger, and I realized he was now just one digit away from giving me the bird. I tried not to be distracted by this as Europeans often didn't attach the same significance to the gesture.

56

"Second, the enemy ship is slow. We'll soon outrun it. Even assuming they duplicate our slingshot action, they will fall a full day's flight behind very quickly."

"Good point, but moot. We're slowing down. Can't you feel the deceleration? I'm going to circle Eden-11 smoothly and gently."

Miklos looked startled. He turned to Captain Sarin, who nodded. I'd already ordered all the ships to slow down, and she didn't like it either.

"Slowing down in the middle of a battle? In the middle of an escape operation? That's not a normal procedure."

"This isn't a normal battle," I said. "On the plus side, the move will give us a chance to pick up our fighters. The numbers on their fuel supply were close—this way, they'll easily catch up and land on the remaining motherships. As an additional bonus, the rest of our fleets will be able to rendezvous with us before we leave the system."

Again, Miklos looked startled. He still had two fingers up, but his mouth was slightly open.

"That was point three," he said.

"What?"

"The difficulty in uniting our fleet."

"Well, put that finger up and consider it knocked down again."

"But sir, do we really want to put our entire force in jeopardy? The enemy might have capabilities we are unaware of. They have already exhibited weaponry and propulsion we don't understand."

"Explain."

"What if they have a longer range than we realize?"

"They would have used it by now."

"We can't be absolutely certain of that. They might have power problems after launching, maybe all their reactors aren't online yet—or whatever it is they use for power. Maybe once they're up to cruising speed and no longer need maneuvering power, they'll be able to apply more energy to their weapons. That is point four, by the way: we can't engage with an enemy we don't understand, it's too dangerous."

"Listen," I said, "you've made some good points that show our weaknesses and demonstrate various frightening unknowns. But we're in the middle of this. We can't just outrun them and leave the Eden colonies undefended. We have to guide them the hell out of here."

Miklos' hand finally sank down. I was glad to see it go.

"Okay sir," he said thoughtfully, "I understand the goal, and the reasoning behind it. We can't fight them, we don't want to outrun them—so we must decide where to take them."

"You've got it now."

"But I still don't think you have selected the best option for a destination. Why not take them to the Macros?"

"Two reasons," I said, then paused, "you know, I might even have three."

With joy in my heart, I lifted my own hand and began ticking off my fingers. Miklos twisted his lips slightly when my hand came up. I could tell he didn't like it any more than I did. I almost showed him my middle finger first, but controlled the urge.

"The first reason is because our battle station is in the way," I said.

Miklos shook his head. "That's a good thing, isn't it? Maybe Welter Station could take this ship apart. They have firepower unmatched by our entire fleet. It would be nice to have the station destroy something instead of just sitting there in space."

I frowned more deeply, now wishing I *had* put up my middle finger first after all. Miklos and I didn't see eye to eye on the subject of the battle station. He thought of it as a waste of hardware that had failed in the past and never seemed to be in the right place at the right time. I thought of it as a fortress, a bulwark securing our flank from attack.

"No," I said, "it wouldn't be a good thing. We don't know if the battle station can destroy it."

"Then take it on past to the Macros. Give them this 'gift', as you called it."

I nodded, seeing his logic. This what he'd been working up to all along. He wanted to ram this monster down

58

the throats of the Macros, and he had a point. It wasn't a bad idea.

"Your plan is to leave the rest of the fleet behind and to fly this taskforce into the teeth of the Macros. If the battle station fails to take it out, we roll it to the Macros and let them do it."

"Exactly, Colonel. In fact, I have written up a set of—"

"Hold on," I said, "I didn't say I agreed with you. We're taking the ship to Earth."

"You said you had second reason—besides the station."

"Yes. I want to liberate Earth from Emperor Crow's grip. I wasn't sure we had the firepower before, but with *Phobos* backing us up, I'm fairly certain we do."

Miklos narrowed his eyes at me, but nodded and crossed his arms. I could tell he was feeling stubborn and abused. I hadn't gotten to my biggest reason, one they all probably suspected. I had already decided to attack Earth and unseat the upstart Emperor before this thing had shown up. Hell, that's why we'd built up the fleet at the expense of everything else. I still meant to keep my appointment back home with Crow.

Miklos suddenly brightened. He leaned forward with a predatory expression. "One more thing, Colonel. We expect mines and fortifications, no? If the big ship is following us, *we* will run into those defenses rather than the Blues. How do we prevent that? How do we make them go through the last ring to Sol first?"

He'd just hit upon a critical flaw in my plan. The truth was, I had no idea how to make them go first, or if it could even be done. In response, I fell back on any old standby technique of mine: I bullshitted him.

"Don't worry about that!" I said. "I have a plan. It will be unfolding shortly."

"Right after the one about getting the enemy to follow us?" asked Captain Sarin, reentering the conversation.

I gave her a dark look. "Exactly."

"But Kyle, what if Earth can't handle *Phobos*?" Captain Sarin demanded. "What if it beats them all? What then?"

"I'm sure the ship will be damaged at least. At that point, we'll have to finish the job. Likewise, if the big ship is easily destroyed, we'll still have the rest of Earth's forces to contend with. Listen, people. This isn't going to be easy. There are no certainties here. If anyone has one, I'd like to hear it."

"I'll give you a certainty," Jasmine said. "If we fail, we'll have brought death to our homeworld."

"I'm not sure about that. It could be the Blues just want to punish me—or Star Force in general. They might not be genocidal."

"You can't know that. They built the Macros and the Nanos."

"And the Nanos helped us, remember? Several of the Blues themselves have expressed regret for having released the Macros by mistake."

She nodded but seemed unconvinced.

The meeting broke up after that because we were reaching the slingshot point, and it was time to lay in the course. I walked back onto the bridge and ordered the entire task force to make a lazy loop around Eden-11 and set course for the Helios ring.

Within a few minutes, we were sliding sideways around their planet

"Don't do so much as ping their world," I ordered. "Don't give them any excuses to injure our civilians later."

The crew looked glum. I knew they were thinking about the time we'd bombed their planet. I had to admit, this uprising by the Blues did appear to be related to that decision. But I also knew that at that time the Blues had been cooperating with the Macros, bringing a monstrous battle fleet to this system to eradicate us. War was still war, and it always came with regrets.

It took a few hours, but soon we'd gone around the gas giant in a half-circle, building up a little velocity and a new course. We sailed away ahead of *Phobos*, toward the distant ring.

"Miklos," I said, "get Marvin up here. I want to have a little chat with the Blues."

The crew looked at one another in concern. The last time I'd "chatted" with them, one of our carriers had disappeared shortly afterward. I refused to accept the blame for that, however.

When Marvin appeared, I looked him over carefully. He had changed his configuration over the last few hours.

Marvin was a robot, but he was unlike any robot in known history. Not only was he sentient due to an incomplete download of his neural chain mind, but he had a creative streak that rivaled the best geniuses in Earth's history. He was often fascinated by doing something bizarre and unnatural—especially to biotic species like us. But in addition to his medical experimentation, he liked to explore. He'd been forbidden to do so as on too many occasions he'd flown off and gotten us into all kinds of trouble.

Today, I frowned at his structure in suspicion. He had a number of flat plates under his body, and was no longer dragging himself around with his nanite tentacles.

"Marvin, I recognize grav plates when I see them," I said. "What're you doing with those plastered all over the bottom of your chassis?"

"'Plastered' is an archaic reference. They're attached with nanite bonding. Essentially, chains of—"

"I don't care how you attached them. Those are contraband."

"Not specifically, Colonel," he said. "According to my recorded orders, I'm allowed to possess a sufficient number to allow me ease of movement through the ship."

"That's right, but you've got enough plates to lift a tank."

"A Star Force standard issue tank weighs approximately—"

"Stop it, Marvin, just stop it. I'll tell you what. Just tell me why you outfitted yourself with a half-dozen heavy grav plates and I'll decide if I'm willing to let you keep them."

Marvin's cameras panned and zoomed, getting my face from every angle, I could tell he was deciding if he should keep dodging or trust my judgment. Since he wasn't saying anything, I knew I'd given him a tough choice.

"Well?" I demanded. "Answer, or drop the plates now."

"I've calculated a sixty one percent chance this vessel will be destroyed within four days."

I nodded. I didn't doubt his figures for a second. Also, I suddenly got it.

"Ah," I said. "I see. You want to be ready to jump ship in case we're hit."

"The possibility crossed my mind."

"Right. Well, good luck with that. From what we've seen so far, we'll be smashed like a bug hit by a hammer if they catch us."

"Do I correctly surmise from your statement that I can keep the propulsion systems?"

I sighed. "All right. Just get up here and start translating. I want to talk to the Blues."

"Excuse me, sir?" Marvin asked promptly. "Do you wish me to relay our signal from a different ship?"

"No, just send it from this ship. Beam it directly at them."

The rest of the crew squirmed as I said these words. I ignored them so I wouldn't have to reprimand them. Why did they think I should attempt to get the enemy to fire on a different ship? We were all Star Force people, and the other crews had as much right to live as we did. Besides, right now we were safely out of range.

"Channel request sent," Marvin said. Less than a minute later, he added: "Channel open."

"This is Colonel Kyle Riggs," I boomed into the microphone. "I was under the impression there was a ceasefire between your people and mine. By attacking us, you have broken the peace and proved yourself to be dishonorable scum."

I wasn't sure how Marvin would translate "scum" into cloud-talk, but I figured it was the thought that counted. We waited a minute or two, giving them time to reply.

"Anything?"

The comm officer shook her head.

I sucked in a deep breath, and turned back to Marvin. "Let's send them another message."

"Ready."

"Addressing the aggressors following my ships," I began in a loud, authoritative voice. "I'm hereby ordering you to stand down. Return your vessel to your planet and await further instructions. Your surrender has been accepted, and your ship will be processed at our convenience."

I closed the channel again and waited, arms crossed. During the interval, Captain Sarin came close to me.

"Sir? What are you doing?" she whispered.

"We have to talk to them," I said. "They don't *want* to talk, so I'm trying to get a response—anything is good. I just want to start up the conversation."

"Your messages don't sound like good diplomacy, Colonel."

I shrugged. "I think I'd have made a better police negotiator than a diplomat."

She wandered back to her side of the table and went back to tapping at her screens. I was glad I'd given her the *Gatre*—she'd done well. It was also stimulating to have her back on the same bridge with me.

"Sir," said Marvin suddenly, "incoming message."

"Translate and pipe it in via our bridge speakers. Let's hear what the gas-bags have to say."

Everyone paused and looked up. Jasmine looked at me, smiled, and shook her head. I think she was surprised I'd managed to get them talking—but not too surprised.

"This is the being known as *Tolerance*," the message began. "We must take issue with your slanderous statements, Colonel Kyle Riggs. We did not initiate this conflict. Nor have we given any indication we wish to surrender. Your thought patterns are in error, and your mind is nothing but wind."

I nodded appreciatively. If I wasn't mistaken, I'd just been called an airhead. That was pretty unique, coming from a talking cloud. I felt a surge of pride. As far as I knew, I was the first man in history to be directly insulted by the Blues.

"Tolerance!" I shouted, motioning with a spiraling finger toward Marvin, indicating he should keep translating and transmitting. Once you have a fish on the line, you don't let go. "Old buddy, I haven't talked to you for a long time. I'm glad to hear it's you. We can communicate, you and I. We've done it in the past and avoided unnecessary destruction for both sides."

"We have indeed spoken before. At that time, I warned you that the annihilation of dense-things such as yourself was near at hand. You set this ship I fly within into motion, Kyle Riggs.

63

You brought the events that are about to unfold upon your people. They will soon sing their final songs."

I frowned. He didn't sound like he was talking about just taking out a few of our ships. The bridge crew seemed to have the same idea. They whispered amongst themselves and their eyes were all glued on me.

I recalled the conversation I'd had with this particular Blue. He'd said something about having the power to wipe humanity from the cosmos. At the time, I'd judged that talk to be threats and bravado from a beaten people. But perhaps—just maybe—this monster ship we were calling *Phobos* was the doom he'd been bragging about.

"All right, Tolerance," I said. "You have my full attention now. What is it you want? How can your anger be appeased?"

There was a longer delay than usual before the response came in.

"The being known as Colonel Kyle Riggs must be destroyed. That is our first priority."

"Little old me? Why am I first on your list?"

"Because you have personally insulted, injured and annoyed us for far too long."

I nodded, unable to argue with that one.

"Also," the gas bag continued, "we have determined that as the military leader of your species, destroying you will ensure your defeat."

"That's quite complimentary," I said.

"It was not meant in any way as a compliment."

I chuckled. "So, you're saying you still fear us? Even with this large ship chasing us around?"

"We do not fear you."

I paused, thinking hard. I didn't believe Tolerance. They *did* fear us, or at least they feared me. I'd ordered my ships to bomb them. As an arrogant people who thought of themselves as above the squabbles of lesser beings, that had shocked them. I'd actually managed to reach down into the dark soupy ocean of gas they called a home and I'd blown a few of them up. That singular event must have stunned their society. They impressed me as an inward-looking culture, rather like the Chinese dynasties of ages past. That bygone culture had possessed the power to explore the Earth and possibly even conquer it. But they'd turned up their noses at the idea. Everything interesting was in China, so they felt they'd had no need to bother with the barbarians outside their civilized paradise.

For the Blues, I was the Mongol at the gates. Terrifying, unknown and unexpected. The barbarian that could not be ignored.

The question was, how could I use that?

"I've spoken with some of your individuals before about honor and mistakes. They said it was a mistake to have released the Macros upon the universe. They said they did not mean to allow them to destroy world after world. Do you personally agree with that sentiment?"

Another long pause, then: "If you're trying to absolve yourself of guilt by calling your actions 'mistakes', I'm afraid that will not work. You have been tried in absentia, and found guilty of countless crimes. Think of me as an enforcement body seeking to apply appropriate punishment."

I leaned forward, interested now. I thought I saw an angle I could work with. "I see, so you're a policeman, then?"

"I am much more than that. I am a judicial system."

"Judge, jury and executioner?"

"Your references are unclear."

"Never mind then, tell me Tolerance, if one of your people is found guilty of a crime, are all the Blues in the region destroyed?"

"Destroyed? No. Our punishments usually involve chastisement and isolation. None will taste the cloud that is bitter."

"I see. But what of the clouds the guilty party has touched? What of those that are progenitors of the guilty party? Are they punished as well?"

"Only if they are guilty of performing the same crime themselves."

"Ah," I said, beginning to smile. "Is it justifiable then to annihilate a world because of the actions of an individual?"

"I see where you're headed with this, Colonel Riggs. Really, it is a pathetic attempt to dissuade an officer from pursuing his legal duties. You're not solely responsible for the actions of your species. There are many beings aboard your ships. Thousands of them. They have each caused us harm."

"But you don't understand," I said. "I'm a military leader. I have been given command of these ships. The beings that attacked your world did so while following my orders. They had no choice in the matter."

There was another pause. I sweated during this one. I'd thought I had him, but now I wasn't so certain.

"You've made an interesting point. I know that dense-things operate differently than we do. You're telling me that the creatures aboard your ship, even those operating it, are not all there of their own free will?"

"Essentially, yes," I said. "They are under my command. I am responsible for everything these vessels do."

I spent some time explaining our hierarchical system of command to him. The Blues seemed to have no precedent for it.

"What did you think 'Colonel' meant?" I asked.

"I assumed it was a moniker, a naming aberration without meaning."

"No, it is a title. It is the highest rank currently in Star Force, and I am the office holder with that title. Tell me, Tolerance, how many crewmen do you have aboard your ship?"

"I have no crewmen. I am the only being operating this vessel."

This caused something of a stir among my own people. That ship was so huge, and yet Tolerance ran the entire thing. It brought many new and interesting ideas to my mind, but now wasn't the time to explore them.

Tolerance said one final thing then: "I have found this discussion stimulating. I will report back every thought and nuance when I return from this mission. I do not wish to forget the important details. If you would be so kind, I would ask you to slow down so I could finish my task now."

I laughed. "You want me to stop my ship so you can blow it up without a chase?"

"Yes. It would be a convenience. A favor done for an officer executing their sworn duty."

"I'm afraid I must deny that request, Tolerance."
"That is unfortunate."

-7-

As the chase continued, it soon became evident that the Blue's ship had strengths and weaknesses not shared by our own vessels. As it flew closer to Eden-11, it sped up as we did, but when it flew around the planet and followed us, it did so ponderously. It was as if the ship was a heavy tanker and couldn't maneuver as well as our lighter craft.

I ordered my fleet to slow down further, and the captains all along the line began applying braking jets. This didn't make my crews happy; they wanted to leave *Phobos* behind. But I didn't think we had any choice. I didn't want to lose Tolerance and give the crazy cloud any ideas about attacking other targets in the system.

"Colonel," Jasmine asked me, coming to my office specifically to complain. "Are we seriously going to brake in the face of the enemy to keep them within close range?"

"Have you ever played with a kitten, Captain?"

She squinted at me. "What?"

"A kitten—you know, a baby cat."

"I don't understand…well, yes. I suppose I have."

"Well, I have too. The trick is to get their attention with a small, moving object. A piece of tissue paper works well. With a bit of string tied to it, you can have hours of fun pulling it away and having the cat chase it. But you know what happens when you yank it away too far? Out of range?"

68

She sighed and rolled her eyes at me. I would have been annoyed at the gesture, but she had very pretty eyes and I was being an irritant on purpose.

"The cat loses interest," she said.

"Right. Now, I don't know if the Blues will operate the same way, but so far their military strategy has been extremely simplistic. They don't even know how a military command structure works, and I don't think they have any heavily hierarchical structure in their society."

"And the significance of that cultural detail is...?"

"I suspect they're less socially sophisticated than we are in certain ways. I believe they can be manipulated—tricked. They won't see a deception or manipulation until it is too late."

"You're saying they're a race of country bumpkins?"

"Sort of," I said. "They understand argument and rhetoric, but they don't understand military tactics."

She nodded. "I hope you're right, Kyle. I really do."

She left me and went back to flying her ship. I believed her when she said she hoped I was right. If I wasn't, we were probably all as good as dead.

I went back to studying what we knew of the strikes against our ships. I had to figure out how their weapon worked if I was to have a hope of defeating it. I brought it over to the weapons people, one of which was Marvin. He wasn't really part of the weapons staff, but as our general science officer, any odd alien tech was in his jurisdiction.

"Hello Colonel Riggs," Marvin said brightly.

"Hello, Marvin. What have you got in the way of a theory concerning the operation of this weapon? How does it work?"

"We don't actually know. But I would hesitantly theorize that their ship generates a compression field of some kind. The field might create a region in space where mass is effectively greater, or it might apply crushing force like a hand squeezing into a fist."

"I guess that makes some kind of sense," I said, looking at the data. "But we're still in the dark about how *Phobos* is propelling itself. Even more importantly, the ship has a weapon we have no clue about, and no defense against—other than staying several million miles away."

"Sir," Marvin said promptly, "I have some theories in that regard as well."

"What theories?"

"I need more data in order to present a complete hypothesis."

"Well Marvin, the only way we could get more data would be by visiting the damaged ships directly. What happened to that pinnace I sent out there to investigate the first wreck?"

"That vessel was destroyed, sir..." Marvin said. "Unfortunately."

I frowned at him. He didn't sound like he thought it was unfortunate, but it was hard to tell with Marvin. He might just be using his usual neutral inflection.

"How did that happen?"

"The enemy vessel targeted and destroyed the pinnace when our fleet was in close proximity. There were no survivors and the mission was not executed."

"Why wasn't I informed another vessel was hit?"

"It was only recently discovered. I'm sure with all the excitement of assaulting *Phobos*, the detail wasn't reported to the flag officers."

"Hmm," I said. "We're swinging back by there soon on our way to the Helios ring. We're also going pretty slowly. Can you run some numbers to see if we can reach—"

"Here they are," Marvin said quickly. His tentacles rasped on the big screen. I soon saw that we could make it out to the wreck and back if we used a fighter on full burn. We'd only have about a twenty minute window to make the launch, however.

As I studied the display, which showed a dashed green line out to the wreck and a curving return course, I noticed the display and calculations were very detailed. Marvin had even programmed a narrowing cone of operational time to make the mission happen. I began to get suspicious.

"You had this ready to go before I got here, didn't you Marvin?"

"Yes. But I must ask for your decision now, Colonel. Are we going or not? The launch-window is rapidly closing."

70

"Yeah, I see that," I said, not liking this. I felt I might be in the middle of one of Marvin's grand schemes. But I had to agree with him, if we wanted to see that wreck the decision had to be made now.

Then something else he'd said clicked in my mind. "You said 'we' are going? Meaning yourself?"

"Of course. As your science officer, it would only make good sense."

"Yeah, right," I said, then sighed. "All right, let's suit up and go. I'll fly the fighter."

"An appropriate vessel has been placed on hold in the launch bay. All weapons have been removed, giving us extra fuel and sensory equipment for contingencies."

"No way," I said. "Put at least the forward gun back on there. I'm not flying an unarmed fighter into hostile space."

"Sir, that will hamper—"

"We have time. I can see your numbers, Marvin."

His tentacles squirmed in distress. I could tell he was mentally weighing the time he'd have to waste trying to convince me to do things his way versus just complying and getting into space as quickly as possible. In the end, he gave up and rushed for the launch bay.

"Please follow me, sir. There isn't a moment to spare."

As I left the bridge, Jasmine intercepted me. Her brow was furrowed with worry.

"He set this up, you know that don't you?"

"I would guess that he did," I said. "But I want to know what we're up against, and I don't have time to burn him at the stake like I should."

"Sandra wouldn't have wanted you to go off with Marvin alone."

I smiled. "You're right about that. But she's not here right now."

Still, I hesitated. She had her hand on my chest plate. I could have easily brushed past her, but I didn't. I knew she had some feelings for me, and it was nice to know someone gave a damn whether I lived or died.

I thought for a second she was going to give me a kiss or a hug, but she didn't. She was standing in front of a lot of her personnel after all, and they were all watching us while trying to pretend they weren't.

My helmet buzzed with a personal channel call.

"Colonel Riggs? Is there a problem? I have the fighter reconfigured now. It is on the pad and ready for launch. Are you coming or am I going to be forced to fly this ship alone?"

"You're not permitted to fly anything unless it is an emergency."

"We could discuss the parameters of what kind of event constitutes an 'emergency', but I would prefer not to. There isn't sufficient time."

Finally, Jasmine removed her hand. I smiled at her and gave her a slight hug. I could tell she liked it, but she cleared her throat and nodded to me instead of reciprocating.

"Until you return, sir," she said.

Then just like that, I found myself hurrying down the long central passage to the launch bays. When I got there, I found a fighter with Marvin in it. Really, it was more like Marvin had wrapped the ship around his body. I could tell now that what he'd meant by 'extra sensory equipment' was himself. The parts he'd left out were not sensor boxes, but parts of his own body. There were segments lying here and there around the ship, discarded. They dripped oil and left yellowish puddles on the decking.

"How did you squeeze into that thing, Marvin?" I asked, laughing.

"Please Colonel, could we just launch? There will be plenty of time for jibes and pleasantries during the flight."

I climbed into the cockpit, which I found cramped. He'd scooted my seat up. I felt the instrument panel was too close and the stick—well, it was almost in my crotch.

"Give me one more inch, will you? Just shove backward a bit."

I heard groaning metal and scratching sounds. A hatch opened and three cameras spilled out, cracking on the deck plates. He'd jettisoned some of his tentacles along with the cameras.

"I should have brought a smaller pilot," he complained.

"I should have brought a smaller passenger," I replied.

72

I engaged the engines and the ship went live. A moment later, a smart metal hatch opened under us and the tiny craft was sucked down into the breach. We were loaded like a shell into a cannon and soon that cannon fired with an ear-splitting boom.

Coming out of the long launch tube of a carrier in a fighter was always exhilarating. Every time I did it, I wondered why I didn't pull rank and go patrolling with the escort ships every day just for fun.

I gunned it once we were at a safe distance and had clearance from the CAG. I whooped as our huge exhaust plume almost engulfed *Gatre* for a brief moment. Flying fighters was fun, and having an excuse to fly at maximum acceleration was even better.

Once we were up to cruising speed, we had a few minutes to talk before I had to perform the reversal maneuver to flip around and aim the engines in our direction of travel. Fighters had only one real engine, and they had to use it to accelerate and decelerate.

"All right, Marvin," I said, "now it's time to talk."

"When I suggested that, it was a metaphorical reference—"

"No. No way. You're going to answer some of my questions right now or I'll turn this ship around and take you home."

"That would be highly counterproductive, Colonel."

"Yes it would, so talk."

"What would you like to talk about?"

"How you engineered this. What exactly happened to the pinnace I sent out here?"

"I fail to understand your references, Colonel Riggs. Are you asking how I altered the fighter to carry my person, or—"

"Knock it off, Marvin. I'm asking what you did to make sure you were the one to fly out here to this wreck."

"I volunteered myself for the mission, if that's what you mean."

I could tell he was going to evade the point until we ran out of time. It was a common tactic for him. Marvin could have taught a class on the subject: Stonewalling 101.

"Hmm," I said. "Let me see if I can piece it together for you. You were curious about it, right? Some kind of new technology we'd never encountered before. You had to see the results up close and personal, but without dying in the process."

"I found the topic stimulating, yes."

"All right then. You must have been disappointed when I ordered the pinnace sent out to survey the wreckage."

"Disappointed? I would not employ that term."

"Well, I would. How to do it..." I thought for a moment, then snapped my fingers. I had it.

"Where did you relay that last message? The one they never answered?"

Marvin squirmed.

"I did as you instructed. I made it seem as if the transmission didn't come from *Gatre*."

"Right," I said. "Meaning you relayed it through the pinnace after the first carrier was hit. You baited them into destroying the pinnace so you'd later have a chance to check out the carrier wreckage first hand."

"I was only following orders. *Your* orders, Colonel."

I nodded slowly. In a way, he'd done us a favor. Instead of losing another carrier at that point, we'd lost a smaller ship. But it was also unacceptable that he would knowingly cause the death of a pilot by baiting Tolerance—even if the rest of us had yet to figure out what was happening at the time. Events often went this way with Marvin.

I heaved a sigh. When it came to ethical conduct, Marvin was in a category all by himself. He was very perceptive, but instead of sharing his insights he used them to achieve his own strange goals. When he acted on information, he applied his own twists. He knew he was dooming a ship by relaying my message through it, even if the rest of us hadn't figured it out yet. Was that evil, or just the careful utilization of a gift the rest of us didn't have? I was ambivalent about it on this occasion.

"I'll have to decide if there will be repercussions for your actions later," I said. "Right now, I want you to focus on gathering as much data from the wreck as you can."

"We're already close enough for a preliminary scan. Very interesting. Can you slow down? It would be optimal if we could circle the wreck in a low-velocity sweep. Thank you, Colonel."

I played chauffer for the next minute or two while we swung around the crushed ship. I soon tired of that and set down on the flattened aft of the wreck. The entire thing looked like a car that had been through a demolition machine—twice, maybe.

"This is unbelievable," I said as I climbed out of the fighter and walked around on the hull. "What kind of force could exert so much pressure? It's like you said, a compressing field came at the vessel from all sides and smashed it."

"I don't think so, Colonel," Marvin said. "Not now that I've seen the damage up close."

He extracted himself from the fighter with difficulty. He wouldn't have been able to do it at all if he hadn't discarded much of his structure. He'd kept only a few of his large cubical units and most of his body consisted of tentacles, sensors and cameras. The cubes, I knew, housed his central power unit and his overly-large brainbox.

"What do you mean, Marvin? Do you know what kind of technology we're facing here?"

"Yes. It seems fairly obvious."

I looked around, dumbfounded. The hull resembled a run-over can on the side of a highway to me. Floating bits of glass and other debris were everywhere around it. Being in space around a large object like this was sort of like walking on the bottom of the ocean. My every movement caused clouds of particulate matter to rise up in swirls.

"It's not obvious to me."

"Let's do some simple deductive reasoning," Marvin said.

Coming from most people, these words would have sounded condescending. But I knew that Marvin was only enjoying himself in his own, weird way. I decided to play along.

"All right," I said, "we've got a crushed ship that has apparently suffered a high-force blow from all sides at once.

75

Looks like an implosion more than an explosion, if only due to all the small debris floating around."

"Excellent. You're making progress. I'll show you another clue."

I sighed in my helmet while Marvin lifted and tapped at a sheet of polymer that must have been from inside the ship somewhere. As I examined it, I frowned. It was peppered with slivers of other, more fragile materials.

"Hmm," I said. "It looks like something on the outside of the ship popped and shot slivers into the interior. Maybe one of the viewports?"

"Close. This material has been identified as having resin compounds that match your vac suit."

I stared at it. "But my suit is smart metal. This stuff looks like shards of stiff plastic."

"When great forces are applied, nanites often take on this configuration."

"That reminds me, I said, looking around. "Where are all the nanites? Are they all dead?"

"Yes. They're more than just dead, actually. They're fused into brittle metal masses. Like clumps of frozen snow scooped up and pressed together."

I grabbed samples of these materials as we examined them. Marvin did the same, but I didn't trust him to not damage the samples. I wanted pure ones to give to my science people.

"This stuff is made up of crushed-together nanites?" I asked. "That supports my compression theory."

"Not at all."

I looked at him. "Just stop beating around the bush and tell me what you think happened. And yeah, I know there are no bushes out here."

"What propulsion systems do we currently know about, Colonel?"

"Chemical, nuclear…anything that throws mass away from the ship quickly to cause it to move the other way."

"Those are common, outdated systems. But there is one more."

"You aren't talking about the rings, are you?"

"No, I'm talking about grav-plates."

I looked around and laughed. "You think gravity manipulation could do all this? That would take a couple of *huge* grav-plates! And a fantastic level of power, too. Our best plates can make a tank or small ship fly at low speeds, but that's it."

"For just a moment, let us assume the Blues have technology superior to our own."

"Yeah," I said, looking at the nanites in my hand. They crumpled to a fine, silvery dust when I handled them roughly. Whatever had killed this ship had done a thorough job. "That's easy to do."

"Superior technology indicates by definition that either entirely new techniques are being applied, or that known techniques are being applied with improved effectiveness. I'm suggesting that the latter is the case here."

All the while he spoke, he kept moving his cameras, taking samples and doing readings. Watching him work was fascinating. He could multitask better than any human that had ever lived.

"Let's get back to the ship," I told him. "We have less than two minutes before our return window closes."

We managed to stuff ourselves into the fighter again, but only barely. Our flight weight was mysteriously high. I noticed this as I closed the cockpit and kicked on the jets.

"Marvin, how many samples did you bring with us?"

"About six hundred kilograms worth."

I grunted, thinking of my five or six baggies of random wreckage.

"Are you sure we can fly back with all that?"

"Yes. I ran the calculations as we flew out here."

"Why so many damned samples?"

"Full acceleration will be required to match speeds with *Gatre*. I assumed that many of the samples would be damaged."

There were many crashes and tinkling sounds coming from the back of the ship as I put the pedal down and we sped away.

"Where did you put all that mass?"

"The only available storage areas were the in empty dorsal fuel tanks."

"The fuel tanks? I better not suck dead nanites into my engines."

"That shouldn't happen. The samples have been isolated with smart metal barriers. I also took the liberty of disabling several valves that connect those tanks with the engines."

Great, I thought. *More tampering.* But at the same time, I thought I'd figured out what he meant about employing improvements to known technology.

"You really think the Blues' ship did all this damage with gravity manipulation?"

"Yes."

"If they have better, more refined gravity control, that would explain a lot," I said. "But doing it on such a scale and with such great range—it would require massive generators."

"Enough to fill a small moon?"

I looked out in the direction of *Phobos*. I couldn't see the ship with my naked eye, but I could see Eden-11, a brownish-white disk. The big ship was in the sunward direction, following my remaining fleet doggedly across the system.

"It does fit. Their super weapon crushes things, I can't deny that. What I don't understand is how they do it at range. Our grav plates only reach a few feet."

"That's a power-relative range," Marvin said, "but still, I don't think they used gravity plates to achieve this destruction over such a long distance. Again, they used known technology but with superior techniques."

"So, they somehow caused the ship to implode? At about a million mile range?"

"Yes, exactly. They didn't place their gravity plates around the ship, but instead caused a gravity effect—an anomaly, if you will—to occur within the hull itself."

"Ah, I see what you mean now. That's why everything is crunched down and nothing blew apart. They sucked it all together by making a high gravity field inside the ship. How large would that field have to be?"

"Very difficult to say without further analysis. But really, it's not a matter of the size of the field. If a single point in space sparked into existence, full of collapsed atoms, it could apply sufficient force."

78

I thought about it all the way back to *Gatre* and the more I did, the less I liked it. I had to admit, the theory fit the facts as we knew them.

If Marvin was right in his theories, the Blues could essentially form a tiny black hole wherever they wanted to—and they'd chosen to do it in the middle of my ships. How could my fleet defend itself against that?

-8-

By the time I'd reached *Gatre*, I had a few new ideas as to how we could damage the monstrous ship that was now tagging along behind us—slowly—across the star system.

"Mines," I told Miklos at our next briefing, after Marvin and I laid out our theories concerning the nature of the enemy weaponry.

"Mines, sir?" he asked skeptically. "But such devices have already proven ineffective. Our small ships and missiles were destroyed by an unfocussed gravity field when they got in close. What makes you think a mine would do better than a fighter or a missile?"

"Timing and surprise," I said. "The Blues—or in this case the one Blue, Tolerance, should be easy to fool. They're not expert strategists. They lack experience in warfare. Hell, they barely know what a commanding officer is."

"When do you expect to employ these mines?" asked Miklos, crossing his arms.

I could tell right away, looking at him and the rest of my staff, they weren't impressed with my idea. Miklos liked ships, the more the merrier. And he was right that mines had been surpassed as useful weapons in recent times. The best place to employ them had always been on the far side of a ring where an enemy ship would run into them blindly. But recently in our wars, combatants had become wary. Every fleet commander had learned to send missiles through the rings to blow up mines

80

before sending ships through, as well as using other techniques to defeat them.

The Blues, however, did not have the benefit of our experience. I felt it would be possible to fool them with an old trick.

"We'll lay the mines where we always do, just on the far side of a ring."

As we looked it over, Miklos became more convinced it might work. Everything Tolerance had done so far hinted on naiveté. With luck, we could lure him to his death.

"I'm liking the idea more and more," Miklos said. "Except I suggest we plant one monstrous mine. A gigaton hydrogen bomb—at least that big. A planet-buster. That's what we need to destroy *Phobos*—a huge single blast."

I was impressed by his willingness to gamble. "Why one huge mine?"

"Because we're only going to get one chance to destroy the ship. After that, Tolerance will not fall for the trick again. The ship will turn on its defensive fields or maybe send a weapon through each ring to clear the way."

"Yeah," I said slowly. "That would make sense. Unless we want to warn *Phobos*."

They all stared at me. Even Marvin seemed startled. His cameras had been floating around aiming at everyone but me. I'd noticed over recent weeks this had been a growing tendency on his part. During our command meetings, I usually did most of the talking. But Marvin seemed to have heard enough from me. His roving cameras were focused on anything else when I spoke. Now his cameras snapped around and caught my face from every conceivable angle.

"That's right," I said. "I want to build mines, not to destroy *Phobos*, but to teach its neophyte captain what's in store for him. How else will he break through Earth's defenses if he just barrels in and gets blown away?"

A storm of protests began after that. They could not believe I was seeking to aid the enemy ship in any way. They complained at my own naiveté. After a while, I cut them off with a chopping gesture.

"Listen up," I said, "I want to retake earth. That's the goal, here."

"But what about the Macros and the Blues? We can't just ignore them."

"We have to take them out one at a time. I consider the Macros to be safely controlled for now on the far side of our battle station. But Earth is a wild card with a fleet that we must assume they've been building up for months. They had strong defenses when the Macro's hit them and wiped them out. We have to assume they've built back up since then. I want to let this big dumb ship barrel in there and take the initial hits for us. Then we'll follow and mop up."

"Sir," Miklos said, standing up, "we've yet to hear your plan for getting our own ships through Earth's defenses."

"We'll get into that when we reach the Alpha Centauri system," I told him.

The following days went by slowly and painfully. Usually, the entire trip to Earth took no more than a week's time. But with this lumbering ox of a ship in tow, we had to go much more slowly. We were still in the Eden System, but we'd almost made it to the ring that led to Helios.

I didn't want to chance losing *Phobos*, so we didn't get too far ahead. The last thing I needed was Tolerance getting ideas about visiting other targets in our home system. Fortunately, whatever else he was, Tolerance didn't seem to be an imaginative tactician. He stayed on our tails as if he believed he was going to catch up to us any minute.

I stretched and climbed out of my seat, leaving the bridge. I recalled then that Dr. Swanson had left me hanging on the subject of a second date—or rather, a second *attempt* at a date. I don't think either of us felt entirely comfortable getting together yet. Sandra had only been gone for three or four months now, and the whole business of being back "in the game" felt strange to me. I didn't know what Kate was thinking, but it seemed to change from one meeting to the next.

I headed for the med lab, but I didn't even make it to the main corridor before Jasmine showed up. She smiled at me and I couldn't help but smile back.

"That Blue really wants you, Kyle. I think at some point you really upset him."

"I'd have to agree," I said, looking back toward the screens. We were standing in the hatchway, half in and half out of the bridge.

"Are you headed below-decks?" I asked.

"Okay," she said, as if I'd given her an invitation.

We began walking, and I began thinking fast. I couldn't very well take her to the med lab. She knew the good doctor and I had a little thing going. My mind scrambled to come up with a new destination, all while making it look natural.

"I could really use a beer," I said.

She gave me a slightly reproachful look. "I thought you had sworn off alcohol."

"Well, within reason. No more than a six pack a day. You know the nanites, the only effect that will have on a marine is to make him visit the head a few extra times."

"Is that all? Why drink it then?"

I frowned slightly. She didn't seem to want to go to the wardroom and have a beer. My first idea had been blown.

"We can forget about that," I said. "Maybe you'd rather play a round of pool?"

She sucked in her breath and I caught her rolling her eyes. Sandra had been really good at pool, but she'd been heavily altered. Most of the Fleet people didn't seem to enjoy the game the way the grunts did.

"I would have to have a six pack first before I could enjoy breaking ribs," she said finally. "Let's just go to the bar. You were right in the first place. I shouldn't have complained."

"I understand. There were some very recent problems with me and drinking. I'm not taking your reaction the wrong way. But this ship isn't exactly a shopping mall back home. There's only so much to do when you have free time."

"I've been thinking about that. We should give our people more sources of entertainment. We offer them hard work with very little time off, and you can't even stream a movie out here from Earth that is less than a decade old."

"Yeah."

It was a problem. Being cut off from Earth didn't just mean a lack of provisions and fresh recruits. It also meant we were isolated from Earth's culture.

"I know what we can do," she said suddenly. "I've got some movies to show you. New stuff from Earth. You might not like it, but they can be funny."

"Funny?" I frowned. "All right. Let's get the beer first. Where we going to watch them?"

There was an awkward pause. Our two cabins were quite close to one another, both being located on the officer's quarters deck. But being seen entering either cabin together with a healthy serving of alcohol was going to start rumors for sure.

"I've got it," I said. "We'll go to my office."

Taking beer into my office was nothing new for me. Many of my binges with Gaines had occurred right there at my desk—so many in fact I'd had to really work to eliminate every stash I had in hidden in that small space.

That thought was followed up by a surprise meeting at the door to my office. It was none other than Major Gaines himself. He had his arms crossed and a bored look on his face. But when I came around the corner with Jasmine in tow, his expression changed.

He looked at me, her and the beer in that order. Then he uncrossed his arms, smiled, and saluted.

"Sorry sir," he said, "I was just going to discuss troop-readiness with you. But I can see you have other official business to attend to."

"That's right," I said, "I'll catch you later, Major."

He tossed us a salute and walked off down the corridor. Jasmine and I hurried into my office and closed the hatch before anyone else could catch us.

"I'm sorry if you had other plans," Jasmine said, "maybe I should have left instead of him."

"Nah, Gaines will be just fine. He just knew we had some downtime and probably was going to offer me a rematch in the pool room."

"How you two can spend so much time drinking and firing balls into one another—I don't entirely get that."

"I know," I said, "it's a grunt thing. The pain on the other guy's face makes it worth the pain on your own."

She shook her head wonderingly. She finally got out the beers and offered me one. I hesitated, then took it and fired it into my mouth. I felt some degree of relaxation come over me as I did so. It wasn't the alcohol I told myself, it was the habit. I guess people who hadn't smoked for a long time felt the same relief when they finally broke down and lit up again.

Jasmine opened her own bottle and sipped it. She made a face, but kept going. Our beer wasn't the best, but it was all that we had.

"Where are these movies?" I said, hoping for a good laugh.

She got out a chip and shoved it into a slot on the side of the main monitor. The slot automatically resized itself and read the data. Another nice thing about modern life was universal compatibility. Having smart-metal equipment meant you could shove an old DVD, a USB drive, or what have you into any machine's slot. They would reshape themselves, figure out the format, and start operating.

All that said, I wondered why she bothered to bring the movies on a chip. We had a central net on every ship. We could pull up anything with various levels of security. Any data she had in her cabin she should be able to pull down here. But she'd brought it along in physical form. I was about to ask her about it when the show began, and I soon learned the answer anyway.

The transmission was slightly grainy. It *was* a transmission, I could tell that. I saw the Empire imagery roll up on the screen. Their logo was an eagle formed with angular, geometric shapes. It looked like a collage of sharp metal pieces. The music began next. It was tinny, and vaguely martial in nature.

Already, my eyes were narrowing. I didn't find Crow and his Empire funny. The next thing that came up was Crow himself.

I was stunned. I hadn't seen the man for years. He wore an ice cream white uniform and a cap circled by gold braids. There were colorful ribbons pinned here and there on his outfit, and a gold sunburst of metal hung around his neck like a medieval emblem of office.

"Who the hell does he think he is?" I muttered.

"Shhh," Jasmine said. "It gets better."

I grabbed another beer and fired it down while I watched. Just seeing Crow made me want to strangle him. I began to think this whole entertainment idea had been a bad one.

Next, the windbag gave a gusty speech. He talked about the unity of Earth and the plentiful bounty of the Empire. He went on about sacrifice and unflinching dedication to duty. I had no idea what he was talking about, but I felt my disgust build.

Crow finally left the lectern. I felt relieved. I was on my third beer by then, while Jasmine still sipped her first. I tried to slow down, and made myself put the beer on the desk for a while.

"Doesn't he look absurd in his costume?" she asked.

"I guess so."

The show continued.

"The captives from the rebel worlds are ready, Emperor," an announcer said, stepping into view. This joker wore black boots, a stone gray jumpsuit and a peaked cap that was as crisply folded as his nose. He was a tall man and he read from a scroll—an honest to god *scroll*—complete with golden tassels hanging from it.

This part struck Jasmine as funny. I tried to smile, but failed.

"The prisoners have been justly tried and found guilty of sedition, treason and refusal to renounce their false loyalties to failed states."

I leaned forward in alarm. "What the hell is this?" I asked, almost shouting.

Jasmine glanced at me worriedly. "This is television from Earth—the evening news. It always begins with executions. Didn't you know that?"

I glowered. I'd heard some rumors, but I was usually so engrossed in military matters and simple management I hadn't had time to really delve into the events occurring back on Earth. I'd felt that if I was working hard to overthrow the

86

government, I was doing all I could. The details were distractions.

The accused prisoners were pathetic, scrawny creatures with their heads clamped in metal cages. They were chained together, with one string of rattling links going from collar to collar. I couldn't even identify them as the cage obscured their faces. I had no idea if they were Star Force people or not.

Eventually, they were executed in a very clean and orderly way. I'd been cringing, expecting to see innocents have their heads lopped off. But instead, they were ordered to shuffle into a chamber—a moment later, the guy with the scrolls announced that the deed had been done.

"What is that thing? Some kind of microwave?"

"Yes. A giant, insta-kill oven. At least, that's what our people think."

The video ended and I squinted at her in disbelief.

"That wasn't funny!" I roared.

She jumped and looked guilty. "The funny part is that they never kill real Star Force people. No one that is even nanotized. Most of the marines that see it laugh at Crow's pompous display and his jingling fake medals."

I had to force myself to calm down. "Yeah, I can see how that's amusing. But we just watched people die. Innocent dissidents that probably pissed off their neighborhood watchman enough to get put on Crow's shit-list."

I got up and began to pace. I was fuming. Jasmine stayed in her chair, looking small and worried.

"I'm sorry," she said. "It's kind of an underground thing. People watch these transmissions and laugh."

"I can see why it's underground. I can see why no one has the balls to show it to their commanders. What I don't get is why *you* think it's funny."

She looked upset. "I said I was sorry. I didn't know it would hit you this way. It's only Crow being absurd and Imperials executing their own kind. I understand that in most cases, the defendants in the dock are Imperial officers. They call them Star Force, but they are their own people. The fiction they maintain is that no Imperial would ever turn against Crow. It's unthinkable, so they pretend it's us."

"Totalitarianism is never funny," I said. "Even if Crow is a caricature of every despot that ever lived, he's still killing real people back home. One of them might have been the father of that girl—the one who...you know."

"Alexa Brighton? The one who killed Sandra?"

I fumed. "Yes, right. Crow maintains power over his people through terror. How can he have become such a monster? He was not a bad guy to have a drink with years back. Now, I don't know..."

"I think he's been getting worse for years. Maybe you didn't see it because he was your friend originally."

I shook my head. "I'm not sure that I would have ever called him a friend. Not exactly. But he was a comrade in arms."

"You have a tendency to be too loyal to people who go bad, Kyle," she said. "I've seen it more than once. Remember Barrera? Or General Kerr? You defended them both, not just Jack Crow."

I glanced at her, not liking what she was saying, but feeling unable to refute it.

"You think I should be on the lookout for enemies even now?"

"Of course."

"Who then? Who in my chain of command is a possible traitor today? Can you name one?"

"I don't know," she said. "What about Gaines? Or Marvin?"

"Gaines, because we became drinking buddies when I was low? Marvin...well, you might have a point with Marvin. He's always trouble. But no one has done more for Star Force than he has. Even if it was by accident half the time."

"Still, if you give everyone a second chance, it can't always work."

I snorted. "Maybe I made a mistake with you in that case. You went to Crow, you worked for him. You came back, and no one knew if you were a real defector or a mole. How can I be sure, even today? Here you are showing me vids of the Imperial Justice system. Should I be suspecting you of treason?"

Jasmine looked upset, and she shook her head.

"Yeah," I said, "that's right. It's not so easy, is it? The day I decide everyone who's had a bad day needs to go to the guillotine, I'll be just like Crow himself. I *like* to give people second chances, Jasmine. That's what Star Force was all about to start with. We have to trust the individual, to push them into a zone where they can grow and do more than they ever thought they could. Sometimes, that will backfire. But overall, I think we have a winning record."

Finishing my speech, I reached out, removed the chip with Crow's evil vid on it, and crushed it with my fingertips. It crunched satisfactorily into tiny silver fragments.

When I turned back around, Jasmine was standing near the door.

"I should go," she said.

I came close to her, but she didn't meet my eyes. I touched her cheek then dropped my hand.

"I'm sorry things didn't go as well as we'd both hoped tonight."

"Me too," she said.

"In fact, it had to be the worst date you've ever had."

A smile flickered over her face, but died. I thought she was going to leave, but she lingered.

I'm dumb, but once in a while I catch on. I kissed her. She let me do it for a few lingering seconds, then disengaged and vanished. I was left wanting more.

"You sure know how to show a girl a good time," I mumbled to myself after the hatch had closed.

I turned around, found the last beer on the table, and poured it out on the floor. It bubbled and fizzed as the nanites sucked it up. My office deck plates were well-trained. They knew all about spilled beer.

-9-

When my entire fleet had gathered at the Helios ring, waiting around for *Phobos* to catch up, I noticed it looked pretty impressive. Even after *Phobos* had nailed us twice, I had a grand total of six super-carriers. They were the latest motherships loaded with four fighter squadrons each. These ships formed the core of my fleet—or rather, their fighters did.

Surrounding the carriers were over twenty cruisers and two hundred gunboats. We had a few destroyers and frigates as well, the old saucer-shaped Nano ships, which we used mostly as scouts. They were faster and more maneuverable than the core ships, but much more lightly armed.

Trailing behind the battle fleet were the transports. There were about sixty of these. I felt ambivalent about bringing them along, but I didn't see how I could expect to take Earth without ground forces.

All in all, the fleet was over three hundred ships strong. We could launch over eight hundred fighters as well, swelling our numbers. These vehicles were tiny in comparison to the rest of the ships, especially the big battlewagons, but they were very sophisticated. I'd been under the impression the ships needed to be updated, but I'd since been informed Miklos had worked on them tirelessly, improving them every few weeks. There were so many versions and plans for these tiny ships I'd lost track of it all during my own downtime. I decided that today was a good day to reacquaint myself with the latest technical data.

My entire armada slipped through the Helios ring in good order, and I felt a familiar shiver go through me as we were transferred from one star system to another. The Helios system had a big red giant star in the middle of it, and every planet seemed all but burnt to crisp. The world of the Worms was here, near the next ring that led to Alpha Centauri. The Worms were an allied species who I quickly instructed to stand down when they saw the Blues' ship following us. I didn't want them to take another beating for us this time around.

In order to consult with Miklos about the fighter designs and other logistical issues, I left *Gatre* and boarded *Relentless*, one of our heaviest carriers. Miklos had taken up residence aboard her after *Defiant* had been lost. I'd yet to give him a new command as I felt he might do better with pure strategic thinking—after all, his ships kept blowing up. *Defiant* had been his third lost command by my count.

"Are we ready to start, sir?" Miklos asked, coming into the conference room. He had a tablet bursting with data he wanted to show me. I could see at a glance there must be twenty windowed tabs open. The volume of stuff made me wince.

"Almost. Where's Gaines?" I asked.

I'd put Gaines in charge of the landing forces. He was a top level marine even if he was green compared to some. I knew he had personal reasons for wanting to return to Earth and remove the Imperials from power. That kind of motivation to win never hurt.

"He'll be up here in a minute, sir. Can I connect to the main display and distribute my data?"

As he said this, he was already doing it. I felt like sighing but let him carry on. Logistics were never as much fun as battle-planning to me. Miklos, on the other hand, seemed to love counting every bolt.

"Where are Marvin and Kwon?" I asked as he worked.

He looked up at me. "Sir? I thought this was a strategic design meeting."

"It is," I said, "but we're about to go into battle. I want my senior people here to listen."

It was his turn to release a tiny sigh. He summoned a lieutenant and relayed my orders. The lieutenant ran off, and I leaned back in my chair.

While we waited, he rattled off facts and figures. We had a shocking amount of men and materials at our disposal—with the emphasis on materials rather than men.

91

"The crews are thin, Commodore," I complained.

"We've automated many basic subsystems, allowing fewer men to operate even the larger vessels."

"That's all well and good," I said, "but what happens when they're boarded or lose a few key personnel? With everyone covering several operational centers, we can't take a hit on any crew without lessening the effectiveness of the ship in question."

Miklos cleared his throat as Gaines walked in.

"Hey, Gaines my man," I shouted. "Take a seat!"

"Thank you, sir," he said, seating himself across from me.

Miklos looked like he smelled something foul for a moment, then went on. "I know that smaller crews are not optimal, but we have to deal with certain realities, sir."

"What realities? I don't want to hear excuses. If just one of these ships is knocked out in the coming action due to undermanning them, I'm going to have to hold you responsible."

"Sir," began Miklos, looking pained again.

Gaines leaned forward and joined the conversation. "If I may speak, sirs."

"Of course," I said.

"What the Commodore is trying to say, Colonel—and do stop me if I'm wrong, Nicolai—is that we're short on men in general."

I looked from one of them to the other. I frowned at them. "What about new recruits? Fresh volunteers from the colonies?"

"There's hardly been enough time for them to breed a new generation, sir," Gaines said.

"Huh," I said rubbing my chin in thought. "I know we've lost a few people, but—"

"Approximately twenty percent in the last year alone," Miklos said.

"That much? And what you're telling me is they've stopped coming from Earth, and they've stopped volunteering from the colonies. I guess all the brave ones have joined already."

"Or died, sir," Miklos said.

I frowned at him. "What's that supposed to mean?"

"Sir," said Gaines, leaning in again. "I had to do the same thing with our marines. You see the troops out there in those sixty transports? They're mostly native contingents."

I made a disgusted sound. "Mostly? Are you saying more than half? Give me a percentage."

"The ground forces following us are made up of more than eighty percent Centaurs, Colonel. There aren't enough humans in the Eden system to fill all those ships. Not anymore."

I nodded and felt depressed. "It's not your fault, gentlemen. We're having manpower problems, that's all. It's plagued many conquerors in the past, you know. The Mongol Horde, for example, conquered countless nations but was mostly made up of non-Mongols by the time they reached Europe."

At the mentioning of an historical precedent, the two men exchanged glances. I ignored this. I felt knowing something about military history was a necessity when trying to comprehend our new, modern form of warfare. Whenever I had a spare moment, I read up on such topics. It provided a man with perspective, and it was an old habit for me. I'd done the same thing long ago while serving in the U. S. military in Middle Eastern conflicts.

Kwon and Marvin arrived shortly after this, and we began the meeting. It was stupefying dull. I liked designing new ships and planning tactics, but this meeting was really about supplies, fuel and the like. I found myself watching the big enemy ship as it came through the ring behind us on the screens. Some had wondered if it would even be able to make it through. The ring was bigger than *Phobos*, but only just. No one had ever tried to send through something the size of a small moon before. We didn't know if the ring could do it, or if it might choke.

I watched with interest as the ring gave birth to *Phobos*. It took nearly a full second to pass through, but it made it.

"Looks like our dogged pursuer has made the jump," I said, putting my tablet down.

Miklos was listing the number of meals each ship had in store, and he managed to make that into a long, drawn-out affair. We could siege them for a year or so with our recyclers working overtime.

"That's all very interesting, Commodore," I said, "and I'm sure you've done an excellent job. But I want to talk to Gaines for a while about the ground forces."

I turned to the Major and nodded to him.

"Well sir, we're ready for anything. We'll assault Earth, the Luna fortresses, or even the Imperial ships, if we have to."

"You know, Gaines," I said, "I originally wanted to hold back on the troop contingent. But I figured we might get an opening if Earth is surprised. If we can get down there suddenly and paralyze their government with a lightning-fast drop from space—"

"Excuse me, sir," Marvin said.

"What is it?"

"There seems to be an emergency situation developing."

We all looked at him. He'd been pretty quiet throughout the meeting. But often, Marvin was the first to know about a recent event. Usually this was because he was tapped into the command centers directly. Occasionally, it was because he'd known disaster was coming for days and hadn't said anything about it.

"What are you talking about?" I demanded.

Before he could say more, the klaxons went off. Miklos and Gaines stood up as if to head for the hatch. I waved them back into their seats.

"The captain of this ship can steer his own command. Bring up the situation on the table, Marvin."

All of Miklos' facts, figures and diagrams vanished. In its place the Helios system appeared, with the big red sun in one corner.

I don't know what I was expecting. Maybe that Earth had shown up with a fleet of their own to intercept us. Or maybe I thought the Worms had gotten frisky, paranoid at the sight of so many "allied" ships in their system. Wildly, I thought maybe a flotilla of fresh Macro ships had just poured out of a hitherto undiscovered ring in the system.

94

None of these scenarios were revealed. Instead, our fleet was displayed moving away from the ring in formation. Behind us, the spherical ship *Phobos* lumbered in pursuit.

I frowned however, tapping at the rear of our formation.

"One of our ships has fallen out of position," I said. "What ship is that, Marvin."

"That's *Gatre*."

I looked at him with widening eyes. I zoomed in until I could read the designation tag. The robot was right.

"What's wrong with her?" I demanded.

"She's been hit, Colonel Riggs. Her engines have been compressed down to approximately fifteen percent of previous mass. Interestingly, the total weight of the engines seems to be close to previous estimates. I can only surmise that—"

"Marvin!" I shouted, standing up and smashing the table with a fist. My hand sunk into the table, and the image of *Gatre* was gone. Fortunately, the surface was made of smart materials, which began reforming themselves around my offending knuckles and tried in vain to gently push me out of their rightful space. "What are you talking about? The Blues can't hit us from this far out. We've ranged their weapons carefully, and we're at more than twice their maximum reach."

"That was our previous estimate, sir," he said with perfect calm. Several of his drifting cameras examined my fist with interest. "You seem to be bleeding, Colonel."

"I don't care about that. Just tell me what happened."

"My report would only be conjecture at this point."

"Give me your best shot," I said, pulling my fist out of the command table and flexing my fingers. My bones were too hard to be broken so easily, but I felt the burn of many cuts and abrasions. Droplets of blood showered the cracked screen as it worked to repair itself.

"There are two reasonable conclusions," Marvin said. "One, the enemy has improved their weaponry and only just gotten the improved technology online."

"You're saying that Tolerance fired a new, long ranged gun the minute he managed to get it working? What's your other theory?"

95

"That the enemy had this capability before, but withheld use of it until we reached the Helios system."

I stared at him. I didn't know why, but I knew he had the right idea.

"That's it," I said. "It's the only thing that makes sense. The timing is too perfect."

Then, I had another flash of realization. The *Gatre* was hit and had lost power.

"Marvin, are there casualties aboard *Gatre*?"

"Yes sir."

I nodded. I desperately wanted to ask if Jasmine and Kate had survived, but when you are in command of thousands, personal fears had to come second to keeping the entire fleet safe.

"Miklos, order the ship abandoned. Order everyone to board the fighters and zoom to a safe distance immediately."

"We should go to flank speed and pull the rest of the fleet out of harm's way as well," he said.

I nodded, pressing my lips into a firm line. "You're right. Do it."

All of us moved then toward the command deck. No further hits had been reported yet, so I figured we had a few minutes while *Phobos* recharged whatever it was that had exerted such awful power. The crisis was on-going, and *Relentless* was full of scrambling personnel.

"Sir?" Gaines asked me in the hallway outside the command center. "If we increase our speed, will the fighters from *Gatre* be able to catch up to us?"

I looked at him sternly. "We'll do that math soon enough. We have to protect the fleet. Let me remind you Major, your transports are in the rearguard."

His eyes widened a fraction, then he nodded firmly. "I understand sir. Where do you want me?"

Usually, a ground commander wasn't needed on the command deck during a fleet engagement, but I had no idea how this was going to play out.

"You can join me at my station on the bridge, Gaines."

We moved to the biggest table in the chamber, and I took the time to tap at the casualty lists. I scrolled the list by flicking

96

my fingers. There were really only two names I was looking for.

Jasmine's name was not there, but Kate Swanson's was. It didn't have an X through it, but it did have a question mark. *Status unknown.* That made sense. Her medical lab had always been in the aft decks, close to the engine rooms.

I tried not to think about it as I closed the list and eyed the screens. Streaks of exhaust plumed from every vessel in the fleet. We were escaping at flank velocity, even though we didn't know if the enemy would hit us again or not.

From the crippled *Gatre*, tiny contacts erupted in a continuous flood. They spread out and flew for all they were worth. The fighters had launched from the doomed ship, and they were chasing us as fast as they could.

-10-

About twenty minutes after the initial strike, we began breathing again. *Phobos* hadn't taken out another vessel—not yet. Maybe firing such a long range shot had taken all the ship's power and it had to build up again. Maybe Tolerance had some other surprise in store for us. Really, we just didn't know. But at least the enemy hadn't been able to take out every engine on every big ship we had in rapid succession. That had been my fear from the start of this new attack.

The bustle around the command deck had settled down to a continuous shuffling. The first fighters escaping the *Gatre* caught up with us and landed, including the one with Captain Sarin aboard. It had turned out they had a much greater capacity for acceleration than the larger ships and were thus able to reach us.

I was happy to see Jasmine's face as she came directly to my command table. She didn't look happy to be here, however. I stepped close to her as she logged into the console and settled in.

"You lost your command," I said, "but it wasn't your fault. I want you to know that."

"I do know that, but it still hurts."

"Of course," I said. "Fortunately, you can be instrumental in getting some revenge right here helping me."

She gave me a confident nod. "Thank you, Colonel."

I looked at the big board, and I didn't like the situation. I didn't like it at all. We had a huge ship with largely unknown capabilities chasing us. What we did know about it made it appear to be unbeatable.

My staff had assembled and everyone was at their stations. The B-team, the staffers I usually left on duty when my top officers were busy or sleeping, had all been shuffled to side jobs or off the deck entirely. Now was not the time for them to get "hands on training". We were in trouble, and I could tell by the looks on every face in the room that the rest of them knew it as well as I did.

I tapped into the overall command channel and hailed all my higher officers in the fleet. After giving them twenty seconds or so to tune in, I addressed them.

"I want all my command personnel to listen up," I began, dropping formalities for now. "We've got a serious situation as you all know by now. The enemy ship we've named *Phobos* is apparently not as toothless as we all thought. I think the fact that we've been able to easily outrun the ship up until now has given us an unrealistic sense of security. But Tolerance, the enemy captain, has just given us all a gentle kick in the ass to wake us up. We're going to have to make some hard and fast decisions. Be ready for anything. Riggs out."

I disconnected and looked at the ring of serious faces circling the command table. This unit was newly designed with a three-D holotank hovering above the table. It was a good setup as I could see the two dimensional layout on the table, which was easier to absorb, while the more precise arrangement of forces was displayed in the tank. The table was laid out along the local plane of the ecliptic for whatever star system we were in at the moment. Usually, that was good enough to accurately place things since most planets, and thus our own ships, were more or less lined up with each other in two dimensions. The tank was better, however, when we got in close. When ships were all over the place in orbit around a single world, for example, two dimensions didn't really do the job.

I tapped at my screen, highlighting the enemy ship.

"What kind of range are we at now?"

Sarin answered first, as I knew she would. Really, it was Commodore Miklos' job, but she'd been my exec for so long she was in the habit of giving me such info, and we all knew she could work the screens better than anyone.

"*Phobos* is about twenty light seconds behind the last ship in the fleet, sir," she said.

"Which is *Gatre*?"

"Correct."

"Could you give us a status report on *Gatre*, Captain?"

"We lost seven crewmen and two fighters. She's crippled, but the ship itself is repairable if the enemy doesn't destroy it on the way by."

I tapped at the casualty list, feigning a professional interest. I found Dr. Kate Swanson's name again. Her name no longer had a question mark by it, and there wasn't an "X" either. I nodded in some relief. She was still alive, at least. I closed the list and looked back up to Sarin, who I now realized was watching my actions carefully. She had to have seen the name I was checking up on.

Under different circumstances, I might have given a guilty start. But what was wrong with wanting to know if a friend was dead or alive? I had nothing to be ashamed of, so I pressed on with the business of the day.

"So far, that one hit was it. We can debate why Tolerance hasn't continued to destroy our ships, but I suspect he can't reach us. Maybe *Gatre* was at the extreme edge of viable range, and now that all the other targets have slipped away, the enemy has to wait for another shot."

"I have another theory, Colonel," Miklos said.

"Let's hear it, Commodore."

"I think the Blue held his fire until now. I think he wanted us out of the Eden system for the same reason we want their ship out."

I stared at him for a moment, then nodded slowly. "They want to protect their civilians? You think that's the motivation?"

"I do. Think about it. Star Force has six inhabited worlds in the Eden System, but the Blues have only one—their homeworld."

"And we've bombed it in the past. You think Tolerance wanted us to move out of the system before he continued the fight?"

"Yes. Because now he's positioned between us and the ring. If we lose the fight, we might want to send some fire toward their gas giant as a form of revenge. This way, we can't do that without passing them by and giving them plenty of opportunity to destroy our fleet."

The more I thought about it, the less I liked it. I'd figured I was leading Tolerance around by the nose. Now, I wasn't so sure.

"What's that ship doing now, Captain?"

She shook her head. "Nothing special. *Phobos* is coming close to the *Gatre* now. The energy readings are stable, its speed..." She looked up at me suddenly. "The enemy is slowing down, sir."

I tapped the screen and zoomed in, frowning. The situation was clear. They were within easy range of the *Gatre* now. Suddenly, the carrier registered some kind of change of status. A glowing red halo appeared around the ship's display.

"*Phobos* is firing again," she said. Her voice wavered slightly, then steadied. "The enemy has crushed *Gatre*, sir."

Jasmine zoomed in, displaying a close-up via long range optics. It had happened over ten seconds ago, but the evidence was clear enough: The *Gatre* was a wad of metal, like a soda can stomped flat.

I nodded, understanding the situation better. "Tolerance held his fire until the target was close. What we aren't sure of is his next move. Will he chase us or linger at the ring and wait for us?"

"With all due respect, Colonel," Miklos said. "I don't think we can wait around until the enemy decides what he wants to do. We have to either run to get out of range or attack him now while he is recharging."

"Run the numbers on an attack. Can we get there in time?"

Fingers tapped madly all around me. There were many variables, but at last the verdict was in.

"We can't really do it. Even if the enemy power system connects the defensive weaponry with their main, offensive systems, we can't get into range in time. They are too far behind us and we're moving at high velocity in the other direction."

I heaved a sigh and examined their work. The numbers didn't lie. The enemy ship would get at least two shots in on us if we attacked with our heavy ships. I knew from the last time that if I sent in only fighters, Tolerance would hold his fire until they got in close then destroy them all with some kind of sweeping field.

"Such simple weaponry, but so effective," I said. "All he has is one weapon with two modes. I think I've underestimated the enemy in this case."

A few people silently exchanged glances. I wondered if I'd won someone a bet—or I'd lost it for them.

"The question remains: what is our response going to be?" Miklos asked.

"There are really only two clear options," I said. "Either we press ahead and hope they follow, or we turn around and charge them."

"I agree. Those are the two choices."

"But I'm not interested in either of those solutions. I'm going to try something different. Marvin, connect me up with the enemy fleet. And the rest of you, keep us gliding away. Not as if we're escaping, but enough to keep us out of range and to give us some maneuvering room."

Orders were shouted and relayed all around us. I ignored them all while I stared at the screens, deep in thought. The Blues had proven themselves susceptible to manipulation in the past. Maybe I could work that angle again.

"Colonel Riggs?" Marvin asked. "What ship should I relay the signal through?"

I looked at him for a second. Everyone around me tensed. No one wanted to be aboard the ship with Colonel Kyle Riggs, at least not today.

"Have we still got a pinnace in the fleet?"

"Yes sir, several of them in fact."

"Release one, have it fly on automatic pilot to a position a few miles away and behind the rest of the main line ships.

We'll relay all conversation through that vessel. If the enemy hits it—well, at least we'll know he cares."

"We'll also get another indicator as to his real maximum range, sir," Miklos said excitedly. "An excellent idea."

We delayed opening a channel until the pinnace was in position. Before I gave the order to call up Tolerance, I asked my staff to do one more thing.

"Jam the ring back to Eden," I told them.

"We've already been doing that, sir," Miklos said. "Ever since we passed through the ring with *Phobos* on our tail."

"All right, good. Hook me up, Marvin."

"Channel open, Colonel."

"Tolerance," I said. "One of my nicknames in my younger days was *Empathy*. I was good at understanding the emotional states of others."

Jasmine coughed lightly, as if she'd choked on something. Everyone looked at her except for me. I pressed ahead, determined not to let her distract me from my plan.

"Do you know what I'm sensing about you today?"

There was a delay as we were at a significantly long range now. Finally, the returning transmission came in, translated and relayed by Marvin.

"You have intrigued me. What is your assessment of my mood?"

"I think you're feeling relief," I said. "In fact, that would be a good name for you about now."

"Relief? That is an odd appellation. I expected you to say, *Exulted* or *Triumphant* or perhaps even *Certain-Of-Total-Victory*."

"Ah, but you and I both know your true goals. You wished to remove my fleet from the Eden System. You've accomplished that. Temporarily, many of my ships are no longer threatening your homeworld. We've been chased from the system allowing your people to relax. Now, you're slowing down. You're hanging back. You have only to guard the ring and keep my ships from returning to your home system.

"You're right to rejoice—for now. Today will not be the final day, the hour of total destruction for your people. That inevitable event has been postponed! Tomorrow,

103

however…well, that's another matter. But at least for this single day, your people are safe. I know what a relief that must be for you, and therefore I rename you *Relief.*"

My statements didn't sit well with Tolerance. As soon as the messages had made their round-trips through space, his voice came back on the speakers: "I've destroyed your ships without effective response. You've run from me like high winds in the distance. But still you persist in speaking as if my people are the ones who should know fear. I would rename you as well, Kyle Riggs, but your new name will be different. I would call you: *Foolishness.*"

People snorted and squirmed at that. I even thought I heard a snigger somewhere near the engine consoles, but I didn't mind as this game wasn't over yet.

"Very well," I said. "You give me no choice but to order the home fleet into action. You might notice that communications with your homeworld have been cut off. My orders have been sent, and now we're jamming the ring. You won't be able to warn your people, which is why it's safe to tell you this now. We left half our ships behind, hidden within the atmospheres of the inner planets. They will reach orbit over Eden-11 within hours. I'm sorry, but bombing will commence upon their arrival."

My staffers, who a moment earlier were all grins and giggles, looked stunned. They nudged one another and spoke in hushed tones. Miklos in particular waved for my attention. I had Marvin mute the channel with Tolerance. I had time to converse with my crew before the response came in.

"Sir?" Miklos demanded. "What home fleet? We'd left behind a dozen or so obsolete ships and a battle station."

I smiled at him.

"Has Riggs gone mad again?" I asked. "That's what you really want to ask, isn't it?"

I chuckled at his whitening face. Miklos was such a straight-man, he rarely appreciated a good joke. Fortunately, the joke wasn't on us this time.

"I know we don't have much left behind, but Tolerance doesn't know that. This monster ship is the first thing the Blues have launched above the atmosphere in who knows how long. They haven't been watching our fleets."

Miklos looked pale, but he nodded. He'd never liked it when I bluffed. Really, the man ought to loosen up and live a little. I signaled for Marvin to unmute the channel.

"Colonel Kyle Riggs," Tolerance said moments later. "Your threats to escalate this conflict are unacceptable for any civilized being."

"Fortunately, we're not all that civilized," I said. "You've pointed that out on countless occasions."

"I will turn this ship around. I will defend my people."

"You can't make it in time. We've done all the math. Your ship is too slow, and you're out of position. The extermination efforts have already begun, I'm afraid. They began the moment you passed into this system. I hate to be the one to tell you, but you are screwed."

The delay was longer than usual this time. Everyone on the command deck was white-knuckling it and sweating. I'm pretty sure I was the only guy on the ship who was having fun.

"I will go back and erase your worlds one by one," Tolerance said at last. "There will not be a single world that will support life within a year."

"Yeah," I said, in a tone that indicated I barely cared. "Those worlds don't mean much to us in any regard. They aren't our homeworlds, just outposts. Our population centers are far from here."

"We've carefully monitored you for years. We know of Earth. Your homeworld is not safe from our vengeance."

"We'll see about that. We've been building up our defenses. Earth's fleets will stop you. We have ten more ships like this one waiting."

"Ah-ha!" boomed the Blue. "Only ten? Such a small force could never overcome this vessel. My course has been set for Earth. Your primary population-reefs will be destroyed without delay. You will be crushed—quite literally crushed—without mercy. *Vengeance* shall be my new name, not *Relief*. Due to your unrelenting savagery, I refuse to speak to your kind further. I will scour you from the cosmos, a legacy that other species will thank me for afterward, throughout eternity."

With that flowery finish, the gasbag closed the channel. My command people were all looking at me and one another in shock. I was surprised to see that I was the only one still smiling.

"Come on," I said, "don't you guys get it? He's going to go for Earth now. That's exactly what we wanted."

"But sir, we're in the way," Jasmine said.

"So? We'll just outrun that barge of his and get out of the way. Navigators, give me a course that sends us around that big red sun once then back into position behind *Phobos*. I'll bet anyone ten bucks that ship will sail right by us and head directly for Earth."

They were all quiet, subdued.

"But," Jasmine said, looking very worried, "what if Crow's fleet can't stop that monster? What if Tolerance breaks through and really does it?"

"What? You mean that business about erasing humanity? Yeah, sure, he's going to try it. But not because of anything I said. That was his plan all along. Don't you remember their threats from last year? The Blues have been talking Armageddon ever since I first bombed them. Touchy bastards."

Jasmine licked her lips and stared at me with her big brown eyes. I was a sucker for that look. "Kyle, I think what has everyone worried is the fear we might not be able to stop them."

"Look," I said, leaning on the command table and eyeing them each in turn. I lowered my voice, but I was pretty sure everyone on the deck heard me anyway. The crowd was pretty quiet. "I figured it out when this ship first showed up. They mean to wipe us out. All of us. This isn't a matter of talking them down and getting them to land on Eden-11 again. They were never going to turn their moon-sized goliath into some kind of natural history museum."

I stared at my staff. I don't know what I expected, but it wasn't glum rejection. These people had faced the Macros time and again and won through. Maybe it was the fact this was a new enemy with new terror weapons to worry about. Maybe that had them rattled. I sighed quietly, figuring they needed a pep-speech.

106

"This is it," I told them. "It's them or us. Or at least, it's that ship or us. You all have to understand that's how this was destined to play out. It's only been a question of tactics since they launched *Phobos*. Right now, I have to say I'm feeling pretty good about our odds. They're better than they were yesterday, I'm certain of that. I laid out the bait and Tolerance ate it up. He's going straight to Earth to get his righteous revenge."

"*This* was your plan?" demanded Miklos. "To fool Tolerance into thinking his homeworld was doomed so he would do the same thing to Earth immediately?"

"Uh-huh. Pretty neat, isn't it? The Blues aren't the best at trickery. Oh sure, they can withhold information, but when it comes to elaborate fabrications, forget it... You know, I'm beginning to think that's our special calling in this universe. If you want a fancy lie told well, you need a human. Anyway, I'll tell you the best part: after we take *Phobos* apart in the Solar System, the Blues back home will never know what happened to their ship! It'll be just like one of those Flying Dutchman stories where some boat sailed away in Earth's history never to be heard from again. Since we're jamming the rings, we can make up any whopper we want and scare the Blues with it when we go back to Eden."

A few nodded, but most of them looked stunned. I wasn't expecting whoops and high-fives, but I'd counted on a smile and a handshake from someone.

I guess a sly man who expects praise for pulling a fast one should expect a long, long wait instead.

Since there wasn't much to do after Tolerance stopped talking, I went to bed. I left instructions for my officers to wake me up in the event anything interesting happened.

Before I knew it, I was fast asleep. It seemed like two minutes later when the door chimed. I sat up with a sudden intake of breath.

"Come on in," I said, then let a deep breath out in a long sigh.

The hatch dilated open and I stopped scratching my head to see who it was. There were no emergency lights or klaxons going, so I figured it couldn't be too serious.

The figure in the hatchway was female in shape. I tapped at the nearest wall, causing the lights to shift up an octave in brightness with each touch. It was none other than Dr. Kate Swanson.

"Hello, doctor," I said. "You look like you're in one piece."

She smiled, crossed her arms and shook her head. "You weren't really asleep, were you?"

"Um...sort of."

"After what you've been through? Do you know how unusual that is? Psychologically speaking? Most people would be up all night, worried and stressed."

I stretched and swept my legs off the side of the bed. My feet found my shoes—or rather my shoes found my feet. Smart clothes could be like over-anxious pets. They adhered themselves to me and began strapping and tightening without any confirmation that I wanted them to.

"Whenever anyone mentions psychology to me, I reach for my sidearm," I said, chuckling.

She didn't seem to think my comment was particularly funny. I paused, frowning. Had I blown a possibly fruitful moment for both of us?

"Unbelievable," she said. "You doomed the entire human race to oblivion, then came down here for a nap?"

I narrowed my eyes, studying her. "Did someone send you to wake me up?"

"No, Colonel. I just thought you might like to see me."

"Yes," I said. "I'd like that very much. Let's go get some coffee, shall we?"

Together, we walked down the ship's primary passageway. I found myself looking around for Jasmine. I didn't really want her to see me with Kate. I knew it was silly, after all Sandra was dead and I was a free man. But old habits die hard.

Fortunately, we met no one who even gave us a second glance all the way down to the wardroom. There, we had our coffee. She had cream, chocolate and some kind of sprinkles on hers. I quietly slipped a shot of bourbon into mine. I silently accounted that as equivalent to a beer and a half.

We talked for a while. I told her I'd checked the casualty lists frequently and was able to give her the exact time her status had gone from a question mark to a known survivor. This gained me a real smile.

"They found me at that time," she said. "I was in one of those medical tubes—you know the ones."

I nodded. Sandra's last days had been spent in just such a coffin-like contrivance. I'd stared into those devices to check on badly injured people more times than I cared to remember.

"It was airtight, of course, and had its own environmental controls. Still, I was close to dying. When the engine room was hit, the hull nanites rushed toward it, trying to compensate. Something blew apart as the walls thinned themselves, and the entire place depressurized. We had on vac suits, as per regulations, but you're never quite expecting sudden catastrophic pressure loss. Several of my staff were sucked out into space. We never recovered the bodies, there was no time."

She sipped her coffee again, troubled.

I touched her hand gently. She put her other hand on top of mine. I thought about giving her a squeeze and pulling back, but I left my hands clasped with hers instead.

"It's always rough to see people you care about dying around you," I told her. "I assume you managed to stay in the chamber, then to get yourself into one of the medical units?"

"Yes. The damage—it was bad, Kyle. The hit was beyond sudden, it was instantaneous. One second, the ship was cruising and everything was perfectly normal. The next moment the engine was the size of a basketball, and the walls around it had been sucked inward, forming strange patterns like melted wax. I'm not sure if that was due to the nanites, or to some side effect of the weapon that hit us."

I gave her our current theory on how the weapon worked. Marvin didn't have many confirmed details yet, but we were learning more each time it hit us.

"So," she said, "why hasn't Tolerance hit us again?"

"Our best guess is he's limited by his power levels. It seems like his ship has one primary gun. It can fire at tremendous range and do great damage, but it drains all his power. He has to let it build up for several minutes before firing again. It's like he's charging a battery to full before each shot."

"You think firing at a longer range made him reduce the scope of the area affected?"

"Definitely. He targeted the engine room specifically and took it out at great range, but he can't do that with regularity. Now that we're pulling away from him and dodging as we fly, he might not be able to hit us at all."

"That's what we thought last time."

I shrugged. "In war, there are always surprises. What's important now is that you're safe, and the fleet is largely intact."

We sipped our coffees and chatted about happier things for a time. Somehow, a near-death experience often puts people into a romantic mood. I wasn't sure as to the cause, but I'd

110

seen it time and again. Dr. Kate Swanson was no exception to this rule.

I'd just begun to wonder if I was going to get lucky tonight after all when she stood up and took her leave. She said she was sore and tired after almost dying a few hours ago. I believed her, but I walked her to her room just in case.

I scored a kiss for my troubles, but that was all. I headed back to my own quarters, sighing. I kept thinking of the two women I was pursuing, and I had more trouble falling asleep this time around.

* * *

It took *Phobos* nearly a week to crawl across the Helios system. I warned the Worms to stand clear of the ship, doubting they could do much if they did attack.

The big lumbering vessel steered after us at first when we headed toward the bloated red sun, but eventually veered off. As I'd hoped, Tolerance had realized two things: that wasn't the way to Earth, and he was never going to catch us.

We were surprised by one thing: when the ship approached the huge star, it slowed suddenly, showing more capacity for deceleration than it had previously, then bounced toward the ring to the next system. I first noticed it when I came to the command deck a few days later and eyed the boards.

"Is that trajectory path right?" I asked.

"Yes sir," Marvin said promptly.

He had a number of cameras tracking me as I frowned down at the big screen and ran my finger along the route the ship had taken.

"That pattern of motion…is that even possible? I mean, at those velocities?"

"Technically, anything is possible with sufficient force."

"Yeah, but it was barreling toward the sun, then it just did a ninety degree bounce away from it. The slowdown and initial acceleration at a new angle…it doesn't make sense."

"No, not given observed behavior and traditional assumptions about their propulsion systems."

I looked up from the puzzling data and noticed all his cameras. There were at least seven watching me.

"All right, Marvin," I said, "if you know something new, tell me about it. And none of your dodging around, this time. We're facing a serious new enemy here."

"Right you are, Colonel," he said, and then stopped.

We stared at one another for several long seconds. My frown deepened. "Do you want something? Is that it?"

His tentacles rattled and slapped for a moment as he sidled closer. He reached out with a single, skinny worm of metal and tapped at the screen. Something lit up with a red circle, something that was far behind the main body of the fleet.

"What's that?"

"*Gatre.*"

I stared at it. "Right, I see it now. The wreck is still flying on a trajectory straight toward the far ring. It's moving at lower speeds, but at a much more direct angle."

I tapped at the drifting ship, projecting its path over time.

"Hmm, she'll be coming close to the ring to Alpha Centauri only a day behind us."

Marvin shuffled and rattled. I could tell he was working up to something, but I couldn't tell what it was.

"There might be new details to learn, about the enemy weaponry, I mean. This ship isn't a total loss. I've taken careful measurements. The fringes of the vessel aren't damaged at all in places. This seems to be because the ship was struck twice. There are spots along the hull that show no damage or a transition from a normal state to a crushed state. By studying the boundary damage—the region where the effect ended—I might be able to make certain discoveries."

"All right, let me see if I understand what you're saying. You want to fly out there somehow and take samples or something? I don't think there's time, Marvin. If we got on a fighter today and flew it out there, we could make it, but there wouldn't be fuel enough to get back."

Marvin looked agitated. "I've done the math. I always do the math before I make a request like this. It *is* possible. But it will take special permission from you, Colonel Riggs."

"Hmm… A request? I think you're attempting extortion."

"A strong word, Colonel."

"Yeah. What new information do you have? I'm not approving anything until you give me an excuse to indulge another of your fantastic voyages."

"Just this, sir: I think I understand the enemy propulsion system. The evidence, in fact, is overwhelming."

It's always difficult for a human to admit they've been successfully manipulated by a machine, but once again I found myself in that position. "All right. Tell me what it is."

"Do I have your permission to—"

"No," I said, "but you have a shot at getting it. Just give me your data right now."

"Very well. The enemy ship is using gravitational control systems for propulsion. Completely self-contained systems."

I thought about it. "There is no exhaust or other form of energy release... Do you think that's how their ship is changing course, too?"

"Absolutely. That was my first clue. They aren't emitting any exhaust, even when maneuvering. That rules out most forms of propulsion. The only known form of propulsion that they could be employing is gravity manipulation. Really, the conclusion is obvious when you consider it carefully."

I had to admit it did make sense. Our ships had gravity systems for stabilizing the vessels and easing high-G acceleration. In smaller systems, we used grav plates to make our armored battle suits and vehicles like tanks fly. But to achieve any real speed we needed more powerful engines.

"So they're using gravity plates to fly a giant ship around," I said, talking to myself. "Nothing else."

"That conclusion is inescapable at this point."

It was obvious, but it was also staggering.

"The power involved," I muttered, staring at a close up of the big ship. "It's shocking. And the grav plates themselves would have to be huge."

"The ship is quite large."

"Yeah. And look at their pattern of motion. It does make sense. The ship was falling toward the red giant using normal gravity to pull it closer. Then it switched on the plates, and the very same force that had been pulling it reversed like a magnet switching polarity. What pulled it faster started pushing it with fantastic force."

"Our own grav plates operate in exactly the same manner," Marvin said. "But on such a smaller, weaker scale. We think of them as systems limited to gliding an object over planetary surfaces. But there is no technical reason they should be incapable of more, given sufficient energy and mass."

After going over the details, I had to admit he'd figured out something significant. The first step to defeating any alien power was to understand their technology. It was beginning to seem to me that the enemy ship did not employ things we didn't understand, but the Blues had built a ship of such vast scale that it could do things we hadn't thought of with the technology we used every day.

"Okay," I said after another ten minutes of study. "Now, tell me about your proposal."

"I want to fly out to *Gatre* and study the damage."

"I know that. How exactly do you plan to get there and back in time? Before the fleet leaves the Helios system. And don't say you want us to hang back for you. I'm not going to let *Phobos* out of my sight for long, even if it is heading toward Earth to attack the Imperials."

"I wouldn't dream of asking for you to hold back the entire fleet."

"Yes, yes you would. But just tell me exactly what you're proposing."

"It's simple, really. I'll need a dozen grav-plates of my own, nothing this carrier can't spare. After cannibalizing a single fighter, the main drives will be attached to the dorsal and ventral..."

He continued, and brought up a detailed schematic. I frowned at it, trying to take it all in. There were sensor boxes, specimen racks, tiny holds and extra power generators. At last, I realized what was at the front of this train wreck of equipment. It looked a tangle of tentacles and cameras.

"Wait a minute, Marvin! Is that you I see up there on the tip of this iceberg of stuff? You're trying to turn yourself into a ship again, aren't you?"

"I wouldn't even propose something like this, Colonel, if it wasn't a necessity."

"A necessity?"

"There's no other way for us to examine the dead ship. There's no other way for us to gain the critical knowledge we need to defeat this terrifying new enemy."

A squadron of cameras studied me. I figured every one he had was trained on me.

I sighed. "All right," I said, "but I think I'm going to regret it."

"Excellent, Colonel! Now, I've taken the time-saving step of drawing up these orders for you to sign. If you would open the folder on the desktop nearest to your right hand, you'll see the files now. It's the icon that's blinking, Colonel."

"I know that," I growled. "I'm just having second thoughts."

"I thought we had a deal, sir."

"We do. But I don't know how I'm going to explain it to my staff."

I was in the middle of signing orders electronically when a new input screen chimed at the corner of the big table.

"Something's coming in," I said, reaching to tap at it.

"Another distraction?" Marvin complained. He almost had me in the bag, and he wanted the deal done.

"It could be important."

"Or it could be a weather report from Eden-8."

I looked at him. It wasn't like him to make a smartass remark. I wasn't sure if he was becoming more sophisticated, or he'd just gotten lucky.

"I can finish this later—"

"Colonel, I'm under a tight time constraint as it is. I need these approvals in order to—"

"All right, dammit," I said, tapping to open each form and quickly signing it. I usually didn't sign things without reading them, but I was getting tired of scanning Marvin's manifests.

"What's this?" I asked, frowning at one of the last items.

"You're almost done, Colonel."

"Bioinformatic permissions? Release of remains? What the hell?"

115

"Sir, the incoming reports are still waiting. In order to access them quickly, you only have to press your right thumb to the lower left corner of each document in the folder. Then you can check on the reports."

I looked at him. "Marvin, how dumb do you think I am? No—don't answer that. Let me tell you something: I'm not signing any more manifests. You got your sensors, you got your fuel, you got your fighter to take apart. That's all you need to get out there and back, and that's all you're going to get. I'm not giving you permission to mess around with the bodies of any Star Force dead you might find floating around out there. You can just forget about that."

Marvin didn't answer. He was frustrated; I could tell by the way he held his tentacles. But that was just too damned bad.

I closed the last three items, leaving them unsigned, then brought up the blinking report. It was from our long range sensor crew.

I read a line or two of the bulletin, then slapped Marvin on the brainbox. "You knew what this was."

"There was no immediate danger to the ship."

"You ignored an incoming report and then tried to use it to snow me into signing for things you don't even need."

"'Need' is a relative term in the investigative sciences, Colonel."

"Yeah, yeah."

I tapped at the displays and called my bridge people to the tactical table. They circled around. Everyone was reading the input and coming to the same conclusions: the Worms were launching their ships.

I'd told them not to. I'd told them to stay put on their planet or to hang around on the far side of their world with their fleets if they wanted to. But the Worms were nothing if not brave and impulsive. They were like the knights of old in that they didn't always do what their own commanders ordered them to do. They were excitable, and I usually liked that about them. But today I had the feeling they were going to be slaughtered.

While we talked about what action we should take, Marvin slipped away toward the elevators. I knew where he was going.

He wanted to get to the hanger deck to begin rebuilding himself.

I looked after him and shook my head. I'd let that robot build himself into a ship before, and things had never gone the way I'd hoped.

Maybe this time I'd get lucky.

-12-

While Marvin scrambled to rebuild himself in the hanger, my tactical ops team scratched their heads about what we could do to help the Worms, if anything.

"I hate to see them lose a single ship," I complained. "We're going up against Earth and the Blues. By the end of this campaign, there's no way humanity will have as many ships in the sky as it does now. The Worms are our only allies with a real space fleet in the known systems."

"I've been working on various options, sir," Miklos said. "The first, naturally, is to attempt some sort of diplomatic steering of their behavior."

Everyone looked at me as he said this. I frowned.

"Sure," I said, "I've managed to talk some people into things, but I'm not a miracle-worker. The Worms have taken in every message I sent them and launched anyway. The trouble is the ship captains themselves. They aren't listening to their central command."

"I gather this is not an unusual circumstance in your experience?" asked Miklos drily.

I gave him a sidelong glance. I was pretty sure he was making a reference to me and my frequent deviations from his script. For Star Force, he represented central command. As an operating field commander, I had, if the truth be told, not always played by his rules.

"Yeah," I said. "They do it all the time. You know, I have a soft spot in my heart for the Worms—and not just due to

118

remorse for having once killed one of their cities. They are a brave and honorable people with a streak of the screaming barbarian in them. Who doesn't admire a true warrior of the old school?"

"Sir, time is pressing, if you don't—"

"Right. Let's get back to the situation at hand. We've got missiles, beams, fighters and cannons. Can we reach *Phobos* with any of those before the Worms hit them? Assuming, of course, that we put the pedal to the metal now in order to catch up?"

Their expressions changed from thoughtful to alarmed. Staffers began tapping and whispering.

"Uh, sir," Miklos said, speaking for the group as usual. "Are you suggesting we're going to attack *Phobos*? I was under the impression the enemy ship was on a course we agreed with and we were going to stay out of it for the duration."

"You thought wrong. The situation has changed."

"But...but, what about the mines? We've been building up a supply. I thought we were going to get ahead of them and drop mines at the rings."

"Forget about the mines. Retool them into missiles. We're behind *Phobos* now, did anyone notice? Damn."

The staffers were white-faced. They scrambled to comply with the changing plan all around us as I spoke.

"Why do we have to get involved?" Miklos asked, not letting the matter rest.

I glared at him. "Allowing *Phobos* to crush the Worm fleet was never in my plan."

"But we would rather them die than us, wouldn't we?"

"Neither of those choices is acceptable. I'm asking for options. What kind of assets could we bring into play?"

Numbers began popping up on the screen. They put them in different colors and a red timer appeared at the top. I could see the layout clearly as they zoomed in and laid out all the details.

We were about ninety minutes behind *Phobos* right now, matching her course and speed. She would hit the ring to the Alpha Centauri system in four hours. But between *Phobos* and the ring was a cloud of some fifty Worm ships. They were spiraling like a swarm of wasps already and heading directly toward the ship invading their territory.

Yellow lines appeared representing predictive paths. These lines gently curved showing a unique route for each group. Our fleet was right behind the enemy, but as I watched, the curve shifted, becoming more linear. They were plotting what we could do if we increased our speed in order to run *Phobos* down.

I crossed my arms and waited. We had some time to spare, and it was important to get these numbers right before making any decisions.

On the screen a series of spheres appeared around our ship. These represented weapons ranges. The spheres looked grossly inadequate on this scale.

"Well?" I asked, becoming impatient as they squabbled over details.

"It's all about the missiles, sir," Miklos said. "That's the only system that can reach the enemy in time."

"And the fighters," Jasmine added.

Miklos looked at her coldly.

"What about the fighters? Can they get into the battle or not?"

"They don't have the range to fly out there, attack, and return."

"Hmm," I said, tapping my fingers on the table. "I see what Jasmine is hinting at. They could fly out, exhausting their fuel. They'd have to drift and wait for pickup afterward. How much tactical time would they have over the target if we did throw them in?"

"Sir, I don't think—"

"Just answer the question, Commodore."

"About eight minutes of heavy fighting. Then they'll be exhausted. But sir, I don't see how we could use the fighters in a strike. We'd just lose them all. The missiles—we could throw them in and afford the loss. We can rebuild missiles with supplies of raw materials aboard our carriers. But the fighters are irreplaceable on the front lines."

I didn't listen to any of them for about thirty seconds after that. I was looking at the tactical displays and thinking hard. Finally, I made my decisions.

"We've seen their weapons in operation several times now," I said. "This could be an excellent opportunity to test a theory of mine."

Miklos looked more alarmed than ever. "Sir, this can hardly be an appropriate time to—"

"Listen: this is all the time we've got. Before anyone freaks out, I want you all to know I'm not going to get anyone senselessly killed. I've got a theory about how their defensive field operates, and I want to test it. That's all. What we're going to do is launch a good-sized barrage of missiles. Let's fire a hundred of them. If I'm reading your map correctly, by firing missiles now we'll strike before the Worms do. Right?"

"That is correct, Colonel."

"Good. Then when we get in closer, we'll launch fighters. Two full squadrons. We have to make it look real."

There was some level whispering about that. On the screen, the proposed attacks were plotted. Lines appeared and moved with ghostly, pulsing contacts. They represented future positions about an hour from now.

"Yeah, that's it. Give the launch order. I want a hundred missiles flying within…eight minutes."

The group broke up now that the order had been given. Miklos didn't leave the table, however. He stepped around it to talk to me privately.

"Sir, I would like to request permission to stand down as your operations officer on this campaign."

"Request denied."

"But sir, I don't feel like I'm doing my job. I've been overruled and ignored on every detail. I—"

"Look Commodore," I said, "I don't have time to replace you right now. You're doing a fine job, anyway."

"You could put Captain Sarin in my position."

I looked him in the eye. I could see he was seriously pissed off.

"I'm sorry for overriding your authority without talking you through the plan," I said. "Sometimes, in space combat, there isn't a week or two to discuss and wring your hands over every decision, each nut and bolt. At those times, I need quick competent support people to carry out my orders rather than individuals with a raft of their own ideas to float. Now, can you explain why you're objecting so strenuously? What's so bad about this situation you want to quit on me?"

"You're risking too much of our strike power in this assault. I believe the enemy ship will destroy everything we throw at it."

"It's a fleet-thing, then. You don't want to lose any more ships."

"Of course not, Colonel."

"It's not just about the fleet, man. The fleet is a tool to reach a goal."

"You're saying that my men and ships are expendable?"

"In the grand scheme of things, yes. I'd kill us all to save the species. That's why we're here, you know. Self-sacrifice is part of the game in any military. But I'm talking about a single dangerous attack. You're making it sound as if we might as well take a nice hot group-shower and slit our wrists together."

"That's about how I would characterize this attack."

I glared at him and he glared back.

"All right," I said. "We have time now, so I'm going to explain my strategy to you in detail. This entire action is a bluff, Commodore. I didn't want to tell everyone that, as I wanted the attack to look as real as possible to the enemy— also, it might turn out to *be* real if we get lucky. We might go through with the full operation if my plan works."

Miklos calmed down, but still looked confused. "What do you mean? How can a fake attack be useful in this situation?"

"The enemy has a very powerful weapon that requires a great deal of energy to use. It doesn't fire frequently, and it has a limited range. The only way past a blanket defensive system like that is to overload it. First, the missiles will reach *Phobos*. If Tolerance takes them out, he'll probably not be able to stop the next wave."

"Which will be?"

"The Worms. Look at the timing, they are scheduled to come in second. The third and last wave will be our fighters.

But I'll only commit them if the Worms are still alive. Do you get the picture? We'll be forcing Tolerance to make hard decisions, testing his defenses. If the missiles are wiped out and the Worms as well, then we pull out our fighters. He only has one shot. If he doesn't stop the missiles, he has to take that strike on the chin and then decide which of the next two waves to target."

Miklos' face cleared. "I understand your logic better now, sir. But I thought you didn't want to destroy *Phobos*. I thought you wanted that ship to clear the way to Earth."

"I highly doubt a few missiles and ships are going to do the job. But we'll have to do it later. If *Phobos* reaches Earth, it will be our task to destroy her then. This is an opportunity to learn how to effectively attack this monster."

He nodded slowly. "I still feel you could have informed me of these details during the planning session."

"Timing was tight. Do you feel that? The shuddering under our feet? Every ship is firing the missiles even now. I wanted them away and on target. I wanted those extra minutes without having to explain it all to you or anyone else."

Miklos sucked in a big breath and let it out. "I'm sorry, sir."

"I am too. You're Fleet, and you love your ships too much. It's clouding your strategic thinking. Due to this, I've decided to take your suggestion."

I gave him a stern, meaningful look. He appeared stunned as it dawned on him what I was saying.

"Yes," I said gravely. "For the duration of this campaign, I'm relieving you of your position. Captain Jasmine Sarin will run tactical ops. You will specialize in logistical management. This may change again in the future, and no ranks will be altered for now. I'm sorry Miklos, but I need people who offer helpful advice rather than paranoid resistance."

He was angry again after my comments. He stood straight and at attention. His eyes avoided mine.

"I see, Colonel. Am I confined to quarters?"

"Don't be dramatic, man!" I said, waving him toward the darkest, least frequented corner of the command deck. "Head

123

over there and start riding those supply nerds. And don't look so upset. Quitting your post was your idea, remember that."

"So it was, sir. So it was."

* * *

Gaines came over to me about an hour later. I looked at him with suspicion.

"What?" he asked right away, seeing my expression.

"Aren't you going to tell me I've been too hard on the Commodore, like everyone else?"

"I'm not like everyone else, sir," he said with an easy smile. "I'm just along for the ride. Until you kick me out into space that is, screaming in my little tin suit."

I smiled. It had been over an hour since I'd smiled, and I wasn't surprised Gaines had been the one to make it happen. He was a true veteran marine: gung-ho, but one step from mercenary in his attitude toward life and death. Orders were orders. Dying was just part of the business, not something to get all ruffled up about.

"You're going to have a lot of company with you when you go."

"Yes sir, and fortunately I like the smell of sheep."

I shook my head. The marine grunts had taken to calling their Centaur comrades "sheep" even though the alien troops were anything but cowardly. I didn't mind, as men since time immemorial have given less than complimentary names to their allies in arms.

"Sir, the real reason I've come to talk to you is about a design-related issue."

I nodded. "All right, I've got a minute. No promises though. Show me what you've got."

He pulled up schematics of the landing pods. My men lovingly referred to these pieces of equipment as "flying coffins". Unlike the standard surfboard-type systems, which were built for space-borne assaults, the landing pods were bigger, torpedo-like affairs. They were designed to insert a marine into a combat zone on a planet with an atmosphere.

This was always a tricky business, as anyone who's done it can tell you.

The enemy almost always shot at you as you came down. In order to avoid being blown to pieces, you had to come down fast. But that created a lot of friction which manifested itself as an armor-melting fireball if it you did it wrong. The trick was to bring the occupant down to the planet surface in record time without cooking him in the process.

"We think the aerodynamics of these units is leaning in the wrong direction, sir," Gaines said, poking at the screen laid out before us.

As he spoke, I turned and looked toward the other staffers. I was beginning to catch on. When Gaines said "we" he meant the nerds in the corner. When he represented his ideas for fixing the design, he did so because they'd put him up to it.

Everyone aboard knew that Gaines and I were drinking buddies. After they'd witnessed my dressing-down of Commodore Miklos, they were probably too scared to give me a good reason to chew on them.

I sighed, trying to pay attention to Gaines and figure out what they wanted.

"You see here?" he was saying, "these lines are some kind of refrigeration tubes. They'll cool down the man inside when the heat gets to maximum. That, and insertion at a softer angle, should allow us to get to the ground faster and more safely."

I smiled at him. "What grade did you get in your college calculus courses, Gaines?" I asked him.

"Uh…"

"That's what I thought. I got Cs and barely passed myself. I hate real math. My point is this: I know the team over there in planning and design put you up to this. But it's cool, as it sounds like a good structural fix that we'll have time to implement long before we reach Earth. Go tell them you've convinced me. Project approved."

Gaines nodded and laughed. "Let me talk to you a bit more, so they figure I had to work real hard."

I glanced at the design team. Some of them were fun to look at. "Trying to get a date, huh?" I asked Gaines. "All right, you've got it."

125

We poked at the designs for several more minutes, but talked about the last time we'd played pool together. We both described in detail the nature of the rematch we'd have after Earth had been liberated. He assured me that I'd walk out of the pool room with a strange gait and a missing bat, while I told him he'd never smile with all his teeth again.

Looking back later, I was happy I'd had that calm minute or two to share with a comrade. Because right about when we finished talking and Gaines walked over to the design group with the good news, bad things began to happen.

-13-

Faced with a multi-wave incoming attack, Tolerance did what any newbie commander would do: he panicked.

"Sir, we have incoming energy emission readings."

I knew what that meant. I stepped back to the tactical tables and waved Captain Sarin over. "Do your magic, Jasmine. What have we got?"

She glanced once in the direction of Miklos, but then quickly got down to business.

"Looks like *Phobos* has fired its main gun again. But we aren't registering any damage."

"That's good," I said, leaning on the table and staring at the display intently.

Our attack was less than an hour from contact. The missiles were green slivers with traced paths ahead of them done in light blue. They were arranged in a wide dispersal pattern and they were going to slam right into the nickel-sized sphere we'd named *Phobos*.

"He's shooting at something. What about the Worm ships in front of him? Have any of them been crushed or fallen out of formation?"

"They don't have a formation in any normal sense," she said, "but as far as we can tell, they haven't been—oh, wait a second. I see it now. We're so far out, it takes our optics time to register anything hitting them."

Deftly working the screens, she brought a timer box that showed how far away in light-seconds each element of the battle was. The Worms were the farthest, a full two hundred light-seconds away. Millions of miles. I shook my head.

"As far out as that he's able to hit them?"

"That's just it, sir—I think he missed."

"What?"

"All the Worm ships are accounted for. *Phobos* fired too early. What I'm detecting is an evasive pattern among the Worms. They're flying in a random tangle of trajectories now."

This was not at all unusual for the Worms. They were always chaotic, but with determination and suicidal bravery. When their ships came at you it was like being swarmed by angry wasps.

"How do we know they're being targeted?" I asked.

"By their reactions. Their spiraling patterns have accelerated. I'm not *certain* they've been hit, but it makes the most sense. They might be monitoring the energy output and taking evasive action just in case—either that or they just took a glancing blow. A strike that didn't destroy any ships, but which they felt."

I watched as calmly as I could. This was all going to come down to a razor's edge.

"If we charged in now, how long would it be until our ships came within *Phobos'* effective range?"

"About forty minutes, sir. The missiles will hit long before that."

"Or they'll be wiped out. I'm curious as to why Tolerance decided to fire on the Worms rather than our missiles."

Jasmine shrugged. "Smaller targets are harder to hit?"

"Maybe. But I think it's something else. I think he's made his decision. He's going use a blanket, close-range blast to take out the missiles. Then he'll let the Worms get in close. Therefore he's not worried about the missiles right now. He knows he can destroy them all when the time comes."

"It could be."

"Hmm," I said studying the screen. "Where's Miklos? Get him over here."

Jasmine looked up, catching me with her eyes. I knew what she was thinking: *Didn't you just fire him, Kyle?* But I didn't care. Now wasn't the time for petty squabbles.

Miklos, once called, wandered over almost in slow-motion.

"Yes, Colonel? Is it urgent? I have fuel calculations to make."

"Yes, as a matter of fact it is. Take a look at this."

Miklos studied the screen and the data. "Am I permitted to speak?"

"Dammit man, why do you think I brought you over here?" I demanded.

"Well, I would say the enemy is more worried about the Worms than the missiles. That could mean Tolerance is confident he can take the missiles out when they get in close."

"Yeah...either that, or he thinks he can ride out the missiles. But I don't get that. Nuclear impacts seem far more likely to do real damage when we're talking about a mile-thick rock armor shell."

"Do you have data on that thickness, Colonel?"

"Certainly not. I'm guessing. But it's got to be at least that thick. Such a huge ship. I wonder how they built the damned thing."

"At least we know the gas giant has a solid core of rock down there somewhere."

I nodded absently, then I came to a sudden decision. "Jasmine: slow down our missiles."

"What, sir?"

"You heard me. Turn off their engines. Let them coast in. Run the projected numbers on impact as soon as you do."

She was startled, but she did as I asked immediately. Miklos stared at me, looking like I'd killed his cat.

That was the difference between these two, I thought to myself. Miklos wanted to be in overall command, which was not his place. Captain Sarin had ambitions, but she didn't firmly believe she'd make a better commander than I would. Therefore, she didn't second guess everything I did. When I gave her an order she followed it first and questioned my sanity second.

The screen changed after she brought up a screen and tapped in the unusual command. Our missiles could be remotely self-destructed, and they could also change course suddenly. But they were so far out, it was going to take a good thirty seconds for any command we gave their tiny brainboxes to reach them.

"Come on, come on," I muttered. "Not much time."

Jasmine didn't even look at me. She didn't get flustered. Her fingers flew over the dialog box she'd popped up on the big screen. A moment later she looked up.

"Transmission sent. We'll have to wait to see the results, though."

It was a long minute. First, our command had to crawl out there, then the missiles had to react. Thirty seconds later we'd be able to see them coasting.

Assuming that the missiles were following orders, the staffers laid in a predicted path for them. I watched the timing boxes carefully. I nodded.

"Now, the missiles will hit second. Not by much, but second."

"Sir," Miklos said, "what if the enemy defensive weapon can now hit both the Worms and our missiles at the same time?"

"Then we're screwed."

He pursed his lips and shut up.

"Timing, Jasmine?" I asked.

"We've got it on the display now. There will be about a minute between the Worm ships hitting and the missiles hitting."

"Okay," I said, "Now, have the missiles hit the gas again. Full thrust. Send them in for that final diving attack. I want them concentrated on the aft area where we identified some structures previously."

Jasmine tapped wildly. Miklos looked at me like I was insane. But, to his credit, he didn't say a word.

When she was done transmitting the order, she looked up at me. "Sir? What was the purpose of that exercise?"

"To throw off Tolerance. He's all alone on that big ship of his, and he's a rookie. I want to rattle him. I want all his plans to be in question. If he makes a mistake, he doesn't have a staff full of caretakers to back him up like I do."

I tossed Miklos a meaningful glance, which he did his best to ignore.

We had about twenty more tense minutes to wait around. During that time, Tolerance fired his cannon—whatever it was—twice more. Both shots were hits, taking out two Worm ships.

"Cut out the engines again," I said.

"Sir?"

"I've been watching the missiles and the timing them very closely. If they coast now, they should still cross that last fifty thousand miles a minute ahead of the Worm fleet. I don't think Tolerance can reload that fast."

"You don't think—?" began Miklos, then he broke off.

Jasmine and I both looked at him sharply. "What was that, Commodore?"

"Nothing, Colonel."

We watched as the missiles flew in deadly silence. Everything was locked in by the last minute or so. One only has so much control over a missile that is millions of miles distant in any case. Soon, projected impacts were blossoming. We had no idea, however, if the projections were real or not. We had to wait for the optics.

"Marvin?" I called. "Where's Marvin? Oh yeah…"

I realized that I'd let him run off to take samples of the wreckage that was once *Gatre*. I hoped he was having fun out there. I pulled up a brainbox substitute and formed a transmission to the Worms.

"What are you going to tell them, sir?" Jasmine asked me.

"To hit whatever they can and get the hell out of there in less than ten minutes. Honor will have been satisfied."

The symbols suggested by the brainbox swam quietly into view on the screen. A warrior, pictured in full retreat.

"No, no!" I shouted. "That won't work! What kind of a second-class box did Marvin build, here? The Worms must be told they're doing something of great import full of honor—no matter what it is."

The box tried again, this time coming up with two pictures: an empty chariot and a setting sun. Or was it the sun rising? I frowned at that, uncertain of the meaning.

"We have to send it soon if they're going to get it in time."

"All right," I growled. "Just transmit it. And switch off our fleet's engines, too.

"The screen is updating, sir."

I watched the main table we all circled with interest. Frequently, I glanced up at the holotank as well. We were in close now and things were getting exciting. The holotank did a much better job of pinpointing a strike on a moon-sized object.

During the next update, the missiles vanished. All but two of them. I whooped with a mixture of relief and excitement. Everyone looked at me the way they usually did at such moments.

"The Worms are still on the board," I explained. "That blanket effect doesn't have the reach to nail an entire wave of missiles, much less the Worms. That's great news. In fact, we should have staggered the missiles into ten small waves. Next time, we will."

"The Worms aren't all the way down to the target yet," Miklos pointed out.

I nodded, conceding the point. "Yeah, but Tolerance has less than a minute to reload."

"True, but we have no data on the reload time of this wide area effect weapon. It could be done in less time than the long range weapon."

I frowned. "Well," I sighed. "We're going to find out soon. Or rather, the Worms are."

They were on their final approach now. Our missiles zoomed down and impact marks appeared. They looked ridiculously small on the surface of that vast ship. It was as if a freshly-birthed moon had just gotten its first two craters.

"They aren't going to be able to do a damned thing," Miklos said quietly.

"Probably not," I admitted. "It'll be a shame if they get wiped out."

The Worm ships swarmed around the two polar points where the vessel was shaped differently. I watched as they utterly ignored my suggestion to retreat. They fired their weapons and churned in spirals. But what could they do? They were gnats attacking an elephant. Tolerance was probably barely aware of the damage they were doing to the surface.

We watched each update as the minutes crawled by. As the clock approached the ten minute mark, I began to wince every time a big redraw came in.

Finally, the inevitable happened. One screen showed Worm ships twirling around, firing rays of accelerated particles and the like. The next showed an empty surface. There were scorch marks, a few dents, and dozens of crumpled chunks of metal. It looked like someone had sprinkled glitter on the poles of *Phobos*.

The Worm ships were all gone. They'd all been destroyed.

"It looks like we have our data, sir," Miklos said.

I looked up at him sharply, not in any mood to be mocked.

"It's good news, actually," Miklos continued. "The enemy's defensive weapon has a timer on it. That has been proven. And it appears to be just as long as the primary weapon's timer. In fact, I would hazard to guess that the weapons are one and the same. Tolerance can increase the area of effect while lessening the range, making a defensive weapon, or he can fire a very tightly focused attack at a distant object. But in either case, it takes a long time to recharge."

I stared at him, unable for a moment to shake my thoughts of all those brave comrades dying at once. They'd been out there one moment, attacking for all they were worth, and then the next they were obliterated.

I gave my head a shake, sucked in my breath and nodded to Miklos.

"You're right, Commodore. This is good news. The enemy has a limitation. Now, it's up to us to figure out how to exploit it."

-14-

The hours slipped by slowly after the failed attack on *Phobos*. I wasn't in the mood to relax having just witnessed the deaths of so many brave allied crews.

I found it odd at times that I could grieve for aliens. I mean, when back on Earth years ago, I might have stepped on things that resembled the Worms without a thought. But somehow fighting against a common enemy brings beings together. It had worked many times in the past on Earth, making cultural enemies into friends.

Maybe it was because of all the aliens I'd encountered, I liked the Worms the best. They were brave, intelligent and would rather die than quit fighting. I could appreciate that attitude, and so I'd started thinking of them as a different kind of human.

I watched as the aftermath of the battle faded. Nuclear clouds of debris dissipated and scraps of crushed ships floated away from *Phobos'* seemingly impenetrable hide to drift in space. We followed in the wake of the unstoppable ship, heading toward the ring that led to Alpha Centauri.

Miklos cleared his throat. I glanced up at him. "What is it now, Commodore?"

"I was thinking, sir, that we should recall our fighters."

I nodded. "Yes. Do it. There is no point to losing them as well."

With a sigh of relief, Miklos ordered the squadrons to stand down.

Turning my attention to the rest of the system, I located Marvin where he was visiting the abandoned *Gatre*. The ship was off course and wasn't going to hit the ring to Alpha Centauri, not anymore. The loss of power from the strike by *Phobos* had altered her course enough to cause her to miss her original destination after a long drifting journey across the Helios System.

"Is Marvin in radio contact with us?"

"Yes," Captain Sarin said. "He has a ring set with him, in fact. We can talk to him in real time."

"What? Why didn't we use him for translations with the Worms, then?"

"He wasn't answering at that time."

"I see. Typical Marvin. Connect me, please. Let's see if he answers the phone when I call him directly."

I waited while a com officer did some magic, shunting our connections to bring Marvin's voice into my ear.

"Hello, Colonel Riggs. If you could excuse me, I'm rather busy at the moment. There isn't enough time to do a thorough analysis, so I'm having to—"

"Not so fast, Marvin. I know you're up to something out there and right now I don't really care what it is. But I do want you to apply your engines to *Gatre*. We can salvage her if we have time later. But not if she drifts off out of the star system."

"Use *my* engines, sir? I don't have sufficient thrust to brake this large of a craft. It would take…approximately four years of steady thrust to bring the *Gatre* to a full halt. Is that what you're suggesting, Colonel?"

"No," I said, realizing he was right. I sighed. "Listen, can you just steer the ship through the ring? Apply enough lateral thrust to put it back on course. That way, it can sail right into the Alpha Centauri system with us."

He was quiet for a second. I wasn't sure if that meant he was doing hard calculations, distracted by whatever the hell he was up to on that ship, or if he was trying to figure out some entirely new dodge. I waited impatiently…for about eight seconds.

"Well Marvin? What's it going to be?"

135

"I can do that, Colonel. In fact, that idea presents some fascinating new possibilities."

"I can't wait. Riggs out."

No sooner was I done talking to Marvin than Jasmine was at my side showing me something on her tablet. It looked like a series of boxes with pictures on them.

"What's this? More Worm dialect?"

"It's a transmission sir, from the Worms—from their command center on Helios. We think it's idiomatic."

I frowned at the images. There was a pair of warriors riding chariots side by side, followed by a picture of a moon or a planet, then two pictures of...little squiggles.

"What the hell are these last two things?"

"Um, Worm young, the computer says."

"Worm young? They sent us a pictogram of comradery, a planet, and two symbols of baby Worms? What the heck does the computer think it means?"

"Like I said, the best brainbox thinks it's an idiom of some kind. A saying that is not clear to us without cultural knowledge."

"Great. Get Marvin back on the phone. I want him to take a look at this."

"It is probably too late for that, sir," she said, directing my attention to the holotank.

I looked up and saw we were about to pass through the ring that led from Helios to Alpha Centauri.

"Send it to him. Now!"

She grabbed the tablet from me and began tapping swiftly. A moment later I saw her hit the send button. A spinning wait symbol appeared.

Then the universe shuddered a little. I knew that feeling all too well. We were now in the Alpha Centauri system, while Marvin had been left behind in the Helios system.

"Did he get the message?" I asked, staring at her tablet. The wait icon had stopped spinning, but that didn't always mean it worked.

"I'm not sure."

"Well, ask him."

"Do you want to stop jamming the rings, sir?"

136

I gritted my teeth. Doing so, even briefly, might let a signal get through from *Phobos*. I didn't want the Blues to hear anything from Tolerance—hopefully, they never would again.

"No," I said. "We'll just have to wait until he comes through the ring riding on *Gatre*."

She looked at me with furrowed brows. "What's he doing back there on my ship? Do you know, Kyle? I don't trust him. I want to disconnect his flight systems again the second he returns."

"You'll have to get in line for that," I said. "And he probably knows it, so it might be awhile."

"Why did you let him run off?"

"I saved the wreckage of *Gatre*," I said. I explained to her Marvin's efforts to guide the ship through the ring after us.

She nodded thoughtfully. "That is a good move, actually. I'm impressed. But we could have just sent a destroyer to play tugboat."

"Yeah," I said, "but I have a feeling we'll need every ship we have and more before this is over."

Jasmine nodded, took her tablet back out of my hands and walked away. I watched her walk. It was a nice walk. It had been months since I'd been with a woman, and I was beginning to feel my eyes wander. Just how long was a guy supposed to mourn? It was a question I'd never been clear on. With my wife, who'd died many long years ago, I'd played it by ear. Essentially, that had meant going on zero dates for years. But somehow after my kids had died and the world had changed, I'd begun to feel free to do whatever I wanted.

It wasn't a good kind of freedom, not really. It was more like the kind of freedom you might feel when you know you're terminally ill. That "what the hell, why not, I'm screwed anyway" kind of freedom. But after losing Sandra, I wasn't sure how I felt about anything.

I sucked in a deep breath and let it out. Back to the here and now, I told myself sternly. Daydreaming about girls was a younger man's game. I had a world to conquer—or rather, to liberate. That was more important than all my hopes, wishes and feelings put together.

137

I took stock of the fleet after the last of them wriggled through the ring. Four hundred ships or so. Was that going to be enough? I knew Crow had been pretty much totaled after I sent a Macro armada through for him to play with. But he'd also had time to build back up.

Miklos came to join me where I stood on the raised deck with the viewports. They weren't actual glass, but they looked like glass. The difference was you could put your hand up to them and zoom in by stretching the amazingly clear image.

"It's a lovely fleet, sir," he said.

"Yes Commodore, it is."

"I would hate to see it wasted."

I looked at him. "Are you trying to annoy me again?"

He laughed. "No sir, that's not my intent. I just don't like to lose ships. You know, when I was a boy, I had a lot of fun building models from kits. I lined them up on shelves in perfect order and painted them for display. What kind of child were you?"

I thought about it and laughed.

"I was the kind that banged my toys together until they broke. Usually, I left them in the dirt overnight, or in the grass. Often, my dad would run them over with the lawnmower and curse about it. I did have some models, but the paintjobs were ratty. Come to think of it, I seem to remember blowing up a few of those every summer with firecrackers."

Miklos nodded sagely. "I'm not terribly surprised."

* * *

Alpha Centauri was a fairly empty system. The stars had a few dull worlds circling them, but they didn't have much in the way of atmospheres or life. It was a stark contrast with the Eden System which overflowed with life, boasting seven organic worlds.

When we'd first encountered the Eden system, I'd been enthralled by its natural beauty. Rather than planets enshrouded in vicious gasses, six of the twenty-one planets were livable for humans. The seventh world to harbor life, we'd figured out over time, was Eden-11, the homeworld of the Blues.

Despite its emptiness, I felt a growing tension as we crossed into the star system. This was the last leg of the journey before we reached home.

Earth. It had been so long since I'd seen her! Years had passed. I could scarcely believe I'd spent so much time exiled in space.

I felt a strange mixture of emotions with every passing hour as we headed for the last ring. What was waiting for us on the far side? Are we bringing death and destruction, or freedom and peace? I didn't really know. At lot of it depended on how Crow reacted, and if he could beat *Phobos*.

I spent much of my time studying the mammoth ship and the records of the attacks. We had a lot of data to crunch on now. From detailed vids and measurements, we were able to construct a good working model of its capabilities. Ranges, power outputs, acceleration—we knew it all now. *Phobos* was no longer a total mystery.

What we didn't know was what the Imperials had built to face her. That represented my biggest dilemma. If I let *Phobos* plow into Crow's fleet, was I doing the right thing? I had options. I could tell the Imperials how to fight the monster ship, sharing the intel we'd learned. That was a safer play as far as Earth was concerned. But would that make things too easy for Crow?

We'd worked out an independent attack plan for *Phobos*. Essentially, it required sustained waves to get to the ship and do damage. The first waves would be missiles, followed by fighters, then maybe assault ships. Every wave that came in could be taken out at once, but with a ten minute window of recharging time in between.

Attacking in waves meant Tolerance was going to have to make some hard choices. Did he ride out the missiles, then obliterate the ships? Or the other way around? Sending in small, targeted barrages was our best plan. We'd dig a hole with missiles pounding at the same point, if we had to. Eventually, there had to be a soft center in that big bastard somewhere, and I meant to dig until I found it.

139

But the Imperials didn't know any of this yet. They were going to encounter something beyond their experience. I wanted it to damage them, but I didn't want everyone to die.

My hand formed into a fist and flexed on the table. I was wracking my brain. What was the best way to play this? After a while, I knew the answer: I would have to play it by ear. There were simply too many unknowns. I was going to have to go in without a clear plan and make changes on the fly.

It was just the sort of non-strategy that drove Miklos crazy. For once, I didn't blame him.

"Colonel? Colonel Riggs?"

I opened my eyes and shut them again. I was lying on my back on my bunk, half-dreaming. Being aboard a modern space craft wasn't exactly an exercise in privacy. When you were command personnel, you were lucky if you didn't have to take calls in the shower.

"What is it?"

"Something unusual, sir. On the surface—uh, I mean the 'hull' of *Phobos*."

I recognized the voice now. It was none other than Captain Sarin herself, my newly appointed lead on ops. I vaulted myself off the bunk and groaned.

"On my way."

I skipped a shower and headed up two decks, taking the tubes. Our tube system was a primitive way of moving around on a large ship that worked better than we'd expected. We didn't have many elevators in our modern carriers. Using a tube was easier and more reliable, especially in battle. They were simply empty shafts with grav plates at the bottom. If you got into the one with the big arrow pointing up, it propelled you up. If you got into the other, you went shooting down.

They were a bit tricky to get used to. Getting off at the right floor required shooting out an arm and catching the edge of the opening when you passed it. Really, it was more like controlled falling than a proper elevator system. Without nanotized strength and speed, it would have been quite dangerous.

When I got to the top of the ship, I must have been blinking. Maybe I was napping, just for a fraction of a second. I rammed my head into a cushion at the top of the shaft and a red light came on, warning me I'd gone too far.

I hand-over-handed it back to the opening and crawled out onto the deck.

"Sleepy, sir?" Jasmine asked.

She was standing over me, smiling. I got to my feet, but couldn't quite bring myself to smile back.

"I need coffee," I said.

She didn't hand me a cup—not that I'd expected her to.

"I'll have a mug brought to the command table," she said. She turned and walked that way.

I followed, rubbing at my eyes and sighing. I grabbed the coffee when it came and downed it. The stuff was too cold and tasted faintly of plastic.

"What have you got?" I asked when I could focus both my eyes at once.

"See this? At the north pole?"

"Dust? You got me out of my bunk after three and half hours for a puff of dust? It's probably just a meteor strike. The thing is as big as a moon."

"Let me back up the recorded vid, sir."

She did so by gliding her finger over a slide bar on a virtual control panel. I was glad she was doing it. I had a hard time nudging those things just the way they liked it. Sometimes, I missed actual physical knobs and buttons.

I watched as the vid played forward again. Instead of a single puff, a dozen of them showed up in sequence.

"Not just one meteor, but a shower? How long has this been going on?"

"For about an hour. We thought it was some kind of shower too, but now we're pretty sure it isn't. Here's why."

She fast forwarded to something from a few minutes ago. Instead of an impact—it seemed like an explosion. An explosion on the surface of the ship.

I grinned. "I like the look of that. What is it? External venting? Maybe all that firepower did break something inside."

"We just don't know. But you left orders to alert you in case the situation changed."

I took a hit off my coffee and winced. Then I nodded. "You did good, Sarin. Let's keep a close eye on—"

Thud.

That was the only way I can describe the sound we all heard then. It was a *thud*, and it came from our hull. Everyone on the command deck looked around, frowning.

"External cameras!" I shouted, my mind leaping to conclusions I didn't like. Not at all.

"Switching, sir."

In sequence, the cameras came up and gave me a one second shot of the hull outside from a dozen different angles.

"Put them all up at once. And sound general quarters."

Jasmine selected mosaic mode. Then she tapped a big red triangle near her hand. The lighting changed on the command deck and various noise-making devices began going off up and down the decks.

We didn't even talk, nor did we answer the queries of baffled staffers who came to circle around. Jasmine and I both stared at each of those external views in turn.

"There it is, on camera fourteen. Select and expand."

The image leapt up into full view. What had been an odd shadow became a much more sinister image. Our visual equipment was excellent, even in starlight.

"What the hell is that thing?" Miklos said.

I glanced at him, then back at the thing crawling over our hull. I felt like telling him he was away from his new post again, but I didn't have the heart and I didn't really care.

"That, Nicolai, is something new. It reminds me of the crawling marines the Macros made to attack our ships once. But it's not Macro tech. It's too humanoid."

We watched it as we talked. It wasn't like flesh, but it wasn't like machine, either. I got the feeling it was some kind of hybrid. A man with robotic parts, maybe. Or a robot with long fingers and dark, ropy arms.

Whatever it was, it didn't have a head. Instead, stalks pointed out from the ribcage—if it had a ribcage—and directed what looked like spherical optical pickups in every direction.

143

"Hmm," I said, watching it still. I never took my eye off it for a second. "See how its prying at all the hatches? It's looking for a way in."

"Could there be some kind of alien race here in the Alpha Centauri System?" Miklos asked. "I don't get it. We should have known if there was something here. We've been traveling through for years."

"There are lots of possibilities, and pretty much none of them are good," I said.

"Give me a few, Colonel."

"It could be from *Phobos*. The Blues might have made themselves a new type of robot. When those puffs fired up, maybe they were launching these."

"Disturbing, but unlikely. I've been reviewing the data. It looks like something was landing there, not taking off."

"Right. Theory two: they're Macros. They've gotten into this area—maybe they've wiped Earth, or are preparing to. This beast is something new they've only recently built to infiltrate our ships."

"I guess it's possible, but not without the appearance of another ring we don't know about."

"What is your third theory, Colonel?" Jasmine asked.

We glanced up at her. I realized I'd fallen into my old habit of talking things over with Miklos and leaving out everyone else. Maybe that bothered Jasmine, but it was hard to tell. She usually kept her face neutral. You had to guess what she was feeling unless she was really upset. Her style was very different from Sandra's—I'd always known what that girl was thinking. She'd always made her feelings extremely clear.

"The third possibility is that this is from the Empire itself."

Miklos scoffed at that. "I would be very surprised. It seems advanced and subtle. Neither term fits the Imperial forces I've seen so far."

"Granted," I said. "But we're now passing on a direct route between the Helios ring and the ring to the Solar System. This is where I would lay a trap or a drone scout, if I had one. Note the timing. First, *Phobos* runs into a series of strange falling objects. Now, we're encountering them."

Miklos' eyes widened. Jasmine's fingers flew.

144

"The timing is about right, sir," she said. "We are at about the same point in space that *Phobos* was when the bombardment began."

I nodded. Theory number three was looking stronger all the time.

"Alert all the other ships. Everyone is to do a sweep of their hulls, looking for intruders."

"Should we destroy them, sir?"

I had to think about that. "Yeah. Fire first and dissect later. I'm going down to the sally port to suit up."

Jasmine opened her mouth as if to object. I knew she didn't want me to personally take part in any dangerous missions. But instead of listing reasons I shouldn't go, she stopped herself and relayed my warning to the rest of the fleet. That was something else I'd never seen Sandra manage to do. If Sandra didn't like what you were doing, you were going to hear about it whether you wanted to or not. Come to think of it, Miklos had been the same way lately. I was glad to have Sarin back on tactical ops, and I thought to myself privately that it might be awhile before she got another command.

I headed back to the tubes. I'd already switched my smart-cloth suit into under-armor mode. That changed the formation, removing rank insignia, pleats and cuffs. The clothing needed to slide easily into the armor shell, like a pair of silk pajamas.

The truth was I was looking forward to taking a couple of marines with me out onto the hull and blasting whatever spy-bot we'd spotted out there. I hadn't seen real action in quite a while.

I made it down two decks and was halfway to the third, the one where the sally ports were located, when something flickered just beyond my range of vision. I turned around, looking back up the tube behind me.

A nightmare glided silently toward me. I knew in an instant what it was—what it *had* to be. It was one of those things, the things I'd seen on the outside of *Defiant*. Only now, it was inside the hull and coming at me with pincher-like foreclaws fully extended.

I forgot about everything else when I saw the little monster. I didn't worry about how it had gotten from outside the ship to inside, or what it could do to me with those snapping claws. All that was in my mind was turning around so I could grasp it hand-to-hand.

The tube was only about three feet across, which made it virtually impossible to turn around quickly. I gave it a try anyway. I formed a ball and did a summersault. All this happened in a split-second while the intruder and I fell toward the lower decks in tandem.

As I flipped around to face the thing, I realized I had a few options. With less than a second to go, you have to make what could be your last choices on this plane of existence count for something.

I could have gone for my com-link, summoning help with a touch. That would have been all I did, however. I chose instead to draw my beamer. I didn't want to be dead in the tube with a few tsking emergency people scraping out what was left an hour from now. Fight first, sound the alarm second—that was my motto.

I brought the beamer up, but the invader was right in my face by that time. Damn, it was ugly. Up close, I saw a smooth black carapace with a metallic sheen. It was veiny and ridged in seemingly random patterns. I could see the optical stalks coming out of the torso, swiveling and tracking me. The two foreclaws extended with fantastic speed, opening wide like jaws. Inside those serrated claws I saw metal. Slivery-bright, like surgical steel. There were spines too, all over the thing. I winced even before we made contact; this was going to hurt.

I didn't have time to fire before we were in close combat. There just wasn't time to get the weapon up, aim and press the firing stud. The fact I didn't have time to do whatever I wanted spoke to the monster's speed. It was, if I had to judge, as fast as Sandra herself. That's saying something, because she had been the fastest human I'd ever met.

As we closed, I reached up my left hand to grab one of those foreclaws. The alien—or whatever the hell it was—tried to snip off my hand but missed. I clamped down on what passed for its wrist, and felt an explosion of blood in my hand. I held on, but I'd just grabbed a load of spines that shot through my palm and out the back of my hand in six places.

146

My right hand, the one with the hand beamer, I played differently. I shoved the gun forward touching the spot where the head ought to be if it had had one. I squeezed the trigger instantly—but nothing happened.

I realized I'd heard a metallic crunch just as I applied pressure to the trigger. The thing had put its second claw around the gun and cut it in half. I guess I should have been glad that it hadn't managed to cut my hand off at the wrist instead, but I knew the night was still young and this dance wasn't over with yet.

What now? That was the thought I had, but my hands were way ahead of my cortex this time. I grabbed the claw that had just chopped my gun in half and shoved it toward the other claw, which was snapping at my face like a springtime turtle.

The move was a crazy one and it cost me another half-dozen puncture wounds, but it was all I had. I was fighting on instinct now. I think my strength surprised the critter. I heard metal squeal, as if ball-joints had been bent in directions planners had never foreseen.

One claw went into the other, and *snap*, there was a spark as something fell off. Fortunately, it was a piece of my dance partner rather than a finger.

It went into a frenzy then. It was as if I'd pained it, which I'd started thinking was impossible. Eye-stalks rolled and the remaining claw thrashed in my grip. I was forced to use both hands to control the one claw, and the monster began bludgeoning me with its stump. I saw stars that had no names each time it connected with my scalp.

Roaring and using my legs against the walls of the tube for leverage, I bent back the second claw. Back and back it went, all the way over into the zone with the eyestalks. It snapped off two of these, and shuddered in what I was sure now was agony.

Then the second arm broke at the shoulder. With a shout of victory, I wrenched it loose, pulling it right out of the socket.

I stared at what came with it. Bones. Metal bones. That's the only way I can describe what I saw. I'd not really known what to expect, but I hadn't expected this eclectic mix of red meat, tendons and shaped-steel bone.

The monster went limp in my arms. I let it go, and it fell all the way to the bottom of the tube system, tumbling and clattering as it went.

I took a few seconds to stare and frown down after it.

"What the fuck was that thing?" I asked no one, breathing hard.

Blood poured from my hands and my scalp. I barely noticed or cared. I tapped my com link with numbed fingers.

"Kwon?" I asked, "could you come to tube eight."

"I'm already at the sally port, sir."

"Really? Is everything all right there?"

"Um, not exactly sir. When I got here, the port was open. Most strange."

"Yeah," I said, "I think I know why. Come to tube eight."

"Right away, Colonel."

I let myself drift down toward the monster which lay limp at the lowest deck level, the entrance to the hold. I moved warily. One never knew what a newly contacted life form was capable of.

When I got close, I became fairly certain it was dead. That presumed, of course, that it had been alive in the first place.

I sensed another gliding presence behind me, and whirled, bringing up my bloody hands defensively.

"What's that you've got there, sir?" Kwon asked.

His hulking form filled the tube to the point where I couldn't see beyond him.

I shook my head. "I don't have a clue. Let's take it to medical."

On a modern Star Force ship, the people in medical had training no human beings in ships of the past had ever received. Healing the sick was only part of their jobs—and a rather small part since we rarely were injured so badly it took more than nanites to repair our bodies. But they had other missions which were just as critical. One of them was analysis and containment of newly discovered alien life.

Doctor Kate Swanson was in medical at the time. Her ship and her medical bay aboard *Gatre* had been abandoned, so she'd been backing up the staff on this ship. When Kwon and I arrived carrying the monstrosity from the tubes, I quickly pronounced her to be our new chief of xenology.

"Here Kate," I said, tossing the remains on a table, "see what you can figure out about that thing."

She didn't move, but the table did. A dozen black tentacles extended from the base and probed the still form.

"Restraints!" Kate said.

The table instantly obeyed, clamping no less than six steel hands onto the thing.

"Was this the alien on the hull?" she asked.

"I believe so. It found a hatch and slipped inside. Not sure how it did that. Not sure how it even functions, or what it is. That's why we brought it here."

Dr. Swanson's eyes were very serious. She walked around it, not getting too close. I approved of her caution. We'd had things like this self-destruct before. I frowned at that memory.

"You'd better do a complete scan. Maybe its mission is a suicidal one."

She nodded and began the procedure. She kept her distance, and brought over more tentacles from a neighboring table to help clamp down everything that looked like it could move on the body.

I shook my hands and sent a splatter of blood flying.

"Sorry," I said. "My hands are stinging and going numb at the same time. Like I slept on them or something."

She glanced at me and Kwon appraisingly. She waved for a nurse, who came over to us nervously. I noticed that none of the other medical people had gathered enough courage to approach.

"Get on that table please, Colonel. We'll do some quick patch-up work."

"Not necessary," I said.

Sure, my injuries burned, but I knew the nanites would fix me up within hours. She looked at me squarely in the eye. Her gaze was stern.

"Are we in a combat situation?" she asked.

"Not at the moment."

"Then get on that table. Do you know your scalp is open and dangling? It will take a regrow if we don't reattach that quickly."

I lifted a torn-up hand and gingerly probed my head. Sure enough, a tatter piece of flesh was hanging there.

"I thought something was wrong," I admitted. "It's hanging by a thread, isn't it? Keeps tickling my neck."

"I thought you liked it like that, sir," chuckled Kwon. "Other people have big earrings hanging down—you cut out the middle man!"

Kwon went off into a gale of laughter at his own joke. I politely joined in, fumbling to pat my scalp into place with damaged fingers.

"I'm experiencing some numbness," I admitted. "Probably nerve damage."

Dr. Swanson turned away from her alien monstrosity and came to me quickly. She probed my hands and face, frowning fiercely.

"Venom," she pronounced. "On the table."

I finally obeyed her. She went to work with quick hands. "Those spines—they're wet, and not just with your blood. You took a grim chance tangling with that thing. What if it had been pumped full of chemical agents tailor-designed to take out our kind, like that girl and her tooth—what was her name?"

"Alexa?" I asked. "Is that what you're talking about? And for the record, I didn't have any choice about engaging the creature. It came after me in close quarters."

"There's always an excuse with you. Why didn't you just shoot it?"

I felt like arguing, but my will to do so was fading. Lying down seemed to accelerate the progress of the venom.

"Did you drug me?" I asked. My voice sounded odd…weak.

"No, the intruder did. I need two personnel over here, now. Prep him for a full blood transfusion. Let's go, people!"

"Shit," I mumbled, then the numb sensation reached my vitals and I lost consciousness.

150

-16-

I've been drugged before, and I've awakened with more than my share of hangovers. Still, even by my standards the next few hours were rough. I puked, raved and caused a few new injuries to appear on myself and the medical staff that tried to help me.

When I was myself again, I opened one eye. The nurses around me flinched, and one skittered away like a kicked dog.

I sat up, grunting. "Did I cause some trouble?" I asked the wary group.

They stared at me and the nearest nurse licked her lips. Her hands were up, as if to defend herself.

"Are you feeling better, Colonel?" she asked.

I looked around, rubbed my temples and did a little swearing. They all watched me silently, worriedly.

"I'm sorry," I said, "did I hurt someone? I was out. This is the first moment I remember clearly, and I've got a monster headache. Anyone have an aspirin?"

"We don't normally allow blood thinners after surgery..."

"Where's Dr. Swanson?"

Someone ran out to get her. When she came in, she looked me over and pronounced me cured.

"The venom might have killed a lesser man," she said. "It was nasty stuff, like a stiff dose of botulism. The nanites and the microbes in your bloodstream must have cleared most of it out. We had to give you back some of your own blood after filtration. It's...unique."

I nodded, unsurprised. I was a party of one when it came to medical matters.

"How long was I out?"

"Long enough for six of our ships to get attacked the way ours did. All of them were carriers."

"Hmm," I said, rubbing ridged flesh. It was scabbing and scarring—but that would fade in a day or so. "Something hit us, but what? Could they have come from *Phobos*?"

Kate shook her head. "I don't think so. We found this on every invader's back."

I looked at the tablet she showed me, which was displaying a photo. I raised eyebrows in surprised.

"The stylized eagle emblem of Crow the Magnificent," I said. "I shouldn't be surprised, but I am. The bastard didn't leave mines out here for us, he left these invaders."

She nodded. "I would have to agree. I've had some time to evaluate the cyborg."

"Cyborg? Is that what it is?"

"Part human, part robot. It can survive in space for prolonged periods. It has blood and flesh inside, but a metal shell and metal bones. The brain seems to be made of nanites. We found the box inside the core of the thorax, here."

She probed the limp form on the table with a long instrument. At no time did she come within reach of those deadly limbs.

"You're showing the monster respect, I approve. That thing is quite deadly. How many men did we lose?"

"Twelve, including you. Seven of them are dead already. You're the only man who is back on his feet."

I didn't like the sound of that. An army of things like this—they could give us real trouble. Fortunately, they didn't seem to have an army. They were probably difficult to make. They looked like sophisticated hybrid technology.

"Crow's nerds have been working overtime," I said. "I didn't really expect new tech from them so soon after getting waxed by the Macros. Let's hope that they're giving Tolerance hell on *Phobos*, too."

Kate shrugged. "I think the technological effort on the part of Earth is admirable. Hardship often motivates people to do their best."

"Hmm. Too bad they're on the wrong side."

152

"They're on the side of Earth trying to stop the machines. These creatures weren't built to kill Star Force personnel. I think they were designed to stop any kind of enemy fleet that sailed through this ring."

I thought about it, and I had to admit to myself the Imperial weapons were ingenious. They were harder to detect than mines since they weren't radioactive and had less metal in them than a motorcycle. Space wasn't entirely empty, especially after we'd fought many battles in and around the rings. Lots of asteroids and floating debris would showed up on our sensors all the time. In general, anything small and anomalous was ignored.

These cyborgs would look like a dead man in a vac suit to our scanners. They could survive for a long time in space, apparently in some kind of capsule. When the time was right, they could come down on any target, probably after pinpointing it with passive sensors. Operating like my marines assaulting a ship, they could do a lot of damage.

But then I had dark thought: how had these aberrations been constructed? "What's your opinion, Doctor? Did they use a human in the construction of this hybrid?"

"Yes, almost certainly. A living one, or one freshly killed."

I got up, and after a few unsteady seconds I was able to walk under my own power.

"I would tell you to get back on the table," she said, "but I know you wouldn't listen."

"Thank you for sparing me the attempt. I like a woman who instinctively knows her limitations."

She huffed at me, but accompanied me to a strange hulk on a nearby table. The cyborg was a mess, as she'd apparently begun a dissection. She showed me around the functional parts, which were an odd mix of electronic, mechanical and biological. There were even Nano elements. I was impressed all over again by the technological blend.

"It's an evil thing. Only the Empire could build it, because I wouldn't let my people serve this way, not even if they consented to being cut up and used for spare parts. Would you do the operation if I ordered you to?"

"Absolutely not."

"Then we're agreed. It's an abomination. But you know, Marvin would love this thing. In fact, I want you to stop working on it."

"Why?"

"Put the shell back on. Let's get it back into as natural a state as possible. Then I'll take a few tantalizing shots of the beast and send them to Marvin."

"You're going to ask him to dissect it?"

"No. I don't want to be so direct, so obvious. He'll suspect what's coming if I do. I'll just show it to him and tell him we don't know what to make of it. That we're baffled and mystified by this new find. Then he'll beg to come running back to check it out."

Kate squinted at me for a few seconds, then smiled and shook her head. "The relationship you have with that machine—it's stranger than this thing on the table."

"Yeah," I said, "I guess it is."

* * *

My play to lure Marvin back into his cage worked. Once he'd guided *Gatre* into the Centauri system, I sent him the pics with a note: "Isn't this cool? We're clueless". The message didn't go out with any orders or requests. That was part of the key to enticing any creature. You had to pretend like you didn't even care what they did.

Marvin couldn't jump off *Gatre* fast enough. He started blasting his way after us about ninety seconds after receiving the message. I grinned, knowing he'd taken the bait. Messing around with the molecular structures of a crushed engine room looked dull when compared to the opportunity to investigate an unknown alien monster.

I was startled as I traced his progress.

"Captain Sarin? Is this reading right? How can that robot have that kind of acceleration?"

She looked it over, frowning. "There's nothing wrong with the instruments, Colonel. He'll catch up with us in a few hours. Looking at this, I believe he must have more thrust than a fighter engine could generate. Either he's redesigned the engine for higher output, or he's built additional propulsion systems onto himself."

I nodded in agreement. "I'd be pissed off about this, but I know he's coming home without a fight and once here it will be easy to disconnect his engines. Hell, he won't even be able to get into Medical without editing himself down to size. He wouldn't fit."

Captain Sarin gave me a flat look. I knew she thought I was too soft on Marvin. Everyone did. Before Sandra had died, she told me she thought he was dangerous. That he might decide to make a million copies of himself and kick us off the evolutionary tree one day. She had a point—they all did. But what they often overlooked was Marvin's usefulness. He was like other great inventions in history in that he was a game-changer. You couldn't very well invent the combustion engine, or electric lights, or the atomic bomb and expect to uninvent it later. It didn't work that way, at least not without the civilization dropping into some kind of dark age first.

"I know you don't trust Marvin," I told her. "But we can't operate without him. We can't afford to play it safe, to take our time. We're going to win or lose this within a month— probably within a few days. Every asset I have is going into the effort, including my crazy pet robot."

"I never suggested anything else."

"I know you didn't. But I also know you well enough to sense what you're really thinking."

Jasmine shrugged and went back to her screens. I looked down and watched them with her. About fifteen minutes later, we were both tapping and frowning. I'd seen something shift. It was as if *Phobos* had shrunken then grown again in a rippling pulse. Dust rose up in eddies here and there, disturbed.

"What's going on?" I demanded. "The surface of *Phobos* has changed."

"That's the external weapon again—that gravity thing that crushes small objects. I believe Tolerance just activated it."

I frowned at the extreme range optics, trying to zoom in tightly while maintaining focus and perspective.

The screen shifted, warped and blurred. I cursed.

"Let me try," Jasmine said.

I crossed my arms as her fine fingers worked the screen. The difference was pronounced. She managed to get the effect I was looking for: a clear view of the surface. *Phobos* now filled the entire screen. Still, it was hard to make out any details.

"Why would the Blue fire his defensive weapon?" I asked no one. "We're not doing anything. Did you register any more impacts? Anything like that little invader that hit us?"

She shook her head. Others were gathering now, and a few offered suggestions:

"Maybe it's an automated mechanism to prevent stealth attacks," said one.

"It could be meteors or debris hitting the front of the craft. We can't see the face of *Phobos* from this angle."

I frowned fiercely at the screen. Several times now there had been odd events in this star system and I wanted to know what was causing them.

"I want a full analysis team working out what is happening on *Phobos*. Figure this one out, people. Being in the dark in the middle of an invasion campaign is completely unacceptable. I want answers and I want them in the next ten minutes. If you don't have what it takes, give me the names of some new people you think can do your jobs better—because after fifteen minutes you're all relieved."

This announcement changed the drifting, baffled looks on everyone's face. They were suddenly focused and engaged. It was no longer a "do you think it will rain tomorrow?" sort of situation. With their jobs on the line, they all began crunching. One team of three went to another table to play the vid files in slow motion of each of these odd events. The rest stood around with their elbows on the table, staring fiercely at the current images Jasmine was zooming in on in real time.

I turned my attention back to Jasmine. "Captain? Do you have a solution?"

"I think *Phobos* is under attack," she said.

"Logical. What kind of attack? Who is doing it?"

"There have been three efforts to stop the ship so far. First we hit it with missiles and fighters. Then the Worms attacked with more missiles from us. Most recently, I believe these cyborgs have landed on the surface."

"One of those three then? Well, we can forget about our people being behind it. We know where they are and what they're doing. We've been pretty ineffectual so far. That leaves us with the Worms and the cyborgs. I'm leaning toward the cyborgs as the Worms appeared to be wiped out."

"They appear to be," Jasmine echoed, "but the truth is that we don't really know how their attack went."

"I know an easy way to confirm some of our suspicions."

She looked at me with expectant eyebrows. It was a very pretty look for her, and I found myself distracted momentarily. I looked back down at the screens to focus my thoughts.

"Open a channel to Tolerance. I want to talk to him."

"What are you going to say, Colonel?"

I grinned. "I'm going to gloat."

I waited until Marvin arrived to attempt communicating with Tolerance. I wanted my star translator available for the job.

When he did finally come aboard, I had to smile. He'd trimmed himself to the extreme. He had only one grav plate, which wasn't enough to lift his full bulk and left him skidding over the deckplates. He barely had enough tentacles left to drag himself from one place to the next.

The moment I saw him, I knew what he was doing. He wanted to show me he'd fully complied with my requirements to return home in a flightless condition. In fact, he'd just about butchered himself.

"Marvin?"

"What is it, Colonel Riggs?"

"I think you need a second grav plate. If only to balance yourself."

"I just wanted to—"

"I know what you wanted. But I'm already tired of hearing that metal-on-metal scraping sound."

Marvin hesitated. "Possibly, I could visit Medical on my way to the workshop. I understand you have a new specimen there that requires close examination."

"Yeah," I said, "but that will wait. If you do a little translation job for me now, I'll let you go straight to Medical afterward."

I had about seven cameras on me now, panning wide for profile shots. I knew he was trying to get as much info on my mood and reactions as he could. In a way, it was flattering that he thought so much of my opinions. But I knew that like any teen, he would forget about me the instant he had the car keys in his possession.

"Open a channel to the Blues' ship for me."

"Channel request sent."

We waited. I began to frown after about thirty seconds. "Nothing?"

"No. The enemy ship has not responded. The channel remains closed."

"Maybe Tolerance has better things to do," Jasmine said.

I glanced at her, then back at Marvin. "Send the request again."

"Channel request sent."

We waited again. I let it go for a full minute, and then I opened my mouth to curse when Marvin finally perked up.

"Channel open," he said.

"Oh...uh," I began, having forgotten exactly what I was going to say. Then I had it. I straightened myself and put on a formal tone of voice. "Tolerance, we request your status. Have you decided to surrender yet?"

This statement got the attention of my bridge crew, if not Tolerance himself. They all looked at me in surprise.

The reply came at last. "Your efforts, although determined, cannot succeed."

"We've barely begun. Our primary forces are still ahead of you. Do you understand the pointless nature of your mission? You can't succeed."

Another pause ensued—a long one. I began to wonder if the alien had cut me off. I was about to ask Marvin about it when the response finally came in.

"Be that as it may, I will not surrender. Though the fabric of my body leaks away, I will fight on to the last."

"Channel closed," Marvin said in his usual vaguely cheery tone.

I frowned back at the screens and at the holotank.

"What the hell is going on out there? He wasn't supposed to agree with me. He's under some kind of attack, and he thinks it's us making the attack."

"Well sir," Jasmine said, "you did indicate by your tone and statements that it was us behind the attack."

"Yeah…" I said, rubbing my chin. "And it wouldn't occur to him to doubt me. So, let's see what we have… Tolerance is under some kind of serious attack. He believes we're behind it, so he must not know the true source."

"Either that, or the real source appears to be Star Force," Marvin interjected. "May I go down to Medical now, Colonel Riggs?"

"No," I said. I turned to Jasmine. "What do you make of this?"

"It's just as you said. It must be the cyborgs…probably."

I released a grunt of annoyance. "Tolerance said something about the fabric of his body and leaking. What do you think that's all about?"

"I think that reference is fairly obvious," Marvin said.

We both looked at him expectantly. His tentacles squirmed on top of one another.

"The creature is gaseous, and with a low pressure zone outside the hull, even a small leak could be catastrophic."

"By low-pressure zone, you mean space?" Jasmine asked.

"He's right," I said, "Tolerance is like the Hindenburg. Just waiting to explode."

"I'm so glad you found my insight helpful," Marvin said. "I'll be leaving now that—"

"No," I said, without even looking at him. "Man your post, robot. You'll get to rip up the corpse soon enough."

"I hardly think the characterization 'ripping up' is appropriate under these—"

I held my hand up in his direction, and he fell into a sulking silence.

I thought about the conversation and the situation with growing alarm. It wasn't supposed to go like this. *Phobos* was supposed to barrel into the face of the Imperials, slamming into Earth's defenses and punching a hole through them for us. Then we would glide in riding in her wake. Instead, it was beginning to look like Tolerance was falling apart before he even reached the Solar System.

"Damned Blues," I muttered. "Gaines isn't going to like this. Not at all."

"What are you talking about, sir?" Captain Sarin asked me.

Marvin panned and examined both our faces, trying to figure out what we were thinking.

"First, I'm going to see if I can even pull this off," I said, baffling them both further. "Jasmine, send Gaines to my office. Kwon too. I'll do the tactical planning from there."

"Sir?"

"What now, Captain?"

She didn't respond. Instead, she turned back to her station and relayed the requests. I knew both Kwon and Gaines were somewhere aboard the carrier, and they would come running when the heard the words 'tactical planning'. I headed toward my office immediately.

Behind me, I heard a scratching sound.

"What do you want, Marvin?"

"I haven't yet been given leave to—"

"I still need you to do more translating. Come into my office please."

"If I may offer some advice, sir?"

I glanced back over my shoulder at him as I touched the hatch and it dissolved, letting me into the chamber. A large ovoid table filled the room. It lit up and displayed local space as I stepped inside.

"Four chairs," I said. The room's brainbox dutifully made them and placed them equidistantly around the table. Chairs clustered around the table, flowering out of the deck like something growing on a potter's wheel.

"Uh, make that three chairs," I said, "leave the fourth open."

One of the four chairs dissolved again. Marvin, recognizing that the open spot was for him, scooted into position.

"I really don't think I'm needed here, Colonel," he began complaining. "In fact, I don't think the entire mission is worthwhile. You should just let the Worms finish their work."

I looked at him with real interest for the first time.

161

"So, you think it's the Worms that are letting the steam out of Tolerance?"

"Your analogy is vague at best, but the message they sent was unmistakable. The Worms are on *Phobos*."

Now he had me staring. The stare slowly turned into a beetling frown. "What? What message?"

"The one the Worms sent. Concerning their commandos being in place on *Phobos*. It was unmistakable—wasn't it?"

"When did you see that?"

"I was tapped into the ship-to-ship network when the Worms transmitted it."

My mouth sagged open. I hated when it did that. Quite probably in my entire lifespan most of these moments belonged solely to Marvin. He never failed to impress me with his odd mix of subterfuge and insight.

I wanted to scream at him, but I held back. I wanted to demand why he hadn't contacted me with this vital information. I already knew the answer, of course. He'd been too busy messing around with the wreck of *Gatre* to be bothered translating for me. Yelling at him now wouldn't do any good, but I almost did it anyway, just to make myself feel better.

Instead, I took a deep breath and tapped at the screen, pulling up the four symbols the Worms had sent to us before we left the Helios system. The translation brainboxes hadn't really known what to make of them, and neither had we.

There was a pair of warriors riding chariots side by side, followed by a picture of a moon or a planet, then two pictures of what appeared to be little squiggles.

"Okay," I said, "guide me through this. Two warriors riding chariots?"

"Comradery and solidarity in battle."

"Good, I'm with you so far. Then a picture of a moon or planet?"

"Right the first time. It is a satellite. In this case, it means *Phobos*."

"Okay," I said, nodding. "Now, the two sets of squiggles?"

162

"Worm young. Eggs hatched into frisking larva. They indicate hope and future happy times. Since the symbols are used together, they indicate all of these things."

"Uh…"

"The entire set must be taken together, of course, with known Worm idioms applied."

"Naturally…just tell me what the hell it means."

"The meaning seems indisputable. The Worms are telling you they attacked *Phobos* with you, and they left a gift of hope behind."

I frowned. "From that, you're sure they left Worm warriors on that rock?"

"Yes, absolutely."

"Why?" I growled.

"Because the only happy, fruitful outcome possible after an attack upon any enemy is the guaranteed death of that same enemy—in the Worm culture, that is."

I thought about what I knew of Worms, and about what was happening on *Phobos*. Tolerance had indicated he was having trouble, that we were beating him. A terrible struggle must be occurring aboard the enemy ship.

I felt a wave of concern rush over me. Whether it was the Worms or the cyborgs or someone else entirely, Tolerance was in trouble.

As these realizations swept through my mind in rapid sequence, Gaines arrived with Kwon in tow.

I looked up at them but didn't speak to them for a moment. I waved them to their seats. Then I cleared the Worm symbols from the screen with a swipe of my hand.

I brought up a shimmering live image of *Phobos*. It looked quiet enough, but I knew better.

"What's up, Colonel?" Major Gaines asked me.

I looked at him, but it took a moment for my eyes to focus.

"We've gotten messages from the Worms, Major," I said. "When their ships attacked, they apparently landed Worm commandoes. Even more amazing, they're apparently still alive."

Gaines seemed unhappy.

"What's wrong?"

163

"Nothing sir," he said, "but I do have the feeling you're about to send some of my men down there on some kind of crazy rescue mission."

"To rescue the Worms?"

"Right."

"Wrong on both counts," I said. "First off, it won't be a rescue mission. It will be an attack. Secondly, I'm not sending your men. All three of us are going to go personally."

"Me too?" asked Kwon, speaking up for the first time.

"Are you all healed up?"

"Fully reconditioned, sir."

"All right then."

Kwon spun in his chair, making the smart metal unhappy. Then he high-fived himself. It would have been an odd display for anyone other than Kwon, and the rest of us ignored it.

"Uh…" Gaines said, looking at all of us like we were madmen. "What about that super-weapon? The thing that nukes everything and everyone who gets in close?"

"The Worms are still alive," I pointed out. "At least, we think they are."

He looked at me unhappily.

"Well, if that's not good enough for you, don't worry. I'm going to use Marvin here to help me talk to Tolerance. Together we'll talk him into holding his fire."

Gaines sat back with his arms crossed. He still didn't look happy.

Kwon, however, was all smiles. He hadn't had a good ground-pounding fight in months.

"I'm so sick of prying crawling things off the hulls of ships and stuff like that," he said. "*Phobos* is really, really big. It will be like fighting on a moon. Are we going to get to go inside, sir?"

I nodded. "That is a distinct possibility, First Sergeant."

Within an hour, I was in contact with Tolerance again via Marvin. My robot wasn't happy with this arrangement, as he still wanted to escape and get down to Medical. We both knew I had him on the string this time, however, so he was doing his job properly—if bitterly.

The first part of any rescue mission is to secure the LZ for the safety of everyone involved. In this case, that was a tall order. Tolerance, despite his name, was not in a tolerant mood.

"Tolerance, let's go over this one more time," I said, gesturing for Marvin to make sure he gave me his best possible translation of meaning. His tentacles were dead still, and his cameras were drooping, but he did the job anyway. "We're not a threat to you. The forces that are currently attempting to depressurize your ship are not under our control. Strangely, we're willing to help you in this instance."

"I find it very hard to believe anything you say, Colonel Riggs. If you will now excuse me, there is a new breach in the aft zones. I have to attend to damage control."

I took a deep breath and let it out slowly. "All we're asking is that you don't fire when we come down to land on *Phobos*. Let us help you."

"Absurd. Your underestimation of my intellectual capacity is insulting. I've already got a dozen of your machines crawling inside my vehicle, and you expect me to allow another large landing? I repeat, creature, you speak in absurdities."

I muted the channel and looked at Gaines, who was standing nearby with a tense look on his face.

"Just my luck," I said, "he finally gets smart and refuses to buy my bullshit when I'm telling the truth."

"He doesn't know that, Colonel. Sounds like the landing is scrubbed. We'll just have to sit this battle out and hope for the best."

"Not going to happen. We're going down there, let me assure you. I don't want *Phobos* knocked out before it even reaches the Solar System."

I tapped at my screen and unmuted the channel again.

"Tolerance. Listen to me: analyze the enemy structures. You said yourself they were machines. We do not fight with unmanned machines. These constructs are not from Star Force. It is our mission to destroy all unmanned machines."

There was a pause after this that stretched for about twenty seconds. I was about to key open the channel again when a response finally came in.

165

"You have won. They have damaged my atmospherics. It is only a matter of time, now. I don't know why you persist in your lies at this point. Possibly, you derive some kind of sadistic satisfaction from the process."

"We might be able to save you. You've got nothing to lose. Tell me: are they machines?"

"My sensors have classified them as primarily inanimate. However, they have flesh components as well. I haven't analyzed these yet, but I've no doubt there is a human inside, operating these tiny dense-thing monsters."

My mind kicked into overdrive. There had to be a way to salvage this situation. If Tolerance died, I didn't want him to leave his ship with every automatic defense system operational.

What could I do? I wanted to beat my fist against my head until I came up with something. I thought back to my visits with these strange people. Perhaps there was a way.

"Tolerance? Are you still there?"

The voice was fainter than before, but it was still audible. "Yes, my tormentor."

"We're not without compassion. Will you allow me, just me, to come down to your ship? I will commune with you. I will taste you, and you will taste me. That way, you will not have passed on completely alone."

There was a brief, gut-wrenching silence.

"I do not wish to die alone. You may come. But if I detect more of your kind, I will annihilate you all as my final act."

"I will come then. Do not dishonor yourself in the name of revenge."

"How little you understand our species."

The channel closed and I gave a whoop of victory.

The rest of my crewmen looked confused.

"Where there's a will, there's a way!" I shouted.

"What are you going to do, Colonel?" Kwon asked, confused.

"What about my men, sir?" Gaines asked, frowning deeply. "Are we going down, or not?"

"No," I said firmly. "That wasn't the deal I made with Tolerance."

"What about just an escort of one, sir?" Kwon asked hopefully. "One man can't piss off that airhead too much."

I shook my head, denying his request. Everyone began a chorus of similar questions, but I calmed them all with upraised hands.

"I'm going down there—alone. I'm going aboard *Phobos* to have a little interpersonal meeting with a gas cloud. As some of you might know they're by nature a social species. On their homeworld they interact by exchanging some portion of their mass with one another. This translates as 'tasting' but really it's more like exchanging gases and gels. Anyway, if Tolerance lets me down there, he must switch off any automatic defensive systems to allow it. That will let me land."

I adjourned the meeting and left my office. Marvin scuttled away in the opposite direction, dragging his bulk toward Medical. He hadn't asked if it was time yet, he'd wised up about that. But I didn't mind. I'd tortured him long enough.

I headed up to the bridge to make preparations and to alert my key personnel.

"But…" Captain Sarin said, her eyes full of concern. "How will you get back? What will you do with all the cyborgs running around the place?"

I shrugged. "It's a big ship. I probably won't even see one. As far as getting back goes, I'm going to have to play that one by ear."

She released an exasperated sound. "You always say something like that."

"Indeed he does," said Gaines. He had just joined us on the bridge. Of all of them, he was the only one who was smiling. I think he was happy he wasn't the one doing a hot landing on *Phobos*.

I was already walking for the exit by this time.

"Come on, Gaines," I said over my shoulder.

He trotted after me. "I thought I wasn't going down?"

"Not with me. But as soon as I secure the situation down there I'm going to need support. I'll call for it, and I expect you to deliver a battalion to my coordinates within minutes."

"Uh, yes sir."

As I reached the launch tubes, Gaines took a ninety degree turn and headed for a pinnace. He was going to have to do a lot of organization to get the assault underway in a timely manner.

"Good luck, Colonel!" he called over his shoulder, throwing me a salute.

I saluted him back and climbed into a fighter. There wasn't time to get into a drop pod, and we were too far from the enemy ship to allow such a delivery system in any case.

A few minutes later, I was rocketing down the tube, howling with the thrill of acceleration. Damn, these birds made fine rides.

-18-

As I roared through space leaving my fleet behind, I did feel a trifle exposed. Creeping doubts entered my mind. What if Tolerance had been bullshitting me instead of the other way around? It was hard to imagine the big steam cloud being able to pull it off, but he'd heard his share of whoppers from me in the past. Maybe he'd learned how to lie like a human.

I began to think of what I would have done in his position. Playing dead and luring the enemy commander in close for a good thrashing sounded like a nice start to any captain's day. Could it be?

Nah. I didn't buy it. The Blues were the straight-men of the universe, and because they had emotions and a sense of honor they were easier to fool than the machines could ever be. What I had to worry about, I told myself, was these cyborg things. Tolerance had never gotten around to telling me just how many were crawling around in the core of his ship.

Still, despite my self-confidence, I felt my guts clench up into a hard ball when I got close to the moon-sized ship. I even began to question my own sanity in coming out here—alone or otherwise.

Phobos was huge. It was just like approaching a planetoid, something I'd done any number of times in the past. It was almost impossible to think of the thing as a ship at all because it was so damned big. It had a curved horizon and the distant suns reflected from the dusty surface with glaring white light.

The only hint that it was an artificial structure lay in its nearly perfect spherical shape.

Squinching up my eyes, I passed the no-return point about ten minutes into the trip. This was where I was within the documented effective range of the enemy blanket weapon. From here on out, Tolerance could crush me with a flip of the switch, reducing my ship and the squishy body inside down to the size of a toaster oven.

It didn't happen, but no one gave my guts the all-clear. I felt a trifle sick by the time I landed on the northern pole of the moon-like vessel and made my way toward the forward sunken structure. Was Tolerance watching me even now, his gaseous finger on a gelatinous button? Was he giggling, thinking he'd let me get almost to the finish line before springing his deadly trap? I had no idea, so I scooted quickly over the smooth ground, kicking up a cloud of dust. My grav boots left furrows on the surface behind me where the force pushed away the sand-like material that coated the hull.

Getting inside the crater-like region at the northern pole was a relief. Deep shadow fell over me plunging me into a relatively cool, gloomy interior. This had to be the main weapon—maybe it was the only weapon. We'd figured out there were only two major, distinguishing features on *Phobos*. One was in the aft region, which corresponded with the southern pole. That was the engine emissions port—only it didn't emit anything that we could determine other than gravity waves.

I was inside the forward structure now. It looked like a parabolic dish, something akin to a giant TV satellite dish. Over a mile wide, we figured it had to be the big gun as it always seemed to be aiming in the general direction of anything that got crunched.

I could have flown the fighter right down into the mouth of this thing, but I hadn't dared. The fighter had weaponry aboard, and I didn't want Tolerance to construe the action as an attack. I wanted to appear as harmless as possible.

I was, in fact, feeling *very* harmless as I plunged down into the conical interior of the structure. Seen up-close, the surface was not smooth. It resembled a honeycomb of hexagonal holes.

Each of these openings was about a meter wide and black inside. I could have gone down into one of those holes, but I didn't dare. Instead, I flew over them and drove onward toward the small end of this monstrous cone.

There, at the very bottom, I found something new. There were oblong black corpses lying and half-floating here and there. The gravity was so low, it left bodies in odd, twisted patterns rather than pulling them down into a flat position. Stains of spilled liquids were everywhere, and they'd congealed into odd patterns. In a vacuum, liquids tended to vaporize, but these didn't. They'd formed nearly spherical beads that glistened in the dim interior.

I had no doubt I was looking at dead Worms. There had to be more than a hundred of them. How had they died? Were they all taken out at once? I didn't know, so I pressed onward.

At the bottom of the cone, I found another kind of dead. These were smaller and metallic. I paused on my journey to examine and film these aberrations. It took me only a moment to identify them.

"I think these things are dead cyborgs," I told my recording system as I scanned the area. "They must have been caught on their infiltration attempt to reach the interior. Either that, or the Worms met up with them and they wiped each other out. I can tell there was some use of gravity weaponry. I can see small black wads of metal here and there about the size of a deck of cards. I think these are the remains of other cyborgs, crushed down by Tolerance."

I was recording my words but not transmitting them. I didn't want to take the chance of pissing Tolerance off. I'd gotten this far—all the way down onto the hull of his ship—and now wasn't the time to give the big bastard the slightest opportunity to change his mind. For all I knew, transmitting my observations would incriminate me, turning me into an instant spy.

I pressed onward, leaving the dead Worms and cyborgs and their clingy balls of blood behind. I found an opening at the bottom of the cone that was as alarmingly large as everything else. It must have been a hundred yards in diameter. This must have been what the previous invaders had been fighting to reach.

Here, there were more bodies. The scene was easy to comprehend. There were both Worms and cyborgs locked in death together. They'd died fighting one another.

It was strange, finding evidence of an open battle with no humans involved. I felt a pang for the Worm commandoes who'd given their lives here. I wondered if they'd lived long enough to see their fleets destroyed overhead. Judging by Marvin's translation of the symbols they'd sent us, I figured they had survived the initial landing. They'd ended up here, dying in combat against a strange new enemy—this time built by Crow's Imperial forces.

I flew down into the abyss at the bottom of the cone and kept going. I could see vague shapes ahead—geometric metal cones, rods and polyhedrons that thrust up from below. They gleamed now and then when the starlight caught them.

I frowned at the interior, baffled. It looked like the inside of an old TV set down here, blown up a thousand times in magnitude. Glimmering things like vacuum tubes and silver exposed wires the size of sewer pipes went everywhere.

Not daring to land on the metallic surface, which seemed to crackle with power, I turned and drifted, using my suit's grav plates. I was looking for a way out of this chamber, a way to enter the craft's core.

Unsurprisingly, the cyborgs showed me the way. Their bodies were evident here and there as I shined my suit lights down on them. I finally found an opening that didn't look like it had been on the original blueprints.

It was a jagged hole at the bottom of the place, in between two large components that looked for all the world like a pair of giant vacuum tubes.

They'd burned their way in. I could see it all now. They'd come down all over the ship, landing like fleas on a passing dog. But then the dog had shaken itself and killed many of them. Fortunately for the fleas, the dog was slow and could only shake about once every ten minutes. After the first bunch had been killed, the next wave made it inside the beast where they were immune to the gravity weapon.

From the interior, they must have burned this hole in the floor. It hadn't damaged the main weapon—at least, not that I could see. But it had allowed them to get in behind the circuitry and to keep going deeper.

I followed their path. The scarred metal was ringed with flanges like a mouthful of razor-sharp teeth. I pressed through, letting these teeth scratch and screech on my suit.

Deep inside the gravity weapon, things weren't any less dangerous. Almost immediately, I found another dead cyborg. This one wasn't crushed down like a bug under a shoe, however. It must have touched the pipe-like exposed silver wires. Fried in an instant, its dry husk lay where it had fallen.

I frowned down at the mess. Its blood had been boiled way, and the immediate area was brown as if a flash fire had occurred.

I didn't like the look of this. Had this one comparatively tiny short disabled this mammoth weapon? It seemed bizarre, but I realized that I hadn't see Tolerance fire his single big gun, not since the cyborg assault.

Looking around, I found nothing non-conductive at hand. I turned on my suit recorder again.

"Hmmm," I said. "I'm going to try to move this dead bug. I think it's worth taking a chance. If I die and this recording somehow survives me, take this as a cautionary tale."

I found one of the big vacuum tube things and put my back up against it. Reaching back, I gripped the tube firmly—but not so hard I chanced cracking it.

Then I aimed the bottom of one of my boots toward the dead cyborg and turned on the grav power.

The boot bucked up against me, and I had to lock my knee. It threatened to push me right off into a spin, but I held on grimly.

Slowly, the repelling forces coming from the bottom of the boot pressed the dead cyborg away. The effect was similar to that which every leaf-blower causes. The cyborg was a particularly stubborn leaf, but he did finally fly away.

I glided close again and examined my efforts. The contact was burnished but appeared dry and serviceable. Maybe there was a breaker somewhere that needed to be flipped, but I could

173

only do so much. As far as I could tell, the short was fixed and the weapon should work again.

I continued on, heading deeper into the interior of the ship. After following a long, winding tunnel I came to a huge chamber. I had to press hard to enter here through the gusty shaft that whistled and bubbled with pressure. I checked my suit readings and realized I was now in a pressurized area.

"I must have passed through some kind of airlock, but I didn't see the hatch," I told my recorder, turning around twice to video everything.

The interior of the ship was dark and smoky. A brown haze like L. A. smog hung inside the chamber. It was so thick and dark I didn't want to even try to breathe it, but I'd made a promise and I needed Tolerance's cooperation.

First, I unlimbered the single piece of unusual equipment I'd brought along on this trip: a conch shell-like translating device. Using a small brain box and what amounted to a megaphone, I began talking to Tolerance—or at least, I hoped I was doing so.

"This is Colonel Kyle Riggs," I said, instantly wondering at the wisdom of clearly identifying myself. There had been times in my life when the simple act of saying those words had brought unfriendly fire in my direction.

I waited, listening to the crackle and hiss of the translation unit. Nothing intelligible came out of it.

"I repeat, this is Colonel Kyle Riggs. Tolerance, are you here? I've come a long way to meet with you."

I waited again, becoming impatient. I reached to key it again a minute later when I thought I heard something. I immediately adjusted the gain.

"...out..."

That was it. I frowned. Was he telling me to get the hell out? As an afterthought, I flipped on the suit recorders again.

"Tolerance, I heard you, but only barely. Are you here? I see some turbulence in the mist locally. We are so physically different—"

I stopped talking, because I thought I heard the voice again.

"...out...your shell..."

174

I'm slow, just ask any girl I've ever gone out with, but I finally got the message. I reached up and spun the releases on my helmet, causing it to open like a tiny hatch. Soon, my exposed head was wreathed in cold, disgusting gasses.

The atmospheres of planets like Jupiter aren't pleasant. They're largely made of methane, helium, hydrogen and various corrosives. In short, they stink like nothing any human has ever experienced back on Earth. But I'd been especially built to withstand this kind of medium. Back when I'd first entreated with the Blues, I'd let Marvin go wild and modify my body for survival in this type of environment. I'd never had him change me back—if such a thing was even possible.

My skin could take splatters of acid. My lungs could breathe what amounted to a mix of farts and jet exhaust without choking—at least for a short period. Surviving in such an environment wasn't the same thing as enjoying it. A gush of nastiness entered my suit and went all the way down to my sweating feet.

Alarmed, my suit beeped and little fans fired up, hopelessly trying to blow away the big stink that had invaded my airspace. I appreciated the effort, despite the futility of it. At least the fans made my feet fractionally cooler and drier down in the bowels of my armor.

I closed my eyes, of course. I didn't need to see Tolerance, and he didn't need to lick my eyeballs.

Slowly, I counted backwards from fifty down to one. I didn't want him to feel shortchanged. When I was done, I slowly closed up my suit again.

After I had the seals back, I still only breathed in hitching coughing gasps. I waited until the filtration system cleared things up enough, and tried to speak. The words came out as squeaks at first, but after a few coughing spasms, I managed to be intelligible.

"Are you happy now, Tolerance?" I asked.

"…no…"

"Well, are you satisfied that I did as I said? That I allowed you to commune with me in your final moments?"

"…unpleasant…"

"Yeah, well, you stink too. But I did what I said I would do. Right?"

"...documented. I can die now..."

I frowned. *Die?* Was all this for nothing then?

"Can I do anything to save you?"

"...you are me...we have mixed..."

Great. I frowned in my suit. I'd always found these guys strange and faintly disgusting. As far as this cloud was concerned, we'd just melded or something and shared one another's essence. I knew that in the culture and biology of the Blues, they considered themselves immortal after melding with other creatures. Part of their gas was forever part of the next guy's each time they met and felt each other up. I didn't like the connotations, and was always left with an urge to rinse and spit.

"Look," I said, "you're still talking. Let us help. Turn off your weapon. Let us fly down here and chase out these cyborgs. I have engineers and plenty of people to help. I even have a crazy robot that might be able to figure out and repair your technology."

"...too late..."

"Just turn off your weapon," I said slowly and clearly. "I've proven to you we're here to help, I've—"

"The weapon no longer functions."

I stopped, mouth agape. I'd come down here alone for nothing? I thought of the damage the cyborgs had done inside the weapon electronics. They'd shorted it out like a moth on a circuit board.

"Why didn't you allow me to bring serious help?" I demanded.

"...only you..."

"Yeah, I know. Now I'm here, and I can't do much by myself. Your suspicious nature has screwed you, Tolerance. I'm now going to call my people. They'll come and land. Possibly, if you hang on long enough we'll be able to save your worthless gas bag life."

I tried to open a channel to my fleet, but found I couldn't. I cursed. I should have left a nanite wire down to here. But I

176

supposed with all the exposed high voltage contacts I'd passed, it would have been too dangerous.

Turning around, I glided up the wall, heading toward the ruptured entrance I'd found. I planned to follow the tunnel out to the surface again. From there, I could call the marines. This place would be swarming within an hour.

"...wait..."

"Wait for what?" I asked.

"...they're almost here..."

I felt an icy chill. *Who* was almost here? There was only one reasonable answer: the cyborgs. The very monsters that had found a way to kill this giant ship.

I heard something new then over my translation device. Faintly, it translated into a bubbling sound. The gases around me swirled and burbled.

I'd heard this before when I'd visited the Blues on Eden-11. Tolerance was laughing.

-19-

I didn't make it to the tunnel. A figure appeared in front of me in the mouth of the gouged-open tunnel. It was unmistakably a cyborg. It's central body had an ovoid shape. Its black arms were crusted by hair-like spines. Seen clearly in my suit lights, it looked to me like a headless, wingless fly.

It crawled out of the hole on its thin, scuttling legs. There were hooks and barbs all over the thing, just like the first one I'd encountered.

With a curse and grunt, I pulled up my laser projector. Connected by a black nanite cable to the power generator on my back, it had a gauge on top. I was thirty percent low already after having flown so far to get into the ship.

I lifted the projector to blast the bug, but it wasn't there. I'd only looked down for a second—where had it gone?

I twisted this way and that, but armored spacesuits aren't easy to see out of. It was like being in car; you couldn't see anything that was too close...

I felt a new weight on my legs, and felt a shuddering sensation through my suit. It was on me. Despite my armor, I shouted in alarm. There's something about having a giant, headless fly latch onto you and starting to dig its way in—call me squeamish, but I felt a chill run down my spine.

The critter was in too close to use the laser projector safely, but I tried anyway. I press the business end to its body and squeezed the trigger.

I half-expected the resulting beam of light to burn a gash into my armor, but it didn't. I managed to burn the cyborg instead. The thing went spinning away, thrashing. Tiny droplets of poison glittered in its wake, left behind by a thousand hair-thin spines. I knew that if they got into my suit and stung me with that stuff before I got off this ship, I'd never make it back to the fleet in time. Paralysis would set in, and I'd be a goner.

With that added impetus, I steered for the tunnel. I planned to go back the way I'd come in as fast as possible and call for help from the surface. Walking back to the fighter across the surface didn't seem feasible now that the enemy cyborgs had located me. If I had to, I figured I could launch myself into space. My suit's repellers were more than powerful enough to reach escape velocity as *Phobos* didn't have much gravity.

Unfortunately, my best laid plans are often no better than my more common off-the-cuff reactions. Before I could even reach the tunnel, more bug-like creatures appeared. Two at first, climbing over one another with their churning, spine-covered legs. Their eye-stalks roamed for a second, then fixated upon me. They seemed eager to make my acquaintance and moved faster when they caught sight of me.

They launched toward me like spiders. I don't know if they screeched because I couldn't hear them through my helmet— but I did. Of all the aliens I'd ever faced, these had to be the creepiest. They were part human, and yet they seemed more evil and unnatural than anything else I'd encountered.

I had time to raise my trusty laser carbine and release a sweeping blaze of energy. The first one was cut in half and sent spinning in two different directions. Its steaming legs and eye-stalks churned futilely.

The second one dodged my opening salvo, scuttling along the wall of the huge chamber. I aimed, but it got in close and sprang at me. My shot went wide. It was much lighter than I was in my power suit, but weight isn't as important in low gravity. The force of its charge sent us both spinning, entwined.

I could hear those spines scratching and rasping on the surface of my scarred armor, trying to find a way in. I tried to

179

put the projector against it, but couldn't. It had crawled up onto my back and I couldn't get the angle right. As anyone who's worn heavy armor can tell you, it's great to have in a firefight, but when an enemy is literally on top of you it can feel like a prison and can hamper your actions as much as it protects you.

My mouth ran with a steady stream of curses, labored breathing and grunts. I dropped the laser projector and reached for my belt knife—but it wasn't there.

A new rasping began on my back. The skin over my vertebrae crawled as I realized the cyborg had my knife and was plunging it into my armor with terrific force. It stabbed and hacked, gouging the tempered steel.

The edge of a Star Force marine standard-issue combat knife is a modern wonder of engineering. Sharpened to a single molecular line at the edge, as perfectly straight as the carbon atoms in a diamond and just as hard, the blade can cut through almost anything. Right now, it was cutting into my power pack and would soon reach the interior of my suit.

There was a hiss of released gas. The interior of my suit rose in temperature, and I could smell the radioactive gases being released inside my very small personal space. I knew that smell; it was like ozone and made your mouth taste like you'd filled it with metal—because you had.

My struggles increased. I had to get this monster off my back. I reached back with both hands trying one angle then the next, but couldn't get a hold on it. My armor was so bulky, it restricted my range of motion. I could no more grab the cyborg than I could scratch the middle of my back while wearing a tight sweatshirt.

I decided it was time to use the laser again, even if it did burn the back of my suit off. I couldn't let this bastard fully breach the integrity of my armor. I reached for the projector, which dangled by a black nanites coil near my right hip.

Just then, the cyborg got big ideas and made a mistake. He slid one of his numerous appendages over my faceplate to get a better grip. I could visualize him back there, stabbing and gouging away with my knife, trying to dig his way into my suit. He needed leverage.

The—I'm not sure what to call it...*claw*, that probably was the best descriptor. The thing's claw was black with spines like a crab freshly hauled up onto a fisherman's deck. I could see it very clearly, as it nearly filled my vision. There was no hand at the terminus, just a few opposable hooks for grasping and manipulating objects.

I reached up and gripped that claw, pulling it away from my visor. I bared my teeth. I had him now. The trick would be to avoid ripping that arm off entirely. If I did that, I'd lose my hold on it.

I began pulling—gently. I dragged the scrabbling monster off my back and around to the front of my armor.

When the eyestalks appeared, they swiveled and squirmed, looking at me. I saw the intellect inside those eyes. They were human eyes. The organs were locked inside some kind of protective clear polymer—but with recognizably human flesh inside. I shivered in my armor as we regarded one another for a perhaps a second.

"What have you done, Crow?" I asked no one. "This thing is worse than a Macro."

Having been dragged off my back, the creature went with the flow. It still had my knife, and the tip of my own weapon came flashing in toward my faceplate.

I winced and grunted, flinching away. The faceplate starred, but held. The next blow, I knew, would plunge that knife through and into my face.

There was no easy way to deal with this thing. It was all arms and spines and I could tell the concept of surrender had never been taught in cyborg school. Taking the easiest approach I could think of, I threw my arms around its body and crushed it against my breastplate.

A bear hug. That's what we'd called it back in school. A crushing, squeezing motion that drove the life out of the victim in a powerful grip. I squeezed with all my strength, which was augmented by the arms of my power suit.

The thing buckled and spasmed. I kept squeezing, feeling it go flat against my armor. It didn't crush down all at once, nor did it go steadily like a deflating air mattress. Instead, my arms came closer to my chest in a series of jerks, as if I were folding

181

it down. I think I was encountering resistance from its metal bones, each of which gave way after a moment of unstoppable pressure.

It stopped flailing, but I kept squeezing. Still, it shivered and scratched at me feebly. I kept on going, roaring now. What is it about a hard fight that makes a man roar with the glory of the kill? I'll never know, but I was lost in the passion of the moment.

Finally, it went limp and I let it sag away from me. It fell with exaggerated slowness toward the bottom of the chamber. I watched it go, wondering if it was capable of human emotions, or if it's mind was as insectile as its body.

Giving one last shiver, I retrieved my knife and holstered my projector. I headed for the tunnel. I fervently hoped there wouldn't be another dozen of these creatures to defeat before I reached the hull of the great ship.

While I struggled through the tunnels, my nanites madly worked to patch holes in my body and my suit. The venom had never penetrated, but the knife blade had. I was slightly nauseated by released radiation and was breathing air heavily laced with radon gas—but I was still alive.

* * *

It took me about an hour, but I managed to reach the outer hull of the ship. By that time, my nanites had repaired the suit enough to allow me to breathe and walk—but the suit wasn't going to be flying again soon. I had to bump along using my fingers and toes rather than grav plates to propel myself carefully. My faceplate was badly cracked, but I could still see the dusty surface of *Phobos* through it. The ship's hull was a strangely welcome sight. The clean, clear star light was a relief after having spent a harrowing time in the guts of this monstrous ship.

I had another scare when I tried to contact fleet. The radio didn't seem to work at first. But then I figured out it had to do with emergency suit power cuts. I adjusted the settings and was able to use my com-link properly.

"This is Colonel Kyle Riggs," I said, broadcasting on an open channel. "Can anyone from Fleet read this?"

"Colonel Riggs?" came a response about a minute later. "This channel is dangerous, please switch over to encrypted—"

"I can't," I said. "My suit's half wrecked. No brainbox left. I can only use manual controls. The nanite repair systems are still up, but they've got no brains guiding them."

"Sir, I can't authorize this conversation according to Star Force protocol."

I mumbled curses. "Jasmine? Is that you? You don't believe I'm Riggs, is that it? Well, then I'll go onto the general channel and tell everyone what we watched in my office the other night. Let me see, what was the title of that exciting vid? Um…"

"That will not be necessary, Colonel," she said primly. "I know who you are."

"Good. Now, come down here and rescue me."

"Your own orders specify that only you have permission from Tolerance to land on *Phobos*."

"True, but Tolerance is dead. Somebody let the air out of that windbag. As far as I can tell, the big weapon is disabled, anyway. Always was. He just wanted me to come down so I could die with him. He almost got his wish, too, that bastard."

"You're injured, Colonel?"

"Yeah, slightly. Mostly my suit is torn up. There are cyborgs here, I don't know how many. I took a few out, but they could come after me in numbers at any time. I need back up. Send Kwon and Gaines. Kwon is bored, and Gaines deserves it."

There was a pause. "They will be inbound to your position shortly. Now, I recommend taking a defensive posture and avoiding all further open transmissions. The enemy is probably monitoring you now and triangulating your position."

I rolled my eyes. Sometimes Jasmine could be like a mother hen, giving you advice that was overly detailed and unnecessary.

But I had to admit, as I rolled over on my back and sat up very slowly to look around, she had a point. The enemy could be listening and on my trail even now. I pulled my projector onto my lap and laid my knife nearby. I planned to take a shot and then grab the knife. I didn't want the next one that attacked me to have any fun slashing me with it.

I turned the suit down to minimum to save power. I couldn't even afford to stand up straight as I was afraid I'd fly off into space if I did.

I sat on my can for the next half hour under the glittering stars. No human trapped on Earth has ever really seen the stars. Our atmosphere is like a foggy lens between the natural beauty of the universe and our seeking eyes. In space they are perfect, like jewels shimmering with icy light.

There were few sounds I could hear other than the hiss of my circulation system and my own breathing. It would have been a peaceful and soul-searching time if I hadn't been straining and craning my neck every few seconds to look for charging cyborgs.

-20-

The next few hours were a blur of activity. The first assault ship came down bearing Gaines and Kwon, as I had requested. Gaines brought along a platoon of his best marines. They secured the LZ like the pros they were, using their suits' shoulder repellers to keep them down on the surface.

I stood up warily and limped closer to them in short hops.

"Your suit looks banged up, sir," Kwon observed.

"You got it in one, First Sergeant."

I turned my attention to Gaines. "You need to know what we're facing here on *Phobos*."

I wired him the suit recordings of my up close and personal interactions with the cyborgs. Playing them on his faceplate made the experience very realistic. He watched the vid, making occasional exclamations.

"Oh shit," he said, wincing and staggering backward.

I chuckled. "You must have reached the part where they jumped me."

"Yes sir…that is one unpleasant hitch-hiker. I'm going to have to pass this on to the men—with your permission."

"Granted. They'll keep a sharp eye out if they know what might attack them."

He dialed up a platoon-net address and transmitted the vid. He then ordered his men to watch it in squads. We enjoyed their visceral reactions.

"Can I watch too, sir?" Kwon asked. "I want to see this."

I gave him the vid while Gaines and I walked aboard the assault ship. I needed a new suit, and the jump-ships always packed a few spares.

Kwon shouted something behind us in Korean. Gaines and I smiled. I figured if we stood around long enough we would learn a few new bad words in Kwon's native tongue.

Inside the pressurized cabin of the assault ship, I donned a fresh suit. The suits could seal and repair leaks by themselves, but there were a lot of specialized parts that couldn't be fixed without a machine shop.

"Sir?" Gaines asked, "about how many of those cyborgs are on *Phobos*?"

"Approximately? I have approximately no frigging idea. I don't think I clocked them all, though. I've only been here a few hours and I've already encountered three living specimens. There have to be more, it's a big ship. The way I figure it, *Phobos* barreled right through a section of space that was seeded by Crow with these cyborgs. They activated and attacked, as per their programming."

"Hmm," Gaines said, nodding. "We did get several of them aboard our larger ships, but this ship was first and it is so much larger...I would have to say a thousand times larger. That would indicate a thousand or so enemy."

I nodded, struggling with the helmet. Helmets were always the hardest part to get right in a battle suit. Believe it or not, people do have differently shaped heads. Unlike my own suit, which had been tailored to my dimensions, this unit was generic. It was able to conform to my shape to some degree, but it would never be as good a fit as a personalized unit.

"The next question is," I said, my voice becoming muffled as the overly-wide helmet clicked into place, "how many of those cyborgs survived *Phobos'* defensive systems? Tolerance must have gotten a few of them when they landed, but not enough to protect himself."

"We'll do a sweep of the northern polar region and get a body count," Gaines said. "But I'm more interested in another detail now."

"What's that?"

"Do you think we can fly this thing, Colonel?"

186

I stared at him. "That's an interesting idea. I'd honestly not considered it until now."

"You were probably too busy staying alive and being probed by Mr. Tolerance."

"Yeah...but you're right. We need *Phobos*. This ship was the basis of our attack plan for the Imperials. If we could get control of the drive system somehow, and get the main weapon working..." I trailed off, thinking hard. "I mean, how complicated can it be? Only one weapon with two modes. A drive system based on repellers, tech we know how to use, but on a drastically larger scale."

I clanked over to the cockpit where a female pilot nodded to me.

"Call up fleet dispatch," I said to her. "Tell Captain Sarin to send a full transport of marines down here. I want more personnel."

"Isn't that risky, sir?"

I looked at her in surprise. "Hell yeah, it is. In case you haven't noticed, pilot, this isn't a desk you're flying. Get them down here."

I walked away and tromped back out of the ship onto the surface. Gaines followed.

"I think Lieutenant Lund was just following orders, sir. Fleet is very jumpy about sending down a large portion of our forces without being certain it isn't a trap of some kind."

"By 'Fleet' I bet you mean Miklos."

"Probably," Gaines admitted. "She also wants to know if we've finished our recon mission here yet."

"Meaning she wants us to get off this rock? Let me tell you something, Major, this mission *was* a trap. A trap laid for me."

I explained briefly how Tolerance had spent his final moments enjoying what he'd hoped was my death.

"As far as I can tell," I said, "he was bluffing to get me down here alone. He didn't have any operating weapons left that I could detect. The cyborgs had knocked them out and let his atmosphere leak away. Any invading force would do the same."

"That was his key weakness," Gaines said thoughtfully. "Maybe that's why the Blues don't go out into space often."

"What do you mean?"

"The Blues are essentially collections of gel, mist and gas, sir. Space has zero pressure. Any kind of leak in his ship's pressurization system would be fatal to one of his kind."

"Yeah," I said, thinking about it. "It wouldn't be about suffocation. A leak, even a small one, would pull his guts out. I guess old Tolerance was brave for one of his kind—even if he was a son of bitch."

After a bit more butt-kicking on the com system with Fleet, I got my full transport load of marines. Having several hundred pairs of boots on the ground made me feel better—or was that hooves?

"You weren't kidding when you said you drew heavily on the Centaurs for this mission, Gaines."

I looked around at the marines, hands on my hips. At least three quarters of them had four legs rather than two.

"No choice, Colonel. Too many human losses."

Something new came down out of the transport then. At first, I thought it was a tank or some other kind of heavy machinery. Then I saw the cameras on sinuous arms.

"Marvin managed to get aboard the first transport?" I asked.

"Couldn't stop him, sir," Gaines said. "Captain Sarin said you might want him to look over the ship's technology."

"All right," I said. "Let's move out. I'm taking company A with me. The rest of you set up camp here and cover the LZ, Gaines commanding. Send the transport back up to Fleet before Miklos loses a kidney from stress."

That earned me a few chuckles. The Commodore's overprotective attitude toward his ships was well known.

"Saddle up, people! It's a long trip."

Marvin took his position at the end of my company of flying marines. I muttered to myself about him as we glided over the surface. The robot usually managed to make people think it was their idea when he got himself assigned to a mission, and apparently he'd pulled that trick on Jasmine. Right now, as far as I was concerned, this was a combat mission. Science officers were supposed to wait until the region was secure before dropping into an unknown and hostile

188

situation. But I had to admit, if we were going to figure out how to fly *Phobos,* I needed him.

I flew toward the north pole of the ship. Behind me, the marines scudded over the surface toward the big nose-weapon area. It looked like a crater from the edge. One would have thought it was a natural structure due to the size of it, but it was just too damned evenly-cut to be natural.

I led them all down into the crater and watched as they bumped over the honeycombed things behind me.

"If this thing goes off while we're this close, I bet we shrink down to the size of dimes," Gaines commented.

"Oh I don't know," I laughed, "Kwon here would probably make a half-dollar coin at least."

"Very good, sir!" Kwon laughed obligingly.

I wondered if he laughed at my jokes for the same reasons I laughed at his. I shrugged, deciding it was as good a basis for a friendship as any.

Soon we found the spot where I'd entered before and began the dangerous journey into the guts of the craft. Marvin almost couldn't contain himself when he realized the size and scale of the find.

"This is fantastic, Colonel. Absolutely fantastic! I want to thank you for authorizing my addition to this exploration team."

"This is a combat mission, Marvin," I said. "And you know full well I didn't authorize anything regarding you."

"Really? Possibly, there was some kind of data-entry error."

"Uh-huh."

We pressed ahead into the tight tunnel that led through the hull to main chamber. While we were in the tunnel, I became wary. Our numbers wouldn't help us as much in a tight space. In fact, the close quarters might even result in friendly-fire problems if the bugs hit us now.

But they didn't. They passed on the opportunity and let us exit into the open primary chamber without incident.

Marvin took flight once he wriggled free of the snake-hole entrance. He flew overhead, looking like Santa's sleigh as he glided his segmented body around.

"This is absolutely amazing," he said, cruising in a rising spiral above my company. "The enclosed cubic space here is larger than anything we've seen—with the possible exception of the Centaur orbital habitats."

"Yeah, it's big. If you're done doing a victory lap, I need you to find the control system and figure out how it works."

"I see something this way. I'll report back shortly."

He left, buzzing into the mist. I watched him go, shaking my head. "That robot is the best and worst thing I've ever done."

"Isn't that what every father says about his kids?"

I chuckled. "Yeah, but most kids don't threaten the species with Armageddon every now and then. Are the rest of those marines in defensive positions yet? I want our exit secure."

"No sir, but they're setting up. About that tunnel we used to enter—I think it's part of the problem."

"What do you mean?"

"It's not natural, and it's not part of the design. I think the cyborgs dug through the rock directly."

I examined the hole. It was smooth and clean, as if a machine had bored it with precision. I'd assumed it was part of the ship's structure when I'd found it, but now that I thought about it, how had the cyborgs gotten in? How had they released the pressure inside?

"They could make something that looks like this, I guess," I said, running my gauntlets over the edges. They were rough at the seams, and there was no hatch to close over the hole. "I'd kind of assumed this was the way Tolerance loaded himself aboard. Being a cloud, he could blow right through here and dwell inside."

"Maybe," Gaines admitted. "But that big of an air exchange would require something on another side to vent the expelled gasses out. Anyway, I think it's too big of a coincidence that the hole leads back to the breach in the weapons system and is just big enough for a human or a cyborg to travel through."

While we puzzled over this, I had the marine company we'd brought inside spread out and watch the interior of the ship. It was too big, dark and hazy to see the far side. There was no way to dig a foxhole, as the hull was too dense. As a

190

result, my marines were standing around in loose squads, playing their suit-lights over the interior and the smoky brown atmosphere inside.

It wasn't long before I heard a chime in my helmet. Marvin was requesting a private channel. I opened the connection and listened.

"I believe I have, it sir. Really, it's the only way."

"What are you talking about?"

"The ship's interface, Colonel."

"You've found it? You know how it works?"

"In principle, yes."

I frowned, not liking that qualifier. But I was happy he'd found anything at all so quickly. I told him to stay where he was working on the problem, located his signal and triangulated my way over to his position.

The flight crossing the central chamber took a good four minutes. This place was *huge*. I arrived and immediately checked my power supply: it was already down to eighty-three percent.

"We're going to have to build some kind of power station network in here," I said, looking over Marvin's find.

I was under-impressed. I'd expected some kind of sophisticated control system. Instead, what I found was a patchwork of hexagons like the honeycomb structure I'd found on the surface. The only difference here was the variable depth of the hexagons. Some were deep holes while others were shallow, and a few poked outward, like a block sticking up from kid's toy. Each of the hexes was about six feet across.

"What have you got here, Marvin?" I asked.

He was cruising around about twenty feet up, poking at one of the hexes. It shifted a little under pressure from his tentacles, sinking inward.

I frowned in concern. "What is that, some kind of button? Don't fool with it if you don't know what it does."

My statement finally gained the attention of a few of Marvin's drifting squad of cameras. A spotlight splashed over me, but he didn't fly down to my level.

"How else will I figure out how to operate the ship?"

191

I ran my eyes over the scene again. Slowly, I was beginning to get it.

"Are you telling me this is it? A control panel built on a fantastic scale?"

"Blues are large beings. Especially in a low-pressure environment."

"Yeah...but none of these buttons are even labeled. How could he tell which one was which?"

"I suspect they are differentiated by the proximity and pressure required to move a given button—I'm not sure as to the details yet. But yes, I am sure this is the control panel. There are few features in this entire vast chamber. As to the lack of labels, well, Blues have no eyes."

The more I thought about it, the more it made sense. How could a massive gaseous being interact with a ship's control panel? He couldn't see it, he couldn't flick a tiny switch—the physical interface had to be simple in structure. It had to be made up of something that could be moved with puffs of air.

I imagined Tolerance hovering here, looking like a slightly darker haze. He could blow into these hexagonal holes—or maybe apply suction. He could push and pull the soft interior material around in each of the hexes, thus controlling the ship.

That was cool, sort of like playing a giant harmonica. But it seemed impossible for a human to operate. You would have to have a dozen people all climbing around tapping on things. What a nightmare. Not to mention we hadn't the slightest clue what any of the controls did.

"Hmm," I said, daunted by the task Tolerance had left us. "Figuring this out is going to be difficult. There must be a hundred buttons here."

"Two hundred and sixteen, to be exact. There are also two other smaller panels higher up."

"Two hundred and...that's going to take months of experimentation to figure out!"

"I hope not," Marvin said, tapping lightly on a protruding hexagonal button.

I saw it move a fraction, and ducked my head instinctively. For all I knew, he was warming up the big weapon to fire.

"You hope not? Why's that? Are we going to plow through the ring to Earth soon? I thought we were on a stable orbital path across the system."

I sensed doom in the midst of triumph. If we rode this monster into the Solar System, that was all well and good, but not if we couldn't control it. We might as well find an asteroid and throw it at the ring. At least an asteroid wouldn't be hollow.

"The ring?" asked Marvin distractedly. "No, we aren't headed that way. Not at all. Hasn't anyone informed you of our new course, Colonel?"

I shook my head.

"Tolerance wanted to be sure, I guess—certain of your death. He set the ship into a death spiral. We'll impact with Centauri B in six days—but the temperature and radiation will kill everyone aboard before that."

I stared up at him.

"Marvin," I said. "We need this ship. We need to ride it like a battering ram all the way to Earth. It can't be that complex. Just figure out the basics. How to engage the gravity drive, how to steer—oh, and how to aim and fire that big weapon on the nose."

I heard a funny noise out of Marvin, one I'd never heard before. If I hadn't known better, I would have thought it was a snort.

"Is that all, Colonel Riggs?"

"No. There's one more thing. I want control of this ship within *five* days. If you manage that, I'll let you fly again, Marvin. I'll strap your engines back on myself, if I have to."

Seven, eight—fully ten cameras panned and zoomed in my direction.

"Is that some kind of joke, sir?"

"No, it's not. I mean it."

"In that case, I will begin my experiments immediately. I'll need a large amount of cooperation."

"Good, what's first?"

"I would like you to dig a new tunnel to the surface in a safe location."

"And second?"

"Get everyone away from the forward weapon. I'm going to try to fire it after repairing the wiring."

"You've got it, Marvin. You've got it. But what about the drive system?"

"Can I please be allowed to carry out my experiments without interference?"

I frowned inside my helmet but agreed readily enough. Marvin was my only hope of grabbing control of the biggest, baddest ship in the known galaxy.

"You've got it. But can you tell me why?"

"I'm under the impression that one of the smaller, simpler panels controls the weaponry. This large one does something else—either operates the sensors or the drive. If I can learn the simpler interface, I can then apply that knowledge to the larger."

"Right!" I said, slapping my gauntlets together with a loud crack. "Right you are. I'll have the northern region abandoned immediately."

I turned and started flying away across the chamber, shouting for my officers. We were going to have five very, very busy days.

-21-

After two hard-working days, I'd landed a lot more equipment and personnel aboard *Phobos*. At last, Miklos couldn't stand it anymore and came down to have look at my crazy project for himself.

He wasn't too happy with any of it. I'd stripped the bigger ships of several laser turrets each with their best brainboxes attached. These were fairly big units, ones that could stop a missile or a small ship with a single burning ray. That hurt Miklos' soul, I think, as he knew it weakened the firepower of his precious fleet. But what bothered him even more was the removal of three factories, one from every other carrier, to manufacture supplies aboard *Phobos*.

He came down to the surface, where I met him with a forced smile. Although we were on the sunside of the hull and his visor was pretty heavily darkened to keep out the radiation, I could see he wasn't smiling in there.

"Commodore!" I shouted, clapping his armored shoulder. "Come on down with me and see what we've done."

He muttered something I didn't catch, and I was pretty sure we were both glad I'd missed it. I pressed on, showing him a small, shuttle-like elevator at the top of the shaft. We got inside, tapped the smart metal panel, and were whisked down into the depths.

"Over a mile of solid rock. The first tunnel was small and winding, but this is much better. We've transported everything inside down through this shaft."

"Only a single exit? What would a fire marshal say about such a design, sir?"

"I've never liked fire marshals. Too obsessive."

He gave me a wry look.

When the smart metal hatch opened again, we stepped out into the interior of the ship. I could tell right away that he was impressed at the scale of it. A cluster of factories, personnel, and habitation bricks circled the elevator shaft as if it were a campfire. They looked lonely in the vast chamber.

"Is this the ship's hold, sir?"

"Yes, essentially. This is where Tolerance himself hung out. Below this deck—if you want to call it that—is an equally vast chamber full of generators and other equipment."

"But how could the Blues...?"

"How could a bunch of clouds build something like this? Well, first of all, realize that deep down in their own atmosphere they would become increasingly dense as the pressure built. Smaller, denser beings would have an easier time manipulating solid objects. The current theory is that they built robots to do most of the finer work—things that probably look a lot like the Macros and the Nanos."

He nodded, fascinated despite himself. He pulled himself together as I reviewed the rest of the encampment with him. He saw a lot of equipment he knew I'd commandeered from his ships and had transported down here.

"Sir," he said, stopping in front of one of the factories. "I must protest. This is very irresponsible. There are less than two days to go now before *Phobos* is scheduled to burn up. Why would we want to have her take these irreplaceable units into the star with her?"

"They won't," I said, "for two reasons: one, I'd pull them out of here first. These factories will be on the first transport— before the crewmen themselves. Two, because Marvin isn't going to fail. He's going to figure out how to fly this thing."

Miklos looked at me with a distinct lack of trust. "I've heard such promises before, especially from that robot."

"Look, man," I said, throwing up my hands, "you should be more excited than anyone about this salvage effort. If it works, just imagine what you can do with it! It will be your flagship.

196

The greatest ship we've ever seen, with you manning the bridge. Hell, I might even give you the command chair."

He perked up slightly, but his face was still sour.

"An incalculable honor, I'm sure," he said.

I continued the tour. I was accustomed to doubters by this time in my career. Sure, Star Force had had more than her share of debacles, but wasn't that to be expected as you explored unknown space? Did people really expect everything to go perfectly the first time they tried it?

"Many of the pioneers of science have had their bad days," I said.

"Yes, and this one makes me think of Edison and his pet elephant."

I frowned at him in irritation. Edison had once used an elephant to demonstrate the dangerous power of his competitor's electrical power generators—by electrocuting the animal. The event had turned into a public relations nightmare.

"An obscure historical reference that bears no relationship to this effort," I said stiffly.

"Uh-huh."

As I led him to the control panel he became more interested. We now had a series of black tentacle arms applying pressure to every one of the two hundred and sixteen buttons. They could pull or push any of them. These arms were linked to a control panel that was human-sized and displayed a related series of sliding virtual controls. You could push in or pull out any tiny variation of power.

"It is odd," I said, "that such a sophisticated people would use what is essentially an analog control system."

"Do we know it well enough to make that determination?"

A voice came down from the hazy air above us, answering his question: "Yes. Yes we do."

Marvin came drifting down out of the sky and settled near the control panel. "We have digitized it to some extent, but the original analog system is more precise. The slightest tug or pull will have an effect on the drive, navigation or propulsions system."

"But so many buttons!" Miklos exclaimed. "How can we ever master them all in time?"

197

"We've determined there are actually two forms of buttons. These you see here do not actually control the ship."

Miklos gaped at the vast array of mega-buttons. "What the hell do they do, then?"

"They are the sensory system," Marvin said. "They provided tactile feedback from the ship's sensors, which told Tolerance what was happening in surrounding space."

"Ah," I said, catching on. "That's very good Marvin. Of course! I should have figured it out myself. How else would he be able to respond to stimuli from outside the ship in space? He read these buttons like a blind giant, reading braille with a thousand sensitive fingers."

"Two hundred and sixteen of them," Miklos said in an odd voice. "Incredible."

I could tell now by looking at him he had the bug. There was something about this ship, this alien monstrosity, that made a man want to figure out its mysteries and gain at least some degree of control over it.

"Exactly," Marvin said. He extended a long black tentacle toward the upper regions, which we could barely see. "Those units up there are the real control panels. They're comparatively simple. There are three, separated by a considerable distance. Each grouping appears to control a different function."

"Navigation, weapons, and—what is the third?"

"I don't know yet. I think it has to do with life support, telecommunications and so forth. I'm focusing on the first two."

Miklos stepped forward and put out a gloved hand. He ran it gently over the nearest hexagonal button. The nanite arm that was attached to that particular button shivered slightly as if in response.

"Very sensitive," he said. "I'm beginning to understand the fascination you've had with this project, Colonel Riggs. I'm glad I came."

I clapped my hands together again and gave Miklos a beaming smile.

"It's great to hear you say that. Imagine the Imperials when they get a look at this thing!"

198

My smile widened into a grin and Miklos shook his head at me.

"What?" he said. "I can tell you have something else to show me."

"You're right. This is the moment. Marvin, demonstrate what you've learned. I want you to fly this monster!"

Miklos laughed, and his eyes lit up with new enthusiasm. "You can fly it? Why didn't you tell me that in the first place?"

"I wanted you to see it all from the start. I wanted you to appreciate the effort. When we turn on a TV, we never think of the wonders going on inside it. You do now, and you'll always know how amazing Marvin's accomplishments were."

We sounded a dozen alarms warning everyone to get to a safe place. We cleared the surface of the vast ship, launching every transport and getting all personnel safely off the hull. After all, we didn't really know what the hell we were doing yet.

Miklos nodded, looking around like a kid in a theme park. His transformation into a believer was complete. Marvin set about starting up the engines. It was for real this time. He engaged them and the ship lurched.

First we were all thrown starboard, then we rolled aft. The ship felt like it was heeling over.

"Let's get to the table!" I shouted.

We pressed ourselves against the navigational table. It was hooked up via a long nanite wire to the surface where sensors had been attached to the exterior. We watched as the ship slowly maneuvered in random directions. Marvin worked the controls with ever more gentle touches.

"Don't touch the screen," I warned Miklos.

Miklos pulled his fingertips away from the edge of the table in alarm. Both of us gripped the border around the edge with clamped on fingers, trying not to touch anything else.

"It's very sensitive, sir," Marvin said. "My apologies for the rough ride."

"Everything is clear to me now, Colonel," Miklos said, "you were so patient with my complaints. I didn't understand your buoyant mood. Now I do. You weren't inviting me for an inspection; you wanted me to experience the ship's maiden voyage."

"Exactly, Commodore."

"I thank you for the experience," he said, gripping the sides of the table less firmly now that Marvin wasn't sending us into a new tailspin every thirty seconds. "One question remains in my mind, Colonel. Why didn't you clear out this atmosphere inside the ship? It's cloudy and roiling now. It must not help anyone attempting to fly the thing."

"We will, we will," I said. "We'll pressurize the entire interior someday with a fresh pine scent. Maybe we'll even have swimming pools, shopping malls and parks. But for now, we lack the supply of gasses to replace what's here. That sort of esthetic will have to wait."

Miklos looked up, frowning and swiveling his head. My eyes were riveted to the control screen. It looked to me like Marvin was doing it. The ship had changed course and was now bouncing away from Centauri B. It wasn't heading anywhere useful yet, but at least we weren't going to burn up tomorrow.

Miklos tapped me. "I'm betting those things are some kind of automated maintenance device?"

"What?" I asked, following his pointing finger.

There was something dark crawling down the nearby wall. My head swiveled this way and that, seeing more and more of them. They were coming from nowhere, hidden in the brown hazy air that hung up there until they got close.

"I'm afraid those are cyborgs, Commodore," I said. "Do you have a weapon handy?"

"I'm never in the field without it."

"Good," I said, drawing my own laser projector and aiming it at the closest cyborg I could see. "Start shooting. We're under attack."

Marvin, who'd been utterly focused on flying his ship, appeared to be startled by my announcement. His cameras rose and panned in every direction.

Everywhere he looked, there were black, crawling cyborgs.

-22-

They'd been waiting for us. Waiting for us to die.

I figured it out as I battled with the crawling hordes. Why not attack earlier, in the middle of the night while we were resting? Because they didn't think they had to. The ship was already as good as dead, spiraling out of control toward a hot yellow star. Why bother attacking the doomed idiots that populated the ship? Let them all burn.

But when we managed to exert control over *Phobos*, they were forced to act. Their mission was clearly to destroy this ship. If we changed course, that was a problem for them.

They came at us in surprising numbers. A week ago it had been Tolerance who'd experienced this sensation of shock. Now, it was our turn.

"Hold the left flank, Commodore, I'll deal with the ones on the right. Marvin, you—" I broke off, looking around. "Marvin?"

He was gone. He'd lifted right up into the stinking haze and flown away. In a way, I didn't blame him. He had no weapons equipped at the moment, but it was never fun to be abandoned.

"We can't hold them, sir," Miklos said, "I suggest we retreat."

"They'll destroy our control system."

"They'll kill us first."

I shot one, then another. The second one got up, smoking, and crawled forward. It was slower, but not finished yet. I glanced over to see how Miklos was doing.

Not so good. One was already on his leg. I realized he had only a fleet officer's pistol. I grabbed him, shot the one attached to him repeatedly, then engaged my grav boots. We glided up into the swirling mist.

They leapt up after us, and I fired repeatedly into the mass of them. There had to be thirty in sight now.

Miklos did a smarter thing—he changed our direction. They didn't seem to have control of their trajectory once they'd taken a leap, so they shot on past us and vanished into the brown haze above.

"Good play, Commodore. We'll go back to the encampment and gather the marines. They'll be destroyed in ten minutes."

"Yes sir," he said, sounding tired. "I'm not feeling so good, however. I wonder if you could take me to the infirmary."

I looked him over. He had holes in his suit. I cursed and shot him with extra nanites. They worked on sealing his suit, restoring pressure and healing his body at the same time.

"You're in for a full blood transfusion. Ever had one of those?"

"No...sir..." he said faintly.

"They suck."

Navigation wasn't easy in a giant brown cloud, but I eventually got my HUD system working and flew to the encampment. I frowned as I landed, seeing the place was overrun with more cyborgs.

"Where the hell is Kwon?" I roared.

"Here, sir!" he shouted, materializing out of the mists.

"Why wasn't this area cleared, First Sergeant? I ordered this entire ship secured days ago."

"The enemy must have been hiding, sir. I don't know where they came from. It's a big ship, Colonel."

"Yeah."

I took the limp Commodore Miklos to the infirmary brick. I had to remove a cyborg who was trying to break into the airlock forcibly. When I keyed in my suit number and gained entry, a bolt whizzed by my head.

"Check your fire!" I shouted. "Friendlies! Wounded!"

A terrorized nurse and doctor rushed forward, gushing apologies. They took Miklos off my hands and told me about things that had been trying to break in.

"Yeah, I noticed. I'm going back out. Keep your guns handy, but make sure you know what you're shooting at. Oh, and the Commodore is going to need a full transfusion and an organ-cleansing."

He moaned. I patted his shoulder and left.

Kwon was standing on top of the medical brick when I got outside.

"This mist is a pain," he said. "I can't see them until they are almost on top of me."

All over the encampment laser fire flashed like lightning in a thick fog.

"How many can there be?" I asked.

"Thousands? I dunno," Kwon said, firing at a crawling figure near the elevator shaft. "They're like cockroaches. Big ones. They're deadly if they get in close on a man. According to platoon chat, we've lost a marine already."

"Dammit. We can't take losses now. Not right before we engage the Imperials. Not to mention, this is cutting into Marvin's time. He needs every hour to get the ship under control."

"What are you orders, sir?" Kwon asked.

"What forces do we have available?"

"Three marine companies are stationed inside, sir."

"All right, I'm going to call up Fleet and order two more transport loads to secure the encampment, the giant control panel and the elevator shaft."

"We can do that with half the men, easy."

"Agreed. After that, my friend, we're going to take five companies and march into the guts of this ship. We're going to burn these cyborgs out, wherever they're hiding."

"A bug hunt? Now you're talking, sir!"

About an hour later I had my reinforcements. The enemy attacks had slackened, but I wasn't sure if they'd run out of troops or had simply retreated to bide their time. In either case, my answer to the problem was the same: burn them out.

Kwon and I marched behind the lead platoon of Company B. Not knowing exactly where the enemy was coming from and having a gigantic ship to search, we'd split up in to five companies. We had a lot of ground to cover and not much time to do it in.

Company B got to explore the generators—which was probably the worst assignment of the lot. The engines were smaller and although the radiation was intense back there, the marines should be able to do a full sweep before any became seriously ill. The plum job had to be the life support systems patrol. Those forward chambers were essentially huge lung-like affairs that pumped and processed the massive volume of atmosphere inside the pressurized portion of the ship.

As I moved between the massive, thrumming generators, I was further impressed by the incredible scale of the ship. It really felt like a ship when you were below decks in the guts of the thing. That's the part I had trouble comprehending. While you were on the surface, or in the elevator shaft—even when you were in the titanic central chamber—you felt like you were on a planetoid of some kind, a naturally-formed, hollowed-out rock. But that wasn't the case.

Down in the bowels of the vessel, in the middle of twisted pipes and unshielded wires the size of fire hoses carrying fantastic currents, you *knew* you were on a ship. The structure was distinctly alien, which was most notable by the sheer size of every component.

There were no decks to speak of. Instead of breaking the ship up into slices ten feet high and calling them decks, they'd bisected it. The upper half of the hollow area was Tolerance's crew quarters and living space. The bottom half was packed with equipment.

Our suit lights illuminated the immediate vicinity, but they could only go so far. Most of the chamber around us was pitch black.

Kwon was just as awed as I was. "This is really amazing, Colonel. I can't even see very far. It's like being miles under the ocean."

"I'd rather be underwater. This place is wide open and unknown."

204

We were half-walking, half-rappelling down a pipe as we talked. Ahead of us was 1st Platoon, with the rest of Company B strung out along the same pipe leading up into the darkness overhead. A combination of repellers and magnetics kept us from falling off.

Headlamps swung every which way as the men attempted to scan their environment for enemies. We walked on that way for about ten minutes with no end to the spiraling pipe in sight.

"This is ridiculous," I said, calling a halt. "We need to get a hovercraft or something. We can't see very far, and we still don't have enough manpower to cover this much territory. Let's back it up and see if we can find a better—"

I broke off then as there was some kind of commotion among the troops in 1st Platoon ahead of me. I frowned down at them.

"This isn't time to be screwing around, lieutenant. Have you made contact with the enemy?"

"I don't know, sir," she radioed back.

"What is the nature of the problem, then?"

As soon as I got those words out of my mouth, I was enlightened as to the nature of the problem. The pipe we were all standing on was…vibrating. It wasn't a violent motion—not yet. But it was definitely disconcerting. As I joined the others in trying to locate a source for the movement a very bad thing happened.

The coiling pipe came apart under our boots and fell into the darkness. Shouts rose up in my helmet, a chorus of freaked-out marines. I engaged the command override on the local channel and spoke to them all.

"Turn off your magnetics! I want every battle suit on powered flight!"

I could see they were already doing it, but some had not moved fast enough. They rode the falling pipe into the darkness. Their suit lights glimmered far away and still they fell.

"If you went down with the pipe, get back up here. Form up floating platoons as you've done in training. Don't get split up. It won't take much power to maintain flight in this low grav environment."

I switched off the override then and let the sub-commanders sort it out. Kwon was at my side a moment later, zooming up from below me. He'd been taken down with the falling pipe.

"Seems odd we have much gravity at all," he said. "This rock is small and hollow—and we're in the middle of it. Shouldn't we be free-falling?"

"It's not exactly gravity pulling us down, it's centrifugal force. The ship is under quite a bit of acceleration due to Marvin's experiments."

"But...how come we feel acceleration when we have gravity control? Isn't this whole ship about grav control?"

I wasn't in the mood for a tech-talk, so I made an exasperated sound. In truth, I didn't entirely understand the science behind gravity-control. To me, it was rather like controlling other physical forces, such as magnetism. Grav control systems worked like giant electromagnets you could switch on or off. By reversing the polarity, you could repel or attract other objects.

But when it came to the edgy parts, such as how gravity control interacted with things like inertia and friction, I was in the dark. Kwon was getting into that gray area, and at a very bad time.

"Kwon, I don't know the answer—and if I did, I doubt I could explain it to you now."

"Sorry sir. Where are we going next?"

"Now that's a reasonable question," I said. I directed my suit lights toward a polyhedron about a hundred yards off. "Let's take our unit over there and do a headcount."

The automatic systems in my command HUD tracked my troops, but didn't give their positions. I liked to see who was with me, not just who was still alive. I was relieved to see everyone was still alive and functional when we reached the polyhedron and perched on it.

As I checked on the status of the other platoons, however, I was shocked to see 4th Platoon had lost seven men. I attempted to contact the lieutenant in charge, but he wasn't answering. Even as I did this, two more dots flickered out. 4th Platoon was in trouble.

"1st Platoon, saddle up," I said. "We're going on a rescue mission."

Without waiting for a response, I launched out into space again. Somehow, flying inside *Phobos* was more disconcerting than doing so in open space. The difference was the existence of frequent dangerous obstacles. They loomed out of the dark and often had sharp edges. Some of them moved in sweeping arcs that could whack a man down like a fan blade hitting a moth. We shot down and to the right—at least that's where it felt like we were going. The men of 1st Platoon were strung out behind me like a swarm of fireflies. Their suit lights glimmered in the darkness.

We came to a broad, flat plane. On the surface of this plane a battle was raging. I watched as lasers flashed and cyborgs chased my men around like spiders catching flies.

No one in 1st Platoon needed any orders. We zoomed down, firing as we came. We landed wherever there was room to put two feet together and joined the melee. The dance floor was soon crowded with struggling forms.

It was the kind of battle the cyborgs dreamed of. We couldn't hold them at range, and we couldn't bring the full weight of our numbers against them. Many men dropped their lasers and drew combat blades right off. Limbs—both human and cyborg, drifted over our helmets.

But the weight of our armor and weapons prevailed. From above us, the other platoons added more personnel until the cyborgs were overwhelmed. Having lost my knife in the chest of one that I'd tossed over the side into the abyss, I began grabbing them and pulling legs off them.

When it was over, Kwon came to me and clapped me on the back. "That was great, sir. Almost as good as fighting Macros. I loved the way you tore pieces off them and tossed them around. You looked like an angry man who hates crabs or something."

I picked up a black, spiny, cyborg limb and examined it. "I do hate these things. They're evil. They're part human—you knew that, right?"

"I disagree," he said, shaking his head. "These things aren't human at all. Just because there is some human meat in there,

207

that doesn't count. That's like calling a man-eating tiger part human because he has someone's ear in his belly."

I decided not to argue with Kwon's logic. I tossed the cyborg arm out into space and did a headcount. Not bad, really. We'd only lost nine men in the entire company, and eight of those had been Centaurs.

"Okay," I said, "has anyone located the source of these attackers? They have to come from somewhere, and I'm willing to bet we're close to their nest."

"I think you're right, Colonel," said a young Centaur lieutenant. "I think they came up out of these holes."

I headed over to the hole he'd indicated and looked inside. I was reminded of a dirty drainpipe from any Earth city back home. "Any volunteers to scout this tunnel?"

Right away, a half dozen centaur troops jostled forward to volunteer. Not a single human did the same. I clapped a young buck on the shoulder and pointed the way. He disappeared a moment later into the dark. I watched as his suit lights dwindled then vanished as he turned a corner.

Originally, the Centaurs had been highly claustrophobic. Marvin with his genetic brain-tinkering had changed all that. He'd been able to give me Centaurs who feared practically nothing—other than dying dishonorably.

"Have we got a nanite line on him?" I asked.

"Yes sir."

I felt bad sometimes about the way I valued a human life more than I did that of a Centaur's. I figured it was a natural human tendency. Not only were humans my own kind, there was also the fact we were relatively rare in the Eden system. People tended to value anything that was rare—just because it *was* rare. I'd be willing to bet if there were only a hundred houseflies left alive on Earth, people would be holding candlelight vigils to save them.

The Centaurs were anything but rare. They were loyal and helpful, but they bred fast and threw their lives away at the slightest provocation. One of the quickest and most honorable ways they'd figured out to do this was to join Star Force and get themselves killed under my command.

"How's he doing, sir?" Kwon asked.

"He's still breathing," I said, checking the readings coming back on the nanite wire.

Not ten seconds after I said that, the readings changed.

"Uh-oh," Kwon said, looking over my shoulder. "Looks like he got nailed."

I turned to him and smiled. "You want to go save him?"

He looked at the pipe dubiously. "I don't know if I will fit, sir."

I gauged Kwon and the pipe, and I had to admit he had a point. I grumbled privately inside my helmet. I didn't want to send a platoon down there into the dark. It could easily be a one-way trip for the lot of them.

"How far down was that? When we lost the signal?"

"At least fifty yards. Maybe twice that. The nanites aren't answering, the line has been severed."

I could see our end of the nanite wire. It was about as thick as a pencil, and resembled a line of mercury. The odd thing about these wires was the way they wriggled and moved on their own. For all intents and purposes, they behaved like long living snakes of metal.

From years of experience, I could tell this wire had just been cut.

Cursing, I vaulted over the side of the platform. I clamped my boots onto what looked like a pipe down there. I was under the metal shelf we'd been fighting on, and it was cramped, but I managed to hang on. I got out my laser projector and burned a hole into the pipe with a single controlled burst.

"You see light in there?"

"Yes sir! That's the one!"

Clanking farther down the pipe, I began to follow it. The rest of the platoon followed me, and the company after that. I hadn't ordered them to do so, but it made good sense so I didn't argue.

We made it down about a hundred yards. A portable sensor unit was giving off a beep, indicating some part of our marine's equipment was nearby. I got out my projector again and did a little custom surgery on an exchange of pipes that came together.

As best I could figure out, we were messing with the atmospheric systems. Probably, the ventilation pipes. This big ship had a lot of them, and since the Blues were gaseous they took these things very seriously.

I no sooner had a circular hole burned than a cyborg arm shot out and clamped itself onto my boot.

"Pay dirt!" I shouted. "Block the rest of these pipes. I want them trapped."

All around me, the rest of the marines began blazing with their lasers. When they'd melted shut the pipes leading to the exchange, we cut our way inside.

We found them in there. A nest of over a hundred cyborgs. They were thick, like a pool full of thrashing fish. In their midst was the torn-apart remains of the Centaur I'd sent down to them on a suicidal scouting mission. There were only scraps of him left.

The cyborgs never had a chance. We killed them all.

-23-

The following few days were relatively uneventful. Marvin's control over the ship improved every hour. By the third day after the cyborg attack, he could hit moving targets with the gravity-weapon and we were gliding on course toward the ring.

It was the last ring. The ring that led to Sol.

Just thinking about that gave me a little thrill inside. Really, no one who hasn't left Earth behind for years can appreciate how homesick space can make you. It's worse than solitary confinement, in a way. Out in space, everything is slightly wrong. There are plenty of odors, but they all stink—and even the stink has a undefinable *wrongness* to it. There are no fresh breezes as good as a mountain pine scent, or a beach wind. The skies, even if they are blue, aren't the right shade of blue. And no planet seems to tug with a gravity that matches what you know in your bones to be right.

I met with my officers and planned the final assault as best we could. The core members included were Captain Sarin and Commodore Miklos, who had recovered completely from cyborg venom. Gaines was there too, representing the marines. Marvin was too busy flying the ship, and I knew Kwon would be out of his depth, so I left them at their stations.

"So," I said, smiling at each of them in turn, "before we begin, are there any updates you'd like to give me? What reports do we have of Imperial activity?"

"Very little since the cyborgs made their move, sir," Miklos said. "Actually, they are being rather quiet. It surprises me. I'd expected them to challenge us by now. I'd imagined Crow or one of his lackeys would transmit a dire warning, telling us we were moving into their space and that proceeding would amount to a declaration of war.

I chuckled. "That does sound like Crow's style. Why hasn't he done it?"

"Maybe they don't even realize we're here," Jasmine said.

"No, I don't believe that. We're being watched. The Imperials laid these cyborg eggs out here to stop invaders. They must have probes beaming back reports. But still, they haven't challenged us. They haven't flown a single ship out here to do so much as flip us the bird."

"Maybe he's hoping we'll go away," Major Gaines suggested. "This is technically neutral territory."

I pointed a finger at him, and shushed the others.

"That's it," I said. "Gaines nailed it. They're hoping we're fighting with this big ship and that we're self-absorbed. Why mess with us if we aren't messing with them? They're weak, and rebuilding as fast as they can. They got a good look at our fleet strength and decided to take a pass. Alpha Centauri is no-man's land. At this point, we could turn around and fly home and no one would say a word about it."

I looked at the group, taking their measure. A few, in particular Miklos, seemed to think that retreating might be a pretty good idea.

I shook my head slowly. "That's not going to happen. We're here, and we have the best relative advantage we're ever going to get. We're pressing the attack."

After that announcement, the planning began in earnest. Not even Miklos mentioned calling the whole thing off. As much as he didn't like the thought of losing ships, I believe he'd been traumatized by the cyborgs. They made it clear Earth was not helpless, that they were still gearing up for war. Who else could they fight, other than Star Force? On the chain of star systems, we were between them and the rest of the universe.

"Let's do this by the book, sir," Miklos said. I thought there might be a hint of pleading in his voice, but I wasn't sure.

"Lay out your plans, Commodore."

The table lit up under our elbows.

"As you can see, we are here, about sixty hours out from the last ring. We can't increase our velocity because this monstrous ship only goes so fast. If the ring was closer to the central star—well anyway, we have sixty hours to go. I recommend the standard missile barrage be fired through the ring right before we arrive. Then, we can at least be certain there will be no mines to encounter when we first break our way into the Solar System."

Everyone glanced at me, checking my reaction. I nodded and said nothing.

"I think we want *Phobos* to go through the ring first, followed by the rest of the fleet."

I watched expectantly, but Miklos shrugged.

"That's about it," he said. "Really, we can't plan a battle with an enemy force we have yet to lay eyes on. We could place a thousand ships there and do a pretend battle with them, but in reality I have no idea as to their numbers or fleet configuration."

"So you just want to wing it?" I asked.

"I thought that might please you, Colonel."

It didn't please me, and it wasn't like Miklos. I wondered if something was up. He always had elaborate plans. I frowned at the screens and slowly nodded. I thought I had his angle: he had a plan, but he wasn't going to show it to me yet. If he showed me his plan now and asked for approval, I could say no. But in the heat of battle, he could present it, and I might well go forward with it without editing.

"All right," I said, "I'm not giving you an A for effort, but I'm in agreement with what you've presented so far. Now, let's go over our ship strength for the battle—presuming there is one. How do we defend *Phobos*?"

They all looked at me in surprise.

"Defend *Phobos*?" asked Miklos as if he had perhaps not heard me correctly. "I was not under the impression this ship needed a special defensive arrangement. We already have a battalion strength marine unit stationed here, and about a hundred laser turrets on the hull. Not to mention miles of rock for a hull."

The others chuckled, but I didn't.

"Let's assume they have more cyborgs—lots more. They got down to the surface before, and they will do it again. When they come here in strength, they'll take the delicate machinery on the nose area apart, disabling the gravity weapon again. A few thousand of them could overwhelm my marine contingent and disable the entire ship."

"Sir," Miklos said, squirming. "I don't know what you want us to do. We can't bring our own ships in close to provide cover. If we do, they will be damaged by the defensive gravity-field if it was fired, which renders it useless. If they stay out of range, they can't shoot down incoming invaders."

"I'm not suggesting we encircle *Phobos* with ships. I'm suggesting we place more marines here. And more turrets."

There was some grumbling at that. Gaines finally spoke up.

"My forces are in space for a reason, sir," he said. "A major element of our offensive force has been the ship-assaulting marine. Every transport has specialists aboard for this purpose. We can—"

"How many?" I asked.

"Excuse me, Colonel?"

"How many of your marines are trained for attacking ships?"

"Well…all of them, actually. But about two thousand of them specialize in such tactics."

"Centaurs, mostly?"

"Yes sir. With human officers leading the units in most cases. We've found the Centaurs tend to get excited and charge enemy ships if they are led by Centaur officers."

"Right," I said, thinking of several suicidal charges I'd witnessed in the past. "Okay. We'll leave forty percent of our ground forces in space, spread out among the carriers, transports and cruisers. That way they can launch a spaceborne attack from many platforms if they're needed. But I want most of your ground-pounders on *Phobos*. I don't want to chance losing the ship."

214

There was quite a bit of complaining after that. I didn't really listen. I signaled Jasmine, and she deftly rearranged the positioning of the ground forces on the map. They were mostly inside *Phobos'* belly before she was done.

"I'm not sure why you want to commit so much of our ground forces to *Phobos*, Colonel," Miklos complained.

His fingers worked, and he kept frowning at Captain Sarin. I could tell he wanted to move the ground forces back onto his ships.

"Because it's the key to our attack. If Earth has serious defenses—and we would be fools to assume otherwise—*Phobos* is the one weapon they can't handle. The ship outranges them with a weapon they probably don't understand. Even more importantly, it's terrifying to behold."

They looked at me with eyebrows riding high. No one seemed to get the significance of what I'd said.

"Look," I said, "we're talking about invading and conquering a world. We have to look scary to do that. If we want Earth to surrender, if we want the local national governments to pull their support from the Imperials, they have to be afraid of us. They have to fear us more than they fear Crow."

"Why can't they like us more than they like Crow?" asked Jasmine. "Aren't we here to liberate them? To free Earth?"

Major Gaines jumped in before I could answer. "The Colonel is right," he said. "I've dealt with people in such situations. They will be shocked, and fear will be their first response. That's just where we want them. We want them uncertain. We want them to hesitate, to hold back."

"Just one more question, Colonel," Miklos said.

I waved for him to talk and get it over with.

"If this ship, *Phobos*, is so key to our victory, what were you planning to do at this point before the Blues built it?"

He had me there. I looked around, and they all knew it. I shrugged.

"I would have thought of something," I assured them.

There was some further argument, but not much. Jasmine's redistribution of the ground forces stuck. Within hours, troops began flowing down onto *Phobos* in great numbers.

The huge ship's outer hull now bristled with weapons and equipment. We were dependent on the Blue's gravity drive to fly it, but even without their primary weapon it was a powerful addition to the fleet.

We had loads of ideas on how to improve it as well. One obvious one was to drill another, broader shaft all the way to the central chamber from the surface. This shaft would function as a launch tube. Miklos' eyes lit up at the idea of storing thousands of fighters and dozens of landing craft within the protective shell of the ship.

But we didn't have time for that much drilling.

"The enemy has already seen this ship and scouted it with cyborgs," I told them on the last day, the final twenty hours before we hit the ring to Sol. "We have to assume they have a good idea of what's inside the ship, and how it operates. The time to strike is now, before they can adapt their defenses to the new threat."

On this point, I had agreement. Not everyone liked it, because they all had their pet ideas on building up for the battle, but they could not argue with the idea that the enemy was out there, building up just as furiously as we were.

I now operated out of *Phobos* myself. We had constructed an excellent command center near the original control systems, and we had gained at least partial control over the weapons. We could fire the big area-effect weapon to knock out missiles and the like without a problem. The long-range weapon, however, hadn't been perfected yet. We'd imploded a number of dummy targets and passing asteroids to experiment. At ranges over a million miles, we usually missed. I suspected that our control system wasn't as perfectly sensitive as the analog one that Tolerance used. That dead cloud's dexterity had been amazingly precise.

The more we learned about the interface, the more I was impressed by it. Most of the push buttons were in fact sensory-feedback. By nudging themselves slightly in various patterns, the hundreds of buttons formed a collective image of the universe outside. They gave anyone touching all of them and sensing their fractional shifts a view of the surrounding space, displaying for a creature like Tolerance information concerning

216

targets and ranges. Fortunately, we didn't have to work with that part of their technology. Just aiming the ship and the primary cannon around was enough, using our own sensor technology.

"Have we got a full charge, Marvin?" I asked, coming on duty after a full set of tests were completed.

"Yes, but my control is still lacking in refinement for long range targets. I can't hit a ship the size of a fighter—and missiles are still out of the question."

"That's all right," I said. "We'll reserve your hammer for the biggest targets. In fact, that's what I think we'll call it—the hammer."

"Dramatic, sir."

"Thanks, I like it too."

I stood on the open deck of *Phobos* beneath a tangle of tentacle-like nanite arms that interacted with the original control boards. We'd move equipment from the fleet to set up the new command center here. I would have liked to have compartmentalized the interior of the huge ship into smaller zones and maybe even pressurize them with bulkheads, but there simply wasn't enough time.

Miklos came to me about seven hours before we hit Sol with a new idea shining in his eyes.

"What have you got, Nicolai? Have the Imperials said anything yet?"

"Still silent, sir. But I do have a possible solution for our decompression problems."

"Let's hear it."

What we'd been worried most about was the possible catastrophic depressurization of the central chamber. It was so large that a big enough hole into space would suck out our crewmen and possibly even our control systems.

"We'll put up smart metal bubbles, sir. Here, and over the encampment that encircles the exit."

We'd set up a shanty town of bricks from the troop ships all around the single shaft to the outer hull. Much of my marine ground force was stationed there, ready to sally out and do battle on the surface or in space itself.

217

"Hmm," I said, looking around. "We won't be able to see much of the interior if we do that. The bubble will be opaque."

We'd managed by this time to pump all of the noxious, corrosive mists out of the central chamber and fill it with breathable air. But it was thin air, and not recommended for human consumption yet. We only had so many gas production units.

"I have a solution for that, too," Miklos said proudly.

I followed him to where he'd begun work on his smart metal dome. In the middle of it was a command table. Marvin followed us out of curiosity.

The table was exposed to the interior of the big ship. It was strange, being in an open space this big. It was like being on a planet—but you could tell you were enclosed. I felt like a mouse on the concrete floor of an empty warehouse.

Miklos had surrounded the command table with what looked like a slurry of melted solder mixed in with hexagonal panes of ballistic glass. As I watched, he tapped a sensitive part on the writhing mess of nanites. They instantly reacted, popping up like one of those dome tents that always gave me fiberglass splinters on camping trips. As they wriggled and unmelted upward, forming walls around us, I was reminded of watching a metal candle melt in reverse. It was impressive.

"Not bad," I said, walking around the structure and looking in through the foot-wide windows.

"This is a small mock-up, of course. We'd have to build larger panes. A full control room would require a hundred barrels or so of nanites."

I made a pained sound. "That's a lot of production, Commodore."

"Come on inside, Colonel."

I looked, and there was a hatch-like door. It wasn't too sturdy. Once we were in there, it felt like you could pop the whole thing with a sharp stick.

"I assume you've done the math on this?" I asked. "It will hold up under depressurization?"

"I helped in that area," Marvin said suddenly, appearing at the entrance. He squeezed inside, making it uncomfortably close.

"Ah-ha," I said. "So, you are in on this too, Marvin? I should have known. Let me guess: you became bored with figuring out how to fine tune the weapons and drive systems."

"The essentials of the alien interface are all documented, Colonel. We already have brainboxes that are as good at operating them as I could be."

"Uh-huh. I don't believe that for a moment. You got bored. But, I'm still liking this. If you're telling me we can use it to enclose a bridge area, I'm willing to go with it. There is a makeshift feel to it all, but I didn't give you much time to come with something solid. Hell, I didn't authorize this project at all."

Miklos cleared his throat and Marvin floated cameras around both of us.

"Sir? Do we have your approval to go forward with this project?"

"You were planning on doing something similar for the brick village near the shaft to the surface, right?"

"Yes, but that would take more time and nanites."

I nodded. "Forget it then. Just build this one small dome for a bridge. Can you get the dome up and safe before we hit the ring?"

"Yes," Marvin said, answering for him. "Absolutely."

"Then you two are on a mission. Do it."

You would have thought I'd given two kids the keys to the candy store. They were both out of there and trotting toward the nanite supplies less than a minute after I gave them the okay.

I walked out of the dome, touched it in a sensitive spot, and watched as it collapsed. I thought to myself that I'd have to make sure the thing could identify Star Force personnel when it took commands. It wouldn't do to have an invading enemy drop our tent on our heads.

-24-

It was just as we made our final approach to the Sol ring that the Imperials finally spoke up.

"There's a single ship at the ring, sir," Sarin told me.

I dropped what I was doing and rushed to the new command center. All around me, others did the same.

"Put up the dome, Commodore!" I shouted.

The newly completed pressure-dome inflated itself from all around us. The nanites had been trained to grow from a foot-high mess on the floor, picking up dozens of large hexagonal windows along the way, and rising up to contact one another at the distant top. There was a hole in the roof for a few seconds, like the smoke hole in a wigwam, until it closed itself and vanished.

Instantly, the sound changed in the chamber. I could tell I was inside an enclosed space. There was something about that I liked, even if the enclosure was relatively flimsy.

"The Imperials are requesting that we open a channel with them."

"Open channel!"

On our holotank, a recording began to play. It started with the Imperial anthem which consisted of pompous, martial-sounding music.

What followed was a series of images. First, there was the stylized metal eagle, the familiar emblem of the Empire. That rolled away and Crow appeared dressed in a white uniform covered in ribbons, medals and insignia. He was holding the hands of two children, and appeared to be talking to them calmingly.

While we watched this, I began to frown and my arms crossed. I could only take so much bullshit, and I was getting past my limit already. I was concerned as they hadn't even said anything yet.

"Approaching transients," came the message at last, but it wasn't Crow saying it. He was on the screen, his voice muted. We got to watch as he handed out small gifts to the children, who appeared to be delighted. "You are about to enter Imperial space. Do not attempt to fly through the ring! If you do, your ships will be destroyed. Long live the Emperor."

The image faded. I shook my head.

"That's it?" I demanded. "They aren't even going to attempt to talk to us personally? How bureaucratic can you get? That looks like a canned message they put out years ago."

"It is heartening," Jasmine said. "Maybe they aren't ready for us. Maybe the crews on the border have not even dared to tell Crow what's coming."

Miklos nodded, looking at her. "That's an interesting possibility," he said. "Dictators are often out of touch when they run a campaign of terror. They are often taken by surprise when the day of their undoing comes."

"Well, we can hope for that," I said, "but we can't count on it. 'Approaching transients.' Huh, they make it sound like we're a pack of space-bums wandering the cosmos out here. Jasmine, send a channel request to the ship at the ring."

She tapped at the screens and I watched the vessel. It was a sleek battleship of the sort General Kerr had flown into our space with some months ago. Events chaining from his visit had led us to the brink of war, and seeing that ship made me think of Kerr and his assassins.

"Channel request refused, sir," she said after a moment.

"Keep trying."

"I've tried several times. They just disconnect."

"Fine," I said, "maybe we should stop talking and fire a barrage of missiles."

A hand touched my elbow. I looked down at it, frowning.

221

"Uh, sir," Miklos said, "we could just broadcast on the open air. I'm sure they're listening."

I frowned at him. I could tell he still entertained fantasies of avoiding fleet losses today. I wasn't seeing things in the same rosy light.

"All right," I said, relenting. "We can try that. Open transmission, Captain Sarin."

"Broadcasting."

"Imperial slave troops," I said loudly. All around me, people winced—and I didn't care. "This is Colonel Kyle Riggs of Star Force. You're about to be liberated...forcibly. If you value your lives and those of your families, surrender your ship now. We do not wish to cause any biotic creature harm. If you do not fire on us, you will not be fired upon. If you wish to join us, indicate your intent with a transmission and join our armada. Any other action will result in death for all hands. Do not doubt our technology or our resolve. You have three minutes to reply. End transmission."

Everyone was staring at me. I didn't look back. I stared instead at the holotank, watching carefully to see what they would do.

"That sounded like an ultimatum, Colonel," Jasmine said.

I looked at her. "Exactly."

We waited for three tense minutes. They passed and the Imperial ship just sat there.

"Maybe they're arguing about it," Captain Sarin said hopefully.

"For all we know there's a coup going on aboard the ship right now. They must be able to scan us—to see the size of this monster headed their way. If they have orders to stand and fight...well, that would be a hard command for any captain to follow."

"Are we in weapons range yet?"

"Hardly sir, look at the boards."

I did, but then I looked at Marvin. He had his own board which controlled the alien weaponry remotely. "Marvin, have you got enough of a handle on that thing to reach out and smash their engines the way Tolerance did?"

"No sir. Not yet."

"Could you try?"

"We're at more than twice the effective range achieved in my prior tests."

"There's always a lucky hit."

"Sir?" Sarin asked. "Maybe we should give them more time."

"We're in sudden-death overtime right now," I said. "Besides, I'm not going to fire if they just stand there. I told them we wouldn't."

"Dangerous, Colonel," Miklos said. "Maybe they've decided to call your bluff, and they'll wait until we are very close before firing."

I shrugged. "There are plenty of ways to commit suicide. If they want to invent a new one, more power to them."

The others exchanged nervous glances. I knew they had been worried about this moment. They'd all privately speculated as to whether or not I could be objective when facing armed Imperials. They should have known me better. These weren't the men who had ordered an assassin to kill Sandra. The only blood I wanted on my hands was still in Crow's veins.

They stood there for a full nine minutes before showing any signs of life. Then, at that point, they turned tail and headed back toward the ring.

My officers all speculated as to their intentions. Maybe they'd been told to run if they had to. Maybe they'd been told to fight to the last. Or maybe, just maybe, a drama had played out aboard their ship and the loyalists had won.

I raised my hands when the Imperial ship was about one minute from the ring.

"Range? Marvin?"

"They are at the very edge of my effective range."

"Are you tracking them?"

"Yes sir."

The rest looked at me. They'd assumed we were going to let them go.

"Are you ready to start the biggest civil war in history, Colonel?" Miklos asked me.

"Yeah," I said, nodding. "That's what we came for, isn't it? They took the time I offered them and more. They think they're out of reach, but they're in for a surprise. Marvin, target their engines."

"That isn't—"

"Just do it, Marvin. I will forgive you if you miss."

"Target already locked in and tracking. Ready, Colonel."

"We should fire now, if we are going to do it," Miklos said. "That way we will have plenty of time to recharge the primary weapon before we reach the ring."

"They don't know they're in our range," Jasmine said. "We can't be sure of their intentions. They didn't fire on us yet."

I glanced at her. Her face was worried. I could tell she didn't want to destroy an Earth ship. I understood that. It had taken a long while for me to get to this point. But now, I was committed. Sometimes, in the name of freedom, bad things happened.

"Fire, Marvin."

The floor quivered under us. It was an odd sensation. I've felt the recoil of countless weapons, and even lasers gave you a kick when they were big enough.

But the gravity weapon was different. Instead of reacting to displaced mass or to a release of energy, it caused a ripple effect. This made everyone aboard feel as if their weight had shifted minutely. As if you weighed a few pounds more on your left side, then on your right. Then you weighed a few pounds less in a similar rippling sensation a fraction of a second later. It was not painful, but it was disturbing.

Our smart clothes writhed on our bodies and the dome overhead ruffled a fraction. I glanced up at it, but it didn't come falling down on our heads.

"Optics?"

"Still waiting, sir. She's about twenty light-seconds away—"

Just as those words were spoken, the display flickered on the screen. The big ship bucked, as if punched in the belly. The middle of the ship was...gone. A plume of gas, flame and debris billowed out.

224

Everyone gasped. The ship went into a slow spin. The engines flared for another few seconds, then went out. But it was enough to change their vector.

"Looks like you missed the engines, Marvin," I said.

"Yes sir. But only by a few hundred meters."

I nodded. He was right. It was a good shot.

We watched as the big ship died. It tumbled and spun— right into the ring itself.

I'd never seen a ship hit the ring before. The resulting explosion was tremendous. That much mass, moving that fast, released a fantastic amount of energy.

"It's on now, Colonel," said Gaines, walking into the tent and surveying the images Marvin was helpfully replaying in slow motion.

I nodded to Gaines. "Yes, Major. It is."

"It looks to me like they're going to fight, sir," Miklos said.

I glanced at him and nodded. "If you call that fighting. We sank their battleship in one shot. They never even got within range. Let's hope the entire war goes so well."

Jasmine seemed distraught. I think the reality of what we were doing was finally sinking in for her. It was one thing to fight aliens out on the frontier, or to occasionally be faced with an Earth ship that appeared to have gone rogue, but now the truth was undeniable. We were about to go to war with our own homeworld. It was easy to see how some would misunderstand the situation and see us as the bad guys.

"So many will die," she said, watching the last bits of the Imperial ship disintegrate. As far as we could tell, there had not been a single survivor. "So many ships will be destroyed…"

I tossed her a glance that said "shut up". She seemed to get it, because she stopped talking.

"I'm going to do a live broadcast now," I told them. "I want to talk to the entire task force."

They all looked at me, some of them nervously. A lot of them didn't like it when I went public. They found my announcements too rough around the edges. I didn't give a crap about their opinions.

I straightened my spine and signaled the one minute warning. Every Star Force helmet for a thousand miles or more

225

around buzzed, letting them know an important announcement was incoming.

When the system engaged, I took a deep breath and started talking. The key to doing these things right, in my opinion, was to have absolute self-confidence. Lacking that—you faked it.

"This is Colonel Kyle Riggs," I began. "The rightful commander of all Star Force. Today, as many of you are aware, we came in contact with an Imperial warship. They ordered us to turn back, and we refused. We then offered them the opportunity to stand down. They did not take that opportunity, and thus became enemy combatants. In order to keep them from rejoining their forces and having to do battle with them later, we were forced to destroy their vessel."

I paused to check the screens. The timers were running, showing me we had five minutes and ten seconds to go before *Phobos* went through the ring. Everything was automated at this point. Unless there was a surprise in store, the brainboxes were running the show until we entered the Solar System.

"There's going to be a lot of sacrifice on both sides in the coming days," I continued. "But I don't want any of you to doubt our cause. There are millions—no *billions* of our fellow human beings on Earth who will be freed if we succeed. I hope, as I know all of you do, that the Imperial forces will see the futility of their cause and abandon their dictator, Jack Crow. But regardless of what they do, we *will* achieve victory. We didn't start this war, but we're by-God going to finish it!"

There was some cheering now; I could hear it in the distance even through the nanite tent Miklos had put up over our heads. The Fleet officers around me were mostly looking pale and worried, but at least I knew my marines were fired up and ready to fight.

The clock hit four minutes then, and our lead missile barrage began firing by itself. A hundred and fifty nuclear warheads sped toward the ring. I hoped the Imperials on the far side were bright enough to get out of the way—but it was a faint hope.

"To everyone: fight well and good luck. Colonel Riggs out."

"Do I have your permission to stand with my men, sir?" Major Gaines asked.

I nodded to him. "Get going."

He raced out and vanished.

We watched the screens. A full squadron of fighters followed the missiles. The real job of the missiles was to clear out mines and any other physical impediments to our flight. The fighters were guinea pigs—or as we liked to call it, a "reconnaissance in force". They would go through and have the first look around, then report back.

Phobos itself was slowing. After all, we didn't really know what was on the far side. I didn't want to go through blind. But I didn't want to look scared, either. It would sap a lot of this big ship's mojo if at their first sight of her she was timid and crawling along.

"Have we got crash harnesses?"

"Yes sir."

"Deploy them. Helmets on for the transition."

Everyone fooled with their equipment for a moment. The fighters went through as we watched, vanishing into nothingness. There was no fancy flare of light as they did so. One second they were there, the next they were just gone. It was as if they'd stepped into a mirror and disappeared into it.

"Anything yet?" I asked, meaning the fighters.

"Nothing sir, they haven't had time to turn around."

They couldn't report back via ring transmissions because both the Imperials and we were jamming the ring. Both sides were better at that now, sending a wave of varied static at a dozen different modulations and frequencies that prevented anyone from using the rings in a stealthy manner.

Part of me wished I was with the boys in those fighters. It would be fun to be the first Star Force pilot to return to our home system. I envied them. They knew they were home again, and that the other side was terrified of them.

I smiled as I dreamed briefly of glory. But this smile faded slowly. The timer showed there were just ninety-six seconds to go.

"They should be back by now. Where are they?"

"Unknown sir."

227

"None of them returned?"

"Negative."

My finger stabbed down onto the big screen. I engaged the fleet-wide com system again.

"I want everyone on the surface of *Phobos* to get below. I repeat: everyone. All following ships, divert your courses to the sides. No one is to follow *Phobos* until we report back what we've encountered. Riggs out."

The effects were gratifying. The ships trailing us began braking, veering. They were going to make it. I could tell.

"Sir?" Jasmine asked me. "What are you thinking? What's wrong?"

"I don't know," I said. "There are a dozen things that could be wrong—very wrong."

I hadn't actually wanted to voice my worries, but Miklos jumped right in at this point and began listing them.

"They might have so many mines or guns that they obliterated our fighters instantly. Or something else could be there that our missiles could not clear out of the way. Our plans have been numerous in ring defense, but we never employed most of them. There are an infinite variety of traps. For example, we considered spreading a mass of sand particles in front of the ring. Such a barrier is difficult to destroy or disperse, and is immune to EMP blasts."

I looked at him sidelong, but he didn't seem to catch my meaning. We were down to less than a minute now.

Miklos threw up his hands and folded his lips into a speculative, euro-looking expression.

"It could even be worse than that," he continued, really getting into the subject. "What if the Imperials have figured out how to control the rings as we have begun experimenting with ourselves? Those fighters might have all flown into the sun, or perhaps the ring only works in one direction now, like—"

"Okay Professor," I said loudly, clapping him on the shoulder so hard he grunted. "Let's man our stations and look sharp. This is it. After all, General Kerr had the balls to come through our ring into our system a few months ago. We're just returning the favor."

Miklos shut up at last. The final seconds crawled by.

228

When the moment came I felt a shiver run through the ship and my own body, telling me we'd made the transition to the other side.

But what was there waiting for us?

-25-

"Surface impacts, sir! Too many to count!"

We'd shuddered while passing through the ring, and now we were *still* shuddering. I felt the entire ship being battered. But how?

Then the big screens went dark. I thought for a second it was a power outage, but then realized the circular shape of *Phobos'* hull was still on the display. Internal readings were fine. But we couldn't see anything outside the ship.

"Report!" I shouted. "Where's my sensory data? What hit us?"

"The sensors were knocked out the moment we came through the ring," Jasmine said. "We're flying blind."

"Hull breach?"

"Negative, sir. But we've lost contact with all our surface personnel and defensive systems."

"I ordered those people to go below."

She gave me a helpless shrug. "They only had ninety seconds to comply, and one elevator shaft, Colonel."

I realized what she was saying. There was no way they could all have escaped.

"Assume we lost them all. Give me a headcount."

She tapped for a few seconds and sent her data to the screens. One hundred seventy one, the counter said. I could have had her add in the fighter squadron, but didn't bother. The data was already depressing. After destroying their battleship, we were in fact about even. Unfortunately, Crow had a few billion more people to lose than I did.

I took a deep breath. "Marvin!" I shouted.

His tentacles jumped. He was manning the control systems that hooked up to the big push-button interfaces on the forward wall of this massive chamber.

"Yes, Colonel?"

"Get your alien sensors working. Tell me what the hell happened out there!"

"At least we know we aren't ramming the sun," Miklos said unhelpfully.

I turned to him. "You're working with Marvin. Come back here in one minute with some damned data."

He moved quickly to his new assignment.

"Should we slow down the ship, sir?" Jasmine asked me.

I felt like chewing my lip, but managed to stop myself. I *wanted* to stop. I wanted to turn around and run screaming back to Alpha Centauri. I had no idea what was going on and the screen was still black. It was like driving through a tunnel at midnight with broken headlights—while doing about a million miles an hour.

It was time to think fast, so I started doing it. My thoughts came out of my mouth the moment they occurred to me.

"If they could redirect the ring, they would have put us right into the sun or some other hard obstacle. We have to assume it was Miklos' sand—something like that."

"But that might not be their entire defense."

"Of course it isn't. What would I place behind an obstacle like that?" I thought for a second. "Ships with heavy guns— maybe more of those cyborgs... Captain, are the impacts still incoming on the outer hull?"

"Negative, sir. All quiet for now."

Jasmine looked at me, and I looked back at her. Then I turned to Marvin, who was really flying this ship.

"Floor it, Marvin," I told him. "Take a hard turn in any direction that helps you get some traction with the gravity drive. Apply maximum speed."

"Engaging drive, Colonel. Data will be coming through soon. The Blues do not have a fast update time on their sensors, and the data is subject to interpretation. I spent all my time studying drive and weapons controls."

"Yeah, yeah," I said, "just relay what you have to my screens as you get it."

Jasmine caught my eye again and leaned toward me, lowering her voice. "When in doubt, do the unexpected? Is that your plan, Kyle?"

I smiled at her. She rarely called me Kyle in public, even more rarely in battle.

"Almost always," I told her with confidence I didn't feel.

I didn't add that firm action was often better than doing nothing. Doing nothing was predictable, and made it easier for your enemy to get off a headshot while you dithered. That was what I figured was happening right now. They'd blinded us, and were maneuvering for the *coup de grâce*. I could feel them out there, closing in.

The deck lurched and the nanite arms sprouting up from the floors gripped us. We were all slipping to the left with about half a G of lateral force. I didn't know where Marvin was heading, and I didn't much care. As long as we were going there fast.

Data finally began coming in. I watched in frustration as the screens crawled. A wire-diagram began to appear.

"What the hell is that?"

"I think it's the ring sir."

"Oh yeah. It's been a long time since I've seen graphics this shitty."

"I could delay the input until it has gone through interpolation algorithms," Marvin said.

"No way. Keep up the raw feed."

The picture kept redrawing itself. There was something big dead ahead of us. Perspectives shifted, and I realized on the new scale *Phobos* was a tiny spec.

"What the hell? What's that thing we're heading toward, Marvin?"

"I do believe its Sol, Colonel. The mass is appropriate. That appears to be the gravity source I've utilized to engage the drive."

232

"Right," I said, thinking hard. "Not much else out here with a strong gravity pull."

If we were in the Solar System, which I had every reason to believe was the case, we were far out past Pluto. The two rings in Earth's star system were farther apart than most. One was on Venus, embedded in the surface of the planet. The second was out here in the Oort Cloud.

"Get a mass reading, Marvin. Is that Sol? Is the distance right?"

"It appears to be, sir. The probability is greater than ninety-nine percent."

I felt somewhat relieved. Some of the worst scenarios were off the list.

As I watched more data crawl onto the screen, I lost patience.

"This sucks," I announced. "Get me Gaines."

Less than five seconds later, Major Gaines was on the line. I had to admit, even if he was a mean drunk, he was on the ball when everything hit the fan.

"Gaines? I need you, personally, to take a company to the surface and deploy sensory equipment. Both passive and active. Go."

"Acknowledged, Gaines out."

I went back to the boards. We'd zoomed in again, which removed Sol from the picture. We were flying away from the ring, and the ring—well, it looked funny.

"What the hell is with the ring?" I demanded. "It looks like it's grown a beard or something. Is that bullshit real, Marvin?"

"Assuming you're referring to the anomalous structures attached to the exterior rim of the ring—yes Colonel, that bullshit is physically present."

"Well? What the hell is it?"

"Unknown, sir."

Gaines worked fast. There were existing nanite leads to the surface that led all the way down to our position here. He hooked up his suit cameras the minute he got to the top and relayed the feed to us.

"Nothing here, sir," he said, looking around.

233

I put the camera feed from his suit onto the tabletop and it whirled with sickening speed. We all watched, glued to our spots.

"Nothing? What about the surface itself?"

He'd been panning space nearby, where no ships or incoming fire seemed to be evident. Now he lowered the view to the ground, where it was a different story.

I frowned at what appeared to be black furrows burned in broad lines across the surface of *Phobos*. The lines crisscrossed it, and each line was as wide as an L. A. freeway.

"What the hell are those?"

"Cratering sir—from whatever hit us. These lines extend as far as we can see in every direction. The entire surface looks like a waffle pattern."

I quickly put two and two together. "Do those look like laser burns to you, Gaines? Like something a really *big* laser would leave behind, doing long burns?"

"Yeah..." he said, panning around. "Yeah, that could be it."

Marvin suddenly loomed over me. I knew because there was a camera over each of my shoulders and one snaking between my legs.

"Getting a good look, Marvin?"

"The evidence is not conclusive, but I believe we've been hit by multiple powerful lasers which knocked out our surface sensory equipment."

"That's right. Now, give me some breathing room, robot."

His tentacles withdrew fractionally.

I told Gaines to set up the sensors and get back into the shaft ASAP. He didn't argue.

I tapped the screens causing the view to return to a middling range, displaying both *Phobos* and the ring we'd just come through on the screen at once.

"Very devious," I said. "It's a trap. They set up a large number of huge lasers, geared to fire the moment anything came through the ring. Our fighters never had a chance—hell, they probably nailed most of our missiles as well. Those big guns are perched there all over the ring itself, and were set to slice and dice anyone who comes through without the proper ID signal."

I turned to Marvin, who was still looming over me with excited cameras.

"Back to your post, mister," I told him.

He scuttled away obediently, and I followed.

"Reverse engines, helmsman," I told Marvin. "Use Sol to repel, rather than to pull us. When we're in range we're going to use our wide-area crush weapon. We're going to wipe out all those lasers at once."

I watched as he worked the controls, and the whole ship lurched. It felt like two railroad cars had just bumped into one another. Suddenly, we were decelerating rather than accelerating.

I'd gotten more used to the gravity drive now, but it wasn't natural to me yet. Essentially, the drive increased or reversed the tug of gravity upon the ship from a given source. By aiming at the sun, you could make it pull you in that direction, or push you away from it. When I envisioned it, I thought of the ship as a spider with the power to shoot lines of webbing toward any large target. You could shoot out a line then use it to pull yourself in that direction, or to slide down the line away from it. The trick was, the objects were things like the sun and the local planets, and the strings we attached to them were invisible. Things became trickier when you wanted to move in a curving arc. You had to work with several large bodies at once to do that.

Miklos looked up from Marvin's station where he'd been working since I assigned him there.

"We're going back to the ring?" he asked. "What if the lasers on the ring fire on us?"

"If they could do that, they would have done so already. Besides, they can't penetrate a mile of rock. They were built to burn ships, not moons."

He nodded and began working with Marvin on the weapons systems.

Before I could return to my own command station, Jasmine was waving to me urgently. I raced closer to her, upsetting my nanite harness.

"Sir, Gaines is back on the line!"

I opened my mouth to speak, but no sound came out. I stared down at the screen where Gaines suit was relaying what he was seeing.

It was absolute chaos. Shapes were hurtling at his helmet cameras. Dark shapes, with spiny, outstretched claws.

The marine company I'd sent up there with him was lighting up that dark sky with their beamers. Flaring light chugged, stitching the ground, the enemy and occasionally other marines, with fire.

A minute or so after that, the feed was cut. We all played with the controls, but there was no way to fix it from here. Gaines was up there getting mauled, and we couldn't even watch on TV.

"Crow's cyborgs," I said. "They've found us."

-26-

"But where's Crow's fleet?" Jasmine asked.

I moved quickly as she spoke to me, donning full battle armor. It was a new suit, with a custom fit. It was a little too snug in spots, but I was sure after it got warmed up in combat I'd like it just fine.

"I don't know where that bastard is hiding his ships. He probably had them stationed out here at the border, but they turned around and ran off when they saw *Phobos*. That would be just like him. He prefers to hoard his ships and never commits them unless the battle is a sure thing. It's a cowardly—but highly effective—strategy."

I turned to Miklos before I left. "I'm putting you in charge while I go check on Gaines."

He looked at me in surprise. "I thought I was on some kind of hiatus."

"Well, it's over. At least until you're dead—or I find someone better."

It was a line I'd used before but usually on grunts, not Fleet people. It always let them know where they stood. They were there to serve and die if need be for the Force. If they didn't like that, they could jump ship right now.

"Very well sir," he said. "I'll keep you up to date on anything else that comes in our direction."

I hurried to the encampment at the base of the shaft that led out to the surface. If these cyborgs were all over the outer hull,

237

they had to be repelled. Just as importantly, we needed to control the exterior of the giant ship in order to defend it.

When I got there, I found the situation chaotic. Two companies of marines were preparing to enter the shaft in combat gear. Another company was doing rescue ops, carrying wounded out of the open hole and transporting them to the medical bricks.

I tapped a gunnery sergeant on the shoulder as he raced by, and he whirled on me with a snarl. Then he recognized the bird on my shoulder and did a double-take.

"Sorry sir—busy sir!" he shouted. He looked like he wanted to run away, but didn't dare.

"Yeah, I gathered that. Are you going in or pulling people out?"

"Going in, sir. We're moving out any minute."

"Good. I'll join you."

I don't know what the man had expected me to say, but that wasn't it. I could tell that I hadn't made his day, either.

Kwon showed up about a minute later while I grouped up with the gunnery sergeant. His grunts looked at me like I was Dracula, fresh out of the grave.

"You're late," I told Kwon.

"Late sir? You didn't even ask for me to follow you."

"Yeah, but you always do. Is your suit ready? We're going down this hole."

"I figured out that part. What's the deal with Gaines? Is he holding on up there?"

"I don't know. We lost contact. The nanite chain and all transmissions to the surface have been cut. That's pretty much why I'm here."

I looked at the gunnery sergeant. He took a breath before speaking up.

"Word is he's pulled back into the mouth of the tunnel, Colonel. The elevator collapsed and we've been left with no choice other than scaling the shaft in our suits."

I nodded. "That's what I figured. Let's go in. If any of them are alive, they'll need relief. If not—we'll need to stop the enemy advance."

238

At the idea the enemy could be advancing down the shaft to our location, the gunnery sergeant's eyes grew comically wide. He checked his weapon again and led the team into the hole.

I followed with Kwon right on my heels. We didn't have much in the way of light or handholds, but we only had a mile or so to go. Using the suit's grav boots, we were able to walk on the sides of the tunnel.

It was an odd sight, looking up and all around. Marines were everywhere, walking all over the walls of the shaft. Since our boots would adhere to any surface and there wasn't much gravity to pull us in any particular direction, I could look directly "up" from my point of view and see more marines walking on what looked like the ceiling from my position.

Behind us, a smart metal hatch closed. The shaft wasn't pressurized like the central chamber of the ship. We were in vacuum now.

The shaft was dark except for our suit lights and a distant circle of glare from the far end ahead of us. It occurred to me that the light from outside was the light of Sol, the *real* sun. The star I was born under. I almost wanted to march the whole way up there just to see it.

Dead ahead, the tunnel flared up with laser fire and my visor darkened to protect my eyes.

"Weapons at the ready," I said on company chat. "Hold your fire until you see what you're shooting at. We have marines withdrawing toward us."

I looked around and realized I needn't have bothered. There wasn't a marine there that didn't have their projector in both hands and aimed dead ahead. Nobody had gone cowboy and begun firing into the unknown, either.

The flare of laser fire grew brighter as we marched deeper into the shaft.

"At least we know some of them are alive," I said. "Hold your fire until we're in close."

A haze of smoke arose, obscuring things. We made several attempts to contact the approaching team, but they didn't respond. I wasn't sure why.

We came up to the edge of the smoke, and being marines, we plunged into it.

I felt my heart pound. My breath came in rhythmic bellows, blasting over the microphone in my helmet and causing a roaring feedback in my headset. This was the stuff! It had been a long while since I'd been in serious action. Hunting down cyborgs hiding in holes in the bowels of this mammoth ship was nothing compared to this. They'd never had the numbers and never had a chance. This was something entirely different.

The first thing I met was a flying marine. He was out of control, spinning into us in free-fall. I could tell he'd let go of the walls of the shaft and fired up his boots, hoping to fly the rest of the way to safety.

Unfortunately, we were in the way. He barreled into the first men in line, knocking them down like bowling pins.

"Let's grab him, Kwon!" I shouted.

Together, we flipped our grav boots to maximum, making them plant us on the side of the shaft. Then we leaned forward, arms outstretched.

He almost took us out. Strong or not, when you're hit by an armored body flying at over a hundred miles an hour, you're hit pretty hard.

I stumbled and felt as if my ankles were snapping off. The servos in my armor whined in protest and the smart metal shivered. Kwon's big hand joined the party, saving the day.

"Duck low if more of them come flying at you!" I shouted. Around me, everyone was duck-walking now into the smoke.

The marine in my arms was limp. I checked his rank and name, which was printed on his helmet and shoulders. PFC Hans Klaus. His vitals were blank—not a good sign.

"Get this man to the rear of the formation! Corpsman!"

More hands soon reached out and handed Klaus to the back of the line. I knew that with luck, he'd make it all the way back out of the shaft and be revived. Our medical was the best—and we were hard to permanently kill. Even though his lungs weren't breathing and his heart wasn't pumping, millions of tiny robots were working inside his body, trying to keep his cells alive.

We pressed forward, and I wondered what we'd run into next. I didn't have long to wait.

240

We could hear them now. I wasn't sure why we'd been unable to get radio before—but now we could. Their com links connected with ours automatically and the chatter came in. None of it sounded good.

"Another group on the right. Keep fire up!"

"Man down! Man down! They've got the corporal and they're tearing the shit of him!"

"I'm out of juice! Can anyone give me a hook-up?"

I took a deep breath and my mouth formed into a hard line.

"Call double-time, Sergeant," I ordered.

He glanced toward his captain, who nodded. Soon, we were trotting down the shaft. I couldn't hear the footsteps of those around me because there was no air to carry the sound, but my boots were clanking and sparking on the melted, fused rock. The material that made up the outer shell had a lot of flint in it, causing us to leave a shower of orange sparks as we ran.

"Relief coming in on your six! Friendlies! Repeat, friendlies!"

We rushed up and joined the men on the front line—what was left of them. I went from helmet to helmet until I found the bluish glow of an officer. It was a Centaur lieutenant, and he was as banged up as the rest of them.

"Where's Gaines?" I asked him.

His eyes were glassy, and I saw he'd lost most of his right foreleg. He still had his projector in his strange Centaur hands, however. He was breathing funny, but I wasn't sure if that was shock or the effects of the venom the cyborgs all seemed to have.

"Gaines!" I shouted at him. "Where's Major Gaines?"

He lifted his trigger finger and aimed it up the shaft.

Great, I thought. *That's where the cyborgs are.*

"Is he dead or alive?"

The lieutenant waggled his head, a Centaur shrug, then he puked in his helmet.

"Withdraw, Lieutenant," I told him. "You've done your part. You're relieved."

When he could manage it, he climbed onto his three remaining feet and staggered toward the rear of the line.

241

I frowned into the haze and laser fire up ahead. How were they getting into our suits like that? The cyborgs I'd dealt with had been mean, but easy to crush in our armor.

Again, I got the answer to my question pretty fast. The cyborgs chose that moment to charge into our line.

The smoke had been doing them a lot of good. It hadn't occurred to me that they might be releasing it purposefully to obscure our vision. But when they showed up with smoke pouring off their bodies, I understood. This stuff wasn't just smoke. It was some kind of artificial agent. It was manufactured particulate matter. Something like an aerogel, which we'd used in fleet battles, but never with ground forces.

When lasers went off inside the smoke, it showed its true nature. It refracted and reflected the beams making them blossom wide in a prismatic glare. The stuff turned a perfect beam of linear light into a thousand splintering rays. If I had to lay money on it, I'd bet the damned smoke stopped radio waves as well, effectively blocking our localized transmissions.

I'd been wondering how the cyborgs could penetrate armor. They did it in a way I'd never expected: they had big machetes—I guess you could call them swords. With blades two feet or so long, these weapons flashed and chopped into their victims, hacking through an inch of steel like nothing.

Those blades—I'd seen their like before. The edges were white, and shone like diamond. They were just like our combat knives, but much heavier. Each cyborg carried two of these in its forward claws, and they swung them like they knew what they were doing.

The results of all these new tactics were alarming. Their smoke obscured them as targets and shielded them from the full power of laser fire even at close range. Once they were in hand-to-hand, the cyborgs had the advantage. They were like dervishes, chopping and slashing with abandon.

"Don't fire unless you have your weapon right up against their bodies," I told Kwon.

"Why not?" he asked, letting fly with a long bolt into the face of a charging cyborg.

The beam flared outward, blinding us and doing little to the enemy other than causing it's carapace to sizzle. The beam had no power in this smoke.

"Oh," said Kwon.

He met the charging enemy with a sweeping foot. He performed a perfect stop-kick. I grimaced, expecting he'd lost his foot. But the cyborg went down. Perhaps it was Kwon's unexpected size and strength. It had begun its swing a fraction of a second late, and before it could chop anything off Kwon, it was flat on its back.

Kwon pressed his projector to the cyborg's belly and pulled the trigger. Steam shot out of it, and it stopped thrashing.

"Yeah," he said. "That works good."

I had two of my own to worry about. Our front line had been pretty well shredded. I didn't think they were all dead, but they were definitely letting the enemy through. Instead of taking Kwon's tactic, I grabbed up one of the enemy blades. Thrusting it directly ahead of me with my arm at full extension, I caught the next one in the chest. It wasn't finished yet, so I jerked my arms and threw it into the next one that came at me while the first was still impaled on the sword.

They both went down together and marines near me shot them to death.

Kwon and I advanced. For once, my improved strength proved invaluable in battle. This was essentially a hand-to-hand fight. I wasn't any faster than the enemy, but my armor was much thicker and I hit much harder. Also, the cyborgs seemed to lack discipline. They charged in a frenzy, reminding me of ancient warriors. They were like screaming berserkers. Once we got the hang of how to deal with them we were able to advance steadily with few losses. We formed up an organized line with the other men and moved up the shaft.

"I should issue shields and short swords," I complained as I hacked and slashed.

Most of my men had swords now, plucked from the dying claws of the fallen. We had our guns in one hand—or in some cases just left them dangling on the ground—while we used the swords to great effect.

The cyborgs were ferocious fighters. They had no fear or pity in them. They were like rabid dogs. But the longer I fought them, I found they had a weakness: disorganization. They didn't adapt well to our effective tactics. They just kept rushing in to die.

Eventually, there weren't any more cyborgs. We'd advanced almost to the top at that point. I called a halt about a hundred yards short of the surface.

Around me, the men leaned on their knees and gasped for air. Nothing quite takes it out of you like prolonged hand-to-hand combat. You exert every ounce of power you have in every move, because it might well be your last. After ten minutes of that, even my men were winded.

"Take a breather," I said. Ahead of us, the opening was a bright circle of light. The sun came into the shaft at an angle, splashing its glare on the southern wall. The round circle of sky we could see clearly now was dotted with stars.

After a ten second rest, I tapped a private's helmet.

"Private, get up there and give me a report."

"Me sir?"

"Dammit, that's what I said!"

Kwon gave him a kick in the butt. That got him going. He scrambled up the final hundred steps to the top of the shaft.

"If you don't like volunteering, don't stand close to an officer," I called after him.

He gave me a perfunctory salute over his shoulder and soon was silhouetted against the starry sky.

I watched as he cautiously stuck his head up there. He looked for all the world like a gopher poking its nose out of a hole.

"Well?" I roared.

"All clear, Colonel. At least, I think it is."

"That's good enough for me. Company, advance!"

We made it out onto the surface of *Phobos*. I had a good look around and was amazed at the mess. Gaines' cameras hadn't done justice to the scene. There were deep furrows burned in huge X patterns all over the place. Our equipment, sensors and turrets were all destroyed.

Worse was the strewn bodies of our dead. Hacked apart, our men lay scattered over the field. I walked from suit to suit, reading nameplates.

Finally, I found Gaines. He'd never even made it down into the shaft. His suit was dead, and he showed no more signs of life than it did.

I fell to my knees and smeared the ash-like dust from his faceplate. Another friend down. How many more would I have to find like this?

I started to get up and leave—but something stopped me. It was a gauntleted hand. Gaines had grabbed my ankle as I turned away. His eyes were still closed, but his hand had reached out and gripped me.

"Corpsman!" I roared. "Get the Major down the shaft. I mean *NOW!*"

I watched them tap nanites into his emergency ports and carry him off.

I smiled. One less dead man would haunt my dreams tonight.

-27-

About an hour later we'd managed to turn *Phobos* around and float back to the Tyche ring. Using the ship's balloon-gravity weapon and some replacement turrets we'd set up on the outer hull, we were able to clean the lasers off the ring. I sent back some messenger ships after that to order the rest of the fleet to come through.

We watched nervously as they began flying into the system behind us. We had good sensory systems set up on the outer hull again, with nanite lines running down to my control center.

Really, the enclosed area under Miklos' tent-like dome of smart metal had become *Phobos'* bridge. I was back there now, watching the screens. They seemed to update more slowly than they did on a carrier, but they were working.

Contacts poured through the ring at a steady pace. As each appeared, it was yellow at first—but quickly was identified as friendly, given contact info with print too tiny to read, and changed to green.

Two carriers, with their surrounding clouds of fighters came through first. After this vanguard a swarm of gunboats followed. Then came the cruisers and more carriers. The wallowing transports brought up the rear.

Just about when they'd all made it through, and I was beginning to relax, a warning buzzer sounded. It wasn't a scratchy, irritating sound, but all of us were attuned to it. Operators jumped and tapped at their consoles. As usual, Jasmine was the first with useful information.

"Contacts sir. Not ours."

"How far out?"

"About an AU away. Not sure where they came from—we were clear, and now we're not."

"At that distance light takes a while to get across space. Maybe our new sensors didn't pick them up until this minute. Are they lined up with the sun?"

Sometimes ships could hide in the glare of the sun. It didn't work with optical pick-ups, but with radar and other sensory systems a ship could hide in the radiation.

"Not exactly, but they are headed toward us."

The fleet formed up together and began heading sunward. It was really the only option as the Tyche ring was far from the inner planets of the Solar System. Even if *Phobos* had been able to move as fast as a fighter, it would still take us a day or two to get to Earth. Since we were crawling with no built-up inertia and not much in the way of gravity wells to pull us faster, it was going to take nearly a week.

"How long until we're within range?"

"Hard to say, they're maneuvering now. At current course and acceleration on both sides, we'll take about sixteen hours to get close."

"Can you get these ships up on the screen? Optical views, I mean?"

"Not yet, but I should be able to get contact positions and counts up right about...now."

She worked the controls as did the other operators around her. The holotank that was suspended at about head-level above the operations table came to life. It had been dark up until now, as we hadn't hooked it up to the new data streams coming from the hull.

I gave a slight intake of breath. It was a mistake, but I couldn't help it. Normally, I never showed surprise around my staff. They didn't need to know when I was surprised. It was always bad for morale.

Somehow, when she'd described "incoming contacts" I'd envisioned something like a hundred ships. A number comparable to what we had ourselves.

247

What I saw was a mass of red contacts. There were hundreds and hundreds of tiny red dots. Each was no more than a pixel or two, floating in layered, disk-shaped formations out here. Rank after rank of them, coming toward us in waves.

When organizing ships into formations in space, there was no need to place them in lines. Lines presupposed gravity and a two dimensional area to be filled. We dealt with ships organized into planes instead. *Sheets* of ships were coming at us. They occupied vast regions of space and were layered one plane behind another.

"I'm still working on a count, sir," she said. "There are so many, the front ranks are occluding the ones behind."

"Take your time," I said, "wouldn't want to get an inaccurate total."

As I stared, it became obvious the enemy could see us as well. They probably had a much better accounting of our numbers than we had of theirs. After all, this was their star system and they had had years to seed space with countless probes and spy-bots.

"How many ranks do they have?" I asked.

"Seven sir. Of that, I can be certain. Right now, I'm estimating that they have around a thousand ships per rank."

Seven thousand ships, I thought. *Holy God, how did Crow manage to build them all?*

My staff was white-faced, except possibly for Sarin. I'm not sure if she was supremely confident in my power to overcome such odds, or simply too busy correlating data to worry about it. Either way, she kept moving while everyone else stood and stared, transfixed.

"That's a surprisingly big fleet," I commented.

"We never could have won with our original force," Miklos said. "We probably can't win now."

I looked at him in annoyance. "Nonsense. Remember we came here planning to hide most of our ships behind *Phobos*. Now, the situation is even better. We have *Phobos* under our control, ready to sweep that fleet from the sky."

As I stared at the enemy line-up of ships, I realized Miklos was right. I'd been crazy to attack Earth at all. I felt like a banana-republic dictator sending my miserable collection of

248

foreign-surplus helicopters and pickup-truck personnel carriers out to attack an organized, first rate armada fielded by a superpower. If it hadn't been for *Phobos*, this entire operation would have been suicide.

But I didn't let any of these thoughts escape onto my face or out through my mouth. I was all smiles and bravado.

"Frankly, I'm surprised they don't have more than this," I lied. "They had all of Earth's industrial might and plenty of time to rebuild."

Captain Sarin had finally looked up and caught sight of the data she'd been busy organizing for us. She seemed mesmerized by the screen. That wasn't like her.

"In manpower alone," she said, "they're a million times more potent than we are."

"But think of what the Imperials must be saying to themselves!" I urged her. "Imagine waking up to see this monster ship bearing down on you from out of nowhere!"

"We don't have to imagine that, sir," Miklos said, "we just experienced that horrible moment ourselves a couple of weeks ago when *Phobos* first rose up from Eden-12."

"Yeah, right you are," I said.

I figured it was time to provide more encouragement. I cleared my throat and went into full-bullshit mode.

"Overall, I take this as a positive sign," I said loudly.

They glanced at me. Most of them gave me their patented "are you crazy?" look. I'm very familiar with that expression. Then they turned back to the impossibly large armada on their screens.

"Don't you see? The Imperials aren't holding anything back. This has to be everything they have. Crow likes to strike that way—all or nothing. He's taken a good look at us, and decided incorrectly that we look weak. He's going to try to knock us out right here on his doorstep."

If anything, my listeners were whiter than before. None of them said anything. No one objected or laughed. They just stared at the screens, then me, then the screens again.

"His strategy will give us a surprise win," I continued. "They won't have time to learn about how to fight this ship. They won't have time to adapt. They'll come in and make their play—one time. We outrange them and have a hull that's for all intents and purposes impenetrable. They haven't got—"

"Colonel Riggs?" Marvin interrupted, speaking up for the first time.

"What is it, Marvin?"

"I believe the enemy armada is firing upon us."

I leaned forward and examined the screen. There they were: fresh contacts. It took a few seconds before all the updates came in. Marvin had access to the raw feeds and so had known sooner.

I eyed the enemy formation as red slivers separated from their fleet. The first rank had unloaded missiles in our direction—lots of them.

"Get a counter going," I said.

"Done," Jasmine answered.

I stared some more. The counter read seven thousand eighty-four ships, and next to that, in yellow, was a flickering number of missiles. The number was already in the triple digits and it was rising fast.

The number stopped at four hundred something. I smiled. "Not that bad. *Phobos* can take out that barrage with one toot from her gravity-horn."

A minute or so later I stopped smiling.

"They've fired another barrage, sir," Marvin said in his ever-perky voice. "Exactly one minute behind the first. Colonel, the gravity weapon will not be able to recharge before—"

"I know!" I barked.

I walked away from the screen and got a cup of hot coffee. I poured some bourbon into it and stirred it with my finger. This burned my finger, but I didn't care.

Jasmine came over to me and stood nearby. I glanced at her, drank my Irish coffee, then heaved a sigh.

"Can I talk to you, Colonel?" she asked.

"Talk."

"In your chambers, sir?"

I nodded and led her away to the brick we'd recently placed adjacent to the domed bridge area.

I walked inside and she followed me. I watched her as she entered. She was prim and sharply-dressed. Every line of her body was hugged by her fleet suit and I eyed her closely, determined to enjoy the view for a few more hours before we were all annihilated.

Behind her, I saw Marvin's cameras craning and zooming. Miklos was lingering too, watching. I frowned. Had Miklos signaled her somehow? I often found my staffers sending little love-notes about me via texts. When they wanted to change my mind about something, they would team up and work in coordination. From the look on Miklos' face and the fact he hadn't come crying to me yet, I figured this might well be the case now.

I closed the hatch in their faces.

"Okay," I said, taking another swig of spiked coffee and setting it down. "What's on your mind, Captain?"

Jasmine leaned forward, passing her nose over my cup. She gave it a sniff, and wrinkled it. She gave me a reproachful look.

"I'm well within my self-prescribed limits," I said.

She nodded. "Well sir…Kyle, we need to turn back."

"Turn back?"

"We're sitting at the Tyche ring. Those missiles will follow us through, but if we play it right, we can destroy them as they come in with PD fire."

I made a growling noise. "I'm not interested in having come all the way out here just to turn tail and run, Captain."

"I understand that, sir. But there are seven thousand ships out there! Who knows what else Crow has—"

"He's got nothing else," I said. "He doesn't play it that way. He likes to fight battles like a man with a sledgehammer. He either goes for it or he doesn't. If we can break this fleet, we'll have Earth."

She shook her head, staring at me with wide, pretty eyes. "You can't be serious! Seven *thousand* ships! Even if we survive all the missiles—and they are still firing by the way— our support vessels won't."

I leaned forward, lowering my voice. "We can't run, Jasmine."

"Why not?"

251

"Because they aren't going to stop coming. Crow has seen my cards. He knows what we have. If we run, he'll follow us—all the way back to Eden. And the battle station is on the wrong side of that system. It won't be able to help."

She looked stunned. I watched her face as she digested this, then she stood up slowly, as if in shock.

"Here," I said, offering her my cup. "You want some of this? Takes the sting out."

She shook her head and didn't look at me. I felt a pang.

Standing up, I reached out and gently touched her hand. She didn't move. I walked around the desk and put my hands on her shoulders. A moment later, we were kissing.

I have a way of picking the oddest moments with women. Call me an opportunist. She kissed me harder than usual, but her lips still felt like butterflies teasing my mouth. Sometimes being unnaturally tough wasn't a good thing.

I released her and I saw she had a single, glistening tear on her cheek.

"I'm sorry," she said. "I'm just thinking about everyone—all those who are about to die."

I laughed. A booming sound. I formed a grin and shook my head. She looked at me with big round eyes, confused.

"I didn't say we were going to *die*! Unless you're grieving for Crow's thugs, you'd better save it. You don't think I'd come all the way out here without preparing for the worst do you?"

She cocked her head and narrowed her eyes at me. She shook her head slowly.

"That's right. Now, send Marvin in here. We have some planning to do. This does change the time schedule of course—but that's all. Crow's head will be on a pike in two weeks. Mark my words."

Jasmine nodded. She gave me a weak smile. I think she knew I was bullshitting her, but she appreciated the effort. She even gave me another peck on the cheek as she left. I marveled at how differently Sandra would have handled the same situation. She'd have kicked me or something.

Marvin was in my office a minute later. I poured myself a fresh cup of coffee and laced it again. I was feeling better already.

"All right," I said. "What have you got for me, robot?"

"Excuse me, Colonel Riggs?"

"I'm asking you what the plan is. How are we going to stop all those missiles?"

"With the outer hull of this vessel, sir."

I twisted my lips in disapproval. "Do you really think the hull can take all of them? Without being punctured?"

"Oh no, Colonel," he said. "By my calculations, the fourth barrage will breach the hull and kill everyone aboard. I could be wrong, of course. It could be the third—or even the second, if my calculations concerning the density and integrity are inaccurate."

"Hmm," I said, taking another belt. "What if we go into a spin? What if we spread the impacts over the entire surface, thus preventing them from damaging any one point too much?"

"Not a bad suggestion. But still, there are now twenty-six separate barrages."

"Twenty-six?"

"Yes—that's how long it's been since the first wave was fired. Each minute, the enemy fleet launches another barrage."

That brought both my hands up to my face. I almost dropped my coffee.

"Still, your idea has triggered additional threads of logic," Marvin said, shuffling his tentacles and cameras. Thoughtfully, he reached out, took my coffee cup with a tentacle and examined it. "Are you aware, Colonel Riggs, that there is a foreign substance in your beverage?"

"Yeah," I said. "It's coffee."

"No, there's another substance. I've detected—"

"Listen, Marvin," I said. "We have a few hours left, then I have to turn tail and run. When I do that, the Imperial fleet will come after us. They'll follow us all the way to Eden. Star Force will be destroyed, and Crow will have won."

"That seems like a large series of logical leaps, sir."

"Yeah, I'm good at that. Oh, and by the way, you'll be destroyed along with the rest of us. Let's not forget about that."

Several more cameras lofted and panned, eyeing me. He finally stopped fooling with my cup and put it down.

"That would be most unfortunate."

"Exactly," I said. "So what were you thinking? You said something about a new logical thread. What did you have in mind?"

"Only the idea of spreading the impacts. If we could spread them over the shield, rather than just a region of the hull, we could destroy them before impact."

I frowned at him, then I slowly got what he was saying. "You mean we could spin the ship, taking the blasts on different regions of the surface. But that would only work if the ship had more than one gravity weapon, right?"

"Sadly, yes."

I was up and pacing. I stepped on his tentacles until he pulled them out of the way.

"How about this," I said. "Could we localize the weapon's discharge? I mean, it can be focused and manipulated, right?"

"Yes, that's how the two primary effects are achieved. A broad, diffused charge crushes everything near the surface. A tightly focused narrow area of effect is utilized to destroy distant ships."

"Right. How about we make a weaker version of the effect? Something localized and diffuse—but only over one portion of the hull? I know the targeting can be adjusted, you've done it before."

Marvin ruminated. "I'm not sure I can do that in the time allotted. Firing a single trigger that catches everything in the ship's vicinity is vastly easier to manage."

"You'll have my entire staff backing you. With any resource you want."

He perked up considerably.

"Anything?"

"Anything within *reason*, Marvin," I said.

He drooped in disappointment.

"Okay, okay," I said. "I'll let you have the cyborgs."

"What?"

"We captured some of them alive. They're half machine and half biotic."

254

"Very intriguing."

"You can dissect them, eat them—make a few of your own. I don't care. You can have them. *If* you come up with a solution to this problem first."

Marvin looked excited. "It might just be possible. The enemy missiles are organized in fairly tight groupings. It's obvious they intend to penetrate the ship's armor with an intense series of blasts over a few square miles."

"Great. Clustered shots right at our hearts, eh?"

"So to speak. But the significance of that would be the localized nature of the threat. If we can put up a gravity effect in the path of each swarm—and do it once a minute—we might be able to survive the battle."

I nodded, thinking of my own adjustments to the situation. I patted Marvin on his rear brainbox as I walked out. He followed me and headed to his station where he began tapping at his consoles.

"Captain Sarin," I said, "I've got new orders for the fleet. They are to move in front of *Phobos* with a wide dispersion pattern. Only the carriers and the transports are going to be allowed to hide behind us. The mission of the forward group is to shoot down every missile they can as they come in."

"Got it, sir…but I must point out that the incoming weapons will be moving very fast. They won't get many shots off before the missiles pass them."

"I'm well aware of that. But every lucky hit we get is one less we have to absorb with *Phobos*."

"Also," she went on, "placing our ships in the front line means they could become targets. The missiles can change targets and take out small ships much more easily than this larger vessel."

I had to think about that one. After studying the screens for a moment, I had to agree with her.

"I think I have a solution. Don't move them up yet. Wait until the missiles are a few minutes away. The enemy fleet is about ten light minutes out. They won't have time to see our maneuver and send new orders to their missiles in time to change their behavior."

She nodded, and we had a plan.

The effect on the rest of the crew was dramatic. Now that I'd come out with new orders, they had something to chew on—something to think about besides getting blown up.

"One more thing, Colonel," she said. "Shouldn't we fire our own missiles?"

"Use them or lose them, eh?"

She nodded.

"No," I said. "If we fail to stop this barrage, we're dead anyway. In that case, I'd rather leave the Earth fleet intact to face future threats."

She went back to her station and went to work. I signaled Miklos, who joined me at the planning table.

"I want you to help Marvin," I told him. I briefly explained the plan, and he admitted it had potential.

"What, specifically, can I do to help, sir?" he asked.

"I want you to keep an eye on him. Make sure he doesn't get distracted. Make sure—make sure he doesn't do anything weird, okay?"

Miklos chuckled. "I'll do my best, Colonel. But no promises."

When it came to Marvin, I knew that was the best anyone could offer.

-28-

The hours crawled by. I slept, ate and worried. When you had thousands of missiles coming at you, it was hard to relax.

Marvin did none of these things. He never left his station, working feverishly on the Blue's interface. He had more hands, eyes and brains than any three of us combined. Plus, he didn't seem to get tired.

Every ten minutes or so, the ship's big weapon fired. We'd cleared the surface of nonessential personnel so he could experiment as he liked. We were too far from the enemy fleet to hit them, of course, but he targeted and destroyed various decoys we placed for him, mostly chunks of floating ice from the Oort Cloud.

When he was ready, we began throwing missiles at *Phobos*. One at a time, the cruisers that followed in our wake launched salvoes with disabled warheads. When they came, *Phobos* shuddered as the weapon activated.

That alone was enough to keep people from resting. My people were like rocks, but it was hard to take relentless impacts and funny noises when you knew doom was out there, speeding along at a million or so miles an hour in your direction.

In all that time, we didn't fire a missile, attempt communication with the enemy, or even budge from the Tyche ring. We looked dead, despite our desperate preparations.

The enemy fleet was sailing toward us during this time as well, but they were taking their time about it. They were cautious. They wanted to see if their missiles could take us out. Under optimal conditions, they could have done it without having to lose a single ship of their own.

I smelled Crow's influence in every action they took. He was probably running this show from his headquarters back on Earth, safely berating his commanders and sipping sherry in his ice cream white uniform.

The thought made me angry. Too often over the long years I'd been dealing with Crow, he'd tricked me or managed to get the upper hand. He'd ordered assassins to kill me and my girl and I was here to return the favor. But I had to stay alive and reach Earth first.

About eight hours before the missiles were due to hit us, I began to get antsy. I went to Marvin and waved my hands around until he turned a single camera in my direction.

"I'm sorry, Colonel," he said. "I'm very busy just now."

I'd found him out working on the Blues' interface directly. He was attaching secondary and tertiary nanite arms to each of the hexes that controlled the weapons system. There were about forty hexes in the weapons panel, and they puffed and sighed as they moved. I watched them for a few seconds before losing patience.

"Are you going to make it, Marvin?" I asked. "If it's time to withdraw, I need to know now."

"I'm going to make it, Colonel Riggs."

"Are you just saying that in order to keep your hopes alive?"

A second camera glanced at me, then returned to his primary focus. "I'm not sure I understand your meaning, sir."

"I mean that I offered you the cyborgs to experiment upon. I'm worried that you might be willing to jeopardize everything for that opportunity."

"That would be irrational, Colonel."

"Yeah, it would. And I'm not putting it outside the realm of possibility. I need some concrete results to prove you can do this."

"What would you suggest?"

"I'm going to fire missiles at *Phobos*. Just two missiles, but they're going to come in five minutes apart. If you can't stop them, I'm declaring this a mistrial."

This statement awarded me no less than six cameras. "I think you're being unreasonable."

"No, I'm being very reasonable. If you can't stop two missiles, we haven't got a chance against thousands."

"When will this test occur?"

"I'm giving you one more hour. That's it. I'm scheduling the launch and putting it on automatic. Stop them, or forget about your cyborg doggy-treats."

"An odd reference. I'll see what I can do, however."

I left him to his work. I knew that if anyone could do it, he could. He was motivated and ingenious. I, for my part, had nothing to lose.

An hour later I fired the missiles. I didn't even bother to give him a second warning.

I watched the screens with arms crossed. Everyone else crowded around, not saying much. They were all hoping, too.

About a minute before the impacts, Marvin came into the command tent—or rather, he crashed into it.

For a split second, I thought one of those missiles had come down the shaft to the surface and landed right on my head. Marvin was in free-fall—he'd gotten a new grav lifter set somewhere—and tore a hole in the smart metal tent we all stood around in.

The ceiling sagged, then ripped open. He came spiraling in, slapped his tentacles on the weapons consoles like a madman doing a drum solo, then flew up and out, back through the same hole.

"Hehe," I said, gazing up through the ceiling. "He's really going for it!"

The rest of my people were still ducking, talking in lowered voices and staring after my crazy robot.

I knew what they were thinking. They'd all seen a last-minute-Charlie before. The homework was due in seconds, and Marvin didn't have his act together.

About then, the first shudder went through the ship. It was a now-familiar sensation. We'd been feeling it for many long hours as Marvin conducted his countless tests.

I pasted on a smile. "There we go," I said. "I'm sure he's stopped the first missile with that one."

I received many doubtful glances. Wincing, I checked the boards.

"Yes," Jasmine said. "The missile was crushed and destroyed. No damage was sustained."

"Set a timer. Five minutes to go."

She pointed to the timer she already had running. There was four minutes and twenty seconds left on it. That may not sound like a lot of time, but when you are as worried as I was, it like was an eternity.

When the clock read twenty-nine seconds, I felt another shudder. I frowned. "Was that...?"

"I think he fired early."

We looked and the missile kept coming. I frowned as it zoomed right down on top of us and exploded. We didn't feel it, but the pickups didn't leave us any doubts. The blast formed a bubble on *Phobos* that quickly vanished.

Jasmine looked up at me in disbelief. "You fired a live warhead?"

"Sure," I said. "I didn't want to hang all our lives on a simulation."

She nodded. "It looks like a failure."

"Yeah. Here comes the professor now."

Marvin bombed through roof again, upsetting the nanites which had been busily repairing the damage from the last time.

"Colonel Riggs," he said, "let's go over the status of the experiments."

"Looks like there is no need, Marvin. The test failed."

"A misfire only, Colonel. Let's do another test."

"Marvin, I told you—"

"But sir, we'll have enough time to escape if it fails. Plenty of time."

"I had other tests planned, but they were predicated on the success of the first one."

"I understand, sir. One more try. I'll be ready in...seven minutes. The trouble was I miscalculated the reset time. When automated, it took less time to engage the firing sequence than I'd anticipated. It ended up being too fast—"

"That's not good news, Marvin," I said. "If the best you can do is about four minutes, we're dead anyway. It has to be one minute apart. No screw-ups."

"One more test?"

I sighed. "All right. Go."

He moved over to the consoles, but did nothing. He just looked at data and flipped through various planning scenarios. I followed him to his station.

"Aren't you doing the test?"

"That's all preprogrammed."

"You mean you set it all up before you asked me? Were you that certain I would approve a second chance?"

He looked at me from several angles, trying to discern my mood. I was incredulous, but I think he has a hard time detecting that one.

"Is my answer going to prejudice you against this endeavor?"

I sighed. "You're right. Keep it to yourself. I don't want to know how big of a patsy you think I am."

"Very well, Colonel Riggs."

The next test went perfectly. We shortened the time down to three minutes, then two. It was hard to break the two-minute barrier. We went all the way down to the wire on that one. He finally managed to nudge one of those hexes just the right number of millimeters to get the precision he needed.

He tried to explain to me that the analog system of the Blues was giving him fits. I understood, knowing analog technology could be a pain. What he was doing was akin to trying to perfectly tune in an old-fashioned AM radio in an ancient car. The slightest tap could bring a station in loud and clear, or make it a scratchy mess. Only in Marvin's case, he was tuning a radio with hundreds of mysterious buttons that an alien race of cloud people had designed. It wasn't easy.

"The trick involves variant pressure on the different angles of the same button. You see, previously I'd been applying

261

equal pressure, causing the button to depress at precisely the same rate on every axis. That was my mistake—"

"Marvin," I said, "I've got a headache. We're doing the one minute test now. This is just like tech back home—you live or die by the demo."

"Reference unclear."

"Shoot down the missiles. All of them. They're coming in now."

I began dropping them on him then, one at a time, precisely one minute apart. I smiled after he got the first four in a row. He was doing it. I turned to Jasmine.

"This is working. He's like a tennis player back home. He's in the zone."

"Can I stress the system?" Miklos asked me suddenly.

I turned to him with a frown. I nodded and stepped from the controls.

Miklos cracked his knuckles and began toying with the ship's helm. He put us into a spin, which applied lateral force to everyone.

Marvin's cameras perked up, but he didn't complain. I figured he knew we were going to stop informing him concerning every detail of the tests at some point. We had to go beyond lab conditions. There was less than an hour to go before the real thing hit us.

I watched the holotank. Miklos was a sneaky bastard. Several of the ships broke formation and positioned themselves in various positions around *Phobos*. When the next missile was scheduled, it came from an entirely new angle. We were spinning now, too.

Marvin was making an odd sound. I wasn't sure if he was humming, laughing or burning a servo. But he did it. He caught them all.

Miklos nodded when he was done.

"It *might* work," he said. "But you're risking all our lives on untested technology, sir."

"We've been doing nothing but testing it for the last seven hours."

"You know what I mean, Colonel."

262

I turned away from him. I knew exactly what he meant. It was crazy—but it *had* to work. We had to win this round. If we turned and ran now it was hopeless.

If the Imperial fleet was so powerful they could stop us while they were still out of our range—well, there wasn't any point to fighting them. We weren't going to survive anyway.

"How many of the enemy ships have fired on us so far?" I asked him, partly to change the subject.

"That is a strange thing, Colonel. We estimate that only the first rank of ships—the first thousand—have fired anything at all. Even half the ships in that first rank have held their fire."

I frowned. "So only five hundred ships out of seven thousand have unloaded on us? That isn't standard procedure."

"No, sir. It wouldn't be for us, at least."

Usually, we fired missiles evenly from every ship in the fleet. If every ship had ten missiles, it made sense to fire five from each, rather than ten from one and none from the next. That way if any of the ships were knocked out the survivors would still have some ammo left for the next round.

Miklos shrugged. "It isn't all that odd," he said. "It may be due to design variations. Maybe all those Imperial ships look alike, but not all were equipped with missiles."

"Hmm," I said. "It's not like Crow. He likes his fleets to be standardized. I don't know if it matters, though. Maybe we just came out here while they were shipping out supplies and surprised them. Maybe they had the ships ready, but without full magazines. Production schedules can be optimized by building a lot of one thing at a time. Maybe Crow doesn't have all those ships fully ready to fly yet."

"We just don't know, Colonel. If we live long enough, maybe we'll figure it out."

We went back to work and I daydreamed about more Irish coffee, but passed. I wasn't going into my last battle sloshed.

I thought about a lot of things as those missiles came zooming in. They were so fast! I'd made a mistake there. I realized during the final minutes that we'd never tested against a target that was moving at such speeds.

Missiles are like tiny spaceships. Our modern units had engines that provided thrust at a steady rate, and the longer

263

they flew the faster they went. Since the Imperial missiles had many hours to build up speed, they were going to hit us very hard and fast. We'd never been in position to test Marvin's focused shielding system against anything going even one tenth as fast as the enemy birds. That meant they might very well get through, despite all our preparations.

I gritted my teeth and wondered if I'd killed us all in the end. At least it would be quick.

-29-

Even a veteran like me finds it hard to ride out a heavy attack in space. Your guts churn and your bowels cinch up painfully tight. Sometimes I thought it was easier to be in a firefight. You aim your weapon, squeeze the trigger—you're doing something. If you do get taken out by enemy fire, you probably never saw it coming.

But while standing on my ship's bridge, watching thousands of brilliant points of death coming at me, I felt helpless to do more than hope I wouldn't die. I've never liked the sensation.

The first wave of missiles was easy. We set up the shielded region of *Phobos*, a couple of square miles of surface area. When the missiles came in, Marvin hit the button, and they all instantly transformed into a shower of wadded-up metal.

I clapped my hands loudly and hooted. "First rank down, set us up for round two, Marvin!"

None of this was necessary, of course. But I wanted the staffers to feel the victory, and they did. A cheer went up when that first wave of missiles vanished en masse. I smiled. I still had the touch. Sometimes my job amounted to playing cheerleader.

It was the second wave, really, that tied my innards into a knot. Marvin wasn't bantering with us as the seconds ticked by—he was madly adjusting his makeshift controls, slapping and jiggling the consoles. I could tell by watching him this was no science. He looked like he was playing pinball and cheating by slamming his knee into the base of the machine and whacking it on all sides.

The second wave went down like the first, and I began to smile. To *really* smile.

"You're going to pull this off, Marvin. I bet you can taste those cyborgs already."

"Taste?"

"Never mind, don't get distracted."

I'm not sure if it was my comment or just fate, but on the third wave he didn't catch them all.

Wham! Wham!

I held onto the command table, but it wasn't that bad. The ship had so much mass, it barely shuddered under the impacts.

"Let's start spinning to spread the damage," I said to the people running the helm, but then turned to Marvin, "will that mess you up?"

"As long as the spin is very predictable, with no acceleration curve, I will be able to compensate with a simple application of a mathematical template."

I winced, knowing that we couldn't apply thrust in a perfectly even pattern to an object this big, not even with the gravity drive. Using the drive would take energy away from his shielding system, too.

"All right," I said. "We'll hold off on the spin for now. Keep swatting down those—"

Wham!

Another one had gotten past and hit us. While I'd been talking to him, the fourth wave had come in and something had slipped past. *Phobos* shook, and I looked at Sarin.

"How many hits? What mega-tonnage?"

"Just one high yield warhead," she said. "I'm estimating seven to ten megatons. According to surface monitoring data, we've got a pall of dust growing over *Phobos*."

I didn't like the sound of that. Dust was a good defense against lasers—but not missiles.

"Move the fleet forward. The Imperials won't be able to retarget the missiles on them. They're too far away now. We need every turret we have to shoot down the missiles."

"The incoming birds are going too fast, Colonel," she told me. "The fleet won't be able to lock on—'"

"Move them up and have them take potshots. If we fail to catch an entire wave just once…"

Jasmine nodded in alarm, visualizing what I was suggesting. She relayed my orders to the fleet commanders, and the situation on the screens changed.

The fleet glided forward into a defensive posture. I hoped none of the missiles were programmed to switch targets in their final seconds—but there was little I could do about that possibility now.

"Start the spin!" I said after the next barrage failed to land a single strike. I'd been looking at the hull damage. It wasn't severe, but it was noticeable. Each strike had left a blackened crater on the surface of my ship. At the deepest, it was no more than a few hundred yards of penetration, but a half dozen more strikes on top of any of these craters would be enough to break through and kill us all. I wanted to make that a hard goal for the enemy to achieve.

Slowly, the big vessel began to spin. We got it moving fast enough to rotate about once every ten minutes and waited. Logically, the missile strikes would now be spread out over ten times the surface area, vastly lessening the odds they could penetrate our outer shell.

As the next wave came in, I dared a grin. The fleet was doing better than expected. Nearly half the missiles were taken out before they reached *Phobos*.

"See?" I said. "This is working. We're getting through this storm."

One would think that by now I would have learned not to tempt the gods of fate. But obviously, I hadn't.

I knew something was wrong about ten seconds before the seventeenth wave landed. I frowned at the screen.

"What…why are they shifting course? Marvin, are you on this? Adjust your shield—"

That was all I managed to get out before the impacts began. *Wham! Wham! Wham!*

Then more fell, and we all gripped our operating stations for dear life. The walls shook, parts of the inner chamber crumbled and fell. It sounded like a distant avalanche in the Alps.

A moment later, Marvin took flight. He shot up out of our command tent, blasting a fresh hole in the writhing nanites. I'd begun to think the whole smart metal tent idea was a loser.

"Where's he going?" Miklos asked.

"I don't know and I don't care. He's got his orders, and you have yours."

"What went wrong, Kyle?"

I stared at the input, searching for the answer to her question. The missiles had shifted with *Phobos'* spin, steering toward a specific spot. I zoomed in with my fingers, spreading them, and examined the surface features. There was a large single cluster of impacts. They'd gone halfway through our armor in a single strike.

"The old craters," I shouted. "Their missiles must be programmed to hit spots that are already damaged. They changed course to hit us there."

I opened an emergency com-link channel to Marvin, without asking permissions from anyone.

"Marvin, set the next shield right over the most damaged, blackened area."

He didn't respond, but I didn't have time to demand an acknowledgement.

"Captain Sarin, stop our damned spinning! Place our most damaged area right in front of the next wave."

She looked at me with fear in her eyes. "But if they get through this time they'll rupture the hull."

"I know, but Marvin's been catching most of them until now. We can take a few more hits. We know right where they're going to strike next. Let's use that."

"Sir?" she said, looking at me with real fear.

"What is it?"

"Kyle—Marvin's leaving the ship. He's in the shaft now."

I froze. My mind froze. I didn't know what to think. Was he truly abandoning us? Running out on a sinking ship? Marvin, the biggest steel rat of all time?

"MARVIN!" I shouted into my headset, firing a channel connection to him he couldn't easily disable. "I know you can

268

hear me. At least set the system to catch these final waves. We know where they'll all land now. Just set the controls on automatic, if you're going to run out—"

"Already done, Colonel Riggs," he transmitted back calmly. "I've done all I can do from my station. Accordingly, I'm heading up to the surface to survey the damage personally. I would suggest you do the same—just in case there is another mishap."

I thought about it. For a split second, I seriously considered running out on my people, just as Marvin had run out on me. But I couldn't do it, of course.

There was no time for a real evacuation. No time to save more than a few, if any of them. I would have to quietly run so as not to be caught up in the traffic jam of thousands trying to escape through that single shaft.

In the end, there wasn't time for anything fancy, anyway. I don't think even Marvin made it all the way out of the shaft and into space before the next wave hit us.

-30-

The lights were out for about ten seconds, then they flickered back on. I had Captain Sarin in my arms by that time. I don't know quite how that happened, but we picked ourselves up and supported one another.

This was easier for me to do than it was for her. I weigh a lot, even without the battle armor. She almost buckled, but held on as I hauled myself to my feet.

The nanite arms that served us as crash harnesses in these situations were limp noodles on the deck. I frowned at that.

"A lot of good these damned things are when you really need them."

"We haven't had time to set up localized power sources," Jasmine said, pushing her hair out of her eyes. She didn't have it cut to regulation length, but I'd never complained. As her only real superior, she'd gotten away with that for years.

Suddenly, I forced myself to stop thinking about Jasmine and her hair. We were still in a battle, after all.

"How long until the next wave hits?"

"I'm not sure," she said. "The operating console is still rebooting, and the holotank appears to be dead. The globe cracked, I think."

I rushed to Marvin's table, where Commodore Miklos and a few staffers were desperately working to get back into the game. This was helm controls and weapons. I wasn't interested in the strategic big picture any more. This was about survival.

"Have we got drive control?" I asked them. "How long would it take us to pull out through the ring?"

Miklos gave me a hooded glare. I knew he was thinking it was a bit late for that, but I didn't care about his problems with authority right now.

"Answer me or stand down!" I shouted at him.

"I don't know, sir. We were hit. The bridge was pretty much knocked out, as you can see. We can't be sure of anything else."

"What about the sensors on the exterior hull?"

"Still operating, but their view is blocked by all the dust and debris. The surface appears to be a mess, sir."

I looked around at everything we had operating. Helm controls seemed to respond. Weapons controls...

"There's nothing coming back from the weapons banks? We're not charging the gens?"

"I don't know—"

"Help me get this ship turned around, one-eighty. That's an order."

Miklos tapped at the controls. They were relatively easy to operate. I saw a central image of the sphere that represented *Phobos*. It was a wire diagram, really an app that Marvin had put together to look at the status of all the drive and weapons systems at once.

Miklos put his fingers on the sphere, began to move it gently in a circle and—

I lost patience. There couldn't be but a few seconds left. I reached over, spun the globe for him and slammed my finger on the execute button repeatedly.

The world spun around me. People screamed, and the ship creaked like an old seagoing vessel in a bad storm. The aft wall of the tent suddenly became the floor, and we all slid toward it. A few seconds later, the ceiling of the tent was the floor, and every bit of equipment we'd failed to nail down was tumbling on top of us.

I was in a tangle of arms and legs. Consoles and tables crashed and popped like giant light bulbs. Coffee ran over my face, burning my cheek. I wished I'd thought to close my faceplate. I heard groans and agonized cries. The nanite

271

harnesses were still dead, I realized, and hadn't held down anything.

We were cast into semi-darkness. People howled under me, and I realized those of us in armor were crushing the Fleet types in their smart cloth suits. I did my best to roll off them and their cries of pain turned into streams of curses.

Miklos was one of the worst offenders. I didn't realize he knew so many foul English terms. I pulled him out of the mess and propped him up. He glared at me in the hazy, flickering light of broken equipment and opened his mouth wide.

"Colonel, without a doubt, you are the biggest—"

He never finished the sentence. The impacts began again at that moment, raining down on *Phobos*. We squirmed and struggled to be free of the wreckage of our bridge, but by the time we were out of the pile, it was over.

"Only one more wave," I said.

"What?"

"One more. We're still alive, aren't we? All we have to do is get the big gens working."

"They're below us, a mile deep."

"Right. But the controls are on the wall out there. Let's go see what we can do."

I grabbed him and headed for the exit. There was quite a bit of smashed equipment in the way, but as the gravity controls had caught up with the ship's new attitude, the generator controls were at least lying on the deck instead of the ceiling.

I rammed a pile of junk aside with my right arm and carried Miklos with my left. He was easy to drag with me, as he didn't weigh much on *Phobos*. Nobody did.

Once out in the open, I was able to fly toward the controls. I could see we weren't going to make it, but I had to try.

Before we reached the controls with their nanite arms, I saw the arms were slack—just like the ones back in the command center.

"No power," I said.

"But the generators—the field is set up. It might—"

We felt it go live then. Every time the gravity field hummed into life, you could feel it in your teeth. Like a

272

powerful, deep vibration. It was like a bass speaker so low your ears couldn't hear it, but your bones could.

"I think its firing," Miklos said.

I set him down on the deck so he could at least die with dignity.

We stood there, waiting for the impacts to begin. Our eyes were narrowed and our jaws were clenched.

But nothing happened.

I blinked at Miklos, and he looked just as surprised as I was.

"Four hundred missiles? Where did they go?"

It took us a while to answer that question. My own Fleet people transmitted the data over an hour later. The last barrages had almost finished our ship, but not quite.

When I'd spun the ship around, the enemy missiles had lost track of the damaged area they were targeting. They spread out, showering a stripe of destruction over the surface. It did a lot of damage, but the hull was not breached.

By the time the last wave came in and slammed into us, the primary generators had been working again and the field fired correctly, stopping them all. After all, the system had had two full minutes at that point to get its act together.

I was now the proud, surviving commander of a smoking ruin. Everywhere around me some kind of damage was visible.

I beamed with pleasure and clapped Miklos on the shoulder. He coughed.

"That was a battle royale!" I shouted, laughing.

"I can't believe we're still alive."

"Damage control. That's what it's all about now. Get your people hopping, Commodore. There could be another attack coming at any time."

While the giant ship licked its wounds and every automated repair-bot and crawler we had was busy replacing equipment, I headed for my private brick and broke into the liquor box.

It was only there for special occasions and official visits, of course. But to my surprise, a half-dead looking Gaines was already sitting in my office when I got there. He had my bottle in his hands, too.

"Major!" I laughed. "You made it after all. Those were some nasty cyborgs. Have you got all your limbs?"

He showed me his left hand—or rather the stump where it had once been.

"They had to take it off. They said the poison was too deep, and it was best I do a regrow. I don't like it."

"No one likes losing a limb," I said, "but it does happen. Part of a marine's life, I guess."

"Do you know, sir, that I lost a limb before? A long time ago, before I even joined Star Force."

I looked at him with mild curiosity. If the truth were to be told, however, I was more interested in the bottle he had in his one remaining hand than I was in his story.

"Hand that over and I'll pour us both a drink while you tell me about it," I said.

The ruse worked. He handed it to me and started spinning a tale of being on an island in the Florida Keys. He'd met his first Macro there and the monster had taken a slice out of him.

"Hmm," I said, sipping and frowning. "I don't want to doubt you, but if you hadn't joined Star Force yet, how did you regrow that hand back then?"

"I was already nanotized at that time, sir," he said, looking at me seriously.

"Really? You're one of the original people from the Nano ships? I thought I knew everyone back then. I don't recall your name on our earliest rosters."

"It's a little bit complicated, but I'll try to explain," he began. "I used to kill people for a living, I told you about that."

"Yes, I do remember that."

I looked at him without flinching while he repeated some of the details of his past. I realized I'd asked the wrong question. It was considered rude to bring up the past with anyone in Star Force. Usually, I avoided these topics like the plague. When people brought up their sordid histories unprompted, I always wanted to make a fast exit. Partly, this must be due to my natural discomfort at hearing anyone's emotional baggage. Ask any woman I've ever dated—they'll tell you I'm terrible at listening to that kind of crap.

But in Gaines case, it went further than that. One of the unwritten Star Force rules was that we forgot about past sins. We didn't provide absolution, mind you. A man could feel just as guilty and haunted as he pleased. But we didn't want to hear about it. Once you joined the Force, you were part of a new family. We liked to pretend the slate was wiped clean. No background checks allowed.

When Crow and I had started up this band of misfits, we'd adapted to the situation and come up with rules that allowed people to leave bad things in their past. This was for several excellent reasons: one, the world was on fire, and we were the only people who had ships to deal with it. The people in those ships weren't pros, for the most part. They were random pick-ups, chosen by machine intelligence for their quick wits and almost animal-like reflexes. I'd lucked out, in my opinion, to have survived those tests.

We'd found out back then that the typical person who lived long enough to command one of these errant star ships wasn't an eagle scout. They were as likely to be a burglar, a bum, or a twitchy guy who slept with guns under his pillow. We had to take whoever we could get.

There were historical precedents for our recruitment strategy. For most of Earth's history, there have been mercenaries and armed rogues wandering around looking for work. France's famed Foreign Legion still operates today, and their original recruitment practices were rather like ours. In the old days when you signed up, they forgot about what you did before, gave you a rifle and sent you out to man a desert fort in the Sahara. Legionnaires even served alongside organized penal military units made up entirely of convicts.

I liked to think Star Force wasn't quite that bad. But there were any number of reasons why a fighting man might want to leave his troubles behind and join an organization with a good reputation that didn't ask any questions.

Listening to Gaines talk about being a paid assassin, therefore, broke all kinds of rules. I squirmed a little, but I decided I had to let him talk. I'd asked the question, and he seemed to feel the need to tell me something.

"There's another detail I have to talk to you about, sir," he said, looking at his hand.

I frowned. This was a bad sign. Gaines was a straight-shooter. He always looked you in the eye and told you what he thought. Seeing him like this—it bugged me.

I sucked in a breath and let it out slow. I pasted on a smile and said: "Tell me about it."

"Do you remember the few ships that didn't follow you and Crow around? The ones that didn't take orders?"

I frowned again. "Yeah...you were on one of those?"

"Yes sir. During the first Macro assaults on Earth, we broke ranks and didn't always help out the rest of you."

"I thought those ships were all destroyed or joined up with us in the end."

"Most of them did," he said. "But I abandoned my ship and left her once the Macros retreated. I wandered Earth in those days. I was unlike anyone else in the general population. While the rest of you flew around in your ships and had parties on Andros Island, I tried to live with the majority of humanity."

"How'd that work out for you?"

"Not good. They sort of kicked me out...it's a long story. Anyway, I ended up killing people for a living."

"So you said."

"But don't worry, I didn't have anything to do with the attempts on your life. But...do you want to know why I ditched my ship and became a mercenary?"

I didn't, of course, but he had me now.

"Sure," I said, hoping it sounded convincing.

He looked down at his hands again. "The Macros hit Earth and bombed it—when I was in my ship. And you and Crow—you guys called for us to come join you, saying you needed every ship to stop the invaders."

I frowned, remembering those dark, terrifying days. Everything seemed more surreal back then. We were playing it by ear, and had no idea what we were up against.

"Yeah," I said, thinking back to the South American campaign.

"I ditched you. Your fleet—I was one of the deserters. One of the few that didn't answer the call."

276

I narrowed my eyes at him. I could tell he was troubled.

"I've always wondered if I could have made a difference. We lost hundreds of millions of people down there. I didn't go to defend them when you called. I've always felt bad about that."

"Yeah..." I said thoughtfully. "I can understand that. But you know, you couldn't have stopped them. We all did our best—and it wasn't good enough. One more ship wouldn't have tipped the balance."

He nodded. "Thanks for saying that, Kyle."

"It's true."

He took a big hit on the booze then, and I joined him. I looked at him sidelong. His story explained a lot. His drinking, his attitude. What haunts a man? We all have a secret ghost or two.

"What made you change your mind?" I said. "Why'd you join up with us, Bjorn?"

He lifted his arm and ran his finger around it in a circle. "It was severed right here," he said. "But I beat the machines then. I figured fighting them was something I was built to do. You know, I think that's what got to me: I realized the Nanos were right. Those little microscopic bastards. They knew who I was and what I could do. They'd believed in me, and had recruited me to defend Earth before Star Force even existed. It just took a while for me to give in and join up."

I smiled and stood up, sensing an opportunity. I slapped him on the shoulder and nodded.

"They made the right choice—and so did you," I told him.

He gave me back a thankful smile.

Then I got the hell out of there.

277

-31-

My little bout of R&R was over. I headed back to the bridge, and looked over all the numbers. They had the tables back together and most of the equipment was operating. It looked banged-up, but it was amazing what a few million nanites can do after a couple of hours.

"No more missiles?" I asked.

"No sir," Sarin answered.

"How are the repairs going?"

"Full speed, Colonel," Miklos said, coming over to me. "Even my arm works again."

"How many did we lose, all together?"

"Ships? Zero."

"No, I meant marines."

"Ah," he said, running his fingers over a console. "Only about six hundred."

"Only... Well, we didn't lose the ship or the battle. At least not yet. What I want to know is why the rest of that flotilla out there hasn't fired their missiles."

Marvin floated near. He was taking liberties now, as I'd allowed him to fly within the pressurized central chamber of *Phobos*. It seemed he was gliding everywhere.

"Possibly, they viewed the failure of the first attack and are biding their time."

I shook my head. "They didn't really fail the first time, they almost had us. If I were the enemy commander, I'd unload five times as many waves of missiles and make them hit us thirty seconds apart. I mean, only one out of fourteen of their ships has fired anything."

278

"There is another possibility," Marvin said in his perky tone. "They may have decided to come in closer before firing again."

I nodded. "That sounds more like it. But that will cost them. They don't know about our range. When will they be in reach of our big crusher?"

"Assuming you mean the gravitational effect weapon— they are within range now."

I frowned at Marvin. "They are? Why wasn't I informed?"

"It is extreme range, I can't be sure I'd hit the target. Also, the weapons systems were offline until the last few minutes."

"Are we as close as we were to that battleship when you killed it?"

"Yes."

"Then I don't care about the details. We should be firing right now."

Miklos stepped up. "I thought we might wait just a few more minutes, Colonel."

"Why?"

"Because I didn't want them to be able to escape. If they close now, they will have a hard time reversing course due to their inertia. Also, if we could hit more precisely than before—"

I didn't listen to whatever else Miklos had to say. I'd heard enough. He was playing the game cautiously again. I didn't see that we had that luxury. There were far too many enemy ships in the field. Every second counted.

"Marvin," I said, turning away from the Commodore. "You're my weapons officer. Is your armament ready to fire?"

"Yes."

"You've been working hard on precision. Is your digitized control system now capable of striking with a more precise, narrowed area of effect?"

"It is a great achievement, if I may be so bold. I've perfected—"

"That's great," I said. "I want you to pick out an easy ship in that line and punch the smallest hole you can in its hull. Make sure it ruptures, that's all that matters. The important thing is that you can recharge the weapon quickly and

279

retarget—the way you did with the missiles. Do you think you can get a shot every minute?"

"More than that. I can—"

"Commence firing! Now!"

Marvin glided away and soon the ship gave her familiar little shiver. I knew the big gun had fired, and all we had to do was wait to see the results. I wheeled and faced Miklos and Sarin, my face was getting red.

"I demand to know why I wasn't called to the bridge the moment the enemy was within extreme range."

"Well sir, the range was extreme, as you say, and—"

"In my office. Now."

I turned and didn't wait for them to follow. I felt a surge of anger that I knew was going to result in a lot of shouting. I didn't like to do shouting and demotions in front of the staffers. It wasn't good for morale, especially during an on-going battle.

I shut the hatch behind them by slapping the interior wall. They looked at me worriedly.

"What's going on?" I demanded. "You two are my most senior officers. If you can't follow basic instructions—"

"I'm sorry, sir," Jasmine began. "But we just don't think we can win this one."

I looked from one to the other, dumbfounded.

"Do I have to start relieving people?"

"That is your prerogative, Colonel," Miklos said stiffly.

"Kyle," Jasmine said, gaining my attention, "there are seven *thousand* of them out there. If we fire once a minute and never miss, it would take days to destroy them all. They will reach us in much less time, and we can't defeat them when they do. They know about our defensive measures and our weaknesses."

I finally reached the point of no return. I was pissed off.

"Do you think I don't know that?" I asked. "I'm not a total fool. I know what the enemy can do. I'm mystified as to why they haven't done it yet, in fact. But I also know what *we* can do. And I know that in every battle there are two wars going on simultaneously: the war of machines and the war of minds."

They looked at me the way my beginning programming students had often done back in my college teaching days—like they were scared and had no idea what I was talking about.

"Morale, people. I'm talking about morale. One side will break first, and it won't be us. If we're tougher than they are, they might buckle even when they have the upper hand. They aren't fighting for a cause they believe in, remember. Once they start taking terrible losses from a weapon they can't even understand—can't defend against at all—they'll start thinking about retreating."

Miklos raised a single finger, requesting permission to speak.

"What?" I demanded.

"Sir, we have no way of knowing if that is true. Those ships are probably crewed by the most loyal of Imperial personnel. They have endured countless days of propaganda, every hour of which has informed them of our evil ways."

"Propaganda?" I asked incredulously. "Propaganda doesn't make a thug lay down his life for a sham emperor."

"Hold on, sir. That statement doesn't hold with history."

I grunted, knowing he was right. There were plenty of cases where good men died for the worst of dictators. They would fight for their homes and their comrades, if nothing else.

"All right," I said. "We'll see how the next phase goes then decide whether it is time to withdraw or not. In the meantime, array our fleet. Launch half the fighters after we punch the first holes in their line."

They agreed, but they weren't happy about it. They didn't want to commit. They were still hoping I would see reason and limp out of the fight through the Tyche ring. Fortunately, I was the one in command.

We all walked back onto the bridge and assumed our places. Staffers looked at us and whispered if they dared. I ignored them all.

We were about an hour out from real contact. For that single hour, we were going to rule this battlefield. Part of me knew that my urge for revenge was driving me. I didn't want to run after a beating like a whipped dog. I wanted them to feel some pain for all the damaged they'd done and the men they'd

281

killed with their missiles and cyborgs. In the back of my mind, I knew that I might reconsider after we'd softened them up and they came close enough to use their lasers.

"Have we got optical confirmation on any hits?" I demanded.

"Not yet, Colonel," Marvin said. His limbs worked his console with blurring efficiency.

I frowned and approached him. I looked at the numbers. He'd already fired several times.

"Why am I not seeing any damage?" I asked.

"I've tried twice to strike this vessel, ship number nine hundred and ninety-seven."

I frowned. The ship was right there on the screen, and it looked untouched.

"You missed?"

"Unknown."

"What do you mean 'unknown'?" I said, raising my voice.

"We should have hit it, but it's still there. Two shots—no reaction."

I stood there, staring. My heart sank. I had all kinds of reasons swimming in my head why this might be the case. None of them were good. Maybe the battle had damaged the unit. Maybe Marvin was missing—or damaged himself. Maybe...worst of all, maybe the enemy had some kind of defense against our weapon.

My face was a mask. "Why that ship, Marvin? Why hit it twice?"

"Number nine hundred and ninety seven is the highest prime number under one thousand. One of my favorites."

"Too bad," I said. "Fire at another one. The one next to it. Fire now."

"That's not a best case target—"

"You're targeting sucks! Follow my orders!"

I knew I was losing it, and I forced myself to take a deep breath to regain control as he tapped the ship I'd indicated and nailed it. A little while later, I indicated more targets, and he shot at them in sequence. I chose even numbered ships every time—just to make sure they weren't one of his happy little prime numbers.

282

Marvin seemed agitated. "Sir, these are not the optimal targets."

"Why not? Explain yourself."

"The even numbered ships have fired many missiles. I was trying to hit the ships that didn't fire at all. Those vessels presumably have full ordnance and are more dangerous—thus they are higher-valued targets."

I nodded, understanding his logic. "I still don't understand why so few of their ships fired at us," I said.

"Colonel!" Jasmine shouted. "A hit, sir!"

I applied my fingers to the screen. I panned and zoomed. She was right. The first one I'd ordered Marvin to fire upon was a puff of gas and twisted metal. From this vast distance, it was difficult to see exactly how the ship had taken the hit—but we could tell it had been destroyed.

I ordered Marvin to keep firing on the ships. I let him choose his targets. I watched with growing relief as five ships were destroyed in short order. They went up one at a time with less than a minute between strikes. Marvin's control over the ship's systems had greatly improved. He was now capable of using small, focused charges with the weapon which allowed for shorter power recharging times. I was certain he could control it better than Tolerance had himself.

But after about five hits, we started missing again. I hurried back to Marvin's targeting screens.

"Put a circle around every ship you fired on," I ordered. "Make the circles yellow on hits, blue on misses."

Soon, they were appearing. I noticed something immediately. "You're firing on odd-numbered ships again!"

Marvin's tentacles writhed. He looked upset. "You gave me permission to choose targets. I went back to firing upon ships that haven't yet released any missiles."

I narrowed my eyes at him and nodded. "Marvin, from now on, I want you to target *only* ships that have fired upon us previously. Do you understand? Leave the rest alone."

"That is not—"

"You have your orders. Carry them out or be relieved as gunner."

I was bluffing, of course. No one else could operate this monstrosity of alien tech.

"There's no need for threats," he said, sounding a little miffed. "I will fire on the approved targets."

I watched as he worked the controls. Soon, we were scoring hits again.

Miklos came over to me and watched. "It might be a few drops in the bucket, but at least we're making an accounting for ourselves."

"How long until our fighters hit their lines?" I asked.

"Twenty more minutes."

"Get me in contact with our wing commanders."

Miklos gave me a strange look. I knew what he was thinking: *here goes Riggs, micromanaging again,* but I didn't care what he thought. I was beginning to suspect something, and if I was right, nothing else mattered.

I talked to none other than Wing Commander Becker. She'd once given me a tour of space in her fighter—and regretted it.

"Becker?" I asked. "Listen, I want you to coast. You don't have to decelerate, but get your foot off the gas and glide in."

"That's not our normal procedure, Colonel."

"Yeah, I know. Just do it."

"May I ask why, sir?"

"I want to destroy a few more ships before you hit them. By our calculations, you won't reach their line for about forty minutes if you start coasting now."

She was quiet for a second, then: "Sir…if we do that, we're liable to take more losses from their counter-fire. These little ships don't have a lot in the way of armor."

"I know that. Sit tight for updates. Riggs out."

Jasmine felt the urge to approach me next. "Colonel, there are seven thousand of them. Our fighters are probably on a suicide mission anyway. If we destroy a few more of the enemy—even a hundred more, it won't make much difference."

"On the contrary," I said. "It will make all the difference in the world."

284

She gave up after that. The battle, if you could call it that, went on.

Battles in space aren't always fair. This one was a case in point. Often, due to extreme ranges and varied ship design, one side or the other had a significant advantage during a given stage of the conflict. At the start of this combat, they'd shot missiles and we had no viable response. We could have fired our own missiles, but with so many ships we'd calculated they would have destroyed them with defensive fire. Because they'd outranged us, they'd been able to work us over and nearly take out our key ship.

But now, things had changed. We had the range on them at this distance, and they had no viable defense against our gravity cannon. I began to smile after we trash-canned their sixtieth ship. The smile just kept growing after that.

Unfortunately, few of the others on the bridge shared my enthusiasm. It was the sheer number of the enemy that daunted them, I knew. In their minds, we'd already lost. I understood their logic perfectly: What did it matter if the enemy had six thousand nine hundred ships, rather than seven thousand? We would still be wiped out when they came in close enough to use their lasers.

I refused to accept that. I wasn't beaten yet. Far from it.

"Colonel?" Jasmine asked me suddenly.

I turned to her, and she looked surprised. Her pretty eyes were wide.

"The enemy is attempting to contact us," she said.

I nodded. "Put them on the screen."

This time, unlike a dozen previous such contacts, we were not treated to a little propaganda vid showing Crow doing something altruistic. Instead, the steel eagle appeared and vanished quickly, replaced by an admiral's face.

I was glad it wasn't General Kerr. I would have liked to kill him, but I hated him so much that I couldn't have enjoyed this situation fully if I'd been forced to deal with him.

"Rebel ship," the admiral began stiffly, "this is Admiral Newcome of the HMS Tasmania. I'm contacting you to discuss terms."

Newcome looked and sounded British. His pink skull and jowls were frosted with white hair. Every last lock of it that hadn't fallen out due to age had been carefully groomed into an individual, spiraling curl. To me, his hair resembled lamb's wool upon a badly shaven lamb.

"HMS?" I asked. "Oh, I get it...Crow is 'his majesty' right?"

"Am I correct in assuming I'm talking to Kyle Riggs?"

"Yes. I'm Colonel Riggs."

"Colonel? A strange appellation for a pirate."

He seemed angry. I smiled at him.

"Yeah," I said. "We pirates make up all kinds of fancy names for ourselves. Like Emperor, for example. Now tell me if I heard correctly Newcome. You wish to surrender your fleet, right?"

"What? Certainly not. We understand you have an impressive weapon with a tremendous range. But you cannot prevail, sir. We outnumber you by more than ten to one. I would suggest to prevent further loss of life on both sides that we—"

"They're fake," I said suddenly, interrupting him.

"What was that?"

"Decoys. Illusions. I'm impressed by your new technological developments as well, Admiral Newcome. And you are quite an actor, sir. But unfortunately, in the calculus of war, a weapon that destroys the enemy is better than a trick— as effective as your trick is."

Newcome looked stunned. He opened his mouth, then closed it again. He looked at me with something new in his eyes. I'd seen that look before: it was fear.

"We outnumber *you*, Newcome," I said. "We always did. Your ships are larger, I'll give you that. But in total tonnage you don't have anything that even comes close to the firepower of *Phobos*."

"*Phobos*?" he stuttered.

"It means terror in Greek, I believe. And that's what this big alien ship is: the embodiment of terror."

It took a moment, but the admiral seemed to regain some of his composure. "Colonel Riggs, this battle is unnecessary. It is,

286

in fact, insane. We should all be facing the real enemy together, the aliens. Why can't you see that?"

At that moment, I decided I liked this guy. I turned my head to Marvin.

"Gunner? Ceasefire."

I turned to Jasmine next, who looked stunned. She didn't seem to quite grasp what was going on, but she was going with the flow.

"Captain Sarin," I said, "Tell our fighters to decelerate. Stop the countdown on the missile barrage. The Admiral and I need time to talk."

I saw her open her mouth, but then close it again. I knew she'd been about to ask me *what* missile barrage I was talking about. None were scheduled as we were planning to hold on to those assets as long as possible. But she didn't say anything to throw off my little stage play.

"Standing down, Colonel," she said.

I turned back to the screen, where Admiral Newcome was staring back at me. He looked very worried, but there was a flicker of hope in his eyes.

I've got you now, I thought.

-32-

Hope can be a terrible thing. When the helpless, terrified man is offered salvation, he always takes it—and he will do anything to get that dangling carrot.

"Admiral," I said, "you're absolutely correct. We should all be fighting the real enemy. The aliens. There are many more of them than there are of us out there. I've seen them, sir. I've strangled them with these hands on many occasions."

He watched me, saying nothing. He licked his lips and straightened his ice cream colored uniform.

"I took this ship from just such an alien enemy," I continued. "I turned it against them. Behind us, several systems away, three worlds that once teemed with trillions of alien lifeforms lie dead and irradiated. Nothing lives in that system now. Do you believe me, sir?"

"I've seen the vids. I know what kind of bloodthirsty pirates you people are. I—"

"No sir," I said. "Come on, you must know most of what you see on the net is bullshit. Let's not be children. Your emperor is a pompous tyrant. He's no fool, but he's at least as much of a devil as I am."

"I—I don't understand. Are we discussing a truce, or—"

"Or what," I said firmly. "Just hear me out. I don't want to destroy your ships. Right now, I'm costing myself lives by not firing on you. If I wipe out half your real vessels before we make contact, that's less trouble for me. But I'm trying to find

288

some common ground, here. I'm trying to end a civil war that will leave humanity weak."

Newcome nodded. He could not argue with my logic. "You realize I'm risking my life by listening to you? All of my crew is?"

I hadn't realized that, but it made sense. That detail moved him up another notch in my estimation.

"Well, if it's any consolation, if these talks end badly, you'll be dead anyway. I'm sure Crow will call you a martyr and a hero back home, for as many days as he has left to rule."

"How did you know? How did you know our ships are decoys? How did you know which ones to fire at?"

"It took a little deductive work, I'll admit. But to put it simply, we shot at a number of your fake ones and they didn't blow up. The ones that had already fired missiles at us did explode. There was only one answer to that riddle."

"Of course," he said, looking defeated. "We've lost nearly a hundred ships. We can't take that kind of loss."

"No, you've only just begun rebuilding after the Macros came through this way last year. I understand. You did make a valiant effort. Earth always does. There is no shame in coming to terms, sir. Let us do so now."

Suddenly, he seemed to grow a spine. He straightened in his chair and brought his fist down upon the arm of it.

"I won't simply surrender. I won't disable my ships, nor will I allow you to board them."

I almost grinned, but I stopped myself in time. Somehow, we'd gone from discussing the *possibility* of surrender—his surrender—to talking about how we were going to work out the details. We were talking terms, and that meant we'd already won the battle.

I signaled Jasmine, and she gave me a quiet, knowing nod. She was already shutting down our attack. The fighters began decelerating, as did *Phobos* and the rest of the fleet. Marvin was still picking targets, but Miklos had stopped him from shooting down any more of their ships. The Commodore had picked up on the changing situation even before I'd told him to shift us into neutral.

Admiral Newcome and I talked for several more minutes. For an Imperial, he was able to see reason very clearly. We worked out a plan that was acceptable to both sides. He would scoot his ships out of my path, setting them on a long, elliptical course that would eventually take him back to a refueling station on Mars.

My fleet, in the meantime, would press on toward Earth. I learned that the Admiral and his senior people had been discussing the possibility of withdrawal even before they began to spar with my fleet. There were certain political officers who would have to be neutralized, but the rest would all join in the ruse when explaining the situation to their crews. They'd tell the rank and file they'd come to terms with the pirates, describing it as a ceasefire.

None of this would be acceptable to Crow, naturally. But he was out of reach. The fleet would stop talking to Earth. By the time Newcome and his ships returned to Earth, it would all be over. The Imperial government would be toppled.

Or so everyone hoped.

"You look like the cat that has eaten the spinster's pet bird," Miklos told me.

Being from Eastern Europe, he sometimes didn't get our idioms quite right, but I knew what he meant.

"The bird cage stands empty, my friend," I said, laughing. I was in an excellent mood. Possibly, this was the best I'd felt since Sandra died.

Miklos was happy it was over, but I could tell he was also slightly annoyed I'd won so quickly after he'd advised me to withdraw. It made him look foolish.

"How did you know, sir?" he demanded when we had a private moment in my office.

This sort of question is often posed to me, and it always represents a dilemma. I could tell him the truth, which was that I'd been unable to quite believe in those seven thousand ships. I'd only figured out they were fake when we kept shooting at them and missing the ones that had never done anything.

But the truth isn't always the best policy. It leads people to think you were just lucky, rather than amazingly good. I'd rather have people think I was some kind of wizard. Morale

290

and discipline are much easier to maintain when people have almost supernatural faith in you.

As usual, I took the middle ground. Something in-between the truth and claiming I was a full-blown oracle.

"I'd begun suspecting something was up from the start," I told him. "There *couldn't* have been seven thousand ships out there—I knew that the moment I saw them. They just *couldn't* be there. Earth's fleet had been smashed less than a year ago. Unless they had a fantastic level of industrial output, those ships couldn't be real."

"But why didn't you test the theory immediately? You could have done so in several ways."

I nodded. Fortunately, I was ready for this obvious back-up question.

"I wasn't absolutely sure they were fake. I was worried, honestly, that when Crow captured the Bellatrix system he might have discovered and captured a number of Macro factories as we did. Just think of that. What if he'd found those new factories and managed to get them working over the last few months? That's the only way I could believe he'd managed to churn out thousands of ships."

"Ah," said Miklos, nodding. "I get it. If the Imperials really had these ships, that would be the only way they could have built them so quickly. With new production facilities we knew nothing about."

"Exactly. They *could* have been real if that had been the case. I also knew for certain some percentage of the ships were real. So, I made my moves conservatively. It looked bad, but I wasn't willing to fold my hand and run for the door. If the ships were fake, we could win. Keep in mind, I didn't know how many were fake. I was kind of thinking the first rank—meaning the first thousand—were real. If they had been, that still would have been a hard, hard battle."

Miklos nodded, staring off into space. He had an Irish coffee in his hand, and he didn't drink much. His eyes were thoughtful and slightly glassy.

I braced myself for the next question: *But sir, why didn't you tell us you thought most of the enemy ships were fake?*

But that question wasn't asked. I'm not sure why not. Maybe he didn't think of it, or maybe my spiked coffee and the natural relief of snatching victory from the jaws of defeat had made him not care.

Whatever the case, the question never came. I stood up and put the bourbon bottle on the table.

"Have another shot, Nicolai. You've earned it."

Then I left and went to review the damage. Overall, it was pretty light. Sure, we'd taken a beating on the surface of *Phobos*, but that was the one part of this fleet we could easily fix. Unfortunately, this was one repair job that was too big for nanites to do on their own. We'd calculated it would take months to get the hull back to full density, but we might as well begin now. Already, the transports were dragging chunks of asteroid rock and ice to drop into the biggest holes. Crawlers were rumbling over the surface of the ship, pushing loose material into the cracks and troweling over the scorch marks.

On the bridge, I met with Jasmine and Gaines. The Major had recovered significantly, only a day after any competent medical person would have pronounced him dead.

We shook hands all around.

"I can't believe you talked them into pulling out without blasting a single ship of ours."

"Hold on!" I said. "Have you seen the surface of this vessel? I'd say we were blasted pretty heavily."

"Exactly where we wanted to take the damage, right on this rock's face, the only place we could withstand the punishment." Gaines shook his head and looked at me with honest disbelief. "I thought we were dead—did you know that?"

"Happens all the time," I told him. "This is Riggs' Pigs, remember."

"It's unforgettable. Well sir, I guess I'm heading amidships for some R&R."

"Whoa," I said, "hold on there. I know you're a little banged up, but you still have a large command full of damaged marines to look after, Major."

"Yes sir. They'll come first."

After he'd left to go back to the barracks, I looked over the flight plan with Captain Sarin. She had it all worked out.

"We'll head toward the inner planets at maximum velocity," she said. "In one way, the location of the Tyche ring is a helpful starting point."

"How so?"

"This ship—this drive system, I mean—it's kind of like sailing, sir. Any large gravitational pull works like the wind. Because the largest wind in any system is the central star, and we want to go almost directly toward it, we're in luck."

I looked over the charts, nodding. I saw our position, far, far out from the Sun. From this position, the inner planets were a long haul. The angle of approach was almost the same for Earth as it was for the Sun itself.

"All we have to do is aim at the Sun and let it pull us," I said. "I can see how that would be easier than crossing a system from one ring to the next. The rings themselves don't have big gravity fields and we have to work with lateral forces pulling and pushing us."

"Right," she said. "Navigating a system like Alpha Centauri was much harder and slower. The drive isn't built for it. You have to kind of tack your way—taking pulls and pushes from planets along the route. Again, it's like navigating a sailing ship with a crosswind."

"How long until we reach Earth?"

"You mean if they just sit there and wait for us?"

I nodded.

"Over a week. Eight days, plus a little bit."

"A long time. But less than I'd thought it might be. I can see Earth is pretty well lined up with the Sun. That makes it even easier."

"There are no incoming contacts, either," she told me before I could ask. "At least, nothing we've detected. No missiles, no ships, no transmissions."

"Excellent!" I said.

She nodded. There was a pause in the conversation. I sensed she wanted to say something, so I kept quiet. Finally, she started to speak, stopped, then started again.

"What are we going to do when we get there?" she asked suddenly.

"Do? We're going to take out the Imperials. We're going to demand they lay down their arms and surrender. And they'll do it, too. Just like their fleet did."

Jasmine zoomed in on Earth. We had some readings from our homeworld by now. I was as transfixed by the image as she was. There were newly scorched areas, I saw. Places that had been green were now brown streaked with gray-black. I noticed a lot more cloud cover than there had been in the old days as well.

"The ecosystem has taken a beating," she said. "They still haven't recovered from the Macro assault. There were bombings—a lot of dust was kicked up into the upper atmosphere. Crops have failed in many key areas."

I looked at my world. It felt odd to be coming home like this. In the past, we'd been accounted heroes. Now, people gazed up at the sky and feared when they heard Star Force ships were coming.

I frowned. "I'm going to fix all that."

"The planet?"

"No—yeah. I mean, not just that. I'm going to get people to believe in us again."

She looked up and met my eyes. "What if they don't surrender? What if they fight out of fear or stubbornness? How many will we have to kill?"

That was a hard question. The hardest I'd heard all day.

"I don't know, Jasmine," I told her quietly. "I guess it's up to them, really."

"Not entirely. We're the ones with the ships and the bombs. You could stand off in space and blast them to dust."

"I don't want to do that," I said with feeling.

"No, but do you really think we can invade? We have a few thousand marines...but not enough to take over a planet with billions of inhabitants."

I lifted a finger and shook it at her. "You need to take a better look at history. Sometimes, grand political events go down without vast bloodshed."

"Civil wars are traditionally bloody."

"Granted. But I don't think this is one. This is more like a coup—or the reversal of a coup. The people don't love Crow. I'm not an outside invader they'll resist to the last man. They may be frightened of me, but if we play this right, they may come to welcome us with open arms."

"I hope you're right, Kyle. I really do."

I was just as worried as she was, but I couldn't say that. I gave her a smile and walked away nonchalantly. I did everything I could to appear calm, confident and in control. Fortunately, these things come naturally to me.

-33-

We sailed onward through space, heading toward Earth. I felt like I was riding an extinction-event asteroid—like the one that was supposed to have killed off the dinosaurs.

It occurred to me that slamming this rock into Earth would pretty much wipe out humanity. My people were so fragile, living out on the surface of an exposed scrap of dirt under an open sky, hurtling through nothingness. The whole thing was crazy. I'm not sure if anyone other than a few Cold War presidents ever felt the kind power I had in my hands today.

As we rolled closer, I kept expecting a new storm of missiles to rise up. Or an entirely new fleet. Hell, they could have at least put up a projected fleet of illusions.

But they didn't. We got closer and closer, and I became uncertain of my next move. If they had nothing, Crow would have called and tried to talk me down. They were up to something down there, I could feel it.

As we had days to go before reaching orbit over Earth and nothing with obviously deadly intent was coming at us right now, I decided to head over to check on our wounded. That would give me the opportunity to talk to Dr. Kate Swanson—a significant bonus.

I found a surprisingly large pile of new bricks in the area. Miklos had said something about trusting *Phobos* now and transferring more personnel from the transports into the interior of the big ship, but I hadn't quite understood the scale he was considering.

There had to be something like four hundred bricks now, stacked three or four stories high. Each was about the size of a railroad car and self-contained. We'd been using these simple systems since we'd first ventured into space in the belly of a Macro transport. The design had stuck because it was easy to produce and worked very well.

With magnets at every corner, the bricks operated optimally on a metal surface. We didn't have a high ferrous content on the inner hull of *Phobos*, so we'd had to make do. Each brick was nailed down with nanite spikes. These were barbed and sunk into each corner of every floor-level brick. The upper ones, when we stacked them up, used their magnetics to clamp onto one another.

The nanite spikes were pretty cool, actually. The best thing about them was that you didn't have to hammer them in. You just put the point where you wanted to drive it in, and the nanites sort of ate their way down to an optimal depth. At that point, they shot out flanges—barbs, really—and hardened into a single mass of metal.

I reached an impressive stack of twenty or so bricks with the painted-on designation MEDICAL. I passed through the airlock and found there was a bustling office inside.

A nurse began to challenge me with a huffy tone, but her attitude changed when she realized who I was.

"Ah...Colonel? Can I help you, sir?"

"Yes," I said. "I understand Dr. Swanson was stationed here. Could you direct me to her office?"

This seemed to fluster the nurse. I wasn't quite sure why, but she turned a new shade of pink. I suspected she'd heard rumors about Kate and I, and was shocked to be in the middle of things.

"I've got a locator right here," she said.

I raised my hand, interrupting her. "No, don't buzz her. Just tell me where she is."

She stared at me for a half-second then regained her composure. "Yes sir. Brick Seventeen, Medical One."

I left before she could ask the questions I knew she was burning to unload on me. All of us had com-links, of course. They served to pinpoint a person as well as provide instant, selective communication. But I'd wanted to surprise her. Walking in on a woman, I'd learned over time, was very effective when you wanted to get a strong reaction. Right now, I was the hero of the hour, and I wanted to collect some laurels while the collecting was good.

I found Brick Seventeen after wandering around for a few minutes. I grumbled about the organization of this non-building. It was a snarl of tubes, ladders and airlocks. The whole time I was wondering if the nurse had already spilled the beans by calling Kate and telling her I was on the way. There were any number of sneaky ways to do this, and that nurse had looked capable in that department to me.

When I finally found her, I wasn't surprised to see she was working on seriously injured marines. We'd taken our share of losses during our battle with the cyborgs. In many ways, those creepy monsters were the most effective thing the Imperials had hit us with yet.

"Colonel," she said, flashing me a smile. She finished up with her patient, who was going through a four-limb regrowth, and turned her attention to me.

We smiled at one another for a minute.

"I suppose you're expecting a hero's welcome," she said.

"Sounds good to me."

She hugged me then, and gave me a kiss on the neck. The reaction from the PFC on the bed was comical. He lit up and grinned behind her back. He would have clapped if he could have. But his hands were only worms of flesh in plastic baggies full of brown stuff and nanites.

"Let's go somewhere," I said.

Kate led me to a cubical in the aft end of Brick Seventeen. It was her office. It was cramped and full of boxes, but she'd only just moved in.

"It isn't much," she said.

"It's the work that counts."

She beamed at me. I honestly had never seen that look in her eyes before. She wasn't maintaining an aloof, professional attitude today. In fact, she looked positively hot.

Kate and I had a strange thing going on. Since Sandra's death, she'd made it clear on a number of occasions she was interested in me. There just hadn't been time for us to get together, however. We were very busy people.

We just stood there and looked at each other for another second or two, smiling. I could see her tongue in her mouth, pressing against her teeth. What did that mean?

"To hell with it," I mumbled, and grabbed her.

She melted. I felt relief. Sometimes when I pull that move, it ends up going badly. Not this time. She embraced me and we got busy.

We'd been making out for a good five minutes when my com-link started buzzing.

I almost turned it off. I swear I almost did.

Kate pulled away. "You've got to answer that."

I heaved a sigh, retrieved my headset and checked the incoming channel.

"Riggs here. What is it, Captain Sarin?"

In the back of my mind I was thinking the woman might have bugged me. Could she be checking my location? Was she wondering what I might be doing in a tight office in Medical, Brick Seventeen and decided to interrupt? I wouldn't put it past Jasmine, who'd had a thing going with me for years.

"Colonel, sorry to interrupt, but we have contacts."

"What kind of contacts?"

"We don't exactly know, sir. At first, we thought it was a shower of ice chunks. Something like a broken-up comet. We're passing Pluto, after all."

"Ice chunks? I'm envisioning platoons of cyborgs in frosty shells. Shoot them down. Don't let anything get to the hull."

"We've been firing on them, but shooting at ice with lasers isn't easy. Almost all of our defensive turrets were taken out during the last action. We haven't had time to replace them."

"Pull in the fleet. Have our ships shoot them down for us."

"Working on that, sir. I just thought I should report the situation."

Kate was walking out the door by then. I grabbed her for one last kiss. Then she slipped away. I left Brick Seventeen and growled in frustration. There had been very little in the way of feminine companionship for old Riggs, lately.

Little did I know that that was about to change—everything was. I contacted Jasmine as I hurried back toward the bridge.

"Have you identified the incoming objects?"

"We can confirm they aren't cyborgs, Colonel. They don't look dangerous at all. Little or no metallic content, shape and size random and apparently natural. But there are so many, and a number have already rained down on *Phobos* over the last several minutes. I thought you should be alerted. I think we should send out a patrol on the outer hull to investigate."

"Do it," I said. "Destroy every one you can. We should have started building our defenses back up faster. We've been too busy, I guess. I'll be right there."

I didn't even make it to the bridge before I knew something was wrong. First, a series of booming sounds rumbled overhead like distant thunder. As a long-term veteran, I lowered my faceplate and tuned in to tactical chat.

"Something on the roof," said a voice, reporting in.

I frowned. The "roof" was the term my marines had begun using when talking about the outer shell of *Phobos*.

I contacted Captain Sarin. At the same time, I urged my suit into a lumbering run which amounted to a series of awkward leaps in low gravity.

"Talk to me, Jasmine," I said. "What's going on outside?"

"We don't see anything, Colonel. Nothing's confirmed. Just chunks of ice impacting with the hull."

"Are there cyborgs in those ice chunks? Are they landing near a particular area, like the main shaft?"

"No sir. Random distribution. Really, the phenomena looks natural."

"Yeah, it might be. But just to be sure, I want you to send out some surface teams to find those ice-balls and recon them—and do it yesterday."

"Already done, sir."

That was the Captain Sarin I knew. She was always on the ball. I could trust her to follow an order and still think for herself on the fly.

I got no further with my bouncing journey from the bricks to the makeshift bridge before a huge series of explosions

300

shook the ship. I didn't think anything as large as this vessel could be rattled, but these bombs were big.

I looked up, fogging my faceplate. I didn't bother shouting for Jasmine's attention. As she was on deck under the bridge dome, I knew she had more than enough to do without spoon-feeding me information over a com-link.

Instead of running and hopping, I stared upward. I thought I'd—yes, there was a *crack* up there. A black jagged line in the endless smooth expanse of the upper dome. It hadn't been there a moment before.

The crack expanded and lengthened. I couldn't believe what I was seeing. All my life I'd figured that when the time came and I saw a disaster in the making before my very eyes, I would be the smart guy. I'd pick up and run, or save someone else.

But like every other sap who can't comprehend his own doom, I watched it come with my mouth hanging open.

"Jasmine, the roof is rupturing! We have a breach! I repeat, we have—"

That was as far as I got before the winds began to howl. The noise wound up quickly into a long, low, roaring sound.

The entire vast chamber was depressurizing. I could see it, and I could feel it even through my heavy armor.

"Seal the bridge! Seal everything!"

I have no idea if they were listening to me on the buzzing command channel, but I couldn't help but shout the instructions anyway.

Behind me, back in the shanty town of scattered metal bricks, a funnel cloud had begun to spiral. I knew I was seeing a tornado—but this tornado was upside down. The dark silvery point of it grew like a twisting finger from the crack in the ceiling, and the broad funnel touched the collection of bricks we'd placed in piles around the shaft.

I reversed my course. I watched as shapes—people and crawlers—were sucked up into the hole in the ceiling.

I wasn't worried about being carried away myself. My heavy armor had grav boots and magnetics that were more than enough to keep me planted on the deck. But many of my

301

people weren't in armor. It was uncomfortable and usually only issued to marines.

I screamed myself hoarse as I ran, but I doubt anyone could make out what I was saying. The inverted tornado was like a freight train of noise. It screamed and rattled everything like a continuous hail of bombs.

I was angry and stunned at the same time. Those ice chunks…if the pattern of distribution had been random, how had they managed to get one perfectly placed where it could rupture the hull?

When I reached the bricks, it was pretty much over. The atmosphere we'd painstakingly pumped into *Phobos* had all been sucked away into the void.

It was strangely silent now. Without air to carry sound, all I could hear was my own footsteps and breathing.

I helped a few people who were lying like broken dolls here and there on the landscape. They couldn't breathe, of course. But if I got them into a medical brick and connected them up to life support quickly enough, they could be revived.

I pushed my way through the airlock of Brick Seventeen. I popped my faceplate and shouted for Kate. A nurse appeared, looking upset.

"What have you got?" she asked, taking the man from my arms.

She was a thin woman, but strong enough to carry him like a baby. She probably could have carried me in my armor as well, if she had to. I'd long ago insisted that all my personnel be nanotized, even Fleet people.

"Broken clavicle, looks like. I found him wrapped around the base of a brick on the first tier. Hey, do you know where Dr. Swanson is?"

She glanced back up at me, giving me an odd look. At that point, I recognized her. She was the same nurse who'd first given me a hard time about locating Kate. She knew I had a thing going with her.

The expression on her face wasn't a good one. It was the face people wore when had to tell you they'd found cancer— lots of it.

302

"She went out Colonel—I actually thought she might be with you. Maybe she wanted to watch you leave, or something… You didn't see her, did you?"

I turned around without a word and went outside.

I didn't bother to shout Kate's name as there was no air to carry the sound. I walked around checking every brick, helping people with the rescues. I should have gone back to the bridge, I knew that, but I felt like I had to find her.

We never did. We didn't even find her com-link. Probably, when she'd been carried off by the funnel to the crack in the ceiling, she'd smashed it on something. Without the com-link, there was no trace.

Finding a body floating in the Oort cloud is pretty much impossible. We retrieved a few of them, but we were flying away laterally from the breach, under acceleration. Kate's corpse was back there floating in space, somewhere in our wake. I knew this, and it bothered me.

"Well Jack," I said to no one as I headed back to the bridge with dampened spirits. "You got me again. But maybe it'll be my turn next."

-34-

Every underling learns to read their boss' face eventually. There was no mystery for my staff when they caught sight of mine. They stopped talking and broke apart as I stepped up to the command table and put my hands on the rim.

I leaned over it and looked at the few brave people who had lingered. Jasmine was there, working the screens. Miklos appeared almost as upset as I was.

"Sir," he said, "I don't understand this latest attack. If they don't have any fleet left, why take a shot like this? Why not sue for peace? On the other hand, if they do have a fleet, why not expose it to us and use it as a threat?"

I swallowed and tried to think. We'd all had to deal with the death of friends and even loved ones. I could tell from Miklos' preoccupation that word of Kate's disappearance hadn't gotten to the bridge yet.

Kate's death was, in truth, occupying my mind. I gave myself a little shake. I had to get back into the game. She was gone, and crying about it wasn't going to change anything. The goal I had to focus on was not losing the rest of my people.

So far, I had to admit, Crow wasn't doing too badly at costing me personnel and equipment. He'd been bullshitting his way through from the start, sniping and dancing away, never letting me know exactly what we were up against or what might be slapping me next.

"Gentlemen," I said, "it's time we hit back."

They looked at me quietly. While they watched, I applied my fingers to the screens and zoomed in on Earth. The blue of the seas, the white of the clouds—our homeworld filled big space between us, bathing our faces in soft light.

"What exactly did you have in mind, Colonel?" Miklos said.

Marvin snaked up behind me out of nowhere. I hadn't even noticed him previously. The bridge had escaped serious harm during the latest disaster. Depressurization was bad for air-breathing humans, but it didn't damage equipment. The bridge area hadn't been hit by high winds, either. The tent surrounded the bridge was still pressurized, in fact. The winds hadn't been as bad at the far ends of the huge central chamber.

I glanced at Marvin's cameras, and they studied me in return.

"I'm not thinking of terror bombing them with missiles, if that's what you mean," I said. "We're not here to destroy Earth, we're here to liberate her."

"What else might we do from this range, Colonel Riggs?" asked Marvin.

I thought, in the back of my mind, that Marvin had already figured it out. He didn't want to let on, however. He wanted my name associated with any accidents—or atrocities—that might ensue. At this point in time, I didn't care.

"We're going to turn the big gravity weapon on Earth. It's a big target—we can't miss."

Jasmine made a gasping sound. "I thought you said we weren't going to engage in terror bombing."

"There won't be any firestorms or radiation. Nothing will be poisoned. We'll just choose targets and scoop them from the surface, crushing them down to size in an instant."

"Very clean and neat," Miklos said.

I thought I detected a hint of sarcasm in his voice.

I threw my hands up in response. "All right," I said. "How do you think we should go about winning this? I'm all ears."

They shuffled around the table and stared at Earth. It was hard for me not to do the same.

"Will you destroy a city?" Jasmine asked. "Which city? Should we draw lots?"

She had me there for a moment.

"No," I said. "I don't think we have to do that. At least, we don't have to start there. I need answers and suggestions, not questions and moralizing. Let's argue after we've heard some proposals. How do we go about subjugating a planet?"

"We destroy their military hardware," Miklos said. "That is standard procedure."

I shrugged. "We already ran off their fleet. If they have more ships, they're in hiding. Give me something doable."

"Then the political leaders must be removed. Their command and control. If we take the head off the snake, the rest will surrender."

I nodded. "Yes, that's what I'm thinking. We're pretty far out to hit something smaller than a city, but I think Marvin might be able to do it. What do you say, Marvin?"

A single camera crept up over the rim of the table. I could tell he wanted nothing to do with this topic, but he was nonetheless intrigued.

"We'll have to take a long time to achieve a lock on a target from this range," he said. "I think we could destroy a single, very large building—but the surrounding area would probably be lost too."

"How big of an area?"

"Will I be held responsible for slight miscalculations in this matter, Colonel Riggs?"

"Only if you withheld the real data."

He perked up at this and slithered closer. I could tell he was excited. He relished the idea of wiping out a city—not because he was cruel and evil, not really. I understood him a little better every day. Marvin craved experience. He wanted to crush a building on Earth precisely because no one had ever done something like that before. He knew it would surprise everyone and would test his technical skills to the utmost. That was just the sort of thing that got him up in the morning.

"Very well," he said, "I would estimate we could take down a minimum of a standard city block—again, I caution that would be minimal damage. Any slight variations would increase the size of the affected region up to a circular area encompassing nine city blocks."

306

"All right," I said. "Let's get down to specifics. Who has a target worth the effort? What will shock the system the hardest?"

"You can't be serious," Jasmine objected. "Nine city blocks? That could include hundreds of thousands of civilians."

"We're not going for targets of that kind," I said. "We're talking military, government—political buildings. Pick one."

"Their military headquarters is in Geneva," Miklos suggested.

"How about Crow's palace in Tasmania?" Jasmine said. "Maybe we'll get lucky and nail him."

"If I may, sir," Marvin said politely.

"Be my guest."

"It occurs to me the target should be one hated by the people. Make them feel glad you did it."

"Yes," Jasmine said, leaning on the table now and staring. She zoomed in on Australia. "Destroy his best house. The one where he spends the most time."

"How do you know that's the one?" I asked.

She looked at me. "I've watched videos, interviews. You've seen some of them."

I cleared my throat. I realized she meant the amusing terror vids from Earth. After watching enough of those, she did know what she was talking about, probably better than most. But her suggestion gave me a better idea.

"Marvin," I said, "would it help your targeting if you were able to trace a signal, a broadcast?"

"Undoubtedly."

I smiled grimly. "Then I've got it. Let's blow away the Ministry of Truth."

Miklos nodded slowly. Even Jasmine flicked her eyes to me and gave me a tiny, assenting nod. We all knew the sort of people that inhabited that center of propaganda and terror. Even the convicts would probably welcome the quick relief from torment.

"Lock onto their signal, Marvin," I said. "Let me know when you're ready to fire."

I crossed my arms, thinking ahead to a second target.

Less than ten seconds later, Marvin surprised me.

307

"Ready to fire, Colonel Riggs."

I looked at him with raise eyebrows. "Already?"

"Yes. I took the liberty of predetermining the most likely targets you would select. I've been working on the targeting. All that was required was to make final aiming adjustments."

"That fast, eh?"

"Yes. I aimed the weapon between Geneva and Brussels. Since the Ministry of Truth is located in Brussels, only a small adjustment was necessary to retarget."

"You could have saved us all a lot of time by blowing it up yesterday," I said in irritation. Sometimes Marvin's tendency to predict outcomes was annoying—especially when he was proved correct.

"No sir," he said seriously. "The ship was out of range at that point."

"Let's wait," Jasmine said suddenly. "Let's talk it over some more. Let's get closer, so we can be more certain of a precision strike."

I could tell she didn't like any of this. I couldn't blame her. I wasn't comfortable with it, either. Was the Ministry a fair target? Since time immemorial, nations at war had targeted communications centers. But this *felt* different. Without warning, from a clear blue sky, mass death stalked thousands. They had no idea it was coming, and we were engaged in the simultaneous roles of judge, jury and executioner.

We were military people who were accustomed to fighting alien robots. We didn't want to kill biotics at all. Unlike most military people of the past, we were unaccustomed to killing humans. But here we were, faced with the realities of the situation. When a commander is forced to conduct an unpleasant war, I knew dithering was always a mistake. It was best for everyone to end it as quickly as possible—in your favor.

"No," I said after a long pause. "We're firing *now*. Marvin, destroy the Ministry of Truth. Do it as precisely as you can. No missing by a quarter mile and taking out a hospital or a nursery school."

A shudder ran through the ship the moment I stopped talking. I stared at Marvin; he hadn't even gone near his

308

consoles. He'd had this ready in advance and preprogrammed. He must have sent the go signal remotely.

"Done," he said cheerily.

I looked back down at Earth. The targeted area was a tiny yellow circle on the northern coast of Europe. I knew the strike had already been made, we weren't able to see the effects yet, not until the light being reflected from Earth reached our eyes. If we had hit them, they were already gone by now. But we wouldn't get confirmation for some minutes due to the distance and the realities of physics.

It was strange to gaze at a building full of people as it once was, knowing that is was rubble and everyone there was already dead.

May God have mercy on their souls, I thought...but I doubted that he would.

-35-

Several of Marvin's previous long range strikes had gone badly, but he nailed this one. The building imploded.

As large and imposing as the Ministry of Truth was, it was positively dramatic as a grav-strike. It had been one of those tall, black-glass specials. Every major city seemed to have one. The architecture was interesting, with curving corners that corkscrewed at the top of the structure.

All of that vanished in a heartbeat. A gravitational force equivalent to that generated by a small star flared into existence for a split-second, yanking everything near it inward. The air collapsed, the glass was sucked together in a billion, hot jagged shards. The rebar and concrete folded up like paper.

Everything and anything living in the vicinity was immediately shredded and crushed into a single dripping mass. When the split second was over, it was as if the fist that had squeezed the building into a lump let go. The crushed remnants fell, but was still so compacted that it stayed together in a single, coherent mass.

We watched this with zoomed-in optics. It was a clear day over Brussels, and nothing was left to the imagination.

"That was awful," Jasmine said.

"They had it coming," Miklos said.

I didn't say anything. Killing of this kind always weighed on me. We could have waited. We could have talked. But that might have cost me more ships and troops.

Maybe, maybe, maybe. It was the unknowns and lost opportunities that ate at a man's soul. Who'd died and left me in charge? It was a question I never posed in front of others, but one that plagued me at times like this. I hadn't asked for this responsibility, this power to decide who lived and who died. Usually, I knew the answer instinctively. But this time it had felt different. There had to be a few people in the Ministry who were innocent. What about the terrified convict in his cell? Or the janitor who had no choice, and had been told by his wife he was lucky to get the job?

I heaved a sigh.

"It's done," I said. "Let's see if they're willing to talk terms."

We began sending signals down to Earth, trying to open channels with someone who was in charge. We didn't have a lot of luck for a while. They seemed to be in a turmoil.

"There are riots everywhere," Jasmine told me after working the com-link for two hours. "Word has gotten out about the Ministry. No one seems to want to talk to us, other than a few rebel independents. They think we're coming to aid them. The Imperials seem to be running around, uncertain. For the most part, they're busy putting riot police into the streets."

"The United States had to drop two bombs to get the attention of the Japanese," Miklos pointed out.

I gave him a dark look. "I'm hoping to do better," I said.

Earth was much closer now. We were about a million miles out. I put *Phobos* into a wide, elliptical orbit about four times as far out as the Moon. We were too far to hit with effective laser fire, if that was their intention. They could shoot missiles at us, but we had plenty of time to stop them.

"Let's use backchannels," I said.

Many of our people had connections with Earth. They had old contacts we could talk to now, even if we had to break into their cell towers and make a simple phone call or send an email.

I tried to contact people I'd known, Star Force personnel I'd left behind. I even tried Senator Bager, who I hadn't had dealings with in long years.

311

Our results weren't good. Most people didn't believe we were who we said we were. Those that did were terrified they would be arrested for aiding the enemy. Senator Begar had been imprisoned long ago. Most of the Star Force people we'd left behind had been executed.

The mood on the bridge grew increasingly grim. To see your home so mistreated, to see those you'd left behind had been living in terror or killed—it was hard to take.

"We should have come back sooner," Miklos said.

"You did the right thing destroying the Ministry of Truth," Jasmine told me. "I think we should destroy more of the Imperial government buildings."

Gaines finally came to the bridge, and he watched what we were doing.

"I might be able to help," he said.

I backed away from the console, waving him forward.

The others look surprised as Gaines dialed up some odd numbers. They clicked and beeped, but finally let him through. A strange voice came on the line.

"Code name."

"Bjorn," he said.

"Confirmation word."

"Bjorn," he said again.

There was a pause. "One moment please."

We all stood there, looking impressed. I knew Gaines had told me a lot of stories about being a spook back on Earth, a government hit-man. But I'd heard other big-mouthed soldiers tell stories like that in bars. Those guys had only wanted to get laid. In Gaines case, I was beginning to think he'd been telling the truth.

A new voice came on the line. It was quiet, and unexcited.

"Who am I talking to?" the voice asked.

"Bjorn Gaines."

"Bjorn Gaines was eliminated years back."

"Then I'm a ghost, Sam," Gaines said with a chuckle.

There was another silence. Gaines muted the channel for a second. "He's trying to trace back the number. Can Marvin or someone bullshit me into New York or D. C.?"

312

"Certainly," Marvin said. He went to work, and after a moment, the stranger came back on the line.

"What kind of tech do you have now, Gaines? Who are you working for?"

"That big new moon you see in the sky," Gaines said.

"Goodbye."

"Hold on, Sam! Hold on! I'm not going to get you into any trouble. I'm just trying to reach someone in charge down there. We need to talk to the Emperor, or one of his people."

"I'm not authorized to do any of this, Gaines."

"I know that. These are not normal times."

"Keep talking."

"Hook me up, Sam. Get me to the biggest name you can. Then vanish."

"Vanish? You're saying you're going to screw me?"

"I'm saying you're probably already screwed. But—"

"You fuck," Sam said quietly.

"Just move me up the ladder and get out of this story."

The mysterious man named Sam fell silent. We waited. I looked at Gaines, but he waved for me to be patient.

There was a strange tone, then the phone was ringing again. Miklos and I exchanged glances. We were impressed. Gaines seemed to be getting somewhere.

"General Kerr's office," a secretary answered.

I released a long breath, and waved Gaines back from the microphone. I leaned forward, taking over.

"Connect me to General Kerr, please," I said.

"Who's calling?"

"Colonel Kyle Riggs."

There was a quiet moment, then: "This isn't funny, Mike."

"This call is being recorded. Alert the General or suffer the consequences."

The secretary sighed. I don't think she believed me, but she connected me anyway.

"Kerr here. I'm busy, so spit it out."

"Hello General," I said. "I'm busy too. I'm deciding my next target."

There was a choking sound on the line. "Riggs? Is that you, you crazy son of a bitch?"

"Yes sir," I said. "I've been working hard to get your government people on the line. Is this any way to run a railroad? Is no one interested in peace talks?"

"We don't deal with terrorists or nut-jobs like you. You're a rebel without a cause, and you should go back out into space where you belong. When the fleet gets here—I don't know how you slipped by them—they'll pulverize your little force. You've got to know that."

I frowned at the screen, which was rapidly flashing views of an earthly city. I realized Jasmine was working feverishly, tracing the call. At last, a blinking yellow circle appeared.

I smiled when I saw where General Kerr was hiding. He wasn't in the Pentagon, NORAD, or even Geneva. He was in Paris just off the Champs-Élysées.

"How do you like the Louvre, General?" I asked.

"What?"

"Haven't got a chance to go sightseeing yet? We've got you zeroed, sir."

I gave him the name of his hotel and the street address. He was quiet for a few seconds after that.

"Don't drop the line, General. I don't want to have to level the entire block just to make sure."

"You wouldn't do that, Riggs. I know you. You're soft."

"Space changes a man, sir," I said. "You should know that. Stay put and keep talking, or I'm taking you out right now."

"All right, all right!" he shouted. "What the hell do you want?"

"I want to end this. Your fleet isn't coming back, General. They've already come to terms with us. Now, we can do this the easy way or the hard way."

"Describe these two approaches."

I smiled. I had him. The yellow circle on my map was staying put. He wasn't running, nor was he hanging up. He was doing exactly what I told him to do. The General was a vicious snake of a man, but he understood a gun to the head as well as the next guy.

"The hard way is rather familiar. We'll destroy every government institution, and the people that run them. Then we'll get down to the military installations. Last, we'll take out

314

your production facilities and infrastructure. Isn't that the normal way one nation beats another into submission?"

"Why not just wipe a few cities off the face of the Earth?" Kerr snarled. "Wouldn't that be faster?"

"Maybe," I said, "but it's not my style. Besides, we aren't here to cripple Earth and make everyone hate us. We're here to remove the Imperial government. They'll cheer us in the streets when we're done."

"Everyone cheers a dictator when they have their balls in a vice."

"You should know all about that, sir."

Miklos signaled me, and I forced myself to calm down. I realized both Kerr and I had been raising our voices and getting angry. I wanted to kill Kerr personally for his part in assassination plots against me and those closest to me, but that wouldn't get today's job done.

"What's the easy way?" he asked after a pause, during which we both exerted self-control.

"A coup," I said. "You help us take out Crow and his cronies, and we'll let you live when this is over."

"It won't be that simple. Crow has a legion of followers. A cult of personality. They won't—"

"Where do the leaders of this political group hang out?" I asked.

"I can't give you that information!"

"You don't have any choice. I have plenty of other lackeys to call up and when I do I'll make them the same offer. I'm giving you one minute to give me a target other than your hotel. Mark...now."

"I'm not going to give you your target, Riggs. You can go to hell."

"Fifty seconds left, General. Marvin, warm up the gravity cannon."

Several cameras swung my way. I thought for a second Marvin was going to blow it and ask me what the hell a gravity cannon was, but he seemed to figure out the situation and waved a tentacle at me while he worked his console. He signaled me again a few seconds later, indicating he was ready to fire.

In the meantime, Kerr treated me to a litany of curses and unpleasant references to my heritage.

"Thirty seconds left, General. Really, I would start talking if I were you. I'm getting bored."

"Geneva," he said at last, "that's where the big people hang out. The financial backers. You must know the address. Most of them are there now, holding an emergency meeting. But without them, who will surrender to you?"

I looked at Jasmine, who gave me a thumbs-up. She was panning the streets, and we soon had a new target onscreen. It looked like some kind of mansion.

"We've got the mansion on our screens now," I said. "But you're still under the gun. Where's Crow? Is he there with his backers?"

"I don't think so. He doesn't announce his movements, especially at a time like this. He's really just a figurehead, you've got to understand that, Kyle. He's the chairman of the ruling politburo, but that's all. It's a purely—"

"Marvin, wipe out that address in Geneva when you have the target locked."

The ship shuddered immediately. I felt only a tiny thread of guilt. These people were evil. If they were backing Crow's empire, keeping the yoke on their own people's necks, they had to be removed. Too often in history, the soldiers in the battlefield paid for the decisions of people like these.

"What did you do?" Kerr asked in alarm.

"Don't worry about the rest of the rank and file on your little committee, General," I said. "I just erased them. Now, are you going to connect me to Crow or not?"

There was a moment of silence. I began to wonder if he'd dropped the phone and run for it.

"General?"

"It's on the news. You really did it. Paint my dick blue, you really pulled the trigger…"

"You know," I said, "I think it's getting easier each time I do it. Don't make me pull it a third time, Kerr."

"You have to understand, Kyle, I'm a dead man if I lead you to Crow. I won't make it out of this building alive. I'm not a free agent. He keeps a leash on me as well."

"Jack was always a wise man," I said. "I should have kept you on a chain when I had the chance. But here's the deal, General. Either you give me Crow, or I take you out—right now."

"I've got an idea," he said. "I think I can make this happen for you, Colonel Riggs, sir. But I need to have immunity. And you have to take me in. Can you transport me to your ship with this magic device of yours?"

Colonel Riggs sir? When had he last spoken to me with such deference? Never…

"It doesn't work that way, General. I can crush things from range, but that's about it."

"That's apparently good enough…" he said. "All right. I'm coming up to you. I'll keep this channel open and I'll talk now and then. I'm going to put you on mute though, okay? Would that be all right, sir?"

I almost laughed. General Kerr usually had balls, but he was also a man who knew when he was beaten. He didn't want to end up looking like an empty beer can on the highway. I could imagine he'd spoken to Crow the same way when he'd declared himself ruler of Oz, working his way into the new Emperor's confidence. I gave myself a stern warning: he wasn't going to get a government post after this was over. Prison maybe, at best.

Kerr spent about an hour reaching a spaceport and fleeing the planet. The Imperials seemed to catch on right at the end. He led them on a merry chase. I had the feeling, while I watched his ship dodge patrol boats to reach orbit at the end, that he'd had something like this planned for years.

It occurred to me as well, when he arrived on *Phobos* hours later, that more than anyone I'd ever known he'd managed to switch sides whenever the switching looked good. He'd been pure U.S. government when I'd first met with him. He'd served as my go-between on many occasions when I ran Star Force, but then he'd tried to take us out. When we'd captured him, he'd turned again, serving us, or at least pretending to.

Most recently, he'd joined Crow's organization and begun calling himself an Imperial. Unscrupulous, yes, but still alive

317

after all these years of war and upheaval. The man was a cockroach that wore sunglasses.

He surrendered himself by climbing out of his tiny ship and waiting on the roof of *Phobos*. I let him bake out there on the sunside of our rock for a time before ordering him retrieved. Sometimes letting a man contemplate his personal demise did wonders to encourage cooperation.

When they brought him down the shaft to the interior, wearing a suit of reflective smart cloth, he stood and looked around in wonder.

"Nice digs you have here, Colonel," he said as I approached. "Where'd you get this crazy ship—or moon, or whatever it is?"

I didn't say anything right away. I let my men move forward until the General was encircled by my marines. He looked at me and frowned.

"Oh, so it's like that, is it?" he asked. "Why'd you bother to bring me all the way up in space if you were just going to wax my tail when I got here? Is the electric bill on your magic gun so high you wanted to save a few bucks?"

"No, General. Honestly, I'm wondering to myself how you can possibly help while you're up here. You were a friendly voice on the inside down on Earth. But now, you're just one more breather on my ship."

"Ah, I understand. Here."

He handed me a small object. It looked like a portable drive for a computer.

"You can still read those, can't you? I mean, you have regular computers on this flying cave of yours?"

"We can read them."

"On that chip is a complete list of government officials, their locations, hangouts mistresses—the works. If they have a nephew on food stamps, it's in the database. Every party member is there—including Crow."

"Intel," I said, looking at the chip. "You're offering me your intel?"

"Not just that. You can choose your time and place. You blast them all from orbit, or enough of them that they don't want it to be their turn next."

318

"Assassination from the skies," I said thoughtfully. "It seems so dishonorable."

"What? Would you rather line up farm boys with muskets and kill a million or two of them? That's the old way we used to do it. Seems to me like the honorable thing to do is to kill the leaders who give the orders. You already started the process with the two buildings you took down. You watch how fast things change. Once they figure out what you're doing, they'll come begging to end the conflict."

In the end, the General was right. We fired the big weapon a total of eight more times. Each shot took down a government center that was full of directors, ministers and their accountants. Then we let the survivors know how they could reach us, using the contact info we'd received from Kerr. The Imperial government of Earth sued for peace the next day.

They'd gotten the message.

-36-

It was a strange experience, signing the peace accords. The Imperials were stiff and formal, wearing their dress whites and dress blacks—depending on what service they were from. The government officials wore stone gray. I thought that was the most honest color among them. They were grim, unsmiling people. They hated me and everything I stood for. Only the threat of death and the collapse of all their support had gotten them to come to the table at all.

Over the last several days, we'd watched the Imperial government crumble. Built on a reign of terror, they could not contain their subjects once the people knew they were powerless.

The mobs had gone wild. All over the globe, there was unrest. A dozen cities had been burned and looted. Whole regions were plagued by rioting. Countless officials and collaborators had been dragged through the streets and hung. The Imperial military dared not intervene. We'd contacted the top brass and let them know we could find them and kill them—thanks to General Kerr's database.

I hoped that today's formal proceedings would put a lid on the unrest, but it was a faint hope. My forces were ill-equipped to police billions of enraged citizens.

The worst concern I had was embodied in the obvious question: *what next?* As has happened so often in history, we'd been focused entirely upon winning the battle, rather than on dealing with the aftermath.

I'd never wanted to rule Earth. But now, for however long it would be until I could give up the reins of power, I'd been placed in that position. I was *it*—there was no one else for the job.

By the second droning hour of conferences and speeches, I was getting bored. My fist was firmly mashed into my cheek, propping up my head. Jasmine was sitting next to me, and she constantly whispered to me, urging me to sit up and appear interested. She was like a mom at church.

I knew she was right. The whole world really was watching live on the net. So I tried, but feigning alertness for so long was more than I could manage.

Things didn't get interesting until we were finally down to pulling out fancy pens and passing papers around. The signing itself wasn't the interesting part. It was who showed up to do the deed that grabbed my attention.

Crow appeared. We hadn't found him all week, despite following every lead in Kerr's database and threatening dozens of security people. We knew he had his own private guards, and that he'd built ways to get into and out of most of the major buildings privately. I immediately suspected he'd used just such a secret entrance to crash the party today.

I sat up ramrod-straight. There he was, no more than fifty feet away. I knew I could leap over the tables that were interposed between us and this white-suited fiend. I imagined ripping off that peaked hat, encircled with golden olive leaves. The ripping off of things would not stop there.

"Kyle!" Jasmine whispered harshly.

I felt the tiny weight of her hand gripping my wrist. I glanced at her, then went back to staring at Crow. The muscles in my cheeks were clenched up painfully tight.

"Don't do anything," she said. "We've won. It's almost over."

I must have looked to her like some kind of guard dog about to charge and bite an intruder. She was right in her assessment, I *was* about to charge.

Crow had ordered a number of assassins to kill me. They'd taken down close lieutenants and even my girlfriend in their failed attempts. He was an evil man.

321

"He might have come here to provoke you," she said. "He's tricky."

I glanced at her again but still said nothing. I was thinking about what I'd do with him after this treaty was signed. We'd promised not to execute the surrendering leaders, of course. They were to be tried and imprisoned in some cases, but not executed.

But that was only a promise. Like many people in my position before me, I was already thinking of ways to fix such mistakes—to make people I didn't like disappear.

I shook my head, forcing myself to gaze down at the desk. The cameras were still on me, I could feel them. They were eating this up. Everyone on Earth knew how things were between Jack Crow and me. Obviously, it was personal.

Crow picked up the pen when it was his turn to sign. Like all of them, he had a pen in one hand, a raft of papers before him, and a lot of microphones under his nose.

He stared at the pen for a moment, but didn't sign. He looked up at me instead.

For the first time in years, we looked into one another's eyes. He just stared at me for several seconds, expressionless.

Then, he smirked. It was a small thing, a twist of the lips with half his mouth. But it was there. A knowing, jeering smirk.

My knees tightened, causing my butt to lift about six inches off my chair. Immediately, Jasmine tightened her grip on my wrist.

It was hopeless for her to attempt to restrain me, of course. I had many times her strength. I could barely feel her touch in my current state of mind. She was saying something. A mantra of quiet, wise words that fell on me like raindrops, washing off my mind. I had no idea what she was saying, but I made an effort to calm down.

She was right, I realized. He was mocking me, trying to provoke me. Why else give me a sly smile? There was no benefit in it for him.

So, I sank back down.

Crow frowned slightly. He glanced at Jasmine, then back at me. Then he gave a small shake of the head. I took this to mean he'd decided to dismiss me from his thoughts.

He lifted the pen again, letting it hover over the papers. He did not touch the tip to the official-looking pile of documents, however. There were countless ribbons and seals—he ignored them all.

At last, he put the pen down. A susurration went through the chamber. People murmured and stirred, talking to their neighbors. Crow leaned forward, grabbed the nearest microphone, and dragged it closer. He cleared his throat.

"I would like to say something," he said. "I would like to speak to the people of Earth. To those who are about to make a huge mistake."

This action was not in the script, naturally. All around us, guards gripped their weapons, officials stared coldly, and people talked to one another.

"I'm sorry," he said loudly. "This won't take long. Please indulge me for a brief moment."

People settled down, but not me. I wanted to kill him more than ever. Jasmine was talking quietly into her com-link conferring with everyone involved.

"The Imperial officials are apologizing," she whispered to me. "They say this is not their doing. He came in without guards, and our people let him in here because his name is on the signing list."

We'd had to put his name on the list. As he was the head of state, it only made sense. He'd been in hiding for nearly a week, and I figured he'd probably stay in his rat-hole, wherever it was, until this was over. But I'd been wrong.

"It's all right," I said. "Let him talk."

"This mistake I'm talking about," Crow continued, "it's the same mistake I made years ago. You're considering replacing me with the rebel known as Colonel Kyle Riggs. I can understand that. He's like a new, tougher dog that has come into the pack and frightened all the other dogs."

"He can't call you a dog," Jasmine hissed. "That's not going to play well in a lot of countries."

"What do you suggest?" I asked her.

323

"You could have him arrested and dragged from the chamber."

I looked at her. She was serious. It might cause a fresh round of riots, but things were looking less organized every moment.

"Excuse me," Crow said loudly addressing me directly. "Do I have your attention, Colonel? Am I boring you? I'm talking about the fate of Earth, here."

"Go ahead and talk, Jack," I called back, unable to help myself.

There it was again. That sly, half-smile. Like he knew something I didn't. Like I was the fool, playing into his hands. That expression sent a fresh jolt of rage through me.

Crow stood up. He lifted his hands toward the crowd and the cameras.

"I'll sign," he said. "It's my death warrant, and it will lead to the end of humanity, but I'll sign. If you all want this new dictator, this foolish tyrant who doesn't care about your lives, who doesn't care about his own women or his friends—who doesn't even care enough to save his own children—"

That was it. I was up and out of my chair. I saw marines all around me come alive, following me, but I waved them back.

I launched myself over the table. I think Jasmine tried to stop me, but she didn't have a hope in hell of even slowing me down.

-37-

The table I'd been sitting at went up and over. I was on my feet and marching to where Jack stood smiling, eyebrows riding high. His hands were uplifted like a priest doing a benediction.

"Here we are," he said. "I want you all to bear witness to the violence inherent in this man. He can't take criticism. Why do you all think I never promoted him to the rank of General? Because he was a poor officer—a narcissist, a megalomaniac. All I want to do today is set the record straight before I'm dragged off somewhere and put to death."

I stopped my march before I reached him. I suddenly understood what was happening. I saw clearly what he was doing, why he wanted to provoke me: He was setting me up for later. He *wanted* me to attack him.

We had a long history of coming down to fistfights, and I wanted to hit him right now more than at any point in our sordid past. But it was a trap. After today, if Crow quietly had a heart attack in his cell, the public would forever believe I'd ordered it.

And they would probably be right.

It was my turn to nod to Emperor Jack Crow. I didn't smile, because I couldn't make my facial muscles do that right now. But I did nod with a steely gaze. I wanted him to realize I knew what he was up to, and that I wasn't going to play his game.

Crow looked mildly disappointed, but he wasn't through yet.

"May I speak?" he asked me. "Or is this just a mockery? I'm willing to sign these documents, but I feel I must express myself to the people. I would rather submit to their judgment than to the mercies of a conqueror."

I nodded briefly. I figured I'd let him talk for a while. No one liked to listen to long, boring speeches. When everyone was getting bored, I'd shut him up and move on. If I pressed for that right now, I knew it would be all anyone remembered from this event.

Crow turned away from me and returned his attention to the cameras and the worldwide audience. I forced myself to relax and tried to appear calm.

"The litany of crimes Star Force has committed against this world is long and frankly unbelievable. No single entity in the history of the human species has caused so many preventable deaths. In each of these instances, Kyle Riggs, your new dictator-to-be, presided over the slaughter."

He proceeded to list events. He started with the South American campaign, in which we lost hundreds of millions. From there he detailed the laying waste of China, southern Florida, much of Europe and places in the Middle East. He had some good points, and some bad ones. He neglected to point out that in the early battles he himself was in charge of Star Force.

He ended with some damning conclusions. "In the final stages, these enemies of their own species allowed a massive fleet to pass them by and fly to Earth. Star Force, a den of traitors, chose not to fight the machines. The alien fleet destroyed ours and nearly wiped out this planet. Imperial forces finally prevailed, but only after a valiant battle. That's a story I need not repeat here, as you all know it well."

I was grinding my teeth, wishing I'd shoved him out of the room before he'd started. I knew that if I did so now, it would appear as if he spoke the pure truth and I feared to hear it. I hung on, forcing myself to breathe evenly.

"And now we come to the most recent events. Trumping up a reason to attack their own homeworld directly—to attack us—Star Force fabricated an assassination plot. It was on this pretext they flew against us when we were weak, and they've managed to win through. Using alien technology, they have defeated us, but not the spirit of those who have survived! I urge you all to resist these invaders—"

"That's enough," I said loudly, unable to withstand any more from him. "This is a peace accord. Everyone here came in the interests of obtaining a ceasefire—except for you, apparently."

"Peace? You dare talk of peace? You bring nothing but death and destruction wherever you go, Kyle. I have held the peace here. Millions did not die, as long as you were away. But no, that wasn't good enough. You had to send your machine minions. When they didn't kill us all, you invented a reason to come back to Earth in person. To do your own dirty work!"

I opened my mouth again, but I saw Jasmine gesturing desperately. She didn't want me to engage him in debate. She wanted me to smile and pat him on the head like a crazy old uncle and be rid of him quietly.

But I couldn't do it. I knew her strategy was a good one. But I wanted to tell my side of this story.

"Twice now," I said, "you made some reference to a trumped up reason for us to go to war with your Imperial forces. Are you attempting to claim that a roster of assassins didn't attempt to kill me and even my girlfriend?"

"That's exactly what I'm saying."

"I have proof, if you want to see it. I—"

"Fantasies! Lies, invented recordings and sheer propaganda."

"Jack," I said dangerously. I was losing it again, I could feel it. "I've heard enough from you. I think it's time you signed those documents—or just got up and left."

"Again with the threats! When something or someone doesn't go along with the master's plan, he crushes the one who dares to speak the truth."

He looked at me then, instead of at the cameras. He looked me right in the eye.

"Was that how it was with Sandra, Kyle?" he asked. "Did you get tired of her, and want to replace her? Or maybe she had too many ideas of her own. I hear you're pretty good with those fists, and I know you assaulted her on many occasions.

What happened the night you killed her and decided to blame it on me—?"

That was as far as he got.

I'm not an easygoing guy, I'll admit that, but under the right circumstances, I can take quite a bit of public abuse. This was not one of those times. I'd been devastated by Sandra's death and I couldn't bear to hear her being used in this way. It wasn't good enough for Crow that he'd killed her. Now he was trying to twist her death to his own advantage.

I charged at him with arms outthrust. As I rushed in he put up his own burly arms. He had a smile playing on his face. I didn't quite understand that. The last time we'd met in hand-to-hand, I'd given him a good beating.

All around us, people shouted and stood up, but they weren't quite certain what to do. The guards stepped closer, but didn't grab Crow the way bailiffs were supposed to do when a convict went ape in a courtroom. First of all, it was me who had gone ape, not the convict. Second, I was their leader, but I wasn't a frail oldster with white hair. I was tougher than any of them, and they knew it.

Nanotized people move fast and the hesitation on the part of the guards allowed quite a bit of action to occur.

With blurring speed, we met. He caught my hands with his, and I felt something odd—a stinging jolt. My right hand felt funny.

He had something in his hand. Something small, like a prankster's joy-buzzer. He'd nailed me with an electrical shock.

Maybe that was supposed to put me down. It did numb my hand and weaken it, but otherwise, it only served to piss me off.

I yanked back the shocked hand and hammered it forward again, aiming for his face. He blocked with both his hands, but my fist blasted through and he was sent reeling.

About then, two of my marines reached Crow. They grabbed for his arms. Crow looked at me, panting.

He grinned. I knew that grin. He was a scrapper. A lowborn bastard from down-under. He liked to fight, and right now, he was enjoying himself.

"Afraid, Kyle?" he asked. "In the old days, men would duel for kingdoms. Don't you want to punch me?"

He had me there. I *did* want to hit him. I really, really did. I couldn't refuse this opportunity. I knew I'd never get it again once he was safely placed in some holding cell. He'd grow old and I'd be bored to death by the bureaucratic details of running a planet. This was the only chance I'd ever get to make him pay personally for Sandra—for all of it.

"All right," I said. "But drop the buzzer."

He nodded and something fell from his hand onto the table. It was small, round and silver, about the size of a quarter.

"You suggested a rule," he said, "so I get one too: no hitting in the face. Let's not end this too quickly."

I agreed then nodded to my marines, who reluctantly let go of Crow.

Apparently, they didn't move quickly enough for his taste. He punched both of them in the mouth at the same time—one with each fist—without even looking at them. His eyes were staring at me the entire time, and he was still smiling.

My marines were caught by surprise and sent reeling away. They had broken jaws. Blood and teeth dribbled from split lips.

Crow came toward me with absolute confidence.

I, on the other hand, frowned in concern. Had I misjudged the situation? What if, instead of getting me to give him a beating, his real goal all along had been to fight me like this, man-to-man?

Just before we met in the middle of the room with a hundred cameras watching, craning on tentacles and buzzing from their drone-platforms overhead, I wondered how this was going to go. I'd been thinking in terms of a traditional fistfight. A battle to beat another man down until he gave up. Such battles normally ended when one man was helpless or even unconscious.

But with two modern combatants such as Crow and I, things didn't always go that way. We were too powerful, too deadly. We could kill with our bodies.

I knew I had been heavily modified, far beyond the level of normal troops. But what about the Emperor of Earth? What had he done to his body to improve it over the years?

He surprised me mildly with a sweeping low kick. He moved fast, but not *that* fast. A normal human would not have been able to blink, but I skipped back and the kick missed. I lunged the moment his foot whistled by and came in before he could regain his balance.

It was his turn to look surprised by my speed. I threw three punches into his ribcage before he pushed me away and got his guard up again.

I hit him hard, but it was like pounding on a steel barrel. He didn't even register pain as we disengaged and circled one another.

"You've been paying the surgeon, Kyle!" he said. "I didn't think you were the type."

I wasn't in the mood for banter, so I came at him again. Punches, kicks, holds and counters. We sparred for perhaps ten seconds. Neither of us landed a blow that could take the other out.

When we separated again, there was blood all over Crow's white suit. Both our fists were bloody as well. Our clothes were ripped in places, as were our skins. Metal showed under there, crawling nanites that were working desperately to repair us. We were breathing harder, but we weren't tired, not yet.

I heard Jasmine calling to me from the sidelines. She had cupped her hands around her mouth.

"This isn't getting us anywhere, Kyle!" she shouted.

She was right, of course, but I didn't really care. I took a step back to talk to her.

Crow apparently didn't want us to talk. He grabbed up a pen from the table—an old-fashioned fountain pen of the type they reserved for these special occasions. He threw it at her with a flick of his wrist.

She appeared not to see it coming in time. The pen caught her in the chest and sunk in, like a thrown dagger.

I looked at her in surprise and anger.

"What the hell—?" came out of my mouth, but that was all I had time to say.

Crow charged at me. I realized even as he barreled in that I'd been tricked. He hadn't injured Jasmine out of spite, he'd wanted to distract me, to make me look at her.

When I looked back in his direction, his foot was coming at my face. The black heel of his dress shoe was scuffed down to the brown leather in places.

I lifted my arms and twisted my head, but that heel connected with my left cheek and slid on into my ear. It hit with such force that it shaved my left ear off. The ear hung down upon my collar, dangling by shreds of skin. Blood welled up a moment later from a dozen severed vessels.

Crow had cheated, I thought for a stunned moment.

What a fool I was. Of *course* he'd cheated. The only reason he'd made up the rule about not hitting one another in the head was so that he *could* cheat. No one watching on the net would know or care. This fight, I realized now, was to the death.

The mistake he'd made, I decided in the next split second, was in not killing me with that single opportunity. If he'd landed his kick square-on, he might have ended this as the victor.

I knew what I had to do. I had to win.

Instead of dancing away howling in agony and trying to put my ear back on, I moved in close. I didn't bother with grabbing his leg or punching his belly—I summoned up all my strength and threw a hammer-blow into his head.

The results were not unpredictable, but they were spectacular. My fist caught him under the chin and applied a couple thousand pounds of force there. Jack Crow's head snapped back—and came off.

I'd decapitated the first and only Emperor of Earth.

One might think, as I did in that moment, the battle would be over. Under any kind of normal circumstances, we'd both be correct.

But technology on Earth had not sat still. Just as we'd made medical advances out in the Eden system due in large part to the twisted genius of Marvin, the Imperials had learned their own share of somewhat gruesome tricks.

His head hung by a flap down his back, thumping there like a backpack, or a slung-back hoodie. But despite gouts of blood, his body did not fall.

What happened instead twisted my guts. Out of his sides, *stalks* sprouted. They were like the eye-stalks of crabs.

331

I looked at them, staggering back. My mouth hung open.

"You're a cyborg," I said. "Are you even the real Jack Crow?"

Crow's mouth worked, hanging there by the spinal cord and flaps of bloody skin. No intelligible words came out, but that was hardly surprising.

He staggered toward me and I backed away, disgusted. As far as I was concerned, this fight was over. He'd lost.

But Jack, apparently, didn't see it that way. He came on, walking oddly, but still functionally. He threw punches at me, and his neck gargled. No doubt he was swearing at me still.

Where is his brain? I asked myself. *He should be dying.*

Jack kept coming and I kept backing away. This seemed impossible, but it was happening.

All around me the crowd of onlookers, who'd at first been circling closer for a better look, now retreated. They were horrified and repelled, and I didn't blame them.

I was glad for the extra room. I wasn't quite sure what I should do. Now that I had time to think about it, I realized why all those blows to Crow's chest had done next to nothing. He really did have a steel barrel underneath his skin. Like the cyborgs I'd fought on *Phobos*, he had a layer of metal, a shell, protecting his innards instead of ribs made of bone.

I thought about ripping his head off all the way, as disgusting as that would have been, but I didn't think it would work. His brain must be inside that central torso. Inside the metal encasement that had replaced his ribcage.

Going for a different tactic, I kicked at his legs. He grabbed my foot, twisted it, and forced me to disengage.

He seemed to move more slowly now that his head was gone. He still had eyes, but maybe he wasn't accustomed to using them.

I jumped up onto a table, still retreating.

"Kill it, Kyle!" Jasmine shouted.

I glanced over to her. She had a vicious look on her face. Not even Sandra could have looked angrier. She'd pulled the pen out of her chest, and a circle of blood ringed the spot and ran down from it. The injury reminded me of a bullet wound.

I decided to man-up and hold my ground. Crow and I traded blows. I grunted as fists slammed into me. I was hitting him harder, and I had better aim, but I wasn't doing any real damage. I might have dented his metal shell, but I wasn't even sure that was happening, as the steel was encased in flesh.

Gritting my teeth, I braced myself to do what had to be done. I've killed aliens in hand-to-hand many times. Ramming one's gauntlets into the guts of a Worm wouldn't be much different, I told myself.

But I didn't want to do it. I didn't want to reach down his severed neck and dig for his brain. I didn't want to rip off the eyestalks. It was just too gross.

In the end, as I was steeling myself for the finish, I was saved by unexpected interference.

Something small and silvery flashed. I shied away reflexively, thinking someone in the crowd, maybe one of the Imperials, had taken a shot at me.

But it wasn't that. Suddenly, Crow's body stiffened. There was a hot, burning smell. Then he shivered and fell, stone dead.

I stood there over him, panting. Around me, there were ragged cheers—but not many. They quickly fell into a stunned quiet.

I turned in a slow circle, eyeing the other Imperials. Over their heads, the cameras hovered and buzzed.

"Does anyone else here object to signing the peace accords?" I demanded.

No one else did.

-38-

Jasmine had done it. She'd thrown that silvery little disk Crow had secreted in his palm to shock me. She'd thrown it well, as only a Star Force trained fighter could. It had landed inside Crow's torso, which had been wide open at the top.

The jolt hadn't been enough to stop my hardened hand, but delivered internally to a cyborg—right on top of an exposed brain—the shock had turned out to be deadly.

After we'd adjourned and cleaned up, the peace accords committee met again. The Imperials were full of apologies and platitudes. I'm sure that if Crow had kicked my ass, things would have been different—but he'd lost in his final bid for supremacy.

The peace treaty was signed. Really, the treaty amounted to an unconditional surrender.

I took my people out of there as soon as I could and headed back up into space where I felt more at home. I thought I'd relish my return to Earth, and in a few ways I'd enjoyed the taste of the air, the sounds of a real city…

But it was harder to get used to Old Earth than I'd thought it would be. I decided to take it slow. If nothing else, there were probably a few million disgruntled loyalists sulking somewhere, wanting to take a shot at me. I figured they'd cool off if I spent most of my time in orbit.

A very busy time passed, and things settled down on Earth. Aboard the reincarnated version of *Gatre*, I met with Jasmine.

She was happy to have her old ship back, and I was happy to return her to a real command.

"You're in charge now, Colonel," she said, giving me a beaming smile. "You're in charge of the whole world."

"Thanks in no small part to you," I said, shaking my head. "I can't believe that whole mess really happened."

"Crow went into the signing ceremony with a plan. I think he knew what he was going to do from the very beginning."

I nodded in agreement. "He thought he could take me."

"He thought wrong."

I looked at her, troubled. "What do you think would have happened if Crow had managed to kill me? What if he'd been standing there alive and I'd been dead on the floor? Would the people have embraced him again?"

Jasmine shrugged. "I don't think he had a chance. He hasn't been fighting for years on the front lines. He was soft."

Privately, I had to disagree. My knuckles were skinless after punching that metal-armored gut of his.

"But what if he had won? People like a winner. They like a king who throws his enemy down."

"Star Force would still be here. We'd still have *Phobos*."

I nodded, frowning. Privately, I thought it would have been a disaster. Miklos and Jasmine would have been left in charge, with Miklos being the higher ranked. Frankly, I didn't think either of them could cut it. Don't get me wrong, they were both fine officers. But some people don't strike me as ready to lead an interstellar civilization. Hell, I wasn't ready myself.

If not Jasmine or Nikolai, then who? And how would Crow have reacted? I figured he would have refused to sign, saying the Imperials needed time to sort things out. I felt sure my people would have let him get away with it, too.

But more important than the level of competition he faced would have been the symbolism of it all. Star Force would have lost in the eyes of the world. With weak successors to my position trying to figure out what to do, Crow might well have secured himself some kind of legitimacy. Perhaps they'd try to place him in exile, like Napoleon on Elba. Historically, that hadn't worked out so well for the French.

I had to struggle to bring my mind back to the here and now. I turned to Jasmine, and looking at her made me smile.

She was glowing. I could tell, looking in her eyes, she didn't share my self-doubts. She wasn't replaying the events with disastrous variations. She had utter confidence in me now. I could do no wrong.

"What now?" she asked me.

"Do you want to go on a date?" I asked. I couldn't help it. Like most guys, I'm a natural opportunist, and the look in her eyes presented serious possibilities.

We ended up back on Earth. I took her to San Francisco, a city every woman seemed to love. We went to a restaurant that had until recently been only available to Imperial party members. The courtiers weren't showing up there anymore, and the place was practically empty.

We didn't go alone, of course. We had about a hundred marines with us. The suited fellows at the door looked alarmed. Burly marines in full kit marched in by the squad. Many of them were Centaurs, and that really freaked out the maître d'. They questioned me about bringing animals into their establishment. I shamed them for their racial intolerance.

Once we were seated—a full company of us—I assured the waiters that they would be paid in full tonight. They seemed relieved. Apparently, the Imperials didn't always settle their debts.

Jasmine was out of uniform, and so was I. It felt strange to be under normal gravity, listening to cars honk on the streets outside. I couldn't get over it.

"This table is real wood," I said, tapping on it.

"It's lovely. Don't break it, Kyle."

"Don't worry, I won't."

But even as I leaned my weight forward on my elbows, I felt it give slightly. I weighed too much for a wooden table. I had to pretend, holding myself rigidly upright while appearing relaxed.

The date went well, but we eventually got around to the topic of politics.

"Are you going to dissolve the Imperial Senate?" she asked after a course of abalone appetizers.

336

"I don't know," I said, scraping my fork on the plate. "You know, these meals are always so light and insubstantial. It's like eating five hundred dollar cotton candy."

"What are you going to do? How will Earth be governed?"

I shrugged. "I thought I might hold a vote. Let them put someone in as president. Everyone seems to be of the opinion we need a single world government. It's their planet. I guess they should be able to run it as they wish."

Jasmine frowned at me. I think it was the first frown I'd seen on her face in a while. She'd been staring at me like I was some kind of holy relic all night.

She slipped a hand over the table and touched mine. "Let's talk about the present."

"Yeah, good idea," I said, thinking about her and our date. She was looking good. I rarely saw her out of uniform, and she looked like the kind of girl I'd never have had a chance with back before the aliens arrived.

"What about an interim government?" she asked. "Before some kind of structure can be worked out, there must be *someone* in charge."

I sighed. "I guess you're right. We have martial law now, and that will stay in place until we sort things out."

Her smile was back.

"Right," she said. "For now, you're the ruler of all Earth."

I didn't feel comfortable with that. I remembered Sandra telling me it would end up this way. I hoped it wouldn't last long. I was a soldier, not a politician. I was better at winning battles than building roads and schools. And I totally sucked at schmoozing.

"So far it's been endless meetings," I complained. "I can't wait until we find someone better suited for the job."

Jasmine frowned at me again. The bread and soup arrived, and I dug in. The bread was the best part of the meal so far. She watched me eat quietly, nibbling.

Finally, she sighed.

"What?" I asked.

"I can't believe you intend throwing this opportunity away."

"Huh?"

337

I was confused. The only opportunity I was interested in involved getting her out of her dress.

She leaned forward and whispered conspiratorially. "You can't just let them vote in some baby-kissing fool, Kyle. Our species is in danger. We aren't playing around. The Macros or someone else could come after us again any day."

"Yeah," I said slowly, not really following her.

"When that day comes, do you really intend to listen to Earth's government?"

I shrugged, but I had to admit it was a troubling thought. When Crow had tried to order me around, things hadn't gone so well between the two of us. The end result had been a bloody mess on live TV.

"You know what they'll do, don't you?" Jasmine pressed. "They'll bring in their own generals and admirals. All of whom will be loyal to them. Pretty soon, they'll give you an order you don't like—something small maybe, just to try it out. Eventually, you'll be kicked out of Star Force altogether and 'retired'. You'll end up doing appearances on net talk-shows and documentaries."

"No I won't. I hate those things."

She rolled her eyes at me. I get that a lot from women.

"They'll try to push you out. They'll have to. You're too frightening for them."

My food was gone by this time, so I pushed my plate away. I didn't like what she was saying, but she had good points. I'd been down that road before with Crow. I remembered the day I'd found out about the three generals he'd appointed to lord it over me. I smiled, thinking of one of them, a man named General Sokolov. I'd disliked him strongly enough to arrange a one-way trip out of the star system for him.

"Let's just eat our meal and enjoy the night, Jasmine," I said. "Our troubles will still be there in the morning."

"Okay," she said. "I'm sorry. I'm such a worrier. I just want you to understand, I'm not fascinated by power. I'm not trying to romance a dictator. I'm just worried about Earth's future."

I gave her a blank look. It was the best I could do, because I figured she was doing all those things and more.

338

"What I'm talking about is *responsibility*, Kyle," she said in a near-whisper. "You've toppled a government—the only government. You can't leave everyone in chaos. And you can't let them choose a random fool to run this planet. They will, you know. And when the time comes, the fool will screw up. After that, we'll all be dead. All of us—forever."

I was finally listening to her. I didn't like what she was saying, but I had to admit, she had excellent points. History strongly supported her case. Normally in the course of human events, rulers came and went. The best of us avoided the task, knowing in our hearts the job was a serious pain in the ass and not worth the perks.

But times had changed. A bad ruler now could mean the end of everything.

"I don't know if I can enjoy my steak now," I complained.

"Sorry."

"Let's forget about it," I said. "Just for tonight."

"But you understand what I'm saying? You see that leadership can't be left to chance now?"

"I know what you're saying. I get it, but I want to enjoy our time together. Can we drop it for the rest of the night?"

Our main course arrived, and when the waiter glided away she leaned closer again.

"Yes," she said, "for tonight. You deserve that."

We had wine and excellent food for the next hour. Then I asked her if she wanted to see the rest of this hotel.

She looked at me almost shyly. "Sure."

I took her upstairs. All the way upstairs, to the penthouse. There was marble, gold, incomprehensible paintings—the works.

Jasmine walked around the place making appreciative comments and sounds. We stood on the balcony outside in the dark, even though I'd assured my security people I wouldn't.

We stared down at the living city. The streets were rivers of white and red lights. A breeze caught Jasmine's long hair and fluffed it around her face.

"I can't believe we're really home," she said. "I didn't think I'd ever get back, you know. I want to thank you for this lovely evening."

"Is it over?" I asked her.

She looked at me seriously. "Not if you don't want it to be."

I guided her toward the couch, where we sat and had another bottle of fine wine.

"What about the rest of the people in this hotel?" she asked. "Won't they be wondering what we're doing? Or taking pictures in the morning?"

I smiled. "There aren't any other people in this hotel. I rented the whole thing. Nothing but marines on the bottom floors, and us at the top."

She melted then, and it was good. I'd waited a long, long time to make love to Jasmine. It was worth the wait.

But later, when she was sleeping next to me, I couldn't turn off my mind.

She'd planted thoughts there that wouldn't go away. How was I going to handle this transition? Was I really going to put a civilian government in place and let them run this planet however they wished?

There were other possibilities, of course. I could establish a local planetary government, but place it under Star Force control. Maybe we'd call it a federation of planets or something.

I was thinking of more than what Jasmine had mentioned. There were so many things to work out. This wasn't just about Earth; it was much bigger than that. The Worms of the Helios were involved, as were the worlds of the Centaurs, and the free humans in the Eden system. I had to remind myself we'd only seen seven star systems so far. There were bound to be more biotic aliens somewhere.

The Macros were still out there as well—and God knew what else. How did one build a government which could easily absorb newcomers for the joint protection of all?

I thought of empires and confederations. None of these plans conformed to the traditions I'd been born and raised with, and that bothered me.

I sighed deeply. Sometimes, I wished I could just go back to my farm in the Central Valley and wake up in the morning, as if from a very long, strange dream.

I listened to the sounds of traffic drifting in the windows with the sea breezes. Earth was alien to me, and yet homey, all at the same time.

The End

More Books by B. V. Larson:

STAR FORCE SERIES
Swarm
Extinction
Rebellion
Conquest
Battle Station
Empire
Annihilation
Storm Assault

IMPERIUM SERIES
Mech Zero: The Dominant
Mech 1: The Parent
Mech 2: The Savant
Mech 3: The Empress
Five By Five (Mech Novella)

OTHER SF BOOKS
Technomancer
The Bone Triangle
Z-World
Velocity

Visit BVLarson.com for more information.

Made in the USA
San Bernardino, CA
10 June 2015